Unfriendly Persuasion

A Tale from the Arbiter Chronicles

Steven H. Wilson

Firebringer Press

UNFRIENDLY PERSUASION
A Tale from the Arbiter Chronicles

Published by
Firebringer Press
6101 Hunt Club Road
Elkridge, MD 20175

ISBN: 978-0-9773851-3-3

March, 2012

Cover Design by Ethan Wilson
Cover Art by Ponch Fenwick

Printed in the United States of America

For Harve Bennett.
Thanks for a lifetime of inspiration.

"...Zeus the Father made a third generation of mortal men, a brazen race, sprung from ash-trees; and it was in no way equal to the silver age, but was terrible and strong. They loved the lamentable works of Ares and deeds of violence; they ate no bread, but were hard of heart like adamant, fearful men. Great was their strength and unconquerable the arms which grew from their shoulders on their strong limbs. Their armour was of bronze, and their houses of bronze, and of bronze were their implements: there was no black iron. These were destroyed by their own hands and passed to the dank house of chill Hades, and left no name: terrible though they were, black Death seized them, and they left the bright light of the sun."

– Hesiod, Works and Days, as prepared by Hugh G. Evelyn-White from the work of W.H.D. Rouse, 1914

CHAPTER ONE

We had two minutes to live. Literally.

The enemy was recharging its weapons. Ours were out, destroyed in a surprise attack by the terrorists who were about to rain death on the birthplace of human civilization, my home planet, Rigel V.

I bought us three more minutes the only way I could, by getting closer to our attacker, moving inside his firing perimeter. Crazy, I know, but there are two places you can position yourself so a gun can't hit you –far outside its firing range, or close to its trigger. The latter was *Titan's* only option.

Even there, in the eye of the storm, our enemy had sent out robot shuttles bearing nuclear warheads. *Titan* was about to die.

I wasn't in command, actually. The whole thing began as a training exercise, a test for *Titan's* five midshipmen, of whom I was proud to be one. Two of the five, interestingly enough, Carson and Metcalfe, are from old Terra.

Metcalfe was in command for the first exercise. Any of us could have been, I suppose, but Captain Atal had chosen Metcalfe and myself to staff the command deck. Metcalfe had proposed a primitive Terran ceremony for deciding which of us actually commanded and which of us piloted the great ship. He called it a "coin toss." I thought at the time it was one more of his quaint religious customs. Being from Terra, Metcalfe still believes that there are, somewhere beyond the fringes of known space, beings called "gods." They're supposed to be very powerful, and, if you speak to them sweetly, they'll do you favors. It brings a delightful diversity to our midst. Still, it's unnerving to go into battle with someone who believes that divine intervention can turn the day.

I've since learned that a coin toss is not a religious custom, exactly. It's a way of making a decision by invoking random chance. (A "coin," for the uninitiated, is a metal disc used in primitive societies as a medium of commercial exchange. Likely you've never heard of one, much less seen one. I know I hadn't, until Metcalfe pulled one from his pocket.)

This day we saw the folly of leaving important decisions to either random chance or Mr. Metcalfe's gods. The very fate of our civilization was in the balance as a ship loaded down with Senterium K was about to make a suicide run on our most populous world, and the man who was in charge of saving our collective skins was, I have to say it, a charity case.

Let me stop and say that I admire Terrence Metcalfe. By the age of 22 standard years, more than half of those born on his world have already died of disease or misadventure. The remaining minority are largely illiterates, scarred with venereal disease and mental illness, who survive only by resorting to crime. Their criminal records would exceed the personal data storage quota of even the richest citizen of Quintil, if they weren't quarantined to Terra. There they go unprosecuted due to a dearth of law enforcement and an even greater lack of interest in maintaining civil order.

Defying the odds, Metcalfe secured an appointment to the Academy and has impressed his officers to the extent that he has been field-promoted to the rank of lieutenant. But let's not fool ourselves, shall we? He has enjoyed the attention and guidance of the Confederacy's finest citizens, namely two members of the prestigious Atal family and the venerated Professor Mors of Phaeton. They see potential in him, and I am certainly not one to deny that which such learned colleagues—one of them my superior in the chain of command–believe they have witnessed. I do not begrudge them the privilege of bestowing their favor on the less fortunate, and giving Metcalfe every opportunity they can to succeed, even if it means promoting him ahead of the more qualified.

But a chimp, even in the finest resplendent regalia, purchased at the finest boutique in Quintopolis, is still... a chimp.*

So, not meaning to criticize, I have to say it was unfortunate that, on such a crucial day, Captain Jan Atal decided to leave his protege in command of the Confederate Navy's greatest vessel, even after the attack began, while he himself was on board and could have stepped in at any time. I do not doubt Captain Atal's wisdom. I only feel pity that he placed so much faith in someone who, in the breech, did not come through.

In short, Metcalfe panicked.

And who wouldn't? Please don't be smug and assume that you would have kept your cool. We were defenseless, reeling from a vicious surprise attack. A freighter had strayed into the field of our mock combat, and, while we were still trying to warn it away, it had fired on us. It was a carefully planned and executed strike, calculated to maximize damage. *Titan*, the grandest ship ever built by human hands, was crippled. Dozens were dead. The Captain and the Secretary of the Navy were trapped in the bowels of the ship. The attacker, a Qraitian named Fehajiq, had finally communicated and told us he was coming around again in two minutes to deliver the death blow. And we had no weapons.

Or so we thought.

* *Much has been made in the media of my treatment of my beloved personal assistant, the chimpanzee named Rourke. I'd like to say for all to witness that I find the tabloid coverage offensive and cruel. Rourke is not a slave, as some have suggested. He is a trusted family friend, adopted three generations ago by the then-chairman of Blaurich holdings, the man who contributed much of my DNA and signed the order for my conception. The fact that I took him clothes-shopping is not evidence of my abuse of animals, but of Rourke's love of fine clothes. He selected the livery in which he was holographed that day. And I did not invite the reporters who shot the images. I merely was cordial to them, as I always am to the media. I would like this matter put to rest once and for all. Rourke stays with me out of love, because I am good to him. He is free to seek other employment any time he wishes. It is not my fault that I own the majority of the gardens in Quintopolis and thus am his only real opportunity for employment as a landscape architect.*

Titan has six weapons arrays, plasma cannons, designated Alpha, Beta, Gamma, Delta, Epsilon and Zeta. They all showed offline after the second Qraitian attack. The ship also carries short and long-range missiles, and bombs of various sorts. At close range, these last would have been quite effective... at destroying the *Titan* along with her enemy.

Metcalfe, in a burst of despair and driven no doubt by his belief in an afterlife, announced that he was going to "ram the Titan right down their throats." He plotted an intercept course with our attacker–not difficult, as they were directly in front of us–and took us full speed ahead to what he expected would be our deaths.

That was when I remembered that battery Epsilon, our fifth weapons array, was not, in fact, offline, but only designated so by the ship's computer for the purposes of the exercise which the computer believed we were still running.

I calmed Metcalfe down. The poor boy was trembling, his face fairly running with sweat. Or perhaps tears. He saw his first command ending in failure and the deaths of billions. Already, in just the past minutes, he'd heard that a shuttle bearing our Bos'n, Aer'La, and his childhood friend Nathan Renfro had been destroyed in the volley between the big ships. It was overwhelming, I'm sure. Once I had his attention and had gotten him to stop muttering prayers to the gods, I gently prodded him. I couldn't say anything too obvious, for the enemy was listening. With a channel open directly to "General" Fehajiq, I could not very well announce, "Hey, Metcalfe, you forgot that battery Epsilon is actually online after all," now could I?

Surprise was key. Fehajiq believed that we were defenseless. He'd been monitoring our communications for hours, courtesy of encryption keys stolen from the data banks of the *Strawbridge*, a Merchant Marine vessel commanded by Metcalfe's friend, the same, late Nathan Renfro. Renfro had himself stolen the keys when he'd been aboard *Titan* months earlier. About the fact that we were under the leadership of a panicking Terran, about to die because of the illegal actions of a second, dishonest Terran, I draw no conclusions for the reader. Wiser heads than mine have turned to the task of deciding whether or not there is something inherently inferior about the Terran psychological makeup, and they have proved nothing.

So I whispered to Metcalfe, "Have you verified the status of all weapons?"

He turned to me, chin quivering, eyes vacant and bloodshot and mumbled, "Wha...?"

I clutched him firmly and warmly by the shoulder and mouthed again, "Status of weapons?"

Poor boy thought I was suggesting a routine status readout. I think he was in autopilot mode now, and any suggestion seemed reasonable as his mind screamed, "What do I do? What do I do? What do I *DO?!*"

He called out across the intraship line, "Armory?"

Kevin Carson answered wearily, "Ready."

"Battery Alpha, status?" asked Metcalfe.

"Battery Alpha, offline," was the response. Of course it was. But what could I say? The enemy was watching.

In fact, the enemy was entertained by Metcalfe's irrational behavior. Fehajiq said, "You're an amusing fellow. It's a pity to blow you up."

Metcalfe continued like a robot drone. "Battery Beta, status?"

"Battery Beta, offline."

I tried to get his attention, to no avail.

"Battery Gamma, status?"

"Battery Gamma, offline."

"Robot shuttles, closing!" I reminded Metcalfe, hoping to snap him out of his fugue and draw his attention to–

"Battery Epsilon, status?"

At last! He had come to the point!

"Battery Epsilon, active!" was Carson's surprised response.

Metcalfe was baffled. "Battery Epsilon wha -- ?" he wondered. Not able to help myself, I backhanded his shoulder and pointed at the enemy on the monitors. Then, finally, with a cough he managed, "Battery Epsilon... fire."

Even as Fehajiq cried out in surprise and rage, *Titan's* mighty cannons lashed out, and the Qraitian's helpless ejaculation was lost in the din of detonations, screams and falling debris which came to us over his open comm channel. Remembering that my place was supporting this poor, failing commander, I reported the direct hit.

Metcalfe, energized by his unexpected success, ordered the destruction of the warhead-bearing robot shuttles. With the ship out of danger, he went on, with only minor prodding, to rescue the survivors and reclaim *Titan's* crew and passengers, who circled round the ship in life pods like bees around a hive.

Lest I belabour the point, it was that one, forgotten battery which stood between all of Quintil and radioactive death. At such moments, it is with calm and cold calculation that we must respond. I don't believe I'm going too far out on a limb in saying that it takes a carefully engineered intellect to deliver that level of calm under pressure, yea, under fire.

Quintil was very lucky. *This time.*

But I've been asked, how did I come to be in this place at this time? Well...

– *Excerpt from* Who'll Stop the Rain: A Candid Account of the Greatest Terrorist Attack Ever Mounted, and How it was Foiled, *by Sestus Blaurich. Copyright 308 PL by Blaurich Industries et al, Quintoplis, Rigel V.*

"And this is *The Naked Truth,* with your host, Vixyn Tantacles. I'm here with author and hero of the Qraitian incursion, Sestus Blaurich. Sestus, Welcome."

"Thank you, Vixyn. It's an honor."

"Please! I'm just the beneficiary of the most spectacular set of mammary glands ever engineered by our civilization. You're an honest-to-commerce hero! Who, I might add, looks even better out of uniform than in."

"Well, Admiral Fournier felt I shouldn't be in uniform, since I'm speaking as a private citizen. Navy regs and all that."

"Allowing you to honor *our* regs, which state that no one comes on *The Naked Truth* wearing a stitch of clothing! And... yum! Look at you!"

"I'd rather look at you, Vixyn."

"So I see. Say, how big–"

"Now, now, my vitals are all public record. Let's not descend to quoting statistics."

"Gorgeous and modest, ladies and gentlemen! I promise I'll keep him here in all his naked glory as long as I can. So, Sestus... Terrence Metcalfe...?"

"What can I say?"

"You've already said a lot."

"Only the truth. I have the utmost respect for what Metcalfe has been able to accomplish, given the hurdles he's had to leap."

"But some of those hurdles have been lowered for him."

"Well... Captain Atal thinks a lot of him."

"But is that high regard misplaced? Yesterday, my guest was Subcutaneous Fraud, the Welzant Chair of the school of psychiatry at the University of Rigel, Quintopolis campus. He suggested that Metcalfe has a martyr complex."

"He did see piloting the ship into the enemy and killing us all as our best option ."

"Do you think he has a death wish?"

"Perhaps not a death wish... I think he wants to be seen suffering for his beliefs. Remember, being from Terra, the bulk of his education has been a religious indoctrination. Terrans idolize people they call "saints," who are supposed to be human beings whose behavior exemplifies everything these god creatures want us to do. Most of these saints, if you look them up, you'll discover they died–horribly, I'm talking, they died in really horrible ways. And I think that's what Terrans admire."

"That they died?"

"That they died in pain, crying out the names of their gods. Professing their faith. There was one, Saint Sebastian, who, like Metcalfe, was given a high military appointment by the Emperor of... something or another. When it was found out he belonged to the wrong religious sect, he was shot full of arrows. But he didn't die. He just inspired a lot of artwork. I think that's what Metcalfe wants. He wants to be seen suffering nobly and praising his deities. So that the folks back home on Terra will point to him and say that he's a local boy made good."

"Wow. That must be hard to deal with. For him and everyone around him. Do you get frustrated?"

"Vixyn, I just try to help the guy. I like him, really. I'm not sure he always likes me."

"But everyone in the Confederacy knows you like him. I've got this holo on permanent view in my office—"

"Oh, no!"

"Oh, *yes*, Sestus. This is a celebration of sexuality if ever I've seen one. Brothers in arms... and legs and tongues and... well... "

"We didn't authorize release of that. It's from Metcalfe's personnel file."

"And it shows you showing your Terran shipmate some very big love."

"It was also a training exercise."

"So? Where do I enlist so you can do that to me?"

"Oh, you don't have to enlist! But seriously, Metcalfe needed a comrade to demonstrate that he didn't suffer from the common Terran perversion of homophobia."

"Homo-what-now?"

"Terrans—most of them—believe that sex should be reserved to one man and one woman for life."

"Ouch!"

"And they're deathly afraid of sex-play between people of the same gender. That's homophobia."

"No, honey, that's just sad."

"Isn't it?"

"Well, I guess Metcalfe doesn't have it, huh? Or maybe you cured him!"

"I don't like to brag."

"I'm embarrassing you! I'll stop. So, you've saved Quintil, hell, you've saved the Confederacy. Let's talk about what happens next."

"Well, obviously we've seen that the threat hasn't gone away. After the Qraitian war ended and the peace treaty was signed, we all heaved a collective sigh of relief. We thought we could go back to business as usual. But I think what we've learned in the last few months is that the universe... it's not a safe place."

"There's a sword hanging over our heads."

"And its name is the Qraitian Empire. I don't think we can pretend that the ongoing peace talks are going to amount to anything. Sure, our leaders might sign on the line and say we're going to make nice; but all it takes is one lunatic who's willing to do something crazy–"

"Like stealing a freighter and loading it with Senterium K."

"And pointing it at our home planet, yes. Exactly. It can happen again. Next time we might not be as lucky."

"Is the Navy taking steps to prevent it from happening again?"

"Big changes are coming. Everyone will be under scrutiny."

"Not me, I hope!"

"Vixyn, anyone could be a rogue, or just an unsuspecting dupe of the Qraitian extremists."

"Sestus, tell me straight: What rights should we, as a free people, be prepared to sacrifice in order to stay safe?"

"We should be prepared to sacrifice *no* rights! That's the meaning of 'a free people,' you horse's ass!" Captain Jan Atal punctuated his remark with a hard slap of his hand on the synthetic glass of the tabletop in front of him. Cups and plates rattled noisily, threatening to spill the remains of a very good breakfast. He was sharing said breakfast with his daughter on his private promenade aboard the *CNV Titan*. His A.I. unit politely inquired if something was amiss. Atal dismissed it.

Kaya clucked her tongue and smiled with one corner of her mouth. "Daddy, it's a recorded broadcast. It can't hear you. And you've never seen a horse, so how can you reliably compare Vixyn Tantacles to the ass of one?"

Her father swore in a language she did not know and shoved hard at the hologram of Vixyn and Sestus with one hand. Instead of shutting off as expected, the medicine-ball-sized sphere containing the images of two attractive nudes bounced off the wall and caromed about the room for several courses before Atal caught it between two hands and made a compressing gesture, causing the interface to switch off.

Kaya laughed hysterically, holding her breastbone with one hand in an effort to avoid choking.

"And you wonder why I never allowed you to watch holos during meals," the Captain growled. "How can the digestive system function when its owner is always angry at the stupidity of his fellow humans as relayed to us so faithfully by programs like that one?"

"I haven't wondered for some time. Not since I was about six years old and realized my father was the sensitive type, prone to lose sleep over the plight of the stupid and less fortunate."

"Sensitive my left buttock! I sleep fine! But I'd sleep better if those two were working where they belong–in Den's cheapest brothel, servicing blitz addicts!–instead of on the highest-rated news show in the Confederacy and aboard my ship, respectively."

Kaya considered it. "Vixyn belongs in a brothel, yes. But it'd be a shame to risk marring Sestus's beauty. He's quite nice to look at, when his mouth is closed. A work of art, really."

"Perhaps you'd like to have him stuffed and mounted in your cabin."

Kaya giggled. "Stuffed and mounted? Well–"

"Stop. Now. I wish you'd show some appreciation for the gravity of the issue, Kaya. Tantacles is a damned fool, but she speaks for all the other damned fools–most of the population! They really are ready to trade their freedom for security. To be searched at every entryway and egress, to have their every move monitored by holo camera, to have their choice of friends, reading material and clothing scrutinized, all so that they can have the illusion of safety!"

Kaya nodded, sober now. "They really are. And they're going to. That decision has been made."

He shook his head. "The majority shouldn't have the power to take freedom away from those who want it."

"The majority takes whatever power it wants, until the individual stands up and resists. Then there's a fight. Fortunately, the majority doesn't have much will power, so it doesn't win a lot of those fights. You taught me that, Daddy. Why are you railing like a student activist?"

Atal set his chin firmly. "Because even with my years of experience, one should never lose one's sense of outrage over injustice... or idiocy."

"I don't think you're in any danger, Father dear." She frowned. "But I do think you're right. The Arbiter's Council is considering another raft of security measures, and the Navy's intel folks are probably way ahead of them, developing new, draconian S.O.P.s–"

"They are," Atal interrupted. "Admiral Fournier is on his way to us as we speak, to invoke a new galactic order."

"Fournier? Talk about ruining my digestion!"

"You can imagine what he has on his agenda. And I imagine he'll be accompanied by a squad of the Navy Press Corps, ready to draft press releases with each syllable he utters." He assumed an exaggerated deep voice. " 'Your Navy, fighting for safety!'"

"You should have been an actor, Daddy."

"I'd probably have gone farther in my career, since all we're doing to protect our populace is spinning journalistic fantasies to lull them into a sense of calm!"

"All Fournier's doing, you mean. I think we've done considerably more. And it's because we stopped Fehajiq and his band of merry men that Fournier's press releases get any attention at all."

"Ninety per cent of the viewing audience would be dead if we hadn't stopped them," said Atal. "Beyond that, you're right. The success of the working few gives parasites like Fournier a lot of clout with the masses."

"And the masses love us right now."

"Most of them," agreed Atal. "But there is a vocal minority who are asking why the Qraitians were able to get so close to accomplishing their goal."

"You mean 'why was a lowly Terran midshipman all that stood between billions and their doom?' That's the question Sestus is encouraging, isn't it? Trying to make it look like Metcalfe bumbled and stumbled through that crisis, instead of keeping his cool and saving all our skins. As if it was only Sestus Blaurich who stayed calm!"

Now she was angry, Atal observed. He voice climbed an octave, as it did when her temper suddenly flared.

"I wonder if the bastard knows that the complete record of what happened on the command deck that day is available?" she went on. "Maybe the public deserves to know that the great Sestus Blaurich was so scared he damn near pissed himself! That he was shrieking at Yank, begging him to let him go to a life pod!"

Atal smiled, unable to contain his pride at the memory of that day. "While you held your post and prepared to go down with the ship."

"While we all did," she reminded him. "Except for Darby, and Sestus, if Metcalfe hadn't made him stay. And now Sestus is taking credit for stopping the terrorists!"

"I'm sure that doesn't sit well."

"Oh, Daddy, you have no idea!"

"I have an idea. I have a lot of them. I'm not the fool on the hill, as you would cast me. But how is Metcalfe? Really?"

Kaya raised an eyebrow. "Ask Pallas."

Since they had transferred to *Titan*, the romance between the young Terran and Pallas, the Phaetonian psychohistorial researcher who'd joined them as a civilian observer, had been the talk of the ship.

"Green is an ugly color on you, daughter."

"Oh, I'm not jealous. Not in the way you mean, anyway. I just mean... he's not talking to us."

"'Us' meaning you and your.. Arbiters' Society?"

"Outsiders may not speak the name, Daddy. We call us 'The Arbiters.'"

"I'm afraid everyone else is starting to. Still. What you're observing isn't new. Metcalfe's ordeal has separated him from his peers. It happens. An officer has to step up and be the one in charge, making life and death decisions. It's hard for people to see someone they consider to be a friend in that capacity, realizing he might decide that their lives have to end for some greater good, assuming it's either greater or good. It's even harder for the one who's singled out, knowing it could come to that."

Not a fan of chairs, Kaya was seated on the floor in lotus position. Now she leaned forward, placing her elbows heavily on the glass. "I'm worried about him."

"You never worry about anything."

"Correction, Daddy. I've worried about you all my life."

"Misplaced concern. I can take care of myself. And I think you'll find that Metcalfe can too."

The giant holo floating over the tables in the officers' mess faded as Vixyn Tantacles enfolded Sestus in her bare arms and legs, insinuating herself about him like she was actually a colony of serpents. It was the traditional farewell greeting for guests on Vixyn's show. More than once, the embrace had continued after the feed was cut, and, more than once, the resultant footage had been released on underground and public networks. Vixyn pretended outrage, but viewers knew it was all part of her P.R. machine.

"Bloody bullshit!" snapped Kevin Carson as the images disappeared. "Making it look as though you were his puppet and he just pulled the strings!"

Across from him, Terry Metcalfe gave a noncommital shrug. It lacked so much commitment that it involved the use of only one side of his mouth and the slightest elevation of one shoulder. He continued to hold his coffee cup in front of him and stare into it pensively.

"Five's just being Five," he observed.

"Five." It was the nickname they had hung on Sestus Blaurich last year when they'd first come aboard the *Titan*. Although Blaurich had arrived before them, indeed, had been assigned to *Titan* first, they'd named him their fifth midshipman on the grounds that he was an outsider in their midst, wherever the Arbiters went being their home turf. The name had stuck, and even spread in usage to some of the casual crew and the ship's Marines. Those who didn't know its simple origins assumed it described the aristocratic Midshipman's mental age.

"What does that even mean, 'Five's just being five?'" Carson demanded.

Metcalfe let out a deliberate breath. "It means we all have our natures and we have to be true to them. Five has to have the spotlight, and so he seeks it out. Hell, the spotlight probably has to have him, too. Maybe light needs to illuminate certain combinations of matter, because light is somehow fed by the appreciation that results."

"Christ, Metcalfe, you're waxing poetic about your mortal enemy!"

"He's not my mortal enemy," said Metcalfe, fiddling idly with his silverware.

Had he always arranged it so carefully on the table after a meal? Carson couldn't remember. Probably not, or he'd have noticed.

"I don't have a mortal enemy," Metcalfe continued.

"So it's okay that he claims credit. You saved the goddamned Confederacy–"

"We," Metcalfe corrected him. "We saved the goddamned Confederacy. And Five was there as much as anyone."

"But you called the shots. You had the plan. And, dammit, Five stayed because you ordered him to! The rest of us stayed even though you told us not to! So why are you suddenly going soft on him?"

Metcalfe chuckled. "Maybe because he was the only one who followed my orders to the letter?"

Carson flung his napkin in his friend's face. "Next time, you bastard–next time you're flying the damned ship on a suicide run, you can bloody well do it alone!"

"I'll keep that in mind."

"Seriously, Metcalfe, why is Sestus the only one who's getting interviewed? Why aren't the rest of us talking about this in the media?"

"Maybe because you and I are both Terrans and they're afraid of getting diseases, Cernaq creeps them out, Aer'La downright frightens them, and the Atals have too much class to appear on *The Naked Truth?*"

Carson grinned. "Could you imagine the Captain on there with Vixyn Tantacles? She'd probably conduct the whole interview seated on his lap!"

"Thus denying the viewers a look at the very thing they'd want to see," observed Metcalfe.

"Be worth it, though, to see the silly little bitch get the cold shoulder."

"I think you just want to see the Captain naked," jibed Metcalfe.

Carson shook his head emphatically. "Too old for my tastes. I'll take my genetically engineered perfection about three decades earlier, thank you very much."

It was oft-observed fact that, though the morals of the Inner Worlds were easy, and public nudity was not only tolerated but encouraged, very few people could say that they'd seen Jan Atal, hero of the Qraitian War and industrial prince of Quintil, nude. Even his officers who had served closely with him for years couldn't say they had, and there were no published holos, though there were many simulations created by fans. It seemed to be all a part of the Captain's mystique.

"I don't see why you're complaining about Five, then," said Metcalfe. "He's 30 years younger and genetically perfect."

"True," Carson agreed. "But, much as I like good-looking boys, I don't see it happening."

"Five wouldn't lower himself, you mean."

"Exactly what I mean, and you know it. He thinks he's better than us. He thinks he's better than everyone. So how can you sit here and let him make you look like the village idiot without even getting a little bit annoyed?"

"By realizing that Five is what Five is, I'm not going to change him, and that it doesn't matter what the drooling masses think happened. I know what happened, and so does everyone who was there. I'll never win a popularity contest with people who are impressed by an empty-headed twit like Blaurich. So why try?"

"Aside from referring to him as an 'empty-headed twit,' nothing in that statement sounds like it came from the Terry Metcalfe I used to know. Where the hell is he?"

Metcalfe's face darkened slightly. "He grew up, and he realized it's pointless to tilt at windmills, especially when the windmills have a dozen public relations professionals in their employ to make them look good."

"Dammit, Terry, I'm serious. You haven't been the same since we fought Fehajiq."

"Of course I'm not the same. Are you the same?"

"I'm not so different that my friends don't recognize me anymore! Last year, if Five had pulled a stunt like this, you would have plotted revenge the like of which no crime boss on Den ever contemplated. Now you just sit back and say, 'Five is Five.'"

"Five *is* Five."

"Yeah! So he is! Congratulations, Doctor of Philosophy Terrence Metcalfe. You've proven that 'A' is 'A.' Would anybody doubt you're shacked up with a Phaetonian? You're starting to act like one!"

"Meaning?"

"Meaning I haven't seen you get drunk in I don't know how long. You haven't come to a night out at the pub in weeks. My god, you *walked out* on the party I threw you when you got promoted–"

"I had my reasons."

That gave Carson pause, and he quieted. Metcalfe had left the party to pray for the souls of the dead. "I know you did. I know... is that it, Terry? Is it Nathan?"

Metcalfe shook his head. "Not really. I mourned Nathan's death... I guess... He was a screwed up piece of shit, but he was my friend. It hurts to realize that he won't be there to bail out any more. I won't get any more calls that he's in trouble, won't see him grinning about the latest stupid, insensitive stunt he's pulled. But then... you know, he died trying to buy Aer'La time, trying to save his crew."

"I know," said Carson.

"I guess that's some consolation. Maybe that's why I can live with it. In the end... there was something good in Nathan."

"Okay, if not Nathan, then–"

Metcalfe held up a finger. "What's that?" he asked.

"What's what?"

Metcalfe reached past Carson's shoulder to place his fingers within the command grid of the news holo. It had automatically quieted and shrunk when two people nearby, namely Metcalfe and Carson, had begun speaking. The interfaces in public areas were programmed to do that. They either shrank and quieted, or muted, depending on the audio intensity of nearby conversations, or they simply bounced away to another, quieter area. There were no quieter areas in the mess this morning.

Making a beckoning and then a stretching gesture, Metcalfe enlarged the holo and brought it closer to him. The volume increased to meet the user's perceived desire to pay closer attention.

A more sedate news program had followed *The Naked Truth*. This particular segment highlighted the opinions of random citizens. Today, cameras were flitting about what Carson recognized as the municipal center of Quintopolis. On the steps and about the open and airy plaza built of a native white stone, demonstrators gathered. Some carried hand-lettered signs, others flashed messages and elaborate animations in holo from their data implants. The camera hovered by one woman who stood on a high step, shouting to her fellows.

"... and we've got to take it as a sign!"

The crowd punctuated this with a cheer.

"We're not *safe!*"

Another cheer.

"We could all have been killed! A civilization gone!"

"Yes!!!" shouted the crowd as one.

"It was Quintil bravery that saved us!"

Cheer.

"One man brave enough to put his life on the line!"

Cheer.

"One man brave enough to kill the enemy!"

Wild cheer.

"Are we going to follow his example?"

"Yes!!!"

"Or are we going to cower in the corner like the Terran?"

"No!!!'

"We're not safe until every last Qraitian is dead!"

Mad, wild, raucous cheers.

"The next signs we carry will be painted on their skins... in blood!"

Noise. Pure and unadulterated.

"What do we want?"

"*WAR!!!*"

"*Idiots!*" Metcalfe punched the holo, sending it flying.

"Whoa!" yelled Carson as Metcalfe's fist nearly struck his chin. Such was the force of it, that, had it landed, he might have lost teeth. "Watch it!"

"Sorry," said Metcalfe immediately. He looked around to see who might have noticed his outburst. He looked even more crestfallen as it became apparent from the stares that everyone had noticed it.

"What the hell, man?" demanded Carson.

Metcalfe shook his head and smacked the table. "Idiots!" he said again. "We save their lives and they want to throw them away in a war."

"No," Carson corrected him. "They want *us* to throw them away in a war. Very different."

"Who in their right mind wants war? Who?"

"People who have never experienced it, or people who have nothing to live for anyway."

"The Quintils have plenty to live for. By that score, you and I should be the ones wanting war." He sat back and attempted to regulate his breathing.

"You okay?" Carson couldn't help but smile.

"I will be." He paused and then threw a piece of toast Carson's way. "What the hell are you smiling about, asshole?"

"It's nice to see you've still got it."

"Got what?"

"The worst temper in the Confederacy. I was really beginning to think Doc Faulkner had lobotomized you. But *that*–" he gestured to where the holo had finally settled over an unoccupied table "–was a classic Metcalfe tantrum."

"So glad to be of service."

"Best to get it out of your system now, anyway."

Metcalfe narrowed his eyes. "Why?"

"Because of the communique I just delivered to the Captain. Admiral Fournier will be on board within the hour. All officers are to report for new orders."

Metcalfe brought his hands to his face and said something which, though muffled, sounded very much like "kill me now."

Session Transcript

4 October 308 PL

LUCINDA GRAE, LT, CMT, PhD

Patient: Lt. Terrence Metcalfe, CN

History: 22-year-old officer who served as commander of Naval forces in a loss-of-life incident. 157 killed, 38 of those terrorists killed by subject's direct orders. Note also loss of close, childhood friend during battle.

Following the Fehajiq incident, Lt. Metcalfe was referred to me for routine CISM screening. Of greatest concern at present is a pronounced and continuing feeling of alienation.

LG: You haven't gotten that angry in a while.

Metcalfe: No...

LG: But you think it was only the news of the demonstrations.

Metcalfe: What else would it be?

LG: Carson has noticed a change in you.

Metcalfe: I've changed. There's no question.

LG: He thinks you're holding back. You're not telling your friends what's going on in your head. Is he right?

Metcalfe: Maybe he is.

LG: Maybe it upsets you that Carson is right. That you can't completely hide from your friends.

Metcalfe: Why would I hide from my friends?

LG: You tell me. Why are you bottling up anger until it explodes in a public place?

Metcalfe: Anger... anger is dangerous. I don't want to show–

LG: You don't want to show anger? As opposed to simply not experiencing it? Or is it that you don't want your friends to see your anger?

Metcalfe: Maybe I'm protecting them.

LG: Maybe... you don't trust them. You don't think they can handle it.

Metcalfe: Maybe.

LG: That is a change for you. We need to talk more about that.

CHAPTER TWO

She tried to gasp, but found she couldn't. To gasp required air, and there was none. Blackness gaped before her, silent and all-encompassing. Death. Black, silent, death. Behind her were still the bursts of light. Shrapnel flew past. It should have whizzed in her ears, but it did not. There was no sound. If a piece came to sever her head, she would never know it. She would just be dead.

Silent, black, death.

She'd be dead in seconds anyway. Ejected from the shuttle as it disintegrated, as Renfro had screamed in his dying agonies, lost in the screams of the others now dead, she had managed to cling to the pressure suit. She had seconds to don it. No human would have even that much.

She gathered it in her hands to pull it onto her legs. It was then that she saw the smashed faceplate. No good. Even if she managed to get it on, it would hold no air. There was nothing to do but open her mouth and suck vacuum and die.

She let our her last breath and wondered what would happen next...

Acr'La awoke, bathed in sweat, gasping for air. She sat up and clutched frantically about her, searching, searching... she'd just had the suit in her hand! She had to get it on! She grabbed fabric and pulled it to her.

As the bedclothes were torn from him, Cernaq snapped awake. Knowing better than to try to touch her in this condition, for she could badly injure him in her panic, he called out with his mind.

Aer'La, it's all right.

"The faceplate!" she cried. "It's broken! I'm going to die!"

You're not going to die, Aer'La. You're safe in your bed. You're with me. The battle ended months ago, and we won.

She tried to wrap her head around it, still gasping.

May I speak now? May I touch you?

She nodded, still unsure of her voice.

His thin arms, wispy, like tendrils of smoke, encircled her. He kissed her neck and spoke gently in her ear. "You're safe, Aer'La. It's over."

She nodded, coughed, and managed, "It was like I was back there, Cernaq. In space. I saw... I heard... Renfro dying. Again. And all his people that we tried to rescue, after Fehajiq attacked their ship and stole the Senterium-K."

"Aer'La," he said gently, "this is the third nightmare this week. You're losing sleep. It's not healthy. Won't you–?"

"No!" she snapped. "I won't go to see a head-shrinker! They'll put me on drugs. I've been drugged before!"

"You were drugged, as a child, by slavers, Aer'La. Their goal was to control you. A therapist will only prescribe drugs to help you recover–"

"No! I don't need drugs! There's nothing wrong with me!"

"There's nothing wrong with you," he agreed. "But there *is* something wrong, Aer'La. Something very wrong. I'm... we're all... worried about you."

"Oh, you've all been talking about me?"

"Not in the way you suggest, but–"

"I'm not weak, Cernaq. I can deal with this. I've been raped. I've seen loved ones... murdered. I've survived it all. Why would this be any different?"

"Because, as a child, you had no frame of reference. No concept of what a 'normal' life should be. You didn't know what you had to lose. Now you do."

"And I can handle it! Metcalfe may need help, but he's not me."

"He's the strongest person I know apart from you," said Cernaq.

"But he's not me! Okay? He may be okay with having some do-gooder playing around in his skull. I'm not! Now drop it, and let's get some sleep. Briefing in the morning, as you keep reminding me."

"They found God?"

Aer'La felt the others glaring at her. She'd blurted out her question out of turn... as usual; but dammit, she *hated* staff briefings! This one had already burned up a half-hour of her time, with no end in sight. *Someone* had to get them to the point.

Beside her, Cernaq muttered that he "didn't realize God had been missing."

"Old joke, Cernaq," said Metcalfe.

"The classics never grow old."

Great. They thought it was all a big joke. Aer'La was actually trying to understand the mission, and they were cutting up.

Admiral Georg Fournier, at the end of the conference table, cleared his throat like the pompous windbag he was. "Gentleman and ladies," he said impatiently. He waited for everyone to stop and notice him. *If I had his face,* thought Aer'La, *I wouldn't want to be noticed!* Damn! He was looking right at her! "Bos'n, your presence here is a courtesy to the Captain. It is not appropriate for you to interrupt. If you are asked to speak–"

Captain Atal spoke up. "Admiral, pardon me, but my officers–the Bos'n included–have been granted standing liberty to speak freely. I find it encourages an environment of intellectual honesty. It makes the ship run more smoothly, and allows potential problems to be identified quickly."

Atal knew Aer'La didn't deal well with this "speak when spoken to" bullshit. That was for slaves, and Aer'La wasn't a slave anymore. The Captain always stood up for his people. That was why they respected him, and drew rude pictures of Fournier on the public nets.

"Bos'n," the Captain went on, "please do not interrupt the Admiral."

Atal also knew how to handle the higher ups.

"Yes sir," Aer'La said.

"Thank you, Captain," said Fournier. "As I was saying..."

Fournier went blathering on about how they were headed for the planet Eleusis, saying it for, what, the eighth time? Like every other colony, it was settled over two centuries ago by out-migrants from Terra. Wasn't that what "colony" meant? And just when it looked like he might finally stop repeating himself and answer Aer'La's question—"the residents claim to have found a physical incarnation of that which Terrans call the Deity" being his way of saying "they found God"—he went and called on freaking Darby to give a report.

Aer'La thought she heard Atal grind his teeth. He did that when he was really pissed. When she saw Kaya nudge her father and whisper, she knew that she was right. Fournier wasn't supposed to give assignments to Atal's crew, but he always seemed to bypass Atal when it came to Darby.

Deputy Captain Phyn Darby was an ass-kisser. Aer'La despised him, and the feeling was mutual. He bullied those he considered to be his inferiors—and that was everyone. He was hopelessly by-the-book in areas where it didn't matter, and sloppy in areas where it did. Above all, Aer'La did not like the way he smelled.

"Eleusis," said Darby, "is one of the more temperate worlds identified for colonization by the early surveys, long before Captain Douglas and Professor Mors began their detailed inventory of the habitable planets in this arm of the galaxy."

Jeez, he sounded like a travel guide! What was the point?

"The settlers were members of the Quaker sect, a religious group on Terra whose official name was the Society of Friends. Like so many such groups, they fled the persecution of the fundamentalist Church of Terra. They left Terra just as Quintil was being settled, employing a generation ship which brought them to Eleusis nearly a century later. They believe in absolute non-violence. "

Translation: Blah blah blah hundreds of years. Blah blah blah they're non-violent. Blah blah blah. Aer'La tried, as sneakily as possible, to settle back into her chair and see if she could nap with her eyes open.

"Not long after their arrival, reports began to reach Quintil that this sect believed they had, as the Bos'n put it, 'found God' on the planet Eleusis."

At last! The only interesting thing that had been said so far! Aer'La sat up.

"Back to my question," she said. "What does that mean? Have they found God?"

"Of course not," snapped Fournier.

"The group now calling themselves the Family of God claim to have made contact with an infinitely powerful intelligence on the surface of Eleusis, an intelligence they believe to actually be the deity their forbears called variously Yahweh, Jehovah or simply 'God.'"

Blah, blah, blah... huh?

"Mysticism and hearsay!" said Fournier. "Darby, we're here to brief your people on the tactical situation."

"Of course, Admiral, my apologies. I find it sometimes helps to capture the attention of the younger officers if one touches on popular culture."

Aer'La thought she heard Kaya mutter something which might have been "condescending pig." She looked to Cernaq, who said in her mind, *Yep. 'Condescending pig.' And he is, isn't he?*

"Strategically," Darby continued, "Eleusis is situated within a cluster of known stable conjugates."

"It's at a crossroads," observed Celia Faulkner, *Titan's* centenarian ship's physician, and a follower of the ancient religion of Wicca. "Mystically significant."

Fournier glared. Aer'La, while she loved Celia dearly, started to lose focus again. Whenever Celia talked her witchcraft stuff, Aer'La felt her eyes glaze, her ears stop up and her brain shut down.

Darby was saying something about Eleusis being "on the way to many strategic locations within both Confederate space and the Qraitian Empire."

"It is therefore a planet to which it's vital the Navy maintain controlled access," Fournier summed up.

"Is that our mission, Admiral?" asked Kevin Carson. "To secure the planet against Qraitian incursion?"

Carson was good at paying attention in meetings. How did he do it? He was also the heaviest drinker, the biggest prankster, the highest scorer sexually, of all of Aer'La's friends. How could he be like that one minute, and then seem to be interested in this crap the next?

"It's a bit more complex than that, Mr. Carson," sniffed Darby. "You see the Family of God maintains that they are not members of the Confederacy. They believe they are brothers and sisters to all living, intelligent beings, and should have no ties or preferences which exclude any others. Therefore... " he paused for effect," they object to a Naval presence in their star system."

"Captain Darby," Metcalfe asked, "are you saying that Titan's visit to this planet is contrary to the wishes of the populace?"

Here we go, thought Aer'La. Nothing got Metcalfe riled like Fournier–or anyone–flexing their muscles against civilians. He was getting pissed already, and it was pissing Fournier off too. Still, if this planet was in a bad place as far as the Qraitians went...

Fournier's tone was sharp. "Mr. Metcalfe, we are going there. If your conscience dictates that you not trample on the delicate sensibilities of fanatics, well, perhaps you need to reconsider your career choices."

Everyone in the room looked uncomfortable. They usually did, when Fournier talked to Metcalfe.

Captain Atal finally spoke, telling Metcalfe that *Titan* wasn't unwelcome on Eleusis, they were just unwelcome to try and send any visitors to the planet away. "The people of Eleusis welcome all visiting ships including military vessels."

"And that," said Darby, "is the biggest complicating factor. 'Military vessels' unfortunately includes Qraitian military vessels. They're in and out of the system all the time."

That, Aer'La simply didn't believe. This was starting to get interesting. "So there are Qraitians already on Eleusis?"

"Worse than that," observed Darby. "Although the Family is scrupulous about maintaining privacy, it has come to the attention of Confederate Intelligence that there are Qraitians who are considered permanent residents, and, indeed, members of the Family of God."

"How the hell did that stay out of the media?" wondered Atal.

"The Office of Confederate Intelligence," explained Darby, "considered it disruptive to public calm for people to know that there were Qraitians living within the established boundaries of Confederate space, and so they—"

"Censored the press," finished Metcalfe. Was he, maybe, being a little overboard today? These were Qraitians, after all.

"Encouraged cooperation by the press and discouraged the publication of speculation about the Qraitian presence on Eleusis."

"They censored the press," agreed Atal. Well, if the Captain said it...

"The key point," said Fournier tightly. "There are Qraitians on the planet; some are permanent residents."

"In addition, the Qraitian military are regular visitors," said Darby. "I have an exhaustive log of their visits in the past month—"

"And how did we get that?" asked Atal.

"Surveillance ships," Fournier replied.

"Are we monitoring traffic in all peaceful solar systems, Admiral?" asked Celia.

"All of those of interest, Doctor," said the Admiral. "These are dangerous and unstable times. The Navy has stepped up observation on all levels."

"And no one objects to this... monitoring?" wondered Metcalfe.

"Many people object. Lawsuits are being filed by the dozens. But we're within our legal jurisdiction."

"Why haven't we heard about increased observation in the media?" asked Metcalfe.

Fournier smiled. "Is there any advantage to stirring up needless concern? We're the good guys, Metcalfe. We're not going to abuse our authority."

Metcalfe looked like he desperately wanted to say, "Yeah right," but he didn't.

"Doesn't the planet have defenses," asked Kaya. "In case one of their guests becomes belligerent?"

"Not a one," said Darby. "The Family of God believe utterly in non-aggression. They have devoted all their energies to making Eleusis a habitable world, and allowing anyone who wishes to settle there."

"If they can afford it," said Fournier pointedly.

"Of course," agreed Darby. "They're pacifist, not socialist. Eleusis is one of the wealthiest planets in Confederate space. There is still ample land which is available for homesteading, but they do not allow squatting."

"Whatever they are," said Fournier, "they do not recognize our authority, or the authority of any government. They will resist our efforts to carry out our mission."

"And that is?" asked Atal.

Fournier harumphed. Again. "To remove all Qraitian nationals from Eleusis and place them in Confederate custody, to establish a Navy Liaison on Eleusis and prepare for the permanent   presence of Confederate protective forces in the system."

"Over the objections of the inhabitants?" asked Metcalfe.

"They may object to their hearts' content. Should they try to interfere, they will be arrested just as the Qraitians are arrested."

"Sir," said Metcalfe, "their history suggests they'll have no problem with that. Further. They may not take direct or obvious action. They may hide the Qraitians among them. On my planet, their ancestors were instrumental in running underground movements to free slaves."

Fournier drew himself up in his seat. "We are not enslaving anyone, Mr. Metcalfe. We are protecting innocent lives against the threat of more Qraitian terrorist activity. You of all people should appreciate that."

Why the hell was Metcalfe bringing up slavery? Aer'La hated to agree with Fournier, but... she spoke up. "Why wouldn't anyone not want to be protected against the Qraitians? Are these Family of God people nuts? Do they know what the Qraitians can do to them?"

Aer'La knew well what Qraitians could do. They could raid a freighter and steal its cargo after slaughtering most of its crew, leaving them floating in bloody pieces in zero-G. They could fire on the shuttle which attempted to carry away survivors, as the shuttle she and Renfro were piloting had done. They could leave a dozen people breathing vacuum, as Aer'La had...

The choking sensation returned. She held her mouth shut tight, keeping the air in her lungs, even as they threatened to explode. She grasped frantically for the pressure suit. Where? Where was it? She reached out–

And grabbed Cernaq's hand.

You're safe, Aer'La.

Embarrassed, she shoved his hand, and with it his comforting presence, away from her. She knew she was safe, dammit! Sometimes the memory just caught up with her, that was all.

It's called a flashback, he said in her mind.

She glared murderously at him. She didn't want reassurance. She wanted to be left alone. She looked away from him, and back to Fournier, who was speaking.

"I'd say they know the Qraitians pretty well, since they have them living among them. I wonder if their reticence to have the Navy on hand is as much about principle as it is about loyalty to the other side."

"So a religious sect that's been nothing but peaceful for longer than the Confederacy has existed is now suspected of what–espionage?" asked Metcalfe.

"Everyone is a suspect," snapped Fournier. "And your tone, Mr. Metcalfe, is bordering on insubordination."

Shut up, Metcalfe! Aer'La thought fervently. She didn't know if she wanted him to do it for his own good, to stay out of trouble with Fournier, or if she was just sick of hearing him talk. Probably the second one. She was sick of hearing everyone talk. Why did they have to have so many damned meetings? If there were Qraitians to beat the shit out of, it was time to go do it!

"Admiral, Captain... " Celia began.

"Doctor?" they both said quickly.

"My people know quite a bit about Eleusis as well."

Fournier rolled his eyes. "Doctor, I'm sure they do, but–"

Celia cut him off. "Eleusis is a dangerous world, Admiral. The legends say–"

"Doctor, this is not the time," said Atal curtly. "This is a mission briefing. If you've got pertinent information, upload it to the appropriate data share; but we must move on."

Anger flashed in the old woman's eyes. Had anyone but Atal said it...

"Thank you, Captain," said Fournier. "You're right, we need to get down to business, because there's a lot to do. Because of the recent... situation, a Qraitian terrorist faction launching an attack on our home soil which failed only—"

"Respectfully, we were all there, Admiral," said Atal, his tone dry.

"So we were. And yet I wonder—were we all aware of what this event means for the future of the Confederacy?" He surveyed the table with one of those meaningful glares which said no one was to dare to answer. Aer'La hated those glares, too, but right now Fournier seemed to at least be making sense.

At last, he answered himself. "It means we can no longer be complacent. We can no longer pretend that the enemy is someone far away and unlikely to enter our sphere of influence."

"Sir," interrupted Atal, "again respectfully... Most of the officers in this room have done their time on border patrol. Recently. I don't think they see the Qraitians as a remote threat. They've encountered more Qraitians than some of the war veterans I know."

"Then why," Fournier demanded, "did this group slip by them, Captain?"

"Begging the Admiral's pardon," said Metcalfe. "They didn't slip by us. They launched a surprise attack on us, and we responded immediately."

Fournier inhaled and considered this. "All right," he said, with unaccustomed civility, "they didn't slip by you. But they made it damned far into our space!"

"And how might we have stopped them?" asked Atal. "They were in a private freighter, broadcasting the correct call signs. We can't just challenge every ship—"

"Can't we?" asked Fournier. "The Admiralty disagrees with you, Captain. We can, and will, challenge and detain any and all non-military vessels found in our space. A security grading system has been established. At the highest grade, ships belonging to more reputable firms and merchants will be subject only to a preliminary review. At the lowest, unknowns and independent operators will be held for as long as it takes to conduct an exhaustive search of their vessels."

"You'll bring interstellar commerce to a standstill!" said Atal.

"Except for the richest companies," observed Celia.

"But we will be safe," said Fournier. "Commercial passenger ships will also be scrutinized. Unknown or suspicious passengers will also be detained. And... as it is possible that the terrorists have agents and sympathizers already in place among settled civilian populations, we're developing a system for monitoring literally everyone who lives in the Confederate Worlds. We're beginning with high risk planets like Eleusis, and also military vessels."

Atal looked as though a chill had run down his spine. "Meaning Titan."

Fournier nodded. "Yes, exactly. It's going to be necessary to carefully monitor everyone on board, especially the civilians. The risk of a sympathizer or actual member of a terrorist group living among the civilian population is just too great to be allowed to continue unchecked."

"What about the casual crew?" wondered Kaya. "They don't go through the background checks that even some of the civilians do."

Aer'La laughed harshly. "Trust me, I know their backgrounds. No Qraitian would dare come into my area. In fact," she grinned, displaying teeth on one side and look suddenly very much like a predator, "it might be funny if one tried. Make a good example to everyone of what would happen if I ever get my hands on one of those bastards. I'll give you what's left over, Admiral... in a little bag. "

Now why was everyone looking at her with such surprise?

Everyone except Fournier, that was. "I may take you up on that, Bos'n. I've no doubt we'll get our hands on some terrorists during the coming shakedown. From this moment on, all civilians boarding *Titan*, leaving *Titan*, or attempting to enter or leave restricted areas, will be carefully screened. In addition, merchants who deal regularly with military personnel will be subjected to background checks and questioning."

"Wait a minute," Atal said. "These are sovereign citizens of Confederate Worlds, Admiral. We can't just–"

"We can," Fournier cut him off. "They are passengers aboard a military transport, traveling at the pleasure of the Secretary," he gestured at himself. "They are not residents on a planet or space station, and you, Captain, are not a governor. I know you think of these people as almost part of your crew, but they are, in fact, my guests. Non-paying guests, most of them. They are subject to military oversight by the Navy. So, effective immediately, screening stations will be set up for all civilian personnel. They will report and undergo questioning and a background check, or they will be arrested and undergo more rigorous questioning."

"And it they object?"

"They may file a complaint. With me. But they will still either cooperate or be taken into custody." His face darkened. "No one has the option of leaving."

"Did you see the look on her face?"

The briefing had dissolved, and Metcalfe and Carson were reporting to their duty stations on the Command Deck.

"Who?" Carson demanded.

"Aer'La, who else?"

"What about her?"

"I don't like the way she's acting. It's like she's suddenly been brainwashed by Fournier, buying into all of this maximum security bullshit. She's too eager to find a Qraitian terrorist. I'm afraid she's going to single out some poor slob who's done nothing wrong. That kind of anger and suspicion gets in the way of her ability to lead—"

"And you know everything about leadership, all of a sudden."

"I didn't say that."

"You didn't have to, it's obvious. Since Fehajiq, every word out of your mouth is about leadership, or priorities."

"I'm just saying we need to maintain a balanced perspective, and Aer'La—"

"Metcalfe, you're overreacting!"

"I don't think so."

"Well I do. You think Fournier's looking for terrorists under every bunk on Titan? I think you're doing the same thing to us–looking for flaws in our leadership style, or our level of commitment. Looking for something you can criticize–some way you can share the benefit of your greater experience and wisdom!"

"I have the same amount of experience as the rest of you!"

"Then act like it!" hissed Carson. "Stop lording over the rest of us like some demigod out of the *Book of Heroes*!"

Metcalfe looked deeply into the eyes of his friend, his expression raw. "You think I'm holding myself above you? That I think I'm better than you are? Kevin, are you kidding? Do you have no idea what's going on in my head? Really?"

"No, I don't," said Carson, still angry, but quieter now.

"I killed dozens of Fehajiq's crew."

Carson started to speak, but Metcalfe held up his hand to stop him.

"I understand I had no choice. I'm not trying to engage in a lot of irrational hand-wringing over doing what I had to do. But... I can't forget what it felt like. On the Command Deck... You told me Aer'La was dead. I knew Nathan had to be too. And... the sheer anger... the rage... I wanted to kill. I wanted to kill Fehajiq with my bare hands. When I gave the order to ram their ship, I knew I had a plan. I knew there was a way to keep us alive, but part of me didn't care! Part of me was so angry that it just wanted to... drive forward and destroy and kill and take us all down to wipe out the ugliness."

"But that part didn't win, Terry."

"No. But I looked in Aer'La's eyes just now and I saw that same naked desire to destroy. It's like looking in a mirror and seeing a scar on my own face."

"And Aer'La will... what? Give into it?"

"She might. You know, she–"

"–She isn't the great Leftenant Metcalfe, with his devotion to peace and understanding!"

"I didn't say– "

"And she's not entitled to her own feelings or her own opinions, because she may be too stupid to handle them!"

"What's the matter with you?" Metcalfe reached out a hand to grasp Carson's shoulder, but Carson slapped it away.

"You think you need to spoon feed Aer'La her feelings, just like you think you need to spoon feed all of us, because only you know right from wrong?"

"Kevin!"

"Maybe what's bothering you isn't you conscience, Metcalfe. Maybe you just need to get the fuck over yourself!"

Session Transcript

5 October 308 PL

LUCINDA GRAE, LT, CMT, PhD

Patient: Lt. Terrence Metcalfe, CN

LG: Is Carson right?

Metcalfe: Do I need to get the fuck over myself?

LG: Are you holding yourself too much accountable? You've admitted to holding back with your friends. Are you actually seeing yourself as not only separate, but superior?

Metcalfe: I don't think—no. No, that's not it. I just... I can't connect with them anymore.

LG: Have you tried?

Metcalfe: (Nods) I can't... focus, I guess. I lose patience. I don't want to talk about silly trivialities. Not after... everything. I guess... I guess I'm trying to... I guess I'm too busy trying to figure out what's going on in my head. That, and making sure... never mind.

LG: No, go on. What are you making sure happens? Or doesn't?

Metcalfe: That I don't lose control again. That I... If I lose my temper, I could screw up. Someone could get hurt.

LG: It's a dangerous job.

Metcalfe: But if I keep myself at peak efficiency, they're safer.

LG: Their safety is your personal responsibility?

Metcalfe: Do I sound that... simplistic? Maybe Carson's right, maybe I do have a messiah complex.

LG: Sestus Blaurich said that.

Metcalfe: Carson's said it too. First, I guess. Scary that they'd agree on something. Especially something about me. Makes me feel like... like...

LG: The world's turning against you?

Metcalfe: I didn't say that. That would be pretty irrational, wouldn't it?

LG: We all have irrational thoughts. Sometimes it's valuable to explore them. Sometimes they're more rational than we at first assume, they're just not fully formed. Don't think, just tell me: what do you want most, right now?

Metcalfe: I want to get away.

CHAPTER THREE

"Want to see a trick?" asked Celia Faulkner, her eyes lively and her tone, well, there was no other word for it... *wicked*.

Shortly before, Kaya had tapped on the open door to Celia's office.

The Doctor was intently studying her tablet, which lay on the oak desktop. The desk was an anomaly on *Titan*, or any naval vessel, for that matter. It was an antique. Faulkner had had it shipped here from her previous posting on *Arbiter*. Apparently, it had been her father's, his father's, someone's mother's... Kaya couldn't keep track. She only knew it wasn't standard Navy issue, and that, though well-kept by its current owner, it was old as hell. The Doctor frequently said that she liked to touch the ancient wood and feel the resonations of its previous owners and users, long dead. Most of her people, the Wiccan residents of Hecate, didn't appreciate antiques. Sensitive to the vibrations of past lives stored somehow within, they found it distracting, unnerving, even frightening to have these objects around. A stray brush of their hands on the surface of one might trigger an intense, emotional, even traumatic episode.

Celia said maybe it was her advanced age that made the difference, or maybe it was just that she was a hard bitch; but she was never overwhelmed by the emotions she picked up from the desk, nor those from many antiques. She found the left over feelings of people now gone soothing and comforting in the technological, information-overloaded culture of the Inner Worlds. It evoked for her a simpler time.

Kaya had touched the desk often and not felt a damned thing. At the back of her mind was a firm conviction that the Doctor was just a bit mad, but it was a madness that her shipmates could tolerate.

Celia looked up at Kaya's knock. Her smile was tight but warm. "Thank you for coming," she said, standing. She came around the old desk and offered Kaya a chair.

"It sounded important," said Kaya.

"It is," the older woman agreed. "Though some might not take what I have to say seriously. It's about Eleusis. And legends."

Kaya sighed. "Dad shut you down in there."

Celia nodded. "The lot of my people. We're usually dismissed by this hyper-rational culture. Still, what I know is important, and I need to share it, before we have dealings with that cursed world."

"'Cursed world?'" Kaya repeated it as the Doctor has spoken it, with the antiquated-sounding double syllable on the first word. "Doctor, I'm afraid you're not going to find me a much more sympathetic audience than my father was. I don't believe—"

"No," agreed Faulkner, "but you will listen."

Kaya wasn't sure if it was an affirmation of confidence in her own generous nature, or a command. She didn't want to ask. She didn't credit herself with a very generous nature.

"The Captain would only dismiss me—has dismissed me, in point of fact. Our Mr. Metcalfe is far too distracted by his own concerns at present to listen. Pallas and Cernaq will both give me a hearing, but... they simply cannot suppress their intellectual natures to glimpse the supernatural in any situation."

"And you think I can?"

The Doctor sat on the edge of her desk, her slight height given the advantage because Kaya was sitting. She looked down at her in what Kaya supposed was a motherly way. Kaya had never had a mother. "I think you're the most persuasive of your fellows, Kaya. While your emotional intelligence is only average—"

"Thanks!"

"Only the truth, kid. Don't be offended by the truth. It's a waste of energy. And don't sulk about it, either. Geniuses on the intellectual front are often compromised by very low emotional intelligence. Not sure why. It certainly doesn't promote the survival of the best and brightest for our geniuses to discourage intimacy."

"I never discourage intimacy!"

"Well-documented," agreed the Doctor. "And that's part of your greatest strength–you know how to play the emotions of others to get what you want–"

"So I'm a manipulative bitch?"

"You can be. And it takes one to know one, trust me. My husbands–no doubt prompted by my youngest, who's an incorrigible–took to calling me 'she who must be obeyed,' for a time. It didn't last."

Kaya grinned. "Why not?"

"Because I *must* be obeyed. When I'm not, things don't go well in the household. There's an old Wiccan proverb–'If mama ain't happy, ain't nobody happy.' I have a feeling your family will someday have the same experience with you. And I think you're the only one who can get the Captain your father to listen to what he needs to hear, namely my people's collected wisdom about the planet we're about to visit."

"Okay," Kaya agreed. "What is it I need to know?"

And it was then that Celia offered to show her a trick.

Kaya once again wondered about her elder colleague's grasp of reality. Was now the time to play games?

"A magic trick?" she asked.

"Not this time. This is technology taking the place of magic." Celia went around and opened a drawer on the old desk. It squeaked as though someone had stepped on the tail of a puppy. From within, she produced a small earpiece, similar to the field radios the Navy sometimes used when neural implants weren't practical.

"This," she said, holding it out for Kaya to examine, "is a vision quest."

"A what? It looks like comm tech."

"It's that too. A vision quest is something my people experience as part of our tutelage in following the path of Wicca. It's not traditionally part of our religion. It's something my ancestors actually adopted from inhabitants of Terra–Mr. Metcalfe's region of Terra, to be precise. They believed that if one could isolate oneself from the distractions of the physical plane and physical senses, one could experience the spiritual in a very real and profound way."

"And they used this?"

Celia laughed. "Oh, no. They used sensory deprivation, partial starvation and sometimes natural hallucinogens. And it took a great deal of training and preparation."

"I don't like hallucinogens–tried them once–and I never deliberately go hungry," observed Kaya.

"Hence this," said Celia, again holding up the small widget. "It's a cheat, which my people tolerate. It simulates the effects of all of those physically demanding practices, temporarily and without physical side effects. It allows the mind to disregard the standard sensory input, and use its spiritual senses."

"And if I don't believe in those?"

"Then you may be in for a surprise. Oh, some people have no spiritual sense. I'm sure our own Captain Darby has none, and I sometimes despair for Cernaq. But I'm sure yours are quite healthy, if untrained and under-utilized. Now, I've had decades to learn the process of vision quest. I don't need something like this. But I'm afraid, given the limited time we have for me to let you experience what I have, this is our only option. It won't be as profound as a true vision quest, but–"

"Can't you just tell me what you know?"

Celia shook her head. "You wouldn't be convinced. Information passed by hearing or reading is only processed, not believed, not experienced."

"And if I don't believe what you show me? Because I know it's induced by manipulating my sensory inputs?"

Celia laughed harshly. "O ye of little faith... I shall open your eyes. You ready?"

"Uh... what do I need to do?"

"Sit back and get comfortable."

"That's it?"

Celia knelt and clipped the earpiece into place. "That. And try to keep an open mind. When you're ready, I'll power on the interface. If you have questions, ask them now."

"What exactly am I going to experience?"

The Doctor chuckled. "Little one, I'm doing nothing short of sending you to hell."

The death of a race.

It begins with the life of a race.

I have no name. I was born on this world. Above ground, in Paradise. I still go there, nights, and revel beneath the moons, my young, perfect body dancing naked, entwined with, enthralling, enrapturing other bodies, young, perfect, naked...

In training as a Warlord, I spend days beneath the surface. I am honed to razor sharpness.

I awake in sunlight. Morning. Springtime. The rising sun warms my bare flesh. There is the faintest, gentlest breeze. I sit up and stretch, reveling in the play of air as it ruffles my hair, loose and free. I so often tie it up for battle, and I hate to do so. I love battle, but I hate the constraint of having my hair confined, captured, beneath an armored helm. They tell me it's my best feature, the boys. The best of many, they say. And I do like the boys to notice me.

The wind tickles my breasts, a pleasant, happy sensation; and I think of the night before, and its pleasant happiness, so rife with sensation. Sixteen lays beside me now, gently snoring, his perfect flesh glowing in the increasing light of day. It was he who brought me such pleasure last night. This morning, his flesh is radiant like fire, bright and hot. Last night, it was cool and silver and perfect as we danced beneath the moons. He chased me up hills and through woods. He caught me and sought his pleasure with me. Then we rested and I chased him, and I caught him, and again there was pleasure.

Now he awakens, interrupting my time alone with morning and nature. Jealous, am I? A little, to have to share this perfect morning. He smiles at me, and I can't resent him. He reaches for me, and I roll away. He rises on all fours, lunges like a beast of prey, launching himself in the air and landing on me hard.

We wrestle, laughing. He has me. We have each other.

This world is perfect. We are perfect. The gods have made us that way, and made the world that way.

I run in darkness. There is no sun here. There are no moons. It is day. The darkness isn't the silvery darkness of the world Above. It's the hot, cramped darkness of the world Below, the one made more by us than by the gods, though they made this world too. We just reshaped it. That's the difference between above and below. Above is untouched, pure, perfect. What the gods gave us. What we want. Below is what *must* be. It is the place we honor the gods by *doing*, by achieving, by building.

There are those who resent what must be, the world Below, the world of war. They are fools. The wise woman wants what must be. We cannot simply live in the Above, reveling in its beauty. Not all the time. The gods put us here to earn their blessings.

It is those blessings which make the world Below a world which must be. The gods created other races. We don't know why. Surely they're not as favored as we are by the gods, for they do not have this beautiful world. They envy us. They want this world taken away from us. If they can't have it for themselves, they'll settle for turning it into a blackened cinder.

And so we must live days in the world Below, preparing. Training. We earn what the gods have given us. We justify their grace through battle with those who would take our gods-given gifts.

Sixteen's arm slashes out, his fist driven in a wide arc towards my jaw. I dodge, and his momentum carries him onward, toppling him. He crashes to the cavern floor.

Cheering. My teachers, my fellow warriors, cheer me.

He recovers quickly, as he always does, as I would. Blood runs red down his beautiful cheek from a gash in his eyebrow. I smile at the sight and lick my lips.

He grins. "Laugh while you can, bitch."

He charges, and the force of his forward thrust takes us both to the ground. We grapple, each trying to pin the other. We roll.

We rolled in the moonlight. We laughed. Naked flesh touched naked flesh.

There is no moonlight. The laughter is different. Armor scrapes armor. I arch my leg and grip his neck with my knee. I pin him between my thighs. He grimaces. Blood stains the synthalloy shell over my groin. I squeeze, and he cries out.

I have seen him look at me in this position before, his head where it is now. But there was no blood, and it was I who cried out.

I squeeze. He bites his tongue.

His tongue. I cried out.

I relax and squeeze hard. A crunch. More blood. Sixteen does not move.

Cheering. My teachers. My fellow warriors. I have made them proud.

My opponent is dead. I didn't mean to kill him. We try not to kill, in training. Neither do we worry over much if it happens. We want to protect our own, but better we kill a few ourselves, and learn that they were weak, than our enemies kill them in battle and we lose our world. Sixteen will never dance in the moonlight again, never run behind me, never fall naked into my arms.

He has lost that right.

I've known him since we were children. I've loved him since I became a woman. He took my virginity and was the delight of my existence.

He was a fool. The world is better off without him.

It is what must be.

Holy Communion is given, before the altar of the gods. I kneel and pray. I thank them for the skill they have given to my care, which belongs, not to me, but to my race. It is my people's gift from the gods. I am blessed to use it, as long as I am worthy.

My sister and brother warriors carry in Sixteen, broken and bloody, as I left him. Over him, the elders join hands, calling out to the gods. Accept his weaknesses, our creators. Forgive him his failings. Forgive us all our failings. We wish only to be strong and worthy of that which you have given us.

The gods sing out their approval. It echoes through the chamber, a heavenly chorus that all is well and we have fulfilled our function this day. We each look up at the ceiling of the place of the gods, a domed cathedral beneath the ground, the center of the world Below. This place which is lit only by flame and by the light of the gods. It rings with their song of approval.

Each elder partakes of Communion. When they are finished, they turn to me, the first among equals this day. Their red faces smile. Their red hands wave me forward. I rise. I walk into the circle amongst them. I kneel again. Sixteen lies before me, broken and bloody. I lean forward and kiss his perfect, bleeding lips. They're cold and stiff. I rear back, open my mouth, and bite his throat, tearing his jugular. I swallow his flesh. I drink his blood. I thank the gods for this Communion.

Then I stand with the elders as each of my fellows drinks. They may not eat. That honor is for elders and for the first among equals this day.

The gods sing their approval. Forgiveness is granted.

Light bathes the broken body, light so intense that it blinds.

When I can see again, Sixteen is perfect, naked, whole and no longer bloodied. He rises, sees me, and smiles. He comes to kneel at my feet.

He thanks me for killing him.

I take his hand, and together we thank the gods for their generosity in restoring his unworthy life. Together with our brothers and sisters, we pledge to keep him worthy, and to use his life in service of our world.

Not everyone is allowed Below. It is the place for warriors. Everyone should be a warrior. Who wouldn't fight for their world, after all? Who would be so selfish as to guard her own life while sisters and brothers die? But not all are warriors.

Sixteen's brother is angry. Sixteen's brother has a name. He has refused to join us, and so has not abandoned his childish identity. It is blasphemous, but he is not the only one.

At the evening revels he shouts in my face, this man-child with a name. He knows what happened. I killed his brother. How could I do such a thing? I try to make him understand. How could I not? If some don't die now, in the practice battle, the practice killing isn't real, then how real will be the death visited on enemies?

I point out that his brother is alive and by my side, thank the gods.

He thanks, not the gods, but our medicine, our technology. He says that the gifts of the mind, not the gods, have made our civilization strong, the envy of every world around. We abandon the mind when we give up our names. We betray the mind when we kill, and risk the loss of the identity. It doesn't matter that sometimes the dead can be raised. He says the violence must stop.

He says the enemies are gone. It's been centuries, he cries. No matter, I say. An enemy unseen is the deadliest of all. We know they're still out there, we, the warrior caste. We train. When they show themselves, we will be ready.

I'm a fool, he says. We have achieved the highest standard of living our world has ever known these last centuries. Above is paradise, I tell him, because below is the pinnacle of technology. The perfect war machines. And the gods of war.

I want to kill him. Right here, right now. If we were Below, I would kill him. Kill him so he could not come back. And no questions would be asked, no reprimand given. I've done it before. Below, insults are not tolerated.

Above they live a soft life, and that is the life we defend. We are not permitted to kill those who lack the courage to go Below. But as I take Sixteen that night, as I fall on him and we give ourselves to each other beneath the moons, I see in my mind my hands snapping his brother's neck. I see myself holding up the lifeless head of the one who mocked me. The lovemaking is the best I've ever known.

As we go Below the next morning, the non-warrior caste lines up in protests and tries to block our way. There is shouting and pushing. Blows are exchanged. There is blood on the soil Above. Blasphemy. Sixteen's brother is among them.

Days later. Months. I do not remember how long. I look at Sixteen's brother through the fence. He and thousands of his fellow conspirators have interfered too often. The elders have ordered them imprisoned, for their own safety, for the safety of our race.

Sixteen's brother says the gods did not ask for this. He says the elders blaspheme their own gods. He says the gods are not real.

He is not a warrior. Only I keep him safe from our enemies. Only the fence keeps him safe from me.

The fence is down. They overloaded it. They're not stupid, these peace-whores.

I taste blood. My own. Not the first time. I've been injured often in training, though I've never suffered the indignity of dying. Tasting your own blood brings no thrill, as touching your own face barely feels like anything.

I was nearly trampled to death in the rush as they escaped. For people so concerned with life, they showed little regard for ours. But we are enemies now. If they find me...

Footsteps. Someone is behind me. I pivot my hips and roll, grasping for my sidearm. It's gone. I go into a crouch, ready for my attacker... of course.

Sixteen's brother. The one with the name.

He casts his gaze to where my sidearm lies beyond my reach. He smiles. Then he goes down, a body flying through the air and tackling him. The opponents land hard, scrabbling, rolling. One ends up on top, his upper body erect and in control. Sixteen. My heart jumps. This is the man I've not dared to tell myself I love. I admit it now. He is perfect in battle. He is worthy of–

Too late, I see the knife in the named one's hand. It slashes out, and Sixteen's blood washes over them both, his throat cut. Before I can react, the knife drives again into his heart. Part of me registers surprise that the weakling can drive in the blade at all. They do know how to fight after all, these peace-whores.

The rest of me screams. I leap, casting aside the body of my dead love. We are Above. There is no bringing him back. The time would pass before I could bring him there. He is dead. He is gone. Forever.

I avenge him. The named one's neck snaps in my hands. I barely notice. I am blind and deaf, senseless in berserker rage. My muscle memory holds the knowledge of how to kill, and I kill. I dishonor my opponent in the ultimate way, severing his head, sawing it off with his own knife. Did it require effort? Ask an onlooker, for I do not know.

I hold the head in front of me by the hair and I spit in its sightless eye.

On the ground, the blood has soaked Sixteen's golden hair, once radiant like the sun. Its light is gone. His light is gone. The blood has covered the sun, and all is darkness, now and forever.

In the cathedral, we commune with the gods. We thank them for our victory over the Above-dwellers. We line up the bodies of the dead on the cathedral floor and we drink the blood.

Sixteen's brother lies before me. I taste his blood, bitter in my mouth. I did not need to tear his flesh. It was torn when I killed him.

The gods do not sing. The dead do not rise. Instead, a cacophony of anger rings out. We rise, hundreds of us, questioning. Are the gods not pleased? We have brought the dead, our enemies, to pay them tribute. These are the bodies of so many who escaped the prisons where we had put them for their own safety.

The gods do not sing. From their fingertips, lightning bolts strike forth, and those who rose in question fall in agony. The dead bodies of the warriors fall amongst the dead bodies of the peace-whores. The blessed nameless die among the cursed named.

We have angered the gods.

All there is to do is flee.

We run, all of us, the nameless and the named. Out of the caverns, away from the hills. We run into the woods. We run from the moving death. It follows us on the wind, a thing alive, sent chasing after us by the gods. It is a swarm of venomous insects. It is a wind which brings death in its touch. It is a fire which will devour us. It is all these things. It is death, and it is alive, and it pursues us. It will never tire.

We run. We will tire. Death will have us. The gods have declared. They have called out to us, their voice thundering. We are the threat. We are the ones who must die now, to preserve the world that is all. Death will have us.

The gods are right. We are the threat. A dozen, two dozen, three? Few of us remain, but we are the threat. It has been decreed, and we have made the decree our own. We will be the threat. We hate the gods. They are the enemy now, they to whom we devoted our lives, sacrificed our lives. They are the enemy. We will destroy them.

The gods will die.

I am back in the Cathedral. It is cold now, and dark. The gods no longer warm it for their worshipers. They no longer light it. I carry a flickering torch, its fuel now nearly exhausted. It will not light my way much longer. It will not have to. I have come far enough. Even the gods must turn their eyes away at times, and I slipped into their Cathedral while they were not looking.

I have brought the final assault. This is our last stand. The last stab at the gods by our race. We built the device together, warriors and peace-whores. I won the honor of delivering it. I fought for the honor. I was trained by the gods to bring death. I would bring it to them, and die with them.

I trigger the final weapon. The light of suns fills the cavern that was dark. It blinds me, forever. As my optic nerves burn away, as I shriek in pain and defiance at the death that comes, I see the dome of the ceiling fall, the debris raining down to form a hole in the world where once there were gods.

No more. I smile and embrace death, welcoming it as the reward for my victory.

But though my eyes are gone, my ears burned away, though I have no flesh to feel, still in the eternity of microseconds before my brain dies I have my divine hearing. And I hear the gods.

They are laughing. They cannot be killed. Only we can be killed. And we have been. The eternal world, the eternal gods, live on.

And they will claim races untold.

Kaya woke, sobbing, her chest heaving uncontrollably in grief.

Celia rushed to her, gathering the girl's head to her bosom.

"Oh Godess," she muttered into Kaya's copper ringlets. "Oh, darling, shhh!" She stroked the girl's hair. "Oh, I'm sorry! I tried to warn you!" She pulled back and lifted Kaya's chin, gazing into her eyes, brushing away tears. "Are you all right?"

Swallowing, putting a hand to her chest to calm her ragged breathing, the girl nodded. "I will be... just... give me a minute."

Celia poured her a drink and handed it to her, admonishing her not to gulp.

Kaya set down the cup and was silent a moment, rocking herself and hugging her own shoulders as she sat upright on the bed in Celia's examining room.

"Was that really Eleusis?" she asked at last.

The old woman shrugged. "Maybe. It was the result of your mind seeking the secrets, the answers to the mysteries."

"They were human?"

Celia shook her head. "Almost certainly not. Whatever you experienced was framed in terms you could understand, filtered through your inner eye, I suppose you'd call it."

"I saw... people... I think I... I was one of them. A warrior."

"That's not uncommon, for the seeker to take the persona of one of the spirits, the one with whom she feels the most kinship."

Kaya shivered. "Kinship? Like hell, Doc. I didn't feel any kinship with this bitch! She killed her lover... she... well, I guess she died trying to save the world. I think that's what I saw."

"I could see you doing that."

"It was all so... hopeless! Like... like I was talking to people who'd lost their battle. They were long dead and defeated, and they knew there was no hope."

"That sounds about right."

"Have you... been there? Wherever it is? Have you seen...?"

"Eleusis? I think so. A lot of my people have. It's a world of great spiritual energy, and not in a good way. Many of us have explored its mysteries."

"Where do the visions come from?"

Again, Celia shrugged. "The vibrations of the universe? Information stored in energy, spread throughout the cosmos? Intelligences we don't understand?"

"Or from inside my own head."

"That is an intelligence you don't fully understand," Celia said, smiling faintly.

"So all that could just be my subconscious, taking out its trash. Showing me a bunch of things I'm afraid of, which have no bearing on Eleusis or our mission there."

"Maybe. That's certainly what most people would choose to believe. A few of us... you, perhaps, know that even if a vision comes to us entirely from within ourselves, it must mean *something*. It's probably not nonsense, coming from such a disciplined mind. And, even if those images were entirely internal to Kayan'na Atal... *how did they get there?"*

"I've certainly never had experiences like that."

"I would say not. Nor have I. But I've seen images of Eleusis in the last days of its former civilization too. And we know from archaeological evidence that there was a civilization there."

"At the end, there was a feeling of... doom. Of a threat so great, it could wipe out anything it encountered." She leveled her eyes on Celia, violet slits, probing. "So what does it mean, Doc?"

"It means," said Celia, "that there's been something very, very dangerous on Eleusis. And the Family's belief that they've literally found God—coincidence? Or have they touched the thing that killed the original inhabitants of Eleusis? I'm speaking of legend, yes, but... you felt it, Kaya."

"Was it real? Or was it just... hallucination?"

"What do you believe?"

"I need to think about it."

"Understandable. But don't think too long, Kaya."

CHAPTER FOUR

Smokin' Joe's was one of the more popular eateries in *Titan's* mercantile district. Catering mostly to lunch clientele, it specialized in smoked meats, as the name suggested. Kevin Carson had discovered it when they'd first come aboard, and organized regular trips there for lunch, when schedules allowed. He said the place "restored his soul."

Joe's was not a high-end bistro of the type which would have attracted wealthy tourists on vacation. *Titan* did not host tourists, despite the occasional quips to the contrary from Aer'La and the ship's marines. The restaurant was a collection of folding tables with checkered cloths and inexpensive chairs, dull from daily cleanings. Its windows looked out on a busy alley in one of the Life Sphere's less expensive areas, referred to universally as "the boulevard." Here, sex workers walked the streets, like something out of old Terran novels, or something from a street on the planet Den.

Titan's sex trade was nothing special, but the ship had the usual coterie of trained professionals and gifted amateurs. Most of the professionals, who bore the license tattoo of the Prostitutes' Guild, had offices in the swankier areas of the City. The Boulevard was home to those too inexperienced, too incompetent, or too jaded, to belong to the Guild. Every city has its low-rent district. The Boulevard was *Titan's*.

Joe's was quiet at dinner time. In fact, it often wasn't open for dinner. Pallas had selected it for that reason. She wanted Metcalfe's focused attention tonight. As he sat glumly across from her, a beef brisket platter barely touched in front of him, she reflected that her selection may have constituted a tactical error. Metcalfe associated this place with Carson, and she read in his mind that he was not at all happy with Carson.

Still, at least here he was away from military concerns. Since the battle with Fehajiq, the entire concept of the Navy was chafing him more than ever. Each order he received caused discomfort and resentment, each evidence of military tradition made him anxious. He was so focused on questioning his place in the Navy that he was unfocused on all else. Others would say—had said—that he was quiet and withdrawn. Of course, no one could be either in the company of a Phaetonian.

"Naturally, you don't have to make conversation," she observed. "It isn't necessary, with a telepath; but one likes to feel that the desire to communicate is mutual. Having to pull the thoughts from your mind is a bit like having sex with a sleeping partner. The reflexes are all there, but—"

"Sorry." He grimaced. He continued to look down.

"Yes," she said, "It *is* something about you."

Now he looked up. "What?"

"You're wondering if your fight with Carson—one of many which are happening more frequently of late—was caused by something about you that's changed. The answer is yes."

"Oh."

"And now you're using monosyllables for response because you don't like that I answered your question for you."

"Because I didn't ask it. It was a private question."

"I... did not mean to intrude." She had overstepped the boundaries of his comfort with her telepathy. She was always afraid of doing that. He had a strongly individualistic personality, and could be resentful of perceived invasions of his privacy. It was, of course, what attracted her to him. He was so like her own Phaetonian people in his passionate selfness, and yet... so different. Reason was all on Phaeton. It wasn't to Metcalfe, despite his high intelligence. He was a conflicting inter-blending of reason and passion. Driven by both, he wasn't ruled by either.

She read guilt in him. He knew he'd made her uncomfortable.

"Sorry again," he muttered. "I guess it's a little silly to expect you not to read what's in front of you, especially if I won't say a damned thing."

"I didn't mean to upset you," she explained. "It's just that I'm aware of the profound effect the Qraitian incident had on you, and I've noticed the changes it's brought about in you. They are changing your relationships with people. Carson is angrier and more resentful now because he doesn't know where he stands with you. You're his lifelong friend, and he's afraid you've outgrown him."

"I didn't know he cared."

"You did know. But you have difficulty accepting the knowledge as personal truth, because he works so hard to maintain an air of disinterest."

"Right."

He was thinking that it was sad, that here he was, separated from his fellows. His experience commanding *Titan* during the attack, almost having to kill them all to stop the mass murder of Quintil, had left him unable to feel a connection with others. He reflected that maybe the threat of great loss had shut down his feelings in self defense. He would have done just about anything to restore them. Here was Carson, on the other hand, who had had no such experience, voluntarily submitting to that same separation from the people he cared about. If he cared.

Metcalfe said none of this. With Pallas, he didn't need to.

"On the subject of the battle–"

"Was I thinking about it again?"

"You're always thinking about it," she replied gently. "When you made me leave the ship–"

"You were safer in a life pod."

"Stipulated. As I was going, though, when you thought you were seeing me for the last time, you said–"

He nodded. "That I wished we'd had more time."

"We have more time now."

"And?"

"And you're not really taking advantage of it, are you? You buried yourself in supervising the repairs to the ship after the battle. You let that be your excuse to be apart from everyone, including me. Now you haven't got the excuse, but the separation is still being maintained."

"I've got a lot on my mind."

"I'm aware of that, of course. Actually, I wasn't referring to your wish that we'd had more time. You also said that you wished we were psychically bonded. Remember–?"

"I remember."

"It wasn't an idle wish. You know what it's like to be joined that way."

For a moment, he reflected on their previous joining. Metcalfe had agreed to test a dream-inducing technology they had found on a planet in the Procyon system. A remnant of a lost civilization, it enforced uninterrupted, lucid dreaming. Celia Faulkner had wanted to explore its therapeutic potential. Captain Darby, seeing a different kind of potential in technology that might control minds, had tampered with her equipment. Metcalfe had become trapped in his personal dreamscape. Only psychic rapport with Pallas had allowed him to find his way out. In that rapport, they'd been forced to confront the depths of their feelings for each other. It was a level of emotional intimacy and complete honesty to which non-telepaths were not accustomed. Thinking he was about to die on the command deck of *Titan*, Metcalfe had wished the bond still existed, so that Pallas would have a part of him within her to live on.

All of this was in his mind. Out loud, he said, "I know what it's like."

"But now, having survived, you feel differently. You don't want that bond between us? "

"I don't know what I want."

"It's possible, you know. Phaetonians establish such permanent connections with each other, occasionally. If I were to imprint your conscious mind with the signature of my thoughts... it's a bit like having the keys to a door. You're always be able to find my thoughts, even though you're not a telepath. My psychic resonance would always echo within your head."

He said nothing.

"Metcalfe," she said levelly, "you're confused. You've been through a very trying experience, one you handled very successfully, I might remind you. Your feelings just haven't caught up to the reality that everything is all right now. For the moment, anyway. You need to master your feelings. I can help you do that. My people have spent centuries understanding the partnership between passion and reason. If we were joined, you would not have to fight this battle alone."

He looked at her, silent. For a moment, his mind was actually blank. Pallas had never encountered such psychic silence in any other being. It frightened her.

"Are you angry with me?"

She immediately saw that he was not, but he answered, "No, of course not."

"I thought perhaps... I know I wasn't very understanding after the battle. The guilt you were ridden with, for killing our enemies. My people don't really understand guilt. We understand noble motives which drive positive feelings. The negative ones... we're not very good with those."

He smiled thinly. "Negative emotions are for the weak?"

"Maybe it is something like that. I don't necessarily agree. Anyway, is that why you're resistant now, to being joined psychically? Is it that I wasn't sympathetic enough?"

He shook his head. "It's just that... I don't where I'm going to be in a year, or a month, even. You see –"

There was a sudden commotion from outside. Shouts of anger rang through the thin windows of the restaurant. Metcalfe leaned over, brushed aside a thin curtain and peered through the glass. "Sounds like a fight's starting." He stood, "I'd better go check."

Disappointed, Pallas nodded quietly. He had to check, of course. A disturbance aboard ship was an officer's responsibility to investigate and control. She already knew what he would find outside.

Metcalfe approached a knot of people clustered at the intersection of the Boulevard and the Main Concourse. It was near one of the main entry portals by which the Life Sphere accessed the secure areas of the ship. There were two such portals at the poles of the great sphere, at the rotational axes. The captive sphere was always under spin, which maintained its gravity. The command, weapons and engineering sections of the ship were stationary, located fore and aft of the superstructure which kept the spinning sphere in place relative to the ship. They had gravity only relative to the ship's acceleration, and thus often had no gravity of which to speak. Civilians largely stayed within the sphere, while officers and crew lived in the sphere and worked outside. Still, a fair number of civilians crossed the portals often, to work as contractors on military projects, and to offer goods and services to the crews while on duty. It was an arrangement which everyone liked.

Stray comments reached Metcalfe's ears as he approached the gathering crowd. They were circled around something or someone. Body language suggested heightened agitation, and phrases such as "no right to do this" and "police state" rang out.

As he drew closer, he heard a woman's dignified voice saying, "You must understand that we are not accustomed to this kind of treatment."

A voice from the center of the throng barked back, "Well, you'd better get used to it, lady. This is the way things are now!"

He knew the voice. It was Aer'La's. Her exclamation was followed by mutterings from another familiar voice, that of Deputy Captain Darby. Metcalfe placed his hands gently on the shoulders of two men at the edge of the group. "Excuse me," he began.

Both men turned and looked him up and down. He was out of uniform, but one obviously recognized him. He said bitterly, "More of you, eh? Coming at us from all directions? You can't make us leave, you know, we have a right to protest!"

Metcalfe withdrew his extended arms and held up both hands in what he hoped was a placating gesture. "I wasn't trying to make you leave. I only want to find out what's going on, and help if I can."

"If you're one of them, then you know what's going on," said the other man he had approached. "They're stopping people from going about their lawful business." The man pointed toward the entrance, whence Aer'La and Darby's voices had come.

Metcalfe issued a mental command which instructed his data implant to display his credentials. His military ID appeared in the air before him, a glowing rectangle with his image, name and rank. "Let me through, and I'll see what's going on. I promise you, I know nothing about this."

Placated somewhat, the two men stepped aside and others followed their example, allowing a clear path to the center of the group, where he found Aer'La and Darby seated at a folding table.

"What's this?" he asked.

Darby looked up. "You're off duty," he said snidely. "It doesn't concern you." The Deputy Captain turned to a woman who stood near the portal. She had apparently just stepped up from the last ring. Entry to the sphere was made by stepping onto a series of rings which moved at increasing speed, allowing a gradual progression from the stationary portion of the ship to the full rotation speed of the sphere. It was less jarring to the body to take hold a of gently spinning ring by handholds, become accustomed to its motion, then grab hold of the next one, which moved more quickly, then the next. The body became acclimated to the increasing rotation speeds, so the final step into the Life Sphere was not like the traumatic feeling of suddenly grabbing a giant spinning top and trying to hold on.

"Display your credentials," he said briskly.

The woman, middle-aged and carrying several heavy bags, looked weary, but complied. The glowing shapes flashed before Darby's face. He scanned them, then nodded. "You may proceed."

The woman shuffled past, grumbling at the protesting crowd to get out of her way.

"Next!" Aer'La barked at the portal.

"Aer'La," said Metcalfe, "what the hell?" He craned his neck for a view through the portal and saw a dozen or more people waiting impatiently. At the Bos'n's call, the first in line began climbing the rings. "Why are you making all those people wait?"

"Orders, Navy," said Aer'La. "Admiral Fournier ordered us to set up checkpoints. You were there."

"I was but... I didn't think Captain Atal was going to allow–"

"Captain Atal has no choice," snapped Darby. "Nor does any one of these people. Really, Metcalfe, if you're going to stay, make yourself useful! Disperse this rabble." He gestured at the group which had just allowed Metcalfe to pass.

"This rabble," said Metcalfe, "are lawful citizens of the Confederacy, gathered to express disapproval of your actions. I can't disperse them. They're not doing anything wrong."

Several people behind him called out in agreement.

"They're gettin' on my damn nerves!" growled Aer'La. "That's wrong enough."

"Hey," called out the young man in the portal, "can I get through?"

"Wait your turn!" Aer'La told him.

"I just want to get home," the young man pressed. "I've been standing here waiting for fifteen minutes. I'm late for dinner, and my husband–"

Aer'La stood suddenly, knocking over her chair. She advanced on her challenger. "You're gonna be waiting a lot longer if I toss your ass in jail!" she told him.

"You should have allowed additional time to pass from the restricted area," said Darby.

"How was I supposed to know you were going to stop foot traffic?" the man demanded.

"It was posted on TitanNet," Darby replied. "Hours ago."

"I don't have time to read–" the young man began.

Aer'La took him by the collar with both hands, lifted him off his feet, and set him firmly in front of Darby. "And I don't have time to argue!" she said. "Now show us your ID!"

"Aer'La!" Metcalfe exclaimed. He'd seen her treat people this way before, including the casual crew members who worked for her. He had never seen her do it to someone who hadn't given her cause by behaving in a threatening, or at least uncooperative manner.

"What?" she demanded. "It's for their own good!"

"These people are just trying to do their jobs," said Metcalfe. "There's no reason to treat them this way. People aren't going to feel more safe and secure if you just find new ways to make them angry."

"Mister Metcalfe," Darby said loudly over the growing rumble of complaints, "*Titan* is Navy property, territory owned by the Confederate government. Everyone here is under martial law, and we all need to remember that. Anyone refusing to cooperate will be jailed and subject to a military tribunal."

He glared at the crowd, obviously hoping the threat would impress them. It obviously did some of them, for their grumbling grew quiet. Then Darby turned back to Metcalfe. "You are off duty, Leftenant, and you are hindering our efforts to carry out orders. Leave this area immediately, or I will place you on report."

Metcalfe did not answer, made one last attempt to meet Aer'La's gaze. She ignored him. He returned to Smokin' Joe's only long enough to pay the check, then left Pallas and his half-eaten meal and disappeared into the crowds on the Main Concourse.

"You look upset."

Pallas didn't need to even glance up. She had felt Cernaq's presence several minutes before he'd entered the restaurant.

"Don't make small talk," she said.

"I'm not making small talk. I'm observing a very unusual phenomenon. I've known you all of our lives, Pallas, and you've very rarely been upset. You're what Aer'La calls 'a cool customer.'"

"Is that what she calls me?" asked Pallas in a wry tone. She was well aware that the Bos'n disliked her intensely. The fact that Cernaq was Aer'La's most frequent sex partner and that Pallas was Cernaq's oldest and closest friend seemed to not mitigate her animosity at all.

"In fact, it does mitigate her animosity," said Cernaq, responding to the unspoken thought. "In her opinion, my friendship for you is what keeps you alive."

They frequently responded to each others' thoughts. In fact it could become confusing for Phaetonians, especially if distracted, to keep track of what was thought and what was merely said. It would have been easier to simply share thoughts without speaking–easier, and more comfortable. Their mentor, Professor Mors, had spent over a century in the company of non-telepaths, however, and had coached them both to speak out loud when in public. It reduced the animosity of the psi-blind toward their kind.

"Why does Aer'La hate me?" Pallas asked.

"Because you're everything that she believes she cannot be: intelligent, respected and, above all, educated."

"That's foolish. She's of above-average intelligence and the Navy affords her vast educational opportunities. Her colleagues respect her, especially you, and your respect is an especially remarkable commodity."

Cernaq smiled and inclined his chin in thanks for the compliment.

"Her fears are irrational," Pallas concluded.

"Most fears are. So are most people, out here."

"Out here" referred to anywhere other than Phaeton, of course.

"But you're not upset about Aer'La's resentment of you. That's been a constant since you met. Right now, you're so emotionally troubled that it shows on your face. You *look* upset, I told you; so something must be very wrong. I felt your distress from the other end of the Concourse. That's why I came here."

"Thank you."

"So, what has Metcalfe done now?"

"Are you prying in my mind, or is his name that evident in my thoughts?"

"Neither. He's just the only person I know of who could shake your emotional balance."

"You probably could too."

"Ah, but I'm perfect," he sighed. "So I know it's not me."

Pallas laughed quietly.

"Better," said Cernaq. "Now, shall we go for a walk on the Concourse so we can discuss this properly, or do you want to sit here and use primitive spoken language to tell me what's happened?"

"I think I'd have trouble filtering out the distractions of the Concourse tonight."

"More proof of how disturbed you are," he observed. "All right. Primitive communication it is. What's wrong?"

"I asked Metcalfe to join in a psychic bond with me," she said slowly.

Cernaq's face showed surprise, which gave Pallas some satisfaction. She didn't like being the only one whose feelings could be seen by others.

"That's... a very big decision. For both of you. It's so rare, even among our own people."

"It is," she agreed. "I wasn't the first to bring it up. Metcalfe himself was intrigued by the openness of full psychic sharing we had experienced in the past. Recently, when he thought he was about to die, he expressed regret that we weren't bonded."

"Regret that we didn't do something does not equate to a wish to do that thing, especially when we think circumstances have made the thing seem impossible."

"More irrationality?" she asked.

He nodded. "It's my understanding that, when confronted with the real possibility of death, people compile mental lists of things that they 'wish they'd done,' but didn't do. These are things they aren't emotionally or intellectually prepared to do now, but hope to fit into their lifetime. They regret that life might end with their desires unfulfilled, but that doesn't always mean they're going to fulfill them if they survive."

"So you think Metcalfe isn't ready?"

"Did he say no?"

"Not in so many words. He said he didn't know what the future held for him."

"Implying that that future might not include you."

She swallowed. "I suppose that's true."

"I didn't mean to hurt you by saying that."

"It's true," she said, shrugging.

"Yes, but... be sure you understand the gravity of the decision that you're asking him to make. Even at home, how many people do you know who've bonded?"

"Three couples, that I knew personally, and one triad."

"Not many," Cernaq emphasized. "Bonding is the ultimate declaration of love. And love is the rational recognition that another person embodies your standards of moral excellence. Most of us never meet someone who does that for us."

"Perhaps I don't embody moral excellence to Metcalfe?"

"I doubt he thinks in those terms. He's Terran. To him love is a less rational process, as it is to InWorlders. But, being Terran, he's more prone to form a lifelong commitment with someone he loves."

"So, do you think it's a good idea, or a bad one?"

"I can't tell you whom to love. I can commend you on your choice. Metcalfe is one of my best friends and one of the finest people I know. But he's not Phaetonian. He hasn't been trained to even consider this possibility. Bonding with a non-telepath... I don't know."

"Would you bond with Aer'La?" she asked bluntly.

For a moment, he was silent. She had caught him off guard, and there was a small measure of pride for her in that.

"She... isn't ready," he said at last.

"Will she ever be? And are you in love with her?"

He looked down at the table and hid his thoughts away. In school, such a response to a direct question would have drawn a student many demerits. It suggested dishonesty.

"Aer'La is not... my ideal of morality or philosophy," he said at last. "I... cannot explain my feelings for her."

Had he not been Phaetonian, he would have blushed furiously. Pallas felt a little guilty now for pushing him. She had unearthed a moral quandary in her friend, and it was possibly greater in proportion than her own current quandary.

"I only know," Cernaq finished quietly, "that I would die–or kill–to protect her."

"Right or wrong?" asked Pallas.

"Right or wrong," he agreed.

Pallas shook her head in amusement. "Check your premises, old friend."

Before he could respond, his data implant flashed a priority message in the air between them. A curt order from Captain Atal instructed him to immediately find Pallas and report with her to the Captain's offices.

Session Transcript

7 October 308 PL

LUCINDA GRAE, LT, CMT, PhD

Patient: Lt. Terrence Metcalfe, CN

LG: And why didn't you say yes?

Metcalfe: I... I told her why. I'm not... sure of anything.

LG: There's little comparable case history available on the subject of long-term emotional partnerships–

Metcalfe: Because your profession fell by the wayside on my planet long ago.

LG: You're right. In some of the ancient, classic texts, however, there's a lot about 'fear of commitment.'

Metcalfe: I am not afraid of commitment! I've sought it actively. I want... I wanted...

LG: A monogamous relationship?

Metcalfe: Someone I could count on.

LG: You don't want that anymore?

Metcalfe: Of course I do. I just don't believe...

LG: 'Don't believe?'

Metcalfe: I mean...

LG: You don't believe you *can* count on anyone anymore?

Metcalfe: Maybe.

LG: What changed?

Metcalfe: Nothing. Everything.

LG: It seems to me that the... incident... demonstrated that everyone close to you could be counted on.

Metcalfe: It also demonstrated how... fragile... everything is.

LG: You mean that any of your friends could die at any moment.

Metcalfe: Yes.

LG: It takes away your sense that things could last forever.

Metcalfe: I suppose it does.

LG: And so you're afraid to invest yourself emotionally in something you could lose.

Metcalfe: (Unintelligible)

LG: Does the fact that something can be taken away mean that it's not worth having?

LG: Why don't we pick this up again at the next session?

CHAPTER FIVE

"Incredible!" barked Georg Fournier. "Does no one on this ship give a damn about the future of the Confederacy?"

"The probability is strong that all of us do," said Cernaq calmly to his red-faced superior. He worked hard to keep his own expression neutral. On Phaeton, to lose control to the point that one allowed one's face to color was actually considered bad manners. It was hard, after years of training in correct etiquette, to sit still through such a display.

Beside him, Pallas shook her head and said, "I'm sorry, Admiral Fournier, but what you ask is impossible."

"What I ask," said Fournier, "is only that you both cooperate in our investigation. The merchants who reside in *Titan's* Life Sphere have never been thoroughly investigated–"

"Admiral, excuse me, but that's incorrect." Jan Atal had sat at his desk and kept his peace while Fournier presented his request. Now, as things became tense, he had clearly decided to intervene. "Every single civilian aboard has undergone a complete background investigation. We are aware that this is a military vessel, sir. No one boards without being identified."

"I'm well aware of the standard operating procedures, Captain. But they were written long ago, when we weren't–"

"They were written when we were actively fighting a war against the Qraitians, *sir*," Atal reminded him. "We are not fighting a war now."

"You think not?"

"In fact," said Cernaq, "we are negotiating to liberalize the terms of the treaty with the Qraitian Empire."

Fournier made a scoffing noise. "That's the stuff of press releases, Midshipman. The Qraitians have once again proved themselves to be a credible threat. For purposes of security, we are at war, and we will behave accordingly."

"Admiral," said Atal, "I've been in a war. This isn't one."

"We'll agree to disagree, Captain. The Admiralty has decided that recent events call for tighter security. Up till now, anyone boarding this ship showed a computer their credentials. There are a hundred ways to pass false ones. There are a hundred more ways to tamper with your legitimate records and remove potential red flags. No, we haven't been thorough at all. Our enemies have. And I believe they've infiltrated agents aboard this ship and many others, agents who are only waiting to strike and blow the *Titan* out of space! We therefore cannot rely solely on past investigations. We must determine the current loyalty of everyone aboard."

"By performing an illegal search of their minds," finished Pallas.

"No act I order is illegal, Doctor," Fournier shot back. "By definition, I am the law aboard *Titan*."

Cernaq exerted special effort to avoid his eyes growing wide or his eyebrows raising. The philosophical flaws in the Admiral's argument were glaring, but he knew better than to point them out.

Pallas did not know better.

"You propose that the rule of man should subvert the rule of law. That is not sound political theory, Admiral. The Articles of Confederation say–"

"Do *not* lecture me on the principals of my government, Dr. Pallas!"

"It's my government too," she said quietly. "The fact that the Articles were drafted on your home planet does not give you ownership of them. Phaeton is as much a member of the Confederacy as any other world, yours included. And your proposed actions are a violation of our worlds' shared beliefs."

Fournier waved a finger at her. "I suggest you remember to whom you're speaking, young lady. Your tone is insubordinate."

"Pallas," Atal began quietly.

"I have an excellent memory, Admiral. Do you?"

"Excuse me?"

"If so, you'll remember that I am not a member of your military, and am not subject to your command or your traditions. I cannot be insubordinate, for I am no one's subordinate. I am your equal in the eyes of the law, and your superior intellectually."

Fournier blanched.

Atal made a noise which might have been an aborted laugh.

Pallas continued. "And it certainly would not be appropriate to take disciplinary action against Cernaq simply because you feel insulted by his countrywoman's honest statements."

"Well of course it wouldn't!" snapped Fournier.

"But you were thinking about it."

"You get out of my head!"

Pallas smiled. "You brought us here to ask us to perform telepathic scans of the minds of every merchant aboard *Titan*–"

"Not every one! Just those whom we had concerns about!"

"–and yet you resent my reading a single stray thought of your own. That is hypocrisy."

"And it's not hypocrisy that you'll read my mind, but not the minds of potential enemies?"

"It is not. Those 'potential enemies,' as you call them, have expressed no position on the reading of minds. You, by advocating the invasion of others' privacy, have essentially stated that you do not value your own. Implicitly, you gave me permission to read your mind."

Gotcha, you prancing bastard! Cernaq nearly started at the intensity of the mental exclamation, which came from his Captain. He wondered if Atal had intended him to hear it.

"Sir," Cernaq said, "respectfully, Pallas speaks for every law-abiding citizen of our world. It is against our most sacred beliefs to enter another mind uninvited."

The Admiral rolled his eyes and muttered. "Religious fanatics."

"Nothing of the kind," said Pallas. "Our beliefs are intellectually derived ethics. We have no religion."

"And yet you're just as pig-headedly... *moral* as your Terran accomplices, Dr. Pallas. So to me it's the same damn thing. Idealism of any kind is rarely practical. And these are times which call for practicality."

"Nonetheless," said Pallas, "we cannot and will not do as you ask."

"Then you're both dismissed!"

Cernaq rose. Pallas remained seated and looked pointedly at the Admiral.

Atal said gently, "Midshipman Cernaq, return to your station. Dr. Pallas, would you excuse us?"

Never taking her eyes off Fournier, Pallas smiled. "Gladly, Captain."

Kaya was about to signal at the door to her father's office when it opened and an obviously enraged Admiral Fournier stormed out. Barely looking at her, he ignored her polite greeting and stalked down the corridor, muttering to himself.

The door being open, she tapped on it with her knuckles and asked, "Bad time?"

Her father, shaking his head in—what? Amazement? Amusement? Disgust?—waved her in. "Overall, yes, it's a very bad time," he said. "But you look as though there's something on your mind. Maybe it will distract me from the stupidity I was just forced to endure."

She sat opposite him, frowning. "I talked to Doc Faulkner... no, that's not right. I... met... with Doc Faulkner. She showed me something."

"The rosewood inlay on her desk?"

"No. And it doesn't have rosewood inlay."

"Sorry. What did she show you?"

"You'll scoff."

"I enjoy scoffing. It relaxes me. And tones the scoffing muscles, which, in most adults, are dangerously under-utilized." When she didn't show the expected amusement, he asked, "So what was it?"

"She called it a vision quest?"

"She fed you drugs."

"No. Some kind of neural interface. I saw... I saw Eleusis. Dying."

"Should we change your name to Cassandra?"

"Who?"

"Sorry. Ancient Terran prophet. All Metcalfe's talk got me curious. I've been reading the *Book of Heroes*. She saw the future. No one believed her. She went mad and was murdered."

"Uplifting story. No wonder Metcalfe's such a downer, reading stuff like that. But I didn't see the future... I saw... I think it was the past. How the original inhabitants of Eleusis rebelled against their gods and brought about the death of their race."

"Who's being a downer?"

"It's not funny, Daddy, it... I think there was some sort of... truth in there."

"You believe you communicated with the long-dead spirits of the Eleusinians?"

"No. Oh, I don't know!"

"Why is Celia feeding you these horror stories?"

"Because you wouldn't listen to her. You shut her down in the meeting."

"Well–"

"Daddy, you did!"

"You're correct, I did. I did so because I didn't want her telling her people's legends in front of Fournier. He would have dismissed her far more harshly than I did, and someone might have ended up getting their feelings hurt."

Kaya cocked her head quizzically. "I doubt the Doc would let Fournier hurt her feelings."

"I was referring to Fournier's hurt feelings when found that Celia had turned him into a frog."

"Don't be silly! Celia couldn't turn him into a frog!"

"Don't be too sure."

"She told me she likes frogs, so I doubt she'd disgrace their species that way. No, I think he'd wind up as a toad."

"In any event, I didn't want Celia to give Fournier more ammunition against her... or the entire crew for that matter. Especially now. He's got the media's attention, and the Council's. He might use his newfound clout to put some of us–or all of us–back on border patrol."

"I hope you'll tell her that. And I'm not sure I agree with your decision. I think there may be something worth listening to in her people's legends."

"Hysterical fantasies, if you ask me."

"Legends, Daddy. And legends are often just distortions of fact. If there's *any* truth behind what I saw, then we need to proceed cautiously."

"Based on a... hunch?" he asked, unable to suppress a wicked smile.

"Dammit, Daddy, I'm worried!"

"Second time in as many days. Seems to be a trend. I'd hate for my only daughter to become hopelessly neurotic."

"You starting to feel the burn in those scoffing muscles?"

"Nothing yet. Better keep up the pressure."

"I saw a whole planet die. No... I didn't *see* it. I lived through it."

"In an artificially induced nightmare."

"What if it wasn't?"

"Then tell me where the information came from. If what you experienced was a genuine account of history, albeit an emotionalized and mythologized one, whose account was it? Where did that person record the data? How did the data survive the extreme span of time since there was a native civilization on Eleusis, and how was that data transmitted to you?"

"Okay... I don't know."

"Correct. You don't know, you *feel*, and that's dangerous. Celia's people are all about feelings and sensations, hunches and premonitions. Theirs is not the world of hard data and scientific analysis."

"Does that make them wrong?" she wondered.

"But don't instinct and legend and gut feelings have their place? Primitive men–even animals–didn't reason. They went with fear and rage to protect themselves and lust to procreate. And their species managed to flourish. There's evolutionary advantage to base emotion. Is it wise to ignore it? Or even scientific? Yes, I experienced something horrific. Yes, I'm emotionally shaken. But my intellect tells me that such things are possible. It would be foolish to discount the possibility without investigating."

He sat back, never losing her gaze, and considered what she had said. "Powerfully argued. You're getting better at rhetoric. I might have to start some sort of vocational training, against the day you take away my job."

"I don't want your job, Daddy, I want Fournier's."

"Good. It's best to keep your goals modest and manageable. So... what's your next action then?"

"Huh?"

"You've told me all the consequences of ignoring Celia's warning, and convinced me that intuitive analysis has merit. But you haven't suggested what, if anything, we should do if we take this mumbo jumbo seriously. You've brought me problems. An officer should bring solutions. Well?"

She paused. "The colonists believe they've found God."

"Yes."

"I... saw... gods."

"All right."

"Coincidence?"

"You think not?"

"I think not. Or... I feel not. And I want to learn what to think of it."

"Good. So?"

"So I'm proposing to go and find out as much as I can about this 'finding God' business, and see if it leads me to any evidence that Celia's fears may be true. I'm going to look for signs of a civilization that destroyed itself aeons before humanity made it to Eleusis."

"All right," he smiled approvingly, "daughter, I'll consider you ship's ghost hunter then."

"You guys mind telling me exactly what's going on here?"

Metcalfe glared at Kevin Carson and Sestus Blaurich. Currently, the three were alone in a small conference room in offices maintained by the

Navy within *Titan's* business district. Just as Metcalfe had entered, Sestus had dismissed one of the local merchants. The woman had left, head bowed, looking as though she were afraid that Metcalfe might strike her for fun.

"We *do* mind, actually," said Sestus.

"Shut up, Five," said Carson. Despite the accustomed hostility toward their unpopular shipmate, Carson's expression was not sympathetic. Nor, Metcalfe supposed, should he have expected anything different. "We're interviewing all the ship's merchants," he explained sullenly. "Performing background checks. As ordered."

Metcalfe pointed at the door. "And what did that lady do? Plot to send contraband potholders to the Arbiters Council?"

"She has some shady contacts on Den, if you must know," Sestus replied. "And family members with criminal records. We've had to place a watch on her."

"How may watches have you had to place on our merchants?" Metcalfe demanded.

"Twenty-seven, so far," Carson sighed.

"Wouldn't be necessary if the damned Phaetonians had an ounce of loyalty," Sestus muttered.

Metcalfe took a step toward him. "Excuse me?"

Sestus stood, arms crossed, and looked Metcalfe in the eye. "I said your girlfriend and your friend Cernaq are disloyal. Why else would they refuse a perfectly reasonable request to perform telepathic scans to determine the threat level here in the civilian sector?"

"Because it violates their principles?" suggested Metcalfe.

"In time of war, principles must be kept in perspective."

"No one knows more about perspective than you, Five." Metcalfe gestured to a device on the desk behind which Sestus stood. "What's this?"

"Look, Terry, why are you here?" asked Carson. "You may not like our orders, but they are our orders–"

"What's this?" Metcalfe asked again.

Carson cast down his eyes on what looked like an ordinary data pad. "You know damned well what it is. We're tracking their vitals to check for physical signs of anxiety which suggest that they're lying. Again, what are you doing here?"

"Saunders came to see me."

"Saunders," acknowledged Carson, "okay."

Saunders owned Smokin' Joe's and was well known to the officers and crew of *Titan*. Carson was particularly friendly with the man, which made it surprising, at first, that he had approached Metcalfe.

"You know he has a record."

"I know," said Carson.

"Well, given the stories that are circulating about your little inquisition, he's afraid he's going to get thrown in the brig and lose his business."

"That's ridiculous!"

"Is it?"

Sestus stepped forward. "It is, yes. Look, Metcalfe, there's no need for you to charge in here playing the champion of the oppressed! We're not trying to frame people or smear their names. We're just performing a lawful investigation... for their own protection."

"If you're protecting them, then why don't they feel safe?"

"Maybe... because they *do* have something to hide," Carson suggested. He didn't look happy about saying it.

Metcalfe pointed disbelievingly at the smirking blond figure of Sestus Blaurich. "You're taking his side? Really? Saunders is a friend of yours, Carson!"

"I'm not taking sides, don't be childish! And I'm not saying I think Saunders has anything to worry about. I just mean that it's natural to get a little antsy when you're questioned, if you have a past you're not proud of. It doesn't mean you're guilty of anything."

"And it doesn't mean the people asking the questions are wrong to ask," added Sestus.
He looked exceedingly pleased with himself to be lined up with Carson in an argument against Metcalfe.

For a moment, the two friends from Terra held each others' gaze, then, finally, Carson looked away. "I have to get back to work," he said uncomfortably, "There are people waiting for their turn."

"Yeah," said Metcalfe coldly. "In fact, Saunders is next."

"Good," said Sestus. "Send him in on your way out, Metcalfe."

Metcalfe snorted. "I don't take orders from you, Five. And, if you don't mind, I'll stay while you question him."

Sestus naturally wanted to say that he very much did mind, but, surprisingly, he looked to Carson for a response. Carson just shook his head and said disgustedly, "Whatever."

"I won't answer that."

The man called only Saunders hung his head and slumped in the chair. It was a big head, though he wasn't a particularly big man. It held a crop of sandy hair, which looked as though it had perhaps never made acquaintance with a comb, much less an A.I.-based personal grooming assistant. He wore an open-collared shirt out of which spilled tufts of graying chest hair, threadbare slacks of linen, and flip-flops.

Metcalfe, a student of Terran history and social custom, could have told the others that Saunders looked like something called a "beach bum." The term would have been meaningless to them, even to Carson. It also would have been inappropriate, given the personal statistics which floated above and behind Saunders for the convenience of his interviewers. The glowing digits showed, among other things, an I.Q. in the genius range, in addition to a sizeable list of convictions for theft, fraud and smuggling. He gave no evidence of the intelligence rating, and made no secret of the crimes. He frequently amused customers in Smokin' Joe's with stories of his criminal past. When asked why he committed such outlandish crimes, he always answered with a glint in his eye, "Because I could."

None of his customers knew how old he was or where he came from. It was tradition to pretend that he was as old as the legendary Lindy Douglas, and that Douglas had found him sleeping in the superstructure after *Titan* was first pressurized. Douglas, a known workaholic, had been hungry on the day of the inglorious first meeting, and had told the stowaway he wouldn't be spaced if he could make a decent lunch.

Thus had been born Smokin' Joe's, *Titan's* favorite eatery... so they said.

In fact, Saunders, who had legally dropped his first name because he hadn't liked it and couldn't come up with a better one, was 42 and born in a bland suburb of Quintopolis. He had completed seven years of a standard ten-year bachelor's program when he'd spent Spring Break on the border world of Den, and he'd never come back home. He had started Smokin' Joe's seven years ago, after completing a year of court-ordered service as a casual laborer on *Titan*—part of a suspended sentence for drug trafficking.

The reality, reflected Metcalfe, killed the legend. He further reflected that it was only reality, not truth. For his part, he would go on believing that Saunders was over a century and a half old, and had been found asleep in the bones of *Titan* by her creator.

"You have to answer," said Sestus, "or go to jail."

Saunders shrugged. "Been to jail. They feed you."

The self-assured pose was just that, Metcalfe knew, a pose. Saunders had earlier confessed to him his real concern over losing his business. But Saunders intensely disliked Sestus, had since the well-engineered young mid had come into his establishment and demanded that he have an A.I. supervise a complete sterilization of all surfaces in the place, and a second A.I. perform contamination rule out. Metcalfe and his fellow Arbiters had not witnessed this, but they'd heard the tale from Saunders. It was exactly the kind of stunt Five would pull, they knew.

Sestus rubbed Saunders the wrong way. Frightened he might be, but he would never let the pompous young aristocrat know it. He'd rather die in searing pain, no doubt, than give Sestus Blaurich of moment of pleasant satisfaction.

Sestus leaned in close to the older man's face and sneered. "It's not that kind of jail," he said silkily, and he smiled, showing perfect teeth. "It's the brig on *Titan*, for now. Then it's transfer to Hydra Station with the spies and traitors. Feeding is not a top priority."

Saunders glared back at him, unflinching. "I want a lawyer."

Sestus smiled more broadly. "Sorry," he said. "Martial law doesn't allow for lawyers. Today, I'm your judge and your jury. Answer my questions... or no one sees you again for a long, long time."

Metcalfe stepped forward. "That's enough, Mr. Blaurich!"

Saunders, who seemed not to notice his ally, shook his head and said bitterly, "Fuck you, boy. I'm not telling you a damned thing."

Sestus shrugged. "Fine." He tapped a touchpad on the desktop, and the door opened, admitting Aer'La. Apparently, she had been signaled quietly some time earlier.

"Trouble?" she asked.

"Just a sec," said Carson. He knelt in front of the recalcitrant merchant. "Saunders," he said quietly, "think about this. You've got nothing to hide, you–"

"Everyone's got something to hide, Carson," the man responded. "*Everyone*. Let people like him," he nodded at Sestus, "start turning over rocks, and you'll find out everyone's guilty. All that stands between any man or woman and jail is who their friends are. And I'm sorry," he nodded to Metcalfe, "but you boys aren't powerful enough friends to defend a man against this kind of ugliness. And I'd rather go to jail and lose my business than cooperate with what's happening here today."

"You're not going to lose anything," said Metcalfe.

"Sorry, Navy," said Aer'La quietly, "but I have to take him in."

"On what charge?" asked Metcalfe.

Aer'La paused, obviously surprised at being questioned. Perhaps she'd thought that her quiet request would placate her friend and superior officer. Now Metcalfe saw in her face the frustration she typically saved for those who worked for her. Her voice raised.

"They don't tell me the charges. My job is to enforce the Captain's decisions."

"This isn't the Captain's decision."

"It's the Navy's decision," put in Sestus. "That makes it the Captain's."

Carson placed a hand on Sestus's elbow and eyed Metcalfe and Aer'La, now facing each other in front of Saunders, their faces only inches apart. "You might want to stay out of this one."

"Whaddya want me to do, Navy," Aer'La demanded. "Disobey orders?"

"Let me check with the Captain," said Metcalfe. "I'm sure exceptions can be made for–"

"–Friends of yours?" wondered Sestus. Carson immediately prodded him.

"For people who have long histories of service to the ship," Metcalfe finished. He gestured to Saunders. "The man just doesn't want to answer prying questions. Everyone's entitled to privacy–"

"Yeah, privacy comes in handy when you're plotting to blow up the ship."

"No one is plotting to blow up the ship!" snapped Metcalfe.

"How can you be so sure?" Aer'La demanded. "What makes you right, and the entire leadership of the Navy wrong? Even Fournier can call it right sometimes, Metcalfe!"

"What makes me right," he said quietly, "is the same thing that made me right last year when Fournier wanted to send you back into slavery!"

Her face went dark.

"That was for the good of the Navy too, Aer'La," pressed Metcalfe. "It wasn't politically expedient for Fournier to defend one escaped slave. Now it *is* politically expedient to deny rights to people like Saunders, people who don't really count.   I can't believe your hypocrisy, having escaped oppression yourself. You'd really help Fournier inflict it on others? Friends of ours?"

Aer'La's jaw twitched. After taking a moment to control herself, she said, "I know what oppression is better than anyone here. Better than you ever will. This isn't it."

For a few moments, they simply stared. Then Aer'La asked, "Well, Metcalfe? Are you going to stand in my way? If so, you'd better be prepared to use a weapon, because you're not going to stop me any other way."

When he didn't answer, she reached to his belt and pulled his pulse gun from its holster. Since Fournier had issued his last orders, they'd all been required to wear them on duty. She jammed it into his hands where he held it only firmly enough to keep it from falling.

"You gonna shoot me, Metcalfe?"

He looked down at the gun, back at the angry eyes of his friend, then around at the onlookers, especially Saunders, whom he had come here to help. Aer'La was right about one thing, the gun was the only tool he could use to accomplish what he'd come here to do, prevent Saunders's arrest. Violence was the only way, right here, right now. He could let one friend down, or attack another.

Without another word, he cast the gun to the deck and left the room.

When Aer'La had led Saunders away, Sestus had gone as well, to dismiss the line of interviewees outside. He'd told them to come back in an hour, once they'd handled this arrest. Then, when all of them had remained to gawk at the spectacle, he had angrily ordered the corridor cleared.

Carson watched after him through the open door. "I would have thought Five would enjoy seeing Metcalfe and Aer'La at each others' throats. Seems to have upset him."

Cernaq, who had slipped in as Sestus confronted the crowd, said quietly, "Such conflicts are emotionally disruptive even for rivals. Mr. Blaurich doesn't like us, but he has recognized, after all that has happened, how beneficial our presence is to *Titan*. And what's good for *Titan* is good for his career."

"Haven't seen Metcalfe and Aer'La go at it like that in years." Carson looked back at Cernaq, who reclined idly against the edge of the desk. "You having trouble deciding whose side to be on?"

"I'm on the same side I always am," observed Cernaq, "my own."

"You don't have an opinion?"

"Several. Aer'La is over-reacting based on her recent experience with the Qraitians. Metcalfe is still suffering–"

"Metcalfe has been suffering since the day he was born!" spat Carson.

Cernaq raised an eyebrow. "Were you there?"

"It's a figure of speech."

"It's an inaccurate statement. You're not old enough to remember his birth."

"Maybe. But you can't deny he's been a complete pain in the ass since that business with Fehajiq."

"He is unsettled by the violence of the encounter. He feels alienated from his friends–"

"Because he is alienating his friends! He's barely spoken to me for a month, except to give orders. Except for Pallas, he's got no time for anyone. And even she–"

"Interesting."

"What?"

"You note that he has time for Pallas. Perhaps you feel she's taken the attention that was once yours?"

Carson smacked the table with both hands. "Is it Intergalactic Be-A-Dick Day or something? 'Cause if it is, I didn't get the memo!"

"Times of adversity, such as this one, bring out the worst in people."

"Your years of experience tell you that, venerated one?"

"No, I saw it on a human relations poster in the officers' mess."

Carson laughed despite himself.

"I didn't mean to upset you," said Cernaq, "by suggesting that you're jealous of Metcalfe's relationship with Pallas. I simply believe... you should think about it. Your friendship is changing. It's leaving a void. If Metcalfe isn't going to fill the role of–"

"Fantasy boyfriend?"

"–of confidant and sibling, then perhaps it's time to start asking yourself who might."

Carson sat down next to Cernaq on the desk. "Right now, I just want to see us get through the day without killing each other."

Session Transcript

8 October 308 PL

LUCINDA GRAE, LT, CMT, PhD

Patient: Lt. Terrence Metcalfe, CN

Metcalfe: I don't know what bothered me more... Carson and Sestus being on the same side–

LG: We've talked about that before–

Metcalfe: –yeah–but I'm also really worried about Aer'La. She's so... angry.

LG: That would seem to be her baseline.

Metcalfe: Quick anger, yeah. A flare-up that lasts a few minutes. Then she hits something... or someone... or she gets laid... and she's rational again.

LG: It's different now?

Metcalfe: It's sustained. She's been ready to bite the head off anyone who says hello since...

LG: Since the incident.

Metcalfe: Yeah.

LG: She almost died.

Metcalfe: It's like she's... I dunno... trying to push everyone away.

LG: Perhaps because emotional interaction distracts her while she's trying to sort out her own feelings? Or because she's realized that friends and lovers could be taken from her easily, and is therefore establishing distance to protect herself from harm.

Metcalfe: Ouch.

LG: I'm just saying.

CHAPTER SIX

"Identification confirmed, Captain," said Metcalfe, zooming the holo display to reveal the frogish form of the ship against the blue-green background of the planet Eleusis. "Qraitian light battle cruiser. Active military registry, not surplus."

Floating by Metcalfe's side, Atal nodded. "It was to be expected. Qraitian traffic has been tolerated in this system. Most of their ships are military, since their emperor legally owns everything. Posture?"

Metcalfe reviewed a series of color-coded icons on the display below the image. "Neutral. No weapons active."

"Let's talk to them."

Metcalfe stabbed an avatar for the alien ship with one finger, and *Titan's* communications A.I. sent an automatic greeting. After a few seconds, the avatar enlarged and glowed green. "The ship's designation is... unpronounceable," furnished Metcalfe.

Atal chuckled. "Yep. Very few vowel sounds in the Qraitian language."

"Her C.O.'s name transliterates as Ustenar. She's coming on."

Before them, the image of Eleusis and the Qraitian vessel retreated and minimized, and the head and shoulders of a Qraitian appeared. Ustenar was female, Atal could tell by the color markings on her skin. Being similar in evolution to the reptiles of old Terra, Qraitian females had no breasts for nursing their young. Secondary sex characteristics could be tricky to spot, but Atal had known a few Qraitians in his day.

"Captain Atal," the Qraitian said. It sound to human ears like "Kuptun Stull." Ustenar was showing a measure of respect to her opposite by actually speaking Confederate Standard, instead of relying on a translator.

"Am I addressing Commander Ustenar?"

"You are. You, of course, need no introduction. Your image is conjured each midday cycle on our worlds to drive the young back into their dens to sleep. Jan Atal, the Qraitian killer." Ustenar let her jaws open, showing fangs.

"That was a long time ago," said Atal. "Today I'm here on a routine visit to one of our colonies."

"Of course, Captain. Our visit is also routine."

"I'm sorry, Commander, but, local custom notwithstanding, incursion on our space by your ships is never routine."

"The Eleusinians–the Family, they call themselves–consider this system a demilitarized zone."

"The Confederacy does not agree."

"Nonetheless, our ships are welcomed here, as are our people... unfortunately."

"How unfortunately?"

"Atal, I wish to be here no more than you wish to have me here. It is an embarrassment to a proud warrior race that any of our number should wish to lay down their arms and stand with peace-lovers. Even an ugly truth must be faced, however; and the truth is that a litter of our people have chosen to join the Family."

"We're aware there are Qraitians living below."

"Then you should be aware that they can never be abandoned by the military sisterhood. Cowards they may be. Traitors they are, but they are still Qraitians. Every Qraitian goes home, be it scarred and victorious or dead and born in honor. Sometimes, yes, even in bondage and disgrace. But every Qraitian goes home to her family. In all my people's history, there has never been what you would call an orphan. Any one of our number who truly had no relations would be required to suicide.

"And because family is sacred, we can never allow a Qraitian to leave our space alone and unprotected. I am here because those below may choose to return. I will be here as long as they live, I or some one of my sisters. Should they die, I will bear their remains home."

"A very tolerant attitude towards traitors," acknowledged Atal. "Please don't be insulted if I say I'm surprised."

"I am not insulted, Captain. You know us as warriors, and that is how we wish to be known. We keep our manner of handling our refuse private, as most races do. Do not think for a minute that there is any love lost on these creatures who have turned to peace. They have forfeited all rights. They possess, under our laws, only the due of family members... a place in our homes, and a ride to those homes, if they are away."

"And if they decide to take that ride?"

Ustenar bobbed her reptilian head elegantly, the Qraitian equivalent of a nod. "There will be celebrations and rejoicing. The prodigal will be embraced by sister-brothers one last time, and then will make formal apology and atonement for her sins."

"Atonement?"

"We will execute her. Lovingly, of course. Family love cannot be destroyed, Atal. But a traitor must die. Any of these who come back to us will be embraced and killed with love."

"Why don't you just arrest them?"

"It is not our way. A Qraitian is never taken into custody against her will. It would be obscene. She must repent and come willingly."

"And if she comes home without repenting?"

Ustenar chuckled. "Then we eat her alive."

Atal knew she meant it literally. "Has anyone from Eleusis taken this offer?"

"Not yet. It will happen. Prodigals nearly always return to embrace a loving death. Unlike your people, we have strong morals."

"To each his own," muttered Atal. "Commander, in light of the progress being made in peace talks between our peoples–"

Ustenar hissed in laughter. "I like your sense of irony, Atal. We both know the peace talks are empty of promise."

"I hope you're wrong, Commander. At any rate... I'm willing to make allowance for your family obligations. If you will assure me that you will maintain your neutral posture in this system–"

"Naturally."

"Then we will pledge non-interference. We're going to check on our people below..."

"And we're going to keep a very close eye, from here, on our people below," said Ustenar. "And on you."

The shuttle hatch cracked and the handful of occupants all inhaled deeply and slowly, savoring fresh air.

Metcalfe sniffed twice. "Pine trees," he said, "and something like honeysuckle."

Pallas followed his example and sneezed.

"And pollen," added Atal.

"Yes, yes, it smells very nice," said Georg Fournier, standing. He stumbled slightly as he adjusted to the gravity of Eleusis. "Now let's see to business, shall we?"

They followed the Admiral through the open hatch and into bright, summer sunshine. Insects buzzed somewhere, and music drifted on the gentle breeze. Hymns? A church service, outdoors, from the clarity of the voices.

Metcalfe had landed the shuttle in a clearing, one of the few identifiable and available. The small population had not made significant changes to the landscape of Eleusis. Nor was there strong motivation for doing so. The bulk of the planet's land surface was in a temperate zone, and was one immense pastoral scene as Shakespeare might have envisioned for *A Midsummer Night's Dream.* Mature forest covered most of the land, and the colonists had cleared only enough for agriculture, homes and community buildings.

"I though Quintil was impressive," observed Atal, craning his neck to observe the nearby wood as it crept up a sweeping hillside. "This is like our biggest city park stretched over a whole planet."

"Quintil is *civilized*," countered Fournier. "This is subsistence living."

The Captain took another deep breath, savoring the air. "I could subsist here."

"You'd give up a sixty-room mansion and award-winning gardens... for this?"

Atal laughed. "Georg, I never saw fifty of those sixty rooms. When I was eight, I moved into a lean-to behind the maintenance shed. Lived there until I was twelve."

"I always figured you for a barbarian, Atal."

Pallas was the first to recognize the approach of locals, sensing them before they were visible. She pointed out for the others four figures as they came out of the wood at an easy jog, coming from the source of the music that drifted on the air.

Fournier squinted and said, "Oh my sainted designers!"

"What's wrong?" wondered Atal.

"Look closer, Captain, and you'll notice that half our reception committee is not human."

Indeed, as the four figures approached, Metcalfe could make out that two of them were taller and had a quite different gait than their obviously human companions. Their limbs moved fluidly, their arms seemed short for their bodies and ended in taloned phalanges that couldn't be called fingers. "Qraitians," he said quietly.

Making eye contact, the four quickened their pace and closed the gap between themselves and their visitors. The two Qraitians were also of different heights, though both taller than the humans. Both were male, evidenced by their bright red throat and facial markings. One was apparently a good deal younger than the other. A human male who was past his middle years walked a few paces ahead with a strong, purposeful stride. The last of the four was a young woman, petite, with wheat-colored hair which hung loose on her shoulders. Like the man, she wore a loose tunic; but her legs were bare beneath the short skirt of it, while he wore loose slacks. The Qraitians wore khakis which resembled the Navy's warm weather fatigues, and also left their limbs exposed and iridescent in the bright sunlight of Eleusis.

"I'm Brock Aronson," the human man said, extending his hand to Atal.

Fournier intercepted the hand, shook it perfunctorily, and said, "Admiral Georg Fournier. This is Captain Atal."

Aronson nodded his bald head and smiled genially. "My mistake, Admiral."

Metcalfe reflected silently that it was an easy mistake to make, assuming Atal led their party. The Captain was a commanding presence. Fournier, while also physically perfect due to genetic engineering, had no charisma and the manner of a minor bureaucrat.

"Are you in charge here, Mr. Aronson?" the Admiral asked. "We had no success finding records about your government."

"God is in charge here, Admiral Fournier," said Aronson with pleasant confidence. "I am a registered minister of the Family of God. People come to me for advice. If I lead, it's only by example."

The girl smiled and looked at Aronson with affection. "Don't let him kid you, Admiral. He's very much in charge here."

"This is Elspeth," said Aronson. "She too will be a registered minister in due time. Her gift is strong."

"Well I need to speak to the people in charge," said Fournier, unable to cloak the contempt in his voice.

Aronson gestured at the air with two spread hands. "Anyone may speak to God."

Metcalfe bit his lip. He had no doubt that Aronson knew he was trying the Admiral's patience. It made him like the man immediately.

Fournier massaged the bridge of his nose with two fingers. "I'm sure that's very kind of God, but I need to speak to a physical person—a *human being* who can make decisions on behalf of your entire colony."

"There is no such mortal person," said Aronson. "I cannot say 'human being' at any rate, since we are not all human here."

"So I see," said Fournier through his teeth.

The elder Qraitian hissed quietly.

"May I introduce two more of our Family?" said Aronson. He gestured at the taller alien. "This is Daedalus, and," he indicated the young Qraitian, "his son, Icarus."

"Really?" wondered Metcalfe. "Those are Terran names."

"Just so," breathed the father Qraitian. "We've found that humans cannot pronounce our names, mine is actually–" Here he broke into a series of hisses and a few clicks, plus some sounds no human tongue or throat could produce.

"I named them," said the girl Elspeth, brightly. "Because Daedalus was a genius who came from a foreign land to share his knowledge with the people of Crete. And because the original Daedalus flew on wings he made himself to escape oppression. Our Daedalus built his own ship to come here. He's a genius too."

"The child overstates my qualifications," said Daedalus.

"The original Daedalus also suffered a terrible loss when Icarus flew too close to the sun," said Metcalfe.

"Friend of yours?" asked Fournier.

"No sir. If the Terran Daedalus existed, he died millennia ago."

"Are you a student of history?" asked Elspeth happily.

"Somewhat," said Metcalfe. "But the story is in the Book of Heroes."

The girl's eyes widened. "You're Church of Terra!" she cried, excited. "I've never met one! I mean... oh, forgive me, I–"

"This is Leftenant Metcalfe," interrupted Fournier testily. "And Dr. Pallas.'

"And it's all right," said Metcalfe. "There aren't many of us in space."

"Mr. Aronson," Fournier almost barked, "we have strayed considerably from the matter at hand."

"And that is?"

"Who's in charge?"

"'Take me to your leader,' eh? I'm sorry, Mister–er, Admiral Fournier. Those who accept divine leadership do not believe that one mortal can make decisions for others. You have kings and emperors in the Inner Worlds. We have no such here."

"We have no kings," protested Fournier.

Aronson raised his eyebrows and nodded at the insignia on Fournier's shoulders. "You wear the colorful braid of royalty, you make decision which affect millions of lives, with no input from those millions, indeed, you have the power to destroy worlds... and yet you are neither king nor emperor?"

Fournier looked as though he'd developed a sudden headache. "In the real world, Mr. Aronson, someone must be in charge. It's impractical to hold an election to vote on strategy when the enemy is actually attacking."

"Admiral," said Pallas, "the organization from which Mr. Aronson's colony has derived does not recognize the concepts of either civic leadership by men and women or military strategy. Historically, on Terra, kings ruled by divine right. If the king and the priest were not the same individual, then the priest had significant influence over the decisions made by the king. In either case, all people were expected to obey the wishes of either king or priest, because their authority was allegedly granted by a supreme being, a god.

"The Society of Friends, popularly known as the Quakers, believed that all humans were of equal value in the eyes of God, and rejected the idea that one human could speak God's will better than another. Thus they never ordained formal ministers to be their leaders. They registered the gift of ministry of any person who demonstrated that gift. They cooperated with non-religious authority only so far as they considered it moral to do so, morality being defined as the laws of the ancient Hebrew and Christian faiths. They–"

"Doctor," Fournier grunted. *"Please."*

But Aronson was delighted with Pallas's digression. "You have versed yourself very well on the history of my people, Doctor. I'm flattered, as I know that religion is not the province of Phaetonians."

Atal smiled. "Did she verse herself, or did she merely pull the knowledge from your head?"

Pallas grimaced. "That would be terribly rude, Captain."

"Phaetonians don't believe in violating privacy," explained Atal.

"We do not, although that is not technically what prevents me from taking his people's history from Mr. Aronson's mind. What I recited were simply facts. They are thus public property. My people long ago ruled that information cannot be owned by individuals. It would be rude, however, to stray into Mr. Aronson's thoughts uninvited. I might uncover personal memories which are his intellectual property."

"Uh... yeah," said Atal.

Fournier spoke up. "Mr. Aronson, if you will not accept responsibility, then I must ask you to gather your people together. There are certain actions which are going to be required of them, and I have no more time to waste."

"And what are your demands, Admiral?"

"I thought you weren't the leader?"

Aronson pursed his lips. "No, but if I don't know the nature of your demands, I may be hard pressed to assemble our people quickly. If I say to them, 'a stranger has arrived and insists on meeting with you all,' some may come from curiosity. Others may feel they have better things to do."

"Well... couldn't I address them at one of your religious gatherings?"

"Certainly."

"Well then–"

"You are moved by the Holy Spirit to speak?"

"Yes, well... what?"

Metcalfe snickered despite himself.

"No one speaks in our gatherings unless touched by God. The Lord whispers words into our hearts, in His still, small voice, and we share His message."

"It's not that kind of message," said Metcalfe.

"Leftenant!" snapped Fournier.

"It is not that kind of message," echoed Pallas.

"Then I'm sorry," said Aronson, "but it would not be appropriate. Please, Admiral, tell me what it is you wish to say. I will see if it interests anyone."

"If it–?!" Fournier's jaw quivered so hard that it looked as though it were trying to shake itself loose of his skull. "Perhaps this will interest your very busy people, then! The Navy intends to close your system's borders. You will accept Confederate protection and a standing military presence on this planet, and you will eject all Qraitian nationals. Will that get their attention?"

Aronson shook his head, "Sadly, I don't believe it will, Admiral. We have a long history of hearing military threats and bluster, telling us who can go where and what imaginary, mortal-created lines cannot be crossed. All the governments which made these threats have fallen, and we are still here. We reject your violent ways, and will continue to live apart from you and from them. We recognize no government but the Kingdom of Heaven, and no law but God's law. We certainly cannot be expected to exile members of our own Family." He nodded at Daedalus and Icarus.

"Then, whether you listen or not, the only alternative you leave me is to order forced relocation. And the Qraitians will be placed in custody." He turned to the father and son and said, "I understand that, if you try to go home, you will be executed. I have no particular concern for your welfare, but I cannot allow that. I need detainees for questioning."

For a moment, anger showed in Aronson's face. It as quickly disappeared, but the calm that replaced it was troubled. "It would be... unfortunate... for you to follow that course of action, Admiral Fournier. I hope we can convince you not to."

"Not a chance in hell!"

Aronson flinched. "Perhaps... if you met my people, you would see there is no cause for alarm. We are no threat."

"Then you can go and be no threat someplace else. No doubt there are other planets you can homestead."

"No other planet where God dwells incarnate," said Aronson quietly.

"I won't listen to this!"

"You must. You don't understand what the consequences of your actions could be."

Fournier almost smiled. "Is that a threat?"

"No."

"Admiral," Pallas cut in suddenly, "Mr. Aronson believes there is grave danger in attempting to use force against his people."

Aronson looked slightly surprised by this outburst.

"Forgive me," said Pallas. "It was a powerful broadcast from your mind."

"I suppose it was," he admitted.

"So you are threatening us!"

"He is not," said Pallas. She looked to the older man. "May I?"

Aronson nodded assent.

"As reported, the Family believe they have encountered God incarnate on this world. They have had contact with a life force dwelling here, with which they have established a rapport. It is powerful, and I sense it might not react well to its... people... that is how Aronson sees it... being taken away."

"Is that all you can say?" Fournier demanded.

"I will not pry further," said Pallas. "If Mr. Aronson wishes to explain..."

"You have explained it sufficiently, Doctor. God wants us to remain."

"Mr. Aronson," said Atal, "two of my officers have expressed a strong interest in your beliefs about this planet. They share your concern that there are forces here which could be a threat, if tampered with. What more can you tell us about the... god... of this world? It really exists? As a matter of fact, not an article of faith?"

"He does exist, Captain," said Elspeth.

"Can we meet him?" asked Atal.

"Only the devout," replied Aronson, "may commune with the Almighty."

Fournier smirked. "Isn't that convenient?"

"I understand your skepticism, Admiral," Aronson assured him. "I would feel the same way in your position. But it's not just a convenient rule we've made to cloak our beliefs in mystery. The simple fact is that non-believers have tried to commune and accomplished nothing. God will not speak to them."

Fournier looked pointedly at Metcalfe. "Well, we have a 'believer' among us. Maybe that's worth something for a change."

Metcalfe bit back an angry response. It wasn't easy to see past the surface hostility of the conversation, but when he thought about the issue at hand–the question of whether or not this planet had a connection to God... "I'm willing to try," he said.

The four Eleusinians exchanged glances, silently deliberating. Finally, it was Elspeth who said, "A Terran Church member who chose to come into space? Your mind must be open to some degree, Lieutenant." She stepped forward and looked intently into his eyes. It made him uncomfortable, with Pallas standing next to him. "I sense you're a seeker."

"I guess I am," admitted Metcalfe.

Icarus, the young Qraitian, said, "We'll take him, Brother Aronson. Elspeth and I."

"I think it's a good idea," Aronson agreed. "Let the young people go to Communion. The rest of us can continue discussing... less spiritual matters."

Pallas had wanted to accompany them. She had made her request aloud to Aronson, and silently in Metcalfe's mind when Aronson had declined it. Not to be prejudiced, he'd explained, but Phaetonians were notoriously the most anti-religious people in the known galaxy. Her presence might interfere with Metcalfe's ability to experience the Communion he sought.

It'll be all right, he'd assured her as her anxious psychic presence appeared in his mind. *You stay here and keep Fournier honest.*

He had felt guilty leaving her nonetheless, and it hadn't helped that, within her range of vision, Elspeth had grabbed his hand to lead him away. He tried not the think of the girl's hand warm in his own, tried to send more reassurance to Pallas between their minds; but hers was oddly silent.

Climbing into the hills which surrounded their landing place, Metcalfe was able to relax. The untouched landscape soothed him, reminding him strongly of his native Virginia. It had been some time since he'd climbed these kinds of embankments. He had been quite good at it, years ago. Carson had called him "the freakin' mountain goat." Now, despite years of drills in all different gravities, he found his mountain legs were out of practice. He stumbled as he followed the other two, and found a strong hand enfold his to steady him.

It was Icarus. Metcalfe reflected that it was the first time he'd ever touched a Qraitian. He didn't know what he had expected it to feel like. He'd always been afraid of snakes, and had never touched one. He was surprised to find the boy's hand smooth, sinuous and cool. After adjusting to the surprise of realizing who was helping him, he found he was not revolted or troubled by the touch.

"It's all right," said Icarus. His jaws parted slightly and a quiet hiss came out. Was that the Qraitian equivalent of a smile? He wondered if the other young man guessed the nature of his discomfort, but then Icarus finished, "I've got you."

"Thanks," said Metcalfe, pulling himself up with help from the proffered grip.

Elspeth looked back at the two of them and smiled. There was no doubt that she picked up on the sub text, if Icarus, younger and more naive, did not. Clearly it pleased her to see two "natural enemies" helping each other in this simple way. "The Communion Ground is right over this rise," she said and scrambled up the hill.

Following her, Icarus led Metcalfe into a grotto with a floor worn smooth by foot traffic, whose trees shaded them from sunlight.

Elspeth stood in the center and spread her arms, spinning a half turn and smiling. "This is my favorite place in the world," she said happily. "It's so peaceful and beautiful!"

"It is that," Metcalfe agreed.

"Sit and rest yourself, Metcalfe," said Icarus. "I think the climb tired you."

Metcalfe grinned. "I think it did." He sat gracefully, folding his legs beneath him, and looked around. "The whole planet is beautiful, Elspeth. I can't think of another one like it."

"I've never seen another one," she confessed, "so I wouldn't know how to compare."

"Have you seen a lot of planets, Metcalfe?" asked Icarus.

"Dozens," he acknowledged.

"Metcalfe." Elspeth seemed to be turning the name over in her mind. "Is that your only name?"

"No. My first name is Terrence. My friends call me Terry."

She tried it on for size. "Terry. I like it."

"May I... call you that?" asked Icarus.

The request was so sincere, and the boy's tone so shy, Metcalfe was taken aback. Without giving it much thought, he said, "Of course." Icarus had noticed that Metcalfe had said Terry was the name his friends used. He was asking if he could be included among the number of Metcalfe's friends. And here, now, Metcalfe found himself wondering, why not? This boy, who could be no older in his own years than a human teenager, certainly had no part in the Qraitian violence Metcalfe had encountered in the past.

Icarus seemed pleased. Like many other teens, encouragement made him talkative. "Terry, do you like being in the military?" he asked.

"I... You know, I've never really thought about it. I left my home because it wasn't... well, life wasn't pleasant there. I wanted to find a better place, a happier place. Joining the Navy gave me a chance to do that. I've made friends. That's been good."

Elspeth frowned. "Brother Aronson says that, throughout history, many people have joined the military because they had no other opportunity to make their lives better."

"I guess I'm one of them. I like to think that I've been able to do some good. We've helped a lot of people."

"Have you had to kill?" Icarus blurted out.

Metcalfe looked away, unsure how to answer.

"Icarus," whispered Elspeth, "have some tact!"

"I'm sorry," said the boy. "I didn't mean–"

"It's all right," Metcalfe assured him. "It's not your fault." He swallowed. "Yes. Yes, I've... had to kill people." He wondered if he should say more, then felt the impulse to be completely honest. "I've had to kill... your people, Icarus."

Surprisingly, the young Qraitian did not react in shock. "Not my people," he said gently. "My people are here, on Eleusis. I am one of the Family of God."

"Still," said Metcalfe. "I'm not proud of it."

"Others among the family have taken lives," said Icarus. "Some who were born elsewhere and came to us later in life, like my father. God forgives all sins, Terry, if the sinner will let him."

Elspeth had stood and walked around behind Metcalfe. She said now, "We should begin Communion, Brothers."

Metcalfe also stood and said, "Of course." He turned to face Elspeth, and uttered an astonished, "Oh!"

She stood before him, her tunic loose, open and falling to the ground. Sunlight through the trees dappled her taut breasts, pale and dusted with freckles. As he watched, speechless, she peeled off the sheer panties which were all that remained of her clothing. She had already kicked off the moccasins she'd worn to climb up here.

Laughing, she said, "Come now, Terry, you've seen a naked girl before, haven't you?"

Trying not to stare, he muttered, "Yes, but... "

"I bet he's never seen a naked Qraitian before," said Icarus.

Metcalfe turned to see that his other companion was also nude. He tried to keep his eyes from widening, and averted his gaze from where it was naturally drawn by curiosity.

Icarus's eyes followed his own, and his jaws again formed the Qraitian smile. "I've been told they're comparatively large," he said. "Don't worry. I know it's rude to use them uninvited."

Them, thought Metcalfe, astonished, and realized that he probably should have paid closer attention in his course on Xenobiology at the Academy.

"This is how we practice Communion," said Elspeth. She nodded proddingly at Metcalfe. "So come on!"

He fumbled with the fastenings of his own clothing, self-conscious as he simultaneously shrugged out of his charcoal gray duty suit and kicked off his boots. The fabric snagged, and he nearly fell.

"Take your time," the girl admonished. "Would you like some help?"

Metcalfe blushed. "I'm good, thanks."

After a seeming eternity, he got his feet untangled and pulled off the flame-red shirt which denoted his rank, then his briefs.

"You definitely improve the look of the place," observed Elspeth.

"Thanks," Metcalfe said, looking away.

"Don't be ashamed, Terry. God made you to be attractive to His other children."

The other two joined hands, then, coming forward, each took one of his own.

Elspeth leaned her head in, and the two males followed suit, their three foreheads touching. "Let us pray," she said.

"Is someone there?"

"I am here, Terry Metcalfe."

"Who are you?"

"Who do you think I am?"

"You speak my language."

"I speak all languages."

"Where are the others?"

"I speak to one soul at a time."

"They said you don't speak to everyone."

"I speak to those who seek me."

"Those who seek God?"

"What do you seek, Terry Metcalfe?"

"I seek... answers."

"The answers that Admiral Fournier sent you to find? Or the answers to greater questions?"

"How did you know–?"

"I know everything you know, and much more."

"I seek... peace."

"Yes. You do. You have tasted war, and it weighs upon your soul."

"I... have killed."

"Do you confess to me?"

"I... I'm just telling the truth."

"You have sinned."

"Yes."

"You took dozens of lives."

"If I had not, billions more might have died. Wouldn't it have been a greater sin to do nothing?"

"Do you make excuses?"

"No. I–I seek guidance. What do you do, when your choices are all evil?"

"Look for another answer?"

"I... didn't have time."

"Did you pray?"

"What?"

"Did you pray?"

...

"Terry Metcalfe?"

"No."

"What?"

"No. I didn't pray."

"All your life you have prayed. Every day. You've brought every problem you ever had to God, but, when you had to kill, you didn't pray."

"I was... frightened. I was angry. I thought I'd lost two friends. I did lose one. So many had already died. I wanted... "

"Revenge?"

"I wanted it to stop. I wanted to stop the evil."

"By committing evil?"

"I... I didn't think about whether it was good or evil."

"You abandoned faith. Then you abandoned reason."

"I did not abandon reason. My plan worked!"

"The plan conceived in anger."

"They killed Nathan!"

"Did killing them bring him back?"

"No! But it saved everyone who was still alive!"

"But is that why you did it?"

"What do you want from me?!"

"What do you want?"

"I..."

"Well?"

"I want... forgiveness."

"From me?"

"From God."

"Am I God?"

"I don't know, but... do you forgive me?"

"I can't."

...

"You were afraid of that, weren't you?"

"Yes."

"But it's not that your sin is unforgivable. I cannot forgive you because you cannot forgive yourself. Can you?"

"I'm... trying."

"What will it take to allow you to succeed?"

"I don't know. Maybe... "

"Maybe?"

"Maybe I should... stop living a life that might require me to kill."

"Is that not just leaving the job to someone else?"

"Maybe... Maybe, if everyone left the job of killing to someone else, no one would kill. Maybe it's a job that would never need doing."

"Good."

"You think I should leave the Navy?"

"I know... It was right for you to come here."

"Where am I?"

"You're in the grotto, among the trees, holding the hands of your friends."

"That's not what I see, not what I feel."

"What do you see, Terry Metcalfe?"

"I see... darkness. But there's light. I see... it's like... I'm underground. In a cave."

"Are you?"

"Is this... where you are? Under ground?"

"Where is God?"

"Everywhere, but this... this chamber... this darkened chamber... I feel... people celebrating... worshiping... there's an altar and... I'm in... a cathedral."

"You are not the first to call it that."

"How many others–?"

"Time to wake, Terry Metcalfe."

"But–I need to know–!"

"Your need to know is less than your need to ask."

"Are you... God?"

"It is good to know you."

CHAPTER SEVEN

"We noticed this from space," said Atal. "It's remarkable."

The Captain and Aronson walked by the side of an enormous lake. After a long session of debate, Fournier had grown increasingly unreasonable. Atal had found it opportune to suggest that he check in with Darby about the course of the investigation on *Titan*. It had been a good excuse to take a break. Atal and Aronson had stepped out for air, and Pallas had decided to explore the village and interview the colonists.

"My ancestors chose the lake as the heart of our settlement," said Aronson. "It supplies an abundance of fish."

"Is it fed by a stream?"

"An underground one, most likely."

"The shape is unusual. A near-perfect circle. Natural lakes are not often symmetrical. Do you know how it was formed?"

"It was here when the first colonists arrived. It has changed little since then."

"When we observed it, I wondered if it was a meteor crater, but there's no other sign of impact. It's more like a sink-hole."

"We've speculated often as to the cause. It was obviously formed suddenly. It has no obvious source and no outflow. No evidence of geologically recent tectonic shifts. No evidence of glacial activity, volcanic activity or landslides. Just a miles-diameter sinkhole."

"As if something underneath collapsed. Perhaps there was an explosion–some cataclysm?"

Aronson nodded, pursing his lips thoughtfully. "There are legends of a great battle or disaster which wiped out the native race of Eleusis. How else to explain that such a hospitable planet is empty of higher life? Still, whatever produced it, it's magnificent. We enjoy it."

"It's beautiful. Restful."

"You should take a boat and go fishing, Captain."

Atal bit out a laugh. "That'll be the day! My fishing days are far in my future, Mr. Aronson."

"Brock."

"Jan."

"You seem to be interested in more than a geological oddity, Jan."

"It may be nothing. Some of my crew are worried about... legends. We're all on edge. It's a bad time out there in the galaxy, Brock."

"We mortals have a propensity for suffering bad times, do we not? Perhaps it would not be so, if we placed God higher in our hearts."

"'Fraid I've never believed in gods."

"You are yet young."

"I have a grown daughter!"

"God has grown children by the billions. Generations of them."

"I stand corrected. Talking to you is a bit like talking to my Mr. Metcalfe."

"A remarkable young man."

"Very. If he weren't I wouldn't trust him to gather intelligence of this kind, or allow him to walk into potential danger,"

"You believe there is danger?" wondered Aronson.

"You know the legends. And you suggested, and Pallas verified that you believed, that something on this planet might bite if we stuck a hand in its nest."

Aronson was silent for a moment. "There is no danger if my people's rights are respected. There is no danger to Mr. Metcalfe. If he is truly a man of faith, he will learn much. If he is not, then he will simply find nothing." He scanned the darkening sky over the lake. "It's getting toward evening. Must the three of you return to your ship, or could we offer you accommodations here? We're too small a community for hotels, but there are many boarding houses."

"Few sailors are ever eager to return to their ships when they've got a warm bed on dry land available. Especially not the first night back on land. But why 'the three of us?'"

"If his Communion is successful, Metcalfe will be gone overnight. The experience itself takes little time, but one must rest and ... meditate afterwards."

"I'm growing a bit concerned. Perhaps I should see him."

"It would be disruptive to the process."

"That sounds a bit suspicious."

Aronson smiled. "It does, I know. Jan, I'm being completely honest with you. If you'd like Dr. Pallas to verify that, I'm more than willing to give consent. After Communion, the focus of the mind is drawn inward. It is a profoundly moving experience. To try and interrupt the natural course of it is akin to trying to wake a sleepwalker. Introducing the mundane world too quickly is jarring, even painful."

"So if I go there now, I'm likely to find a drunken sailor?"

"An apt analogy. The children will stay in the prayer lodge tonight. Come, let's find something for the three of you."

"You're sure Metcalfe's all right?"

Atal sat with Pallas on the porch of a farmhouse, built by hand out of local wood. Few homes on Quintil could touch it for craftsmanship, however. They sat in old-fashioned rocking chairs, also handmade. The young doctor presented an incongruous picture in such a rustic environment: ramrod straight as always, immaculate in her preferred black jumpsuit–civilian, but military in style–not one of her pale hairs out of place. It occurred to Atal that, with her white-blonde hair and alabaster skin, Pallas was made to be seen in moonlight.

And there he left that particular train of thought.

"If he were injured or in danger, I would know, Captain," she acknowledged.

"Aren't you curious what he's up to?"

Her eyes narrowed. "You mean aren't I tempted to slip into his mind and observe his activities." It was not a question. "No, I'm not."

"You are an unusual woman, then. Even in our sexually liberated culture, most people are uncomfortable if their, ah... " he paused, suddenly realizing that her relationship with Metcalfe was something he'd never discussed with either of them before. He had started down a path and wasn't sure if he should be on it.

She finished his thought, "–if their lovers go off in company with someone who might be seen as a rival."

"The girl is very pretty," said Atal.

"I didn't think you meant the Qraitian boy."

Atal laughed.

"She is very attractive. And I didn't have to violate any privacy customs to know that she found Metcalfe extremely attractive."

"Why do you call him 'Metcalfe?"

"That is his name. It's what you call him."

"Yes, but I'm his Captain. You're–"

"His lover. I don't know why you hesitate to use the word."

"Neither do I, really. I suppose it feels like I'm violating your privacy by naming your relationship. I learned long ago not to refer to Kaya's partners as her 'boyfriends' or 'girlfriends.' It made her disagreeable."

"And you feel a parental tie to Metcalfe as well?"

"I suppose I do. There's an old saying, you know, that the Skipper is the father to his crew."

"Skipper?"

"Slang for Captain. Not a clue why. I assure you, I rarely skip."

"But your paternal feelings for Metcalfe are stronger than those you feel for, say, Sestus Blaurich."

Atal snorted and smacked the arm of the rocker. "My paternal feelings for this chair are stronger than my paternal feelings for Sestus Blaurich, but I take your point. I push Metcalfe harder, and I worry about him more."

"And yet you call him 'Metcalfe,' as I do."

"Not quite the same relationship, Doc."

She smiled. "No, it isn't. Phaetonians have only one name. It is for public use, for communication and identification on the spoken level. On the telepathic level, names are useless. You never have any doubt, in telepathic conversation, as to who is speaking to whom. You never have any confusion over which person is being referred to in conversation. Telepathically, identity is certain. That is why telepathy is the preferred communication method of the true individualist."

"That doesn't follow. Telepathy allows the most intimate sharing of thoughts. It crosses boundaries that, for non-telepaths, are never crossed. It violates privacy."

"Only if the telepath is very rude," she reminded him. "Telepathic communication removes all doubt as to the honesty of a statement, or the authorship of an idea. A disciplined telepath can easily identify which of her thought processes are her own, and which have been influenced by others. We are much harder to emotionally manipulate, and we cannot be blackmailed. The traditional weapons of collectivist society are thus rendered powerless. Ironically, in rendering the name–the traditional hallmark of identity–useless, we have secured the uniqueness of the individual identity in a way no society ever has."

"So you don't need a name for Metcalfe?"

"Except when I'm talking to you. He knows when I'm communicating with him. I use his surname, his public name, really as a kind of a joke. And to remind him that we're communicating in a very non-intimate way."

"You're a tease, Doc."

Again, she smiled. "I believe it pleases me to be so described, Captain."

"And you're sure he's all right?"

"There is no inordinate cause for worry this evening."

"Not even from the threat of pretty girls?"

"Captain, among my people, and, more importantly, in my personal code, falling in love is an intensely rational process. It means I have chosen Metcalfe as my moral ideal. Having done so, would it make sense for me to constantly suspect him of doing that which I would not wish him to do?"

"Well, when you put it that way..."

"Neither of us has cause to worry."

On the side of the enormous lake opposite the village, Metcalfe, Elspeth and Icarus strolled in the moonslight. Everything was silver: the ground, the lake, the girl...

Her hand was in his. How long had it been there? She'd led him back down the hillside... when? He didn't remember leaving the grotto, didn't remember awakening. Or was it awakening? Had he been asleep? Someone had been there.

When had he dressed?

Elspeth was saying something, and Metcalfe laughed. He didn't know what she had said. He just felt like laughing. The girl snuggled in close to his arm.

"It's amazing, isn't it?" she asked. "Touching God?"

"I feel like I'm drunk."

"You are, kind of," said Icarus. "Drunk on the Love of the Lord. You get more accustomed to it, but it's always overwhelming."

"It's hot tonight," said Elspeth. "Let's go for a swim. It will clear your head."

"Great idea!" sang Icarus, as much as a Qraitian's voice could be said to sing. He began divesting himself of his clothes.

"Come on," Elspeth said, and started to unfasten Metcalfe's collar.

He gently stopped her hands. "I have to get back... report..."

She giggled. "You can't report anything in this state! Besides, we sleep in the prayer lodge tonight. Your friends know you won't be back till morning."

He made another token objection, but had neither the will nor the coordination to resist as they undressed him. Then he felt the shock of cold as Icarus easily lifted him and tossed him into the water. For a moment, a thousand icy needles cut into his bare flesh and he screamed in protest. This only made his companions laugh more. They dove in and joined him.

Shaking water from his hair and ears, Metcalfe, grinning, arced out of the water and pounced on Icarus. He forced the boy's head under for a second, but the reptilian sinews were not easily held. Icarus snapped out of his grasp like a cracking whip, hissing with laughter, and shoved Metcalfe backwards and under the water again.

He surfaced, blowing water from his nose and at the same time laughing uncontrollably. Weeks ago–was that all?–he'd been locked in life and death battle with Qraitians. Now he was capering in the water with one, like an innocent child. Could both events be real? Could one who killed be one who laughed and played? If not, which did he want to be?

"Come on, boys," Elspeth called out. "Best two out of three! I have money on the purple kid!"

Metcalfe caught Icarus's eye. They both smiled and silently agreed on a plan. Seconds later, each had Elspeth by an arm, and the girl was flipped upside down in the water. As she righted herself, Metcalfe watched the light play off her perfect limbs and felt himself responding. She was beautiful!

"Bullies!" she cried out when she'd regained her voice. "Two against one! That's not fair!" She splashed Icarus in the face, and then propelled herself at Metcalfe, hooking one leg behind his and trying to knock him off balance. He struggled in her grasp, but maintained his stance, even as warm legs rubbed over his, and soft hands pushed at his chest.

He didn't realized he was kissing her until it had been going on for some time. Her mouth was warm and sweet, her tongue yielding but playful against his. Their hands explored.

Where had Icarus gone? He had just been there...

And then they were on the bank, in soft grass. Idly, he registered that something pillowed his head. It might be his uniform, or her tunic. His senses were more drawn to the feelings she was creating as she moved on top of him, warm against him, teasing him, inviting him, loving him.

He was loved. He was loved and... he was forgiven. There was still good in him. He could laugh and play and be accepted by these innocent people. God loved him. Yes, God was here. God was with him. He felt God still, in his head. He felt God in her playful caresses, in the sweetness of her kisses, in the warmth of her skin pressed firmly to his.

When she'd drawn him inside her, sighing happily, she leaned in close to him. Her teeth gently grazed his ear, and her breath was hot inside it. She whispered, "Icarus is watching."

Metcalfe made to turn his head and see where the boy was, but she stopped him with on hand to his chin. "Don't look," she breathed. "It doesn't bother me. Does it bother you?"

Nothing in the world or all the worlds there were bothered him.

"He's curious. There's nothing wrong with that."

She fell silent as their motions grew frantic, and he rolled her under him. They both cried out. She dug her fingers into his flesh, urging him on.

As orgasm overwhelmed him, he heard a voice–hers? Someone else's? "It is good to know you."

Metcalfe awoke to the welcoming smells of coffee and bacon. Almost unbidden, he swung his legs out of bed to seek their source. At home... on Titan... the smell of coffee was there every morning. His cabin's A.I. knew when to have it ready for him. Bacon, on the other hand, would have to be sought in the Officer's mess, or in one of the eateries off the Main Concourse.

He took a moment to assess his surroundings, having awoken from one of those hard sleeps which robs one of the memory of where one fell asleep hours before. Then he remembered the lake and the girl and recognized what must be the interior of one of the many log cabins that dotted the perimeter of the lake. A prayer lodge, she had called it. Simultaneously, he realized he was naked and was immediately uncomfortable.

Nudity was not particularly a taboo for him anymore, and he preferred to sleep naked. Still, he had spent years on Terra, and old training died hard. To sleep naked in the home of strangers, even when one had prayed and swum naked with them the night before, well... On the farm, no one would have considered retiring in less than briefs and a nightshirt. Modesty was rigorously enforced. At the Academy and on *Arbiter*, he'd shared a room with Carson. Terran standards of propriety had carried over, although late nights with their friends and the liquor cabinet had often relaxed them.

Now, in his own private quarters, it would have been silly to wear clothes to bed. Years out from earth, he was comfortable with skin. His own, and anyone else's.

Comfortable, but not indifferent.

He remembered the first time he had seen Pallas nude. She'd caught him by surprise, having invited him to her stateroom on *Titan*. She had said she wanted to collect experimental data on human sexuality. He'd had a good idea what that had meant, but had been stunned speechless when after closing the door, she'd pressed the clasp on her jumpsuit and let it fall to the floor. She wore no undergarments. His mouth had hung open and gone dry.

She'd given a little smile. "Are you surprised that I undressed? Isn't it required?"

"It–that is–I–thought there'd be preliminaries. Discussion. A drink?"

She'd given a small gasp of realization. "I've forgotten the emotional importance of suspense! Should I get dressed again?"

Surveying her carefully, he'd answered, "Seems pointless now."

She had met his gaze. "Am I properly constructed to serve as your sexual partner?"

And again, he hadn't known what to say. There were advantages to being with a woman who read minds.

Now, in the cabin by the lake, the door opened and Elspeth walked in, carrying a tray and wearing a loose robe which hid little. She had probably only donned it to protect herself as she'd cooked.

"Good morning, Beautiful," she said happily. Then, noticing the effect his memories of Pallas had had, "Ready and waiting for me, I see?"

He felt himself blush, two counts of embarrassment registering. "You don't call men beautiful."

She grinned. "I do. All the time. And you are. And so is this." She indicated his other source of embarrassment.

He pulled away, covering himself with a sheet and causing her to frown.

"Is something wrong?" she asked. "You weren't this shy last night."

"I... shouldn't have done that. What we did last night."

"Whyever not? You're very good at it!"

"Thank you. It's just that I'm... involved... with someone."

"Oh." She was silent for a moment. "What exactly does that mean?"

"It means–I'm actually not sure what it means."

"You're not married?"

"No."

"Engaged?"

"What?"

"Planning to get married. I can't believe I know an old earth term that you don't!"

"No. Not engaged. Just... involved. I mean... "

"You're in love with her?"

"Yes."

"And she's in love with you?"

"Yes. I mean... she says so."

"Why do you doubt it?"

"I don't!"

"Then why did you spend last night in bed with me?"

"... 'Cause I'm an unfaithful jerk?"

She wrapped him in her arms and stroked his hair. "You most certainly are not! Even if you promised her you wouldn't be with anyone else–did you?"

"I guess I didn't. I just intended not to."

"So you broke a promise to yourself, not to her. And now the question is why? Why did you break your promise, Terry? Why did you make love to me?"

"After... after last night... what I... felt... in there... I... dammit, I can't even put it into words!"

"You were so overwhelmed, so filled with the sense of the Spirit, that you had to try and reach out, to make contact, to connect. The Spirit is life, so you reached out to the life that was nearest."

"How did you know?"

"Been there, done that."

"Is it like that every time?" he wondered.

"Oh, no! The first time is like... well, the first time you made love!"

The first time Terry Metcalfe had made love had been not that long ago. He'd been nineteen, and a midshipman at the Academy. His first time had been with an instructor, Captain Angela Baron-Danaker, now an Admiral. Such contact was not forbidden in the Inner Worlds, as it would have been on Terra, and the older woman had told him she couldn't resist his innocence and passion. They'd parted dear friends. They still spoke now and then via L-Space comm.

During the first encounter, he had been nervous, excited, terrified, and as aroused as he'd ever been in his life.

"You're right," he conceded to Elspeth's comparison.

"So... maybe you don't need to beat up on yourself?"

"Maybe."

"And a second encounter is–?"

"Not a good idea," he said sadly.

She nodded, keeping her expression neutral. "She's a lucky girl."

"I hope she thinks so."

"Breakfast is getting cold. Let's eat."

"Okay. But give me a minute to check in, okay?"

"So did you find God?"

Atal's image, rendered by the data implant, hovered in the air before him. Metcalfe had dressed for the occasion. Atal looked rested, had a cup of coffee in hand, and was apparently seated outside on someone's porch.

"I found... something. Or it found me."

"Intelligent?"

"Definitely."

"You communicated?"

"In some way."

"Did you learn anything?"

"Not about it. It asked most of the questions."

"'Not about it?' What did you learn about?"

"Myself."

"Oh." There was a pause. "Metcalfe, I would never question your loyalty, but you are privy to a great deal of sensitive information–"

"It didn't seem at all interested in strategic intel, Captain. It asked the questions I'd expect God to ask. I felt like I was... you're familiar with the concept of Judgment Day?"

"I've heard of it. Some god named Pete puts you on trial?"

"St. Peter. And he's not a god. But yes, that's how it works."

"It was an interview? Spoken out loud?"

"It was... inside my head. Kind of like a dream."

"Are you sure it really happened?"

"I... something affected me. Profoundly."

"Like a dream, you say. Like an hallucination?"

"Maybe."

"Could you have been drugged?"

Metcalfe considered it. He'd spoken to a god, left the physical world behind, played with a Qraitian as though they were innocent children... he'd slept with a girl he barely knew. It would sound to an objective witness as though he were a sailor out on a drunk. Was he?

"I can't rule it out, sir."

Atal sighed. "It troubles me. It's too much like Kaya's account."

The Captain had briefed him on Kaya's vision quest. Metcalfe hadn't had time to give it much thought. Now he compared what he knew of Kaya's experience with what had happened to him.

"You thought Kaya was communicating with her own subconscious. You think that's what happened to me."

"You said yourself you're not sure what happened."

"I also said I was profoundly affected. I am."

Last night, the world had spun so fast, he'd had no time to think. He'd only just awoken and begun immediately to wrestle with his guilt, but despite the frenzy of events and the emotional static, a certain clarity emerged. Where it came from, he did not not know, but Metcalfe felt a peace and a resolve that he hadn't since... No. He had never felt this way.

"Are you all right?"

"Never better, Captain. It's just... like I said, I learned some things about myself last night."

"Go on."

"I know your people think of Terra as backwards. They think that Church of Terra's just a collection of inbred, uneducated bigots. I've fought that belief all my life, but... I also know it's not entirely a fantasy. There's a lot of hate, a lot of wrong-headedness that comes out of my people's beliefs."

"Are you questioning your faith in those beliefs?"

"Far from it. Despite all the negatives, the core of my faith is right. We believe in the Golden Rule."

"Does that have something to do with money?"

Metcalfe smiled. "Not really. It says to only do to others things you wouldn't mind having done to yourself. We also believe in loving our enemies."

"Tall order."

"It's supposed to be. Being a human and carrying the spark of the divine isn't supposed to be easy. We're supposed to try to be, well, like God. Or the gods. That means recognizing that there's good in everyone. Last night I prayed with a Qraitian. We talked. Really talked. We went swimming together and laughed and carried on like a couple of old friends. They're not... they're not *aliens*. They're people."

"I never doubted it."

"I guess I did, sir. Although I knew intellectually that they were intelligent beings, I never recognized, deep down, that, well... maybe they're God's children, too."

"Is this about Fehajiq?"

"Partly."

"You did what you had to do."

"I know that. I accept that. But I'm asking myself if I should let myself be in a situation where I might have to do it again."

Atal's voice took on a strange edge. "Metcalfe–"

"Sir, can I really continue to be part of a group which uses violence to achieve its ends, when violence is contrary to everything I believe? To everything I was put here to accomplish? These people are the first ones I've met who actually built a society on the idea that, above all, we must not use violence against each other. I know it sounds crazy and sudden. In a way it is. It snuck up on me and hit me, but it's also something I've been thinking about for quite a while."

"What is?"

"Sir... I've been looking for an answer. I think I've found it. I want to stay on Eleusis."

CHAPTER EIGHT

Official Memorandum from the Desk of Fournier, G. Admiral
To Atal, J, Captain
Re: Metcalfe, T, Lieutenant

Please review the *Standards and Code of the Confederate Navy* (CNV-001.238), Section 3, subsection 5.8.9: Desertion. Metcalfe's intent is to violate both the letter and the spirit of this regulation. It is possible to recommend court martial based upon his statement to you, but, since you were so careless as to not record said conversation, there might not be sufficient evidence to convict.

You are hereby instructed to record all future conversations with Lt. Metcalfe and submit them for review by the J.A.G. Since he is still on assignment on Eleusis, his presence there, unfortunately, does not constitute statutory desertion. If you were to order him back to *Titan*, and he refused, we could act decisively. You are so ordered to require his return...

"... and so I ordered him to remain and continue to collect data on the intelligence or life form, or whatever it is."

Celia Faulkner clapped her hands with glee and sank back into Atal's couch, putting her feet up on the glass coffee table. "Have you told Fournier yet?"

"I have not."

"He'll charge you with insubordination."

"Won't be the first time. But I can hold him off. Metcalfe–by Fournier's own order!–has made contact with an unknown intelligence. This is possibly a first contact situation with a non-human life form. I can't pull from the field the only officer who's made contact, now can I?"

"I'm convinced. Will Fournier be?"

Atal shook his head. "Not a chance. But my argument will stick with the rest of the Admiralty, Fournier knows it, and will back down before they ever hear it, for fear of looking stupid in front of his peers."

"Good. Then what?"

"Then what what?"

"Then when this mission is over, and Metcalfe still doesn't come back with us?"

"I'll cross that bridge when I come to it. Dammit, Celia, I thought Kaya was being a mother hen, but now I'm worried about the boy. He's not behaving rationally."

"Isn't he? He's found a world where they live according to his most closely held beliefs. How many people can say that?"

"Can't you?"

"Yes, but I was born there. I didn't find it later. Terry's grown up believing a very gentle philosophy, but he was surrounded first by ruffians and then by, well..."

"Shallow dilettantes? Don't be afraid to say it. It's what we InWorlders are."

"Fair enough. Can you blame him for feeling he's come home?"

"I can blame him for deserting his post!"

"You can. And he knows it. But will you, Jan?"

Atal didn't care to answer that, not even in his own head. "What if this... Communion... has affected his mind?"

"There's no question it's affected his mind. As he told you himself, it brought a moment of unique clarity."

"Which caused him to doubt the course of his entire life!"

Celia narrowed her eyes. "Jan, have you considered that perhaps Terry's destiny does not lie with the Navy?"

"I don't believe in destiny!"

"That doesn't mean it doesn't exist. Even so... here, with us, may not be the best place for him to be."

"I refuse to accept that."

"Because having him by your side is best for you?"

"This isn't about me!"

She emitted a loud "Ha! I think I prefer Phaetonian selfishness. It's more honest. Anyone who tries to claim he's not thinking of himself is lying."

Atal glared at her, mostly because he was not sure she was wrong. "This 'moment of clarity' could as easily be some kind of emotional breakdown."

"Terry Metcalfe having an emotional breakdown? Listen to yourself. He's self-righteous, stubborn and temperamental, but there's no saner man in all the galaxy. Just because he's choosing a path other than the one you would choose for him—"

"—Or maybe he's being influenced by an outside force. If his account is accurate, there's an intelligence down there we don't understand."

"True enough." Celia rested her hands on her knees and leaned forward. "So. What are you going to do about it?"

"You mean, am I going to force him to come back to the ship or face Court Martial?"

"I know damned well you won't do that. You know damned well that forcing the issue could change him—destroy the Metcalfe you think of as a son, whether you admit it or not. Find a way to make it work, Jan. He needs to work through this. Put him on detached duty—you have the authority. Or I can arrange for him to be medically discharged."

He stroked his chin and considered her suggestion. "No," he said finally. "That would leave him with no way to turn back. I'll order him to continue intelligence gathering. Even Fournier has to agree that we need a man on the inside, to evaluate the threat. And the Eleusinians accept him."

"Speaking of the threat," she said, "have you given any more thought to my warnings?"

"I have. There is something... unexplained... about this planet. Having Metcalfe there to observe isn't the worst plan ever. Nor is doing a little additional digging."

"Well, I haven't seen many places of worship," said Kaya, "but this certainly doesn't look like what I've been led to expect."

She and Pallas stood in the midst of the grotto which Metcalfe had told them was the place of Communion.

"I've never seen a place of worship," said Pallas. She had her hands stuffed in her pockets, an especially informal gesture, for her, as she walked the circular perimeter.

"I've seen holos. The Terrans often spent the bulk of their wealth constructing them."

Pallas nodded. "Because they were also centers of political power. I believe that use of them corrupted their true purpose. This is probably more appropriate. 'The happiest man is he who learns from nature the lesson of worship.'"

"Huh?"

"Ralph Waldo Emerson."

"Who?"

"You haven't studied any philosophy?"

"I read Brand Greer's *Get Happy*."

Pallas laughed quietly. "I'm ashamed of you. You read a book on finding spiritual fulfillment written by a twelve-year-old musician?"

Kaya arched an eyebrow. "Brand just turned fifteen, I'll have you know."

"I don't keep track of such things."

"It was headline news the day we kept Quintil from being bombed. We came second."

"The media display their usual sense of priorities, then."

"Anyway, I wouldn't call Brand a musician, either. He just looks cute on stage."

"Not that I mind being enlightened on popular culture, but what are we looking for?"

"Evidence of the existence of... God. This is where they claim they talk to him. The Captain asked me to perform a search and see if there's anything here that's out of the ordinary. He called it my ghost-hunting mission."

"And you thought me an experienced ghost-hunter?"

"No. I wanted an objective witness, someone who could also sense non-physical evidence."

Pallas looked up at the trees, turning slowly in a complete circle. "I sense nothing," she said finally. "Background noise from fauna. Nothing more."

"I've never thought about it; can you read the mind of an animal?"

Pallas shook her head. "I can feel the presence of the mind of a mammal. I can't sense thoughts because they don't really have them. As I said, noise. The difference between static on a radio channel and actual communication."

"Maybe they have the thoughts but on a different wavelength?"

"Phaetonian research suggests not. If there is intelligence with a brain chemistry similar to a human's, I can feel it when it is close. There is no such intelligence here."

"But Metcalfe says something spoke to him, in his mind."

"That memory is very clear for him, yes. The rest of his experiences last night are–I believe the word is 'fuzzy.'"

"So you've scanned him," said Kaya.

"Briefly, when I saw him this morning. He was just about to meet with your father, so there wasn't much time to talk."

"Then he hasn't talked to you about his decision?"

"To stay on Eleusis? No."

"Do you think he'll really do it?"

"He very rarely fails to do what he says he's going to do."

"Doesn't it concern you? He spends a night in the woods, talks to some... being... that we can't find any trace of, and suddenly he wants to resign? What if his mind's being tampered with?"

"Your father is wrestling with the same questions. I saw no evidence of tampering. His intellectual and emotional processes are consistent with what I know to be his norm. His decision was sudden, true. It did follow a period of disorientation, similar to drunkenness, the cause of which is unknown. He does believe there is a presence still communicating with him, which was particularly apparent during the Communion ceremony, and during his sexual congress with the girl Elspeth. He—"

"Whoa!" said Kaya. "Back up! What sexual congress?"

"Metcalfe and Elspeth had intercourse last night," said Pallas matter-of-factly.

"He told you that?"

"He could not hide it from me. He felt strong sensations of guilt about it when he saw me this morning. I don't really understand why."

"Because he's a noble Terran, and they believe in monogamy."

"I'm aware of that, but Metcalfe has put aside many of his culture's irrational taboos. He certainly doesn't have to maintain partial celibacy for my sake."

"Are you sure it's an irrational taboo?" wondered Kaya.

"That's an odd question, coming from you, Kaya. You've always believed strongly in the InWorlder tradition of open sexuality."

"I have, yes. But knowing Metcalfe has taught me some things. And one of them is that spreading love—not just sex, but love—spreading it around to too many people dilutes it. It cheapens it, I guess. If you're intimate with everyone, what does intimacy mean? If you have no secrets, why should anyone make the effort to get to know you? Maybe that's where the Terrans are coming from on the whole monogamy thing."

"Are you planning to adopt monogamy?"

"Doubtful. Daddy says I'd never find a man or woman who would put up with me in the same bed for more than a week. Apparently, I'm overwhelming."

"I do not find you so, but most people have far weaker personalities than I do. Perhaps you are intimidating to a majority of those around you."

As always, Phaetonian honesty walked a fine line between being like a refreshing breeze and a sudden gust of wind which blows sand in one's eyes. "Maybe that's why humanity moved away from permanent domestic partnerships. We're all too disagreeable. If anyone really gets to know us, they don't want to hang around."

"I have no frame of reference," said Pallas. "My people don't practice physical intimacy."

"Does it bother you at all, that Metcalfe slept with that girl?"

"Should it?" Pallas studied Kaya's face. Then her eyes widened slightly, and she looked suddenly embarrassed.

"What's wrong?" asked Kaya.

"I... I apologize, Kaya. I read a thought from you which I had no business reading."

"It's okay. I guess I know what it was."

"It bothers you, that Metcalfe and I are lovers."

"Sometimes."

"May I ask why?"

"Because... I guess it's just a case of missed opportunities. He offered me the same kind of monogamous commitment he seems to want to offer you. I turned it down."

"And now you wonder if you should have."

"Not really. I know I couldn't live that life. But sometimes I miss the attention he used to pay me. Pretty selfish, huh?"

"There's nothing wrong with selfishness, Kaya. What most humans refer to as 'selfishness,' though, is not rational self-interest at all. It's an irrational impulse to satisfy immediate whims or cravings, without regard to the consequences for self or others. Stealing is often labeled a selfish act, but it is in fact a terribly non-selfish one. The consequences far outweigh any financial gain brought by the theft. The discord it brings, the breakdown of social custom, the need for increased security, the–"

"You're lecturing."

"Sorry."

"But I get it. A selfish act–an act of rational self-interest–would be insisting that I be paid the salary I'm worth."

"Based on market data, yes."

"Or making my education a priority over doing charity work."

"Precisely. You will benefit others more if you realize your potential. And no, your feelings about Metcalfe are not selfish."

"Thanks."

"They are irrational and self-destructive."

"Oh."

"But we have something in common."

"What's that?"

"I also miss the attention he used to pay me. Since the battle with Fehajiq, he has been conflicted, distracted. I believe the colloquial term is, 'he's pulling away.'"

Pallas abruptly halted her circular wandering. She held up a hand for quiet.

"What–?" Kaya began.

Pallas shook her head frantically. Then Kaya heard, in her mind, Pallas's voice saying, *Someone's coming. Someone not human.*

Qraitians? Kaya wondered, and hoped Pallas could "hear" her. *Daedalus and Icarus?*

No. I sense a belligerence not present in the two I met yesterday. I suggest we stay out of sight. They seem to be making for this grotto. They are armed, and would become violent if challenged.

Indeed, Kaya could now hear heavy footsteps approaching, and the low, grumbling hiss of male Qraitian speech. At Pallas's mental suggestion, the two exited the grotto, going farther up the hill in into a rocky outcropping. There was a natural opening in the rocks, what appeared to be the mouth of a cave. Kaya started for it, but Pallas grabbed her by the arm and held her back.

I sense that the cave is their destination. They move with purpose. They have reconnoitered this area before.

Together, the two women from *Titan* backed away from the cave entrance and ducked behind a cluster of large rocks and scrub brush. As they watched, the Qraitians, uniformed warriors both of them, advanced and entered the cave. They exchanged what sounded like harsh words–a disagreement.

I don't speak Qraitian, Kaya thought.

Nor do I, said Pallas in her mind. *But I can sense what they're arguing about. The larger one, the one with the blue coloration along his spine, says that they've already searched and found nothing.*

So they've been here before. They're as interested in this place as we are? That's a bad sign.

Indeed, Pallas agreed. *The other Qraitian says that... the source... not sure who that is... told him that this is the place of power.*

'The source?' Can't you read who that is?

I told you that I can sense mammalian minds and human thoughts. The Qraitians are neither. I can pick up their conscious, focused rationalizations—what's 'at the front of their minds,' so to speak. Essentially, my telepathy allows me to translate Qraitian speech, and little more.

You don't mind eavesdropping when it suits you, I see.

They are trespassing.

So are we.

Not strictly. Brock Aronson said all were welcome here. But the fact that they are prepared to use weapons against any they encounter suggests that they are coming here unknown.

Why are they here, on the planet? If they're not members of the Family --

There is no immigration office on this world. People come and go as they like.

One of the Qraitians raised his voice in something resembling a shout. It came out as a loud hiss. He gyrated his tail bone as he did it, a snake's manner of attracting attention and appearing threatening.

He is attempting to elicit a response from the intelligence within, Pallas explained. *He believes 'it' lives in that cave. The other says that they have tried this before, unsuccessfully. Again, they refer to information... intelligence... reports from 'the source' that there is something here.*

Do they have a spy among the Family?

It's one possibility, Pallas admitted.

The smaller Qraitian made a coughing sound, which Kaya interpreted as a cry of alarm. His corresponding gesture of tapping frantically on his comrade's back seemed to reinforce her assumption. The first Qraitian pointed down the hill, where Kaya now heard footsteps.

Members of the Family, coming to pray, supplied Pallas.

A young man and two children, humans, chatted happily as they ascended the hill toward the grotto. The Qraitians backed away toward the cave, attempting to hide, but drawing their weapons. They moved too slowly. The adult human saw them and called out to them, merely recognizing their presence, not particularly challenging.

The larger Qraitian raised his weapon and made to charge.

He's going to kill them! Kaya snapped. *We've got to stop them!*

We are unarmed, observed Pallas. *The Qraitians will simply kill us as well.*

Sorry, Pallas, I can't let that stop me. Civilians are at risk, and I have to protect them. You stay here, and—

Wait! Pallas commanded her. *There's something happening. Within the cave...*

Down the hill in the grotto, the two children, now recognizing the threat, cowered behind their adult companion. Pallas informed Kaya that he was their father. The young man held up his hands in a placating gesture, telling the Qraitians there was nothing to fear in this place. Despite his assurances, Kaya could read naked fear in his eyes.

The lead Qraitian stopped his charge only when he came within firing range. He raised his pistol.

The children screamed as their father attempted to shield them with his body.

A shot rang out. Kaya charged forward, determined, somehow, to stop the Qraitian before he claimed all three of his victims. She had taken only a few steps, however, when she realized that the shot had not made its mark. At point blank range, the Qraitian could not have missed, and yet the father and the two children still stood, alive and well and amazed. Their eyes were wide as they looked at... nothing.

Kaya followed their fearful gazes, and saw that where their attacker had stood was now an empty space. Somehow, in mid-shot, both the Qraitian and his weapon had—

"Vanished?" Atal demanded.

"Vanished," Kaya confirmed. "Vaporized, as far as we could tell. His cohort turned tail and ran. Literally."

"And this happened when they threatened the colonists?"

"More than threatened, Captain," said Kaya. Her tone was consciously formal thanks to the presence of Admiral Fournier, who reclined on Atal's couch, listening impatiently. "He actually fired on them."

"Bullets?" asked Fournier. "Or pulse gun?"

"Some kind of projectile, Admiral."

"What the hell happened to it?"

"The same thing that happened to the Qraitian, presumably," Kaya replied. "It... went away."

"Was there a visible source of the attack?" wondered Atal. "A beam, a blast, something?"

"Nothing, sir. Dr. Pallas reported that she sensed activity within the cave they were about to explore. Coming from her, I assumed that to be some form of mental activity. But she wouldn't even confirm that. She said she sensed... intent. Not intelligence."

"And where is she?" wondered Fournier.

"She stayed to interview the family members who were attacked."

"That interview should be conducted by military personnel," said Fournier.

"It is being so performed," said Atal. "Mr. Metcalfe is with her."

Fournier rolled his eyes. "You know my feelings about that situation, Captain. He should have been ordered back."

"He's the most qualified representative to remain down there," Atal countered. "He has gained the trust of the colonists, and, need I remind you, he's proven he can deal with Qraitians?" Atal smiled pleasantly and turned back to his daughter. "Continue, Ms. Atal."

"One of the Qraitians kept talking about information they received from 'the source.' Someone who knew a lot about the Family's Communions with... whatever it is."

Fournier slapped his knee. "I knew it! A spy!"

"Dr. Pallas and I consider it likely," said Kaya. "One of the alleged Qraitian Family members may be passing information home. That, or they've turned or interrogated one of the human colonists. In any event, it's clear there's something about this planet that has caught their eye, and they're not just kept here by racial or family honor."

Atal crossed his arms and regarded his daughter sternly. *Teacher mode,* Kaya recognized. *He's going to ask me questions in that tone which suggests I'm an idiot child if I don't know the answers.*

"Speculations, Midshipman Atal? What would draw the Qraitians out of their space, to a planet of pacifists, risking attack by our military and sudden death at the hands of forces unknown?"

"Power," Kaya said firmly. "Weaponry of some sort."

"*Powerful* weaponry," agreed Atal. "It vaporizes opponents on contact."

"But why?" she wondered out loud. "Why did it... they... whoever's behind the weapon, decide the Qraitians were the opponents?"

"They were the aggressors," suggested Atal.

"Perhaps the unknown enemy shares the Family's commitment to non-violence?"

"Doesn't share it very well, since it vaporized the Qraitian. As I understand it, the philosophy of the Family is to meet violence with compassion and passive resistance."

"Do we *know* it vaporized him? I didn't see vapor, sir. I saw a man–a Qraitian–vanish utterly. There was no residue."

"You're suggesting a perfect conversion of matter to energy?"

"It's possible."

Fournier held up his hand. "Stop," he said firmly. "This is idle speculation."

"Hardly idle, Georg," said Atal. "We can't be prepared for the possible scenarios we'll encounter unless we envision them."

"Impractical, Atal. I won't have you wasting my time daydreaming. Our goal is to minimize the threat posed by this planet. Before we prepare ourselves for unknown dangers, let's eliminate the *known* dangers, shall we?"

"You mean the Qraitians," said Atal.

"I do. We have a Qraitian warship in orbit. Our first order of business is to enforce our treaty with their empire, and require them to leave."

"They won't leave their people below, Georg. And I believe the treaty has enough wiggle room that they can make that an argument for hanging around."

"Not if we also expel the Qraitians below. You may recall that I've already informed Aronson we're going to do just that."

"You may recall, Georg, that he promised to resist such an effort. Promised very politely, but promised nonetheless. You go looking for those Qraitians they've adopted into their family, and they'll hide them."

"I can arrest resisters," said Fournier.

"They'll *all* resist, Admiral. It's what they do. Are you prepared to arrest several thousand of them? Because I'm not. *Titan* doesn't have the facilities to hold them all in custody, and it would take more time than you have for us to improvise a prison camp on Eleusis.

"You underestimate the ship's Marines, I think."

"Granted they're very good, but–"

"Dammit, Atal, what the hell is your end-game, anyway? Where do you see this going? Left to yourself, you'd just keep Titan here until the end of time, I suppose, blithely monitoring as the Qraitians seek out this weapons technology that may be below, and further infiltrate themselves into Confederate space, using Eleusis as a jumping-off point!"

"Sirs, if I may?" Kaya interrupted quietly. "Let's not forget the strong possibility that there is a double-agent amongst the Family. Someone could be feeding information to the Qraitians, using a privileged position to gain access to the secrets of Eleusis."

"I'm glad to see one of you displays the sense that made Atal Holdings an interstellar power!" said Fournier. He didn't quite smile at Kaya. She didn't know if she could have held down her lunch if he had. "The sooner we round up and interrogate those Qraitians below, the sooner we find that spy and learn what he knows!"

"Sorry to disappoint you, Admiral," Kaya replied, "but that wasn't what I meant. I was thinking that, if it were revealed to Aronson and his people that one of their number might be a spy, they might be more willing to come to a compromise solution."

Fournier's jaw tightened. "There is no compromise, young lady! Atal, you will contact Colonel Druelinger of the Marines and make arrangements to take any Qraitians on the surface into custody immediately. We will contact Commander–"

"Ustenar," supplied Atal.

"Yes. We will tell her she's leaving immediately."

"Begging the Admiral's pardon," said Atal formally.

"Eh? Yes?" Fournier looked annoyed but intrigued. Atal never showed him the formal politeness he desired. It was a clear ploy to get his attention, whether the Admiral was bright enough to recognize it or not. In any event, it worked.

"Sir, if Commander Ustenar leaves, we may never know what it is that she knows."

"About what?"

Atal nodded at his daughter. "Midshipman, an exercise for you. What could we learn from the Qraitians?

Kaya paused and stroked her chin, a deliberate imitation of a gesture she so often saw from her father. She wondered if he noticed. "Fact," she began, "there's something on Eleusis which is capable of making matter–and living people–disappear without a trace. What triggers it is unknown. Since the attack was on three of the Family, they may control it. Fact: The Qraitians are aware of that something, and probably know more than we do. *If* they can figure out how to control it, the threat to the Confederacy is great."

"And what action do you propose?" asked Fournier testily.

"I'd like to place the facts in context first, sir," said Kaya.

"If you must."

"Legend has it that there's something down there powerful enough to wipe out a civilization."

"I'm not concerned with legend!"

Kaya nodded. "As you say, sir. But the facts point toward something which tends to support the legend: that immense power is in play. Together, fact and legend suggest we need to learn everything the Qraitians know, and we need to be very careful with... whatever it is."

"And your proposed action, Midshipman?"

"Don't order the Qraitian ship away. Put someone on board who can find out what the Commander knows. They're spying on the Family, let's spy on them."

"There's a problem," said Fournier. "The Family welcomes Qraitians. Commander Ustenar will not welcome humans."

Kaya looked at her father, then said to the Admiral, "Sir, I was raised on tales of the Qraitian War. I know as a result that human spies have infiltrated Qraitian ships and outposts disguised as Qraitians."

Fournier nodded. "It's risky, but it's been done, using exo-suits."

"Since there are already Qraitians among the population below," said Kaya, "and the stated purpose of the military contingent is to give them passage home, should they change their minds, a spy could pose as a returning prodigal."

"I'd point out that, during the war, more than half of such spies were discovered and executed."

"The stakes are high, sir," said Kaya. "I think it's worth the risk. "

"I'll make that decision, Midshipman," snapped Fournier. "But you have a point. Trouble is, it would take days to get an espionage team on site and injected."

Atal shrugged. "I have some experience in this area—"

"Out of the question," said Fournier. "I can't risk you."

You mean you can't control him, thought Kaya; but then she wasn't altogether disappointed. "Sirs, I'd like to point out that I had the highest scores in espionage of any Academy graduate in the last ten years."

"Modest as always," muttered Fournier.

"Don't even think it!" Atal said directly to her.

"That doesn't sound like a Captain talking," said Fournier.

"Maybe it isn't, but—"

"Captain, putting aside my personal opinions about your... unusual attachment to your offspring, the fact that Midshipman Atal is an officer under your command precludes your option to take your emotions into consideration when making command decisions."

"Dammit, Georg—!"

"Atal, I will not have you speak to me that way in front of our subordinate!"

Kaya heard the distinctive sound of grinding teeth again.

Fournier turned back to her. "Ms. Atal, I find your suggestion completely appropriate."

"And the exit strategy?" asked Atal quietly. "How does she get out, once she's completed the job? Even if this crazy plan works, and she's not discovered, it's a one way trip. The Qraitians who return are going home to die. They're not going to be allowed back off the ship again."

"We could arrange for some kind of criminal charge against the fictional Qraitian, and demand extradition," said Kaya.

Fournier shook his head. "Too complicated."

"There's always a trade," said Atal.

"What kind of trade?" asked the Admiral.

"As I understand it, they'd like nothing better than to bring Fehajiq home to be executed. He's a blot on their honor. They'd give damn near anything to get him back, including a spy."

"You want me to release a man who tried to kill ten billion people?" demanded Fournier.

"I don't want you to try this idiotic scheme at all," Atal replied, adding a pointed, "Sir. But, if you're going to do it, I think you owe your agent the best chance she's got of getting home. Fehajiq would be a guaranteed safe passage for her. And what are we going to do with him? Other than let him rot on Hydra Station? He's got nothing left to tell us. He doesn't know anything. He's a rogue terrorist."

The Admiral considered it for a moment, then finally nodded. "I don't like it, but you're right. I'll arrange to have Fehajiq brought here. He's worthless to us. Eventually, we were probably going to execute him anyway, once we got through the red tape." Fournier slapped his thighs. "Well, then... The Captain will have Dr. Faulkner begin preparation on the exo-suit immediately. You will develop, with Captain Darby, a mission profile and submit it to me within three hours. Are we clear?"

Atal fumed. "Crystal, sir." He threw his daughter a glance which suggested that being killed on this mission might not be the worst of her options.

CHAPTER NINE

The shuttle docked with a heavy jolt against the hull of the Qraitian vessel. Used to human comforts, Kaya and Faulkner had to work hard not to flinch at the impact. Obviously, the impact buffers employed by the Qraitians were less capable of absorbing shock than those on *Titan's* shuttles. In addition, Qraitians, evolved from beings who felt safe and comfortable primarily below ground, kept their ships dark, and had no view ports with which to see space outside the hull. It was disconcerting to humans.

No less uncomfortable were the false skins and prosthetics the two human women wore to disguise them as Qraitians. Faulkner had been able to replicate technology used by Confederate Naval Intelligence, which Fournier had authorized her to tap into.

As they suited up, the Captain had demonstrated the workings of the suits. Kaya suspected her father had used such disguises himself, or at least seen them used. Jan Atal had been closed-mouth about it all. Still angry at her for actually manipulating Fournier into helping her win an argument against him, her father wasn't saying anything but what he had to.

"The false skin breathes," Atal had explained, "but there's no question you'll be hot. There's a built-in circulatory system which should help to cool you, but keep your expectations low.   You're going to be uncomfortable."

Celia Faulkner had grunted as she had tried to stand for the first time with her body limited and controlled by the hardware.

"Celia, you sure you want to do this?" Atal had asked.

"I refuse to allow you to send the child in alone, Captain. And I'm the most qualified technician to keep these monkey suits–"

"Lizard suits," Kaya had corrected her.

"Lizard suits, then, working. I was part of a medical team during the Qraitian War which treated Qraitian POWs. No one still active has a better knowledge of Qraitian physiology than I do."

Before adding clothing, Kaya had noticed the most remarkable feature of the disguise. Looking down, she'd exclaimed, "Really?"

Atal had rolled his eyes. Faulkner had chuckled. "Yes. Two sets of sex organs. One set is completely non-functional. Please don't try to use it. You might be badly injured."

"I hope my daughter can restrain herself for a few hours," Atal had said.

A raspy, coughing voice had replied, "Come now, Daddy, I have to try everything at least once!" Kaya had reacted in surprise, at first, hearing her own words come out in that alien voice, if voice it could be called. The supplied speech synthesizer worked so well, translating Kaya's speech into the hisses and clicks of Qraitian, it was frightening. At that moment, it rendered her words in accented Confederate Standard. A simple adjustment would render them as easily in Qraitian.

Atal had stared at her. She couldn't tell if he was annoyed at her attempt at humor, and about to snap, or if he was just still annoyed. He surprised her by putting a hand on the bulky armor plating of her shoulder. "Whatever you try, Kaya... try to come back to me."

It had been only hours later that they had arrived clandestinely on the surface of Eleusis. They'd reported to the intake station to surrender themselves as defectors from the Family. The station was manned by a skeleton crew of Qraitians. It was no doubt a boring duty, probably assigned punitively, as were assignments to border patrol in their own Confederate Navy. Kaya and Faulkner–or Chhrrlk and Ffffmall, as their assumed Qraitian names roughly transliterated–were the first defectors in the history of the intake point. They were a cause celebre to the phlegmatic junior officer on duty when they came in, the first hint in recent history that perhaps fate didn't intend him to die staring at the doorway of this filthy, dusty little office on this revolting, green planet.

It was the second remarkable event of his day, Kaya knew. Earlier, a Phaetonian intellectual, a female, had visited him, asking all manner of prying questions about the number of Qraitian nationals present on the planet. Kaya could just imagine the disgust which Pallas's questions must have evoked. As if he cared how many disgraceful cowards there were on this backward, muck-encrusted swamp of a world!

Little did the poor slob suspect that he was being visited by a telepath, come to implant in his mind the suggestion that he had seen the two called Chhrrlk and Ffffmall once or twice in passing. Perhaps he'd seen them working the fields like lowly servants, as all the humans here did. Maybe he remembered the contempt he had felt, and how he'd associated it with the cloying sweetness of the spring flowers which had dotted the landscape.

Pallas had warned them in advance that her efforts might prove fruitless. She could easily convince a middle-aged human named Bert Smith, fully four-hundred pounds, that he was a nine-year-old ballerina named Euphemia. Qraitian minds were different, as she'd already warned Kaya. Her implanted suggestions might not take root.

Clearly, however, they had. Vrrrallik, the junior officer, had treated them with contempt, but it was the contempt aimed at two he accepted as his own kind. He was ashamed because they had behaved in such an un-Qraitian manner as to join this cult of pacifists. As he'd processed their orders and arranged transportation, he'd hissed, "At least you both came to your senses. I suppose eating dead meals with the humans became tiresome, eh? I am sorry I will miss your executions. I hope you will do your families the courtesy of dying well."

"Thank you," Faulkner had said. "We're looking forward to it."

Kaya had no idea how the translator had rendered the Doctor's sarcasm, but it did not seem to evoke any strong reaction in Vrrrallik. She therefore resisted her urge to kick Faulkner beneath the interview table. Just as well, really, as the synthi-skin covering her body would probably have kept the doctor from feeling it anyway.

Vrrrallik had shown little interest in them as they'd waited for the shuttle to come and take them on the first leg of their flight of shame. Kaya made a mental note to congratulate Pallas on the job she'd done. It was the easiest way to smuggle the two aboard, they'd decided. It was better to start close to the source, with the intake office, since the Family wouldn't have cooperated in any effort to fool the Qraitians.

Fortunately, the Qraitian military had no desire to deal directly with Aronson's people, and so the intake office was maintained to facilitate re-patriation. Equally fortunate, Qraitian bureaucracy shared with its human equivalent the phenomenon whereby one bureaucrat is supremely disinterested in the business of another; so no one on the warship kept track of the names of the expatriates below. It wasn't their job, after all.

Now, they were docked with Ustenar's vessel, and ready for the ultimate test of their planned masquerade. The hatch dilated, and the Commander herself stepped aboard the shuttle. She hissed at the two who waited apprehensively, shoved to their feet by the guards.

"A pair of traitors," she observed, walking a circle around them.

"My daughter and I," Celia responded, "know that our very presence shames you, Lady. We can ask only swift transport, forgiveness by our families, and merciful death."

"Amidst mercy," added Kaya, "we beg that we not be spared our due suffering. Let death be as painful as our transgression merits."

The wording was ritualistic, and had been prepared after careful research on Qraitian customs. Faulkner and Kaya had rehearsed it several times.

"Pain I can promise you," said Ustenar. "Though what you merit is eternal torment. Had I my way, you would never die, but only be killed forever more."

"My Lady is just," murmured Celia.

Ustenar's jaw opened, and vestigial sacs which, in an earlier epoch had held venom, spat fluid in the faces of first the "mother," and then her "daughter." To this humiliation, the commander added, "Filth!"

But her eyes lingered over Kaya.

"Bring them aboard," she snapped to the guards who attended them. "I shall hear their statements before we prepare for their return home."

Kevin Carson was halfway through a Yorkshire pudding when Sestus, uninvited, slid into the seat across from him. He reflected that this was unusual. Then he reflected that he wasn't sure which was more unusual: Sestus sitting down to a meal with him, or his having ordered Yorkshire pudding for lunch. He only ordered Yorkshire pudding when he was depressed. It was, said everyone, his comfort food, meaning it reminded him of childhood and home, a time and place when he had felt warm and safe and loved.

Trouble was, Kevin Carson hadn't had that much of a childhood. As far as he knew, he'd rarely been either warm or safe, prior to joining the Navy. A half-dozen odd years in the farming community where he had spent the immediate period before the Academy had been relatively stable, yes. Still, food had been rationed, and warmth had been only partially provided by the threadbare, moth-eaten blankets available in Father Vaskis's stores.

Loved? Setting aside sex as being distinct from love, which it almost always was, he had not known a lot of love in his short life. When someone said "love" and "safety" and "warmth" to Kevin Carson, a sense memory crept into his head. He remembered, for an instant, burrowing under the covers of the bed in that old, drafty building. Just where the bed was depended on the time and the number of itinerant children. Sometimes he'd slept in the stone rooms below the house, sometimes out on the wide verandas in warm weather, sometimes–rarely!–in a small room upstairs with only five or six other children. Under the thin blankets, as the fire died, he would edge himself toward the only source of warmth: the body of the boy his own age who was always with him.

The memory never lasted more than an instant, for Kevin always banished it. Best not to admit to anyone, least of all himself, that the words "love," "warmth" and "safety" provoked in him the feeling of being snuggled in bed against Terry Metcalfe.

And yet his friendship with Metcalfe may just have been his earliest coherent memory. None other ever asserted itself in his mind, and he certainly didn't go searching for them. He didn't even know when he'd first had Yorkshire pudding. It was one of the few things in his life that had just always been there, like oxygen and girls who liked to hang on the arms of a boy who knew how to sweet-talk them.

No, Kevin Carson had never really known a home until he'd joined the Navy. Even that had been Metcalfe's idea, and now word had it Metcalfe wanted to go and abandon him... all of them... and take up residence on Eleusis. That left Carson here... with Sestus, sitting across from him at the lunch table. Well, they had been spending a lot of time together lately, interrogating the civilians. To be fair, Five was a bit less obnoxious since Metcalfe had saved them all from the Qraitians. At least, he was less obnoxious in person. His interview on *The Naked Truth* and his book were classic Five arrogance.

"Rough day, eh?" Sestus remarked, neatly unfolding his napkin and beginning to expertly segment a chicken breast into regulation pieces. Good god, did the boy ever take a step that wasn't prescribed by a book of etiquette?

Carson shrugged. "Had worse. Though I thought the lady from the shoe store was going to turn violent."

"I wish she had," Sestus grinned. "It would have made things interesting." His smile lit up his face. His teeth were perfect. Why did such a nice-looking boy have to be such a prick? Carson wondered.

Still, he had no once else to talk to right now. Cernaq and Aer'La seemed to be keeping to themselves. Times he had seen her lately, Aer'La had seemed more dangerous than usual. Kaya was, ship's gossip had it, confined to a bed in the infirmary with a potentially infectious illness. And going to Smokin'

Joe's was not the same, since Saunders was in a holding cell and his employees were running the joint.

So, it was talk to Sestus, or go back to his cabin and swear at Galatea, his A.I.

Galatea was too good at swearing back.

He was thinking of something intelligent to say which would not start a fight when Darby appeared at his elbow, bearing his lunch tray. "Ah, Sestus," said the Deputy Captain pleasantly. He also sat without being invited (he *was* the Deputy Captain) and only seemed to notice the table's third occupant as he unfolded his napkin. "And Mr. Carson. I've been reviewing the day's reports. The two of you have made excellent progress, sorting through all these civilians." He said the last word as though he were referring to a waste product. "I wish we'd had a few more in for questioning. Still..." He turned to his salad and began to crunch too loudly.

"We can only detain the ones who actually reveal something suspicious, Phin," said Sestus.

Darby cleared his throat gently, reminding his young friend, Carson assumed, that he should be addressed as 'Captain' in mixed company. It was a gentle rebuff, its gentility uncharacteristic of Darby, except where Sestus was concerned. The older officer was entirely too conscious of Sestus's family's wealth and connections.

"At the rate you're going, we'll have completed the background investigations before we leave this system. I have to say I'm impressed."

"Thank you," said Carson.

Sestus merely smirked.

"Most of them are just average citizens," Carson said. "Not too good, not too bad."

Darby nodded. "As expected. We have to be careful though, Carson. An average citizen with a secret–something that leaves him open to blackmail–can be a huge security risk."

"As can any who have relatives on Den," offered Sestus.

"Have you found any?" wondered Darby, swallowing as he said it.

"A few," said Carson. "But most of the relatives were moderately successful merchants, who should be safe from Qraitian influence."

"Anything is possible," Darby reminded him. "But yes, those are probably just worth noting. No need to detain them."

Carson trimmed off a slice of beef, marveling at how easily he could slip into casual conversation with these two. The thought did not escape him that, were Metcalfe here, an argument would already have started. Indeed, Darby would never have joined him, and Sestus would have done so only to start said argument. There just seemed to be a scent of challenge in the air when Metcalfe was around.

"Any news from below? I understand there was an exchange with the Qraitians."

Carson registered that Sestus was speaking to him. "Kaya and Pallas did encounter some Qraitian military personnel. I don't know the details. I think Metcalfe's making an inquiry."

In fact, he did know some of the details. Kaya had relayed a message before returning to the ship, describing a violent altercation, with one Qraitian missing, presumed dead. Carson knew better than to reveal the contents of a personal message to the Captain, however. Nor did he find it necessary to share that Kaya would tell him the whole story as soon as she had time. Among themselves, the Arbiters had always displayed a healthy disrespect for military secrets; but only among themselves.

"I'm glad to hear Metcalfe is doing some work down there," said Darby, his voice now holding the tang of disapproval Carson was accustomed to hearing. Of course, he *was* talking about Metcalfe. "I'm surprised he's been allowed to stay."

"You know the Admiral was unhappy about it," said Sestus. "It's a dangerous game the Captain is playing, turning Metcalfe's threat of desertion into an order for long-term cultural observation."

Darby shrugged. "He is the Captain, and it's his decision. He's very good at surviving the disapproval, even enmity, of his superiors."

"I wonder if he would be if he weren't the heir to Atal Holdings," said Sestus.

"Doubtful," said Darby. "But I hope you don't get any ideas, Sestus. Your social standing may be the equal of the Captain's, but it's still in the best interests of your career to avoid making waves. I know I'd never give such a risky order."

Ain't that the truth, thought Carson.

"Will he come back, Carson?" asked Sestus. "Metcalfe, I mean. Atal's giving him time to cool his heels. Do you think he'll realize that, get this... whatever it is out of his system, and come back?"

"I don't know," said Carson quietly. He didn't, in fact, and it troubled him. A year ago, he would never have felt at a loss to predict his friend's actions.

"If he doesn't," said Darby archly, "he's not only putting an end to his career, he's jeopardizing the Captain's as well."

"I think the poor boy's cracking up," said Sestus. Carson wondered abstractly if he should be angry. Until recently, he would have simply thrown something at Five, or threatened to punch him. It was an offhand remark, insensitive, but it sounded less mean-spirited than it might have. Was it possible that Five sensed the gravity of Metcalfe's emotional state, and was actually throttling back the competitive bluster?

"I think Admiral Fournier agrees with you," said Darby.

Carson listened quietly as they speculated further, still asking himself if he should be angry. More to the point, he wondered, why did he not simply become angry? One didn't get angry because it was the right thing to do, one just got angry. It was an emotional response. So why was he debating with himself whether or not to do it? They were insulting his friend. They had been doing it as long as they'd known him. He should be leaping to the defense.

Were their positions reversed, were Metcalfe sitting here, listening to speculation on the state of Carson's sanity, he would respond decisively. Metcalfe could always be counted on. He'd always had Carson's back, and Carson had always had his, even when they were children...

Father Vaskis had been gone for days. He did that sometimes, leaving their small, ersatz village, going out on the road where he might meet up with travelers who would be willing to barter. The village didn't have much to trade. The land was overworked and didn't produce much food. What chickens they had they needed for eggs. Some hearty plants thrived,

146 Steven H. Wilson

but they weren't edible. Tobacco would sometimes grow, and that they could sell. The children had been taught–with the threat of severe punishment for disregarding the warning–that it was unhealthy to partake of it. Still, there was a market for it, and Father Vaskis was willing to trade in the stuff. Kevin had heard murmurings sometimes, among the adults, that perhaps it was immoral to sell tobacco, even to feed children. Father Vaskis had responded that he would sooner answer to the gods for making adults sick by their own choice than for letting children die of starvation.

He returned from this trading venture with potatoes, which hadn't grown here in Kevin's memory. Also there was medicine, something called antibiotics. Kevin knew that was a good thing. Little Lydia was always getting sick. Medicine would keep her well. Kevin liked Lydia. She was a sweet little girl, and always kind to him. More important, when she was sick, Terry would not leave her side, and Kevin would have no one to play with.

It was an overcast summer day. The kids had all been gathered on the stone terrace in the back garden, to greet their returning benefactor. Food would be distributed immediately, carefully rationed. Father Vaskis, though clearly exhausted from travel and days of lost sleep, supervised. Kevin was glad, because the adult women who tended them, members of the Father's church, were not as kind as the aging priest. They were quick to take a ration away, and quicker still to punish a child.

Kevin stood in line with Terry and Lydia, awaiting their share of a lunch less meager than their usual one. As they edged up in line, Jedd, a new boy who'd only just come to the farm a few days earlier, elbowed his way in front of them.

"Look out," he said to Terry, shoving him a step back.

Little Lydia made a face. "Wait your turn!"

Jedd looked down at her, his wide face breaking into a cruel smile. "Gonna make me, little bug?"

Lydia's dark eyes narrowed. "I'm not a bug!"

"Leave my sister alone," said Terry to Jedd. "And go to the back of the line."

Jedd crossed his arms and planted his feet. "I like it here."

A hand settled gently on Jedd's meaty shoulder. Kevin looked up to see Father Vaskis, who had a habit of approaching quietly. "It seems we're getting a little impatient, waiting for our meal," the old man observed.

"No, Father," Jedd responded. The mocking smile and the harshness were gone from his tone.

Father Vaskis smiled. "When we're hungry, we often have trouble staying patient. Hunger can even make us mistreat our brothers and sisters. But I'm sure Terry can tell you, Jedd," the priest looked sideways to where Terry stood, one arm protectively about his little sister's shoulders, "about how hungry the five thousand were the day they came to hear Jesus. There was a boy there about your age, Jedd, who set a fine example. You should listen to that story."

Jedd shrugged. "I guess so."

The priest stood to his full height. "I am weary, children. I need to rest after this long journey. I will see you all at evening prayers."

As he walked away, Jedd's sneer returned. He said to Terry, "Try to tell me a story, you won't have any teeth to eat your lunch with." He raised a dirty fist to emphasize his point.

One of the women called them forward to fill their plates, ending the conversation.

When the three had taken their seats on a crumbling brick wall, however, Jedd returned to them.

"What do you want?" Terry demanded.

Jedd looked over his shoulder, checking to see that no adult was watching.

"I didn't get enough to eat." he snapped back. "And it looks like y'all need a lesson in how to chew your food a little faster."

He reached out and seized Lydia's plate.

"Hey!" she cried out.

Terry smacked Jedd's hand away, only barely preventing the food from spilling on the ground. "I said to leave her alone!"

"She don't need as much food as the rest of us," said Jedd. "Ain't much to her. Just a runt."

Lydia's lip quivered.

"She's been sick, you jerk," said Terry. Kevin could think of weightier insults, learned before he had come to the village. Terry never swore, though.

"Sick of looking at your face?" wondered Jedd, his chin doing a dance as though it were proud of his wit.

Terry looked away from him. "Go away," he said quietly.

"No," spat Jedd. "I told you, I'm still hungry." He shot his arm out, grabbing the plate again and this time snatching it away. He shoved a whole roast potato in his mouth and began chewing it sloppily, sending chunks of it flying from the sides of his mouth.

Lydia began to cry. Terry set down his plate and shot up.

Kevin handed his own plate to Lydia, patting her shoulder. "Don't worry about it, Terry, she can have mine," he said quickly. Not quickly enough.

With a snarl, his friend launched himself at the larger boy, one hand clutching at his ragged shirt, the other, curled in a fist, ready to strike. Jedd grabbed Terry's shoulders and shifted his own weight, carrying them both to the ground. Terry was quickly on his back, pinned by the other's superior size and weight.

A crowd of children gathered around, shouting, energized by the fight. Across the yard, the adults had noticed. Two women came bustling toward the impromptu arena formed by a circle of yelling boys and girls. Both of them stopped only long enough to pluck switches from one of the scraggly bushes on the edge of the garden. As they made for the fight, they stripped the leaves from them.

Kevin had witnessed such scenes before. The fighting boys would be switched until they released their holds on each other. Then, any child involved in the fight, winner or loser, bully or victim, would be led into the house for a lengthier, more formal session of punishment. The women from the church were firmly of the belief that fighting would be discouraged only if the marks from the punishment beating lasted longer than the bruises made by other children's fists.

Terry and Jedd were both in for it, and there was nothing Kevin or Lydia could do.

The women forced their way through the onlooking children and, switches flying, attempted to pull Jedd off Terry. The bigger boy resisted, even as angry, red welts rose on his hands. He seized Terry's hair and rubbed the boy's head in the dirt and gravel. When he finally gave up and allowed himself to be pulled back, Terry was bleeding from his nose and a cut on his jaw. His breathing was ragged, and his whole body shook. Kevin saw no tears in his eyes, though, and sensed the valiant effort his friend was making not to be broken.

Beside him, Lydia sobbed at the sight of her brother and the knowledge that, once his wounds were tended, he would be subjected to another beating by the women.

Surveying his victim, Jedd smiled, and, before he could be pulled fully away, reared back and kicked Terry in the ribs. Kevin saw his friend cringe and roll into a fetal position. After that, he forgot everything around him, save his friend's pain and his attacker's harsh laughter.

"You son of a bitch!" he shrieked and charged forward. As the crowd of children gasped at the outburst of profanity–a mortal sin, as far as they knew–Kevin tackled Jedd, tearing him from the hands of the two women. The force sent both boys to the ground, Kevin landing on top. Not taking a moment to let Jedd recover his breath, he rained blows on his opponent's face, satisfied by the grunts of pain and especially the blood that began to flow from the bastard's nose.

Behind him, the two women screamed and clawed at him. Their switches lashed out, striking his hands and his neck. One bit into his cheek as their frantic attempts to stop his violence increased. The pain of the lashings increased until he cried out from them. He tasted blood and his own tears. He made no effort to stop them. He ceased his attack only when Jedd's own sobs drowned out all else. Then he allowed himself to be hefted to his feet.

"I see you boys have enough energy to fight," said one of the women. "I don't think you need anything to eat." She took Kevin by the collar and started to pull him toward the house, where the violence would continue, but there would be no fighting back.

Her companion moved towards Terry, telling him harshly to get up and stop pretending he was hurt. Kevin pulled away from his captor and ran to kneel by his friend. "Get away!" he shouted to the woman who was reaching down to haul Terry to his feet. He gently placed one arm under Terry's shoulders and eased him up, supporting his weight. Together, they stood, Terry leaning heavily on him.

"I've got him," Kevin said to the astonished women. "You leave him the fuck alone!"

Father Vaskis had stayed the execution of further punishment. They had still gone without food. It was all gone now. By the time the bruises on Terry's face had faded, Jedd was gone. He disappeared in the night, looking for a better situation, no doubt, where the other kids didn't fight back.

Carson hadn't hesitated, then, to rush to his friend's defense, despite the punishment that loomed. Nor would it have been a trivial punishment, had Father Vaskis allowed it to proceed. Scars from authorized violence often lasted much longer than those from fights in the backyard. Some were even permanent. Of course, that level of punishment happened in Father Vaskis's absence, and without his consent.

So why did he not now feel the urge to leap to Metcalfe's defense, or even a twinge of anger at the words being exchanged by Darby and Sestus? He didn't believe he had become a coward. He didn't feel any fear.

Come to think of it, he didn't really feel anything at all.

The process of returning home after joining the Family was, for the Qraitians, an intensely formal affair. First, at the intake station below, they'd been counseled. It wasn't heartfelt. Vrrrallik's cohort on duty had read to them from his implant, coldly and stiffly. He'd played some of the session back on holo, as it had been pre-recorded by someone back home whose job in some way resembled that of a human psychologist. Whether the Qraitians had a field of psychology was, to Kaya, unknown. The ones she had met thus far did not seem an empathetic lot, but perhaps that was merely indicative of the quality of people the military dispatched to undesirable assignments like Eleusis.

They'd been asked repeatedly if they knew they were to die. They'd been asked if they harbored any remaining allegiance to non-Qraitian belief systems. They'd been asked what their duty was to home and family. Fortunately, enough knowledge of Qraitian culture was amassed in Confederate data banks that their answers appeared to have been acceptable. Otherwise they might never have been passed on to the ship in orbit, and the next phase of their repatriation.

Faulkner had just undergone the next phase, a personal interview with Ustenar, incorporating their right to a formal deposition by the state, as embodied here by the Commander. Now it was Kaya's turn. She was escorted to the flag cabin, or whatever they called it, and invited to seat herself on a slab of black stone. Her guard departed immediately, and she was left alone to examine her surroundings. She wondered if she should activate her implant and attempt to record. She wondered if there was anything worth recording. Fortunately, they hadn't found the implant. Qraitians didn't use the devices, They were Luddites that way. Technology to increase personal efficiency didn't interest them. Only technology which benefitted the Empire as a whole was considered worth developing. Since the disguises had worked, Kaya and Faulkner's were implants safe. No Qraitian would have an implant, so no Qraitian would be checked for one.

There was a squeal, soft but frantic, from the other side of a door. It was one of two circular doorways in what appeared to be a sitting room, and the one through which Kaya had not entered. It dilated open like some sort of bodily orifice relaxing, and Ustenar sidled through. From her mouth hung something pinkish-gray which wiggled. The Commander tilted her head back briefly and gulped. The wiggling piece disappeared.

"Apologies," she said, "I was late taking my meal. Rat?"

For a moment, Kaya thought she was being insulted, then realized she was being offered a snack. She declined politely.

Ustenar came and sat beside her on the slab, large enough for three Qraitians, if they were friendly. More, if they stacked, which Kaya believed they sometimes did. Ustenar slapped the stone firmly and hissed gently. "Isn't it comfortable? I wouldn't normally permit a prisoner such luxury. Of course, most officers don't bother with such luxuries aboard ship. But I like something on which to," she narrowed her dagger-like pupils and a forked tongue flicked briefly out between her lips, "*entertain.*"

Kaya thought the stone, cold and hard, the least comfortable surface on which she'd reposed since Sestus had planted her bare ass in a tray of salmon mousse at a party back home. She didn't say this, of course. She knew that someone descended from a reptile would have a different perspective. "It's... cool," she said, aware of both meanings she could be implying, and hoping one would stick.

"Exquisitely so," agreed Ustenar. "It brings on a wonderful feeling of relaxation, but allows me to be alert at a moment's notice."

The Commander turned from admiring her stone couch, and looked intently into Kaya's eyes for several seconds, saying nothing. Kaya wondered if this was part of an interrogation technique, or if the Qraitian had seen something amiss in her disguise.

"You are so young," Ustenar said wistfully.

Good, thought Kaya. Her disguise was sound.

"Your colors are so vibrant, it's as though they were painted on by the gods."

That made Kaya uncomfortable. They *had* been painted on, by replicating machinery aboard *Titan*. She merely said, "Thank you, Lady."

"It's a pity for anyone to die so young," Ustenar observed wistfully. At least, it seemed wistful when she said it. Who the hell knew when a Qraitian was being wistful? For all Kaya knew, the old snake was actually laughing her ass off with glee over her impending demise.

"I understand that I am accountable for my actions," she said neutrally.

"Yes," agreed Ustenar "There is no denying it. I suppose you are eager to die and end this, eh? I would be." She reached out and ran a taloned appendage along Kaya's synthetic jaw. "Even if I were so young."

No, Kaya decided, Ustenar was not mocking her. She was probably feeling maternal. Did Qraitians feel maternal?

"Still," the Commander went on, "you were wise to return. It will go more easily for you than for those who remained on Eleusis. It's only a matter of time, of course, before the Confeds take the entire populace into custody. Our brother/sisters below will have no choice any more about returning home. They will die here, in human prisons."

"You believe the humans will kill them?"

"Possibly not, but I certainly hope so! And I hope it's painful. We've heard tales of torture of enemy agents, and I do pray that they are true. Can you imagine dying, a sinner, painlessly? Or of old age in an enemy prison cell? Think of the brutal fate that would await you in the afterlife! No, if the others are taken, I hope they die in searing pain, and I'm sure they will hope so as well, for the good of their immortal souls!"

"Is there any time for them to change their minds and come back with us?"

"Do you think any of your fellows are close to making such a decision?"

For a moment, Kaya's blood ran cold. As cold as her disguise fooled medical sensors into thinking it was, and colder. Was she going to be asked to produce names of Qraitians among the family?

"I can't be sure. I only think it's a pity."

"It cannot be helped. I sense, based on what their Admiral Fournier said yesterday, that the humans will strike almost immediately."

Kaya felt relief at no being asked for names. She also registered that, since Ustenar knew what Fournier had said to the Family, their suspicions of a spy amongst the people of Eleusis were confirmed.

"You think they'll make everyone leave?"

"I do. And so much the better for us, that the planet be empty."

Kaya decided to take a chance. "Yes, since it would leave us free to examine this weapon."

Ustenar cocked her head. "You know of a weapon?"

"Very little, other than that it is very powerful, and would be of immense benefit to the Empire."

She twitched her head in what must have been a nod. "Good. I can confirm nothing, of course. Though I can't see why anything I tell you would matter. You're not going anywhere. And you're correct. An empty

154 Steven H. Wilson

planet will be far easier to explore and investigate. There *is* something there."

"If the Confeds don't force us out of the system," said Kaya.

"Oh, they shall think they have done so," said the Commander. "We will leave, with the face-saving excuse that we must take you home for atonement. Other ships will not be far, however–well, perhaps I say too much."

"My jaws are locked."

Again, Ustenar studied her. "You are not like the others I've encountered from below. They're all so committed to this human 'Family.' You are far more intelligent than they, and seem so sensible. However did you manage to be swayed?"

Kaya began to answer, but was interrupted by a loud, blaring alert sound.

Looking annoyed, Ustenar unclipped a communications device from her belt and keyed it. "What is it? I'm in the midst of–"

"Lady," said an urgent voice, "I apologize, but there is an emergency. A force of Confederate warships has arrived. A large one."

Ustenar swore a hissing curse and dashed from the room, leaving Kaya to wonder what had happened now.

CHAPTER TEN

"Georg, what the *hell* is going on?"

Atal stood before the Admiral in his superior's guest quarters. He was fuming. Fournier looked up blandly. "Explain yourself, Atal."

"Why are there additional ships arriving in the system? The Qraitians have already assumed defensive posture and begun training weapons! Are you *trying* to provoke an incident?"

Fournier stood and straightened his jacket, a delaying tactic he was fond of. It seemed to give him great pleasure to attempt to slow the pace of conversation on the rare occasions when he drove Atal to anger, instead of the reverse.

"It's time to act."

"Act stupidly?" demanded Atal.

"Careful, Captain," Fournier warned. "Your handling of the situation has been too cautious by half. Frankly, I think you're more concerned about Metcalfe's apparent nervous collapse than–"

"Of course I'm concerned about Metcalfe!"

"But there are thousands more people to worry about up here, Atal! And billions back home! Your own daughter discovered evidence of a powerful weapon on Eleusis, one of which the Qraitians are now surely aware! We cannot allow it to fall into their hands. If preventing that provokes an incident, then so be it!"

"It is customary," Atal said tightly, "for the Admiralty to act only in an advisory capacity when present on a mission. You order my ship to this system, and I am in command–"

"So you are. But I believe your handling of the situation is unacceptable."

"Are you relieving me of command?"

"I..." Fournier paused. "I don't want to," he said at last, with forced calm. "I think it would be better for morale if you simply accept my order and move forward."

"Again," said Atal, "it is customary for such orders to be discussed prior to their execution."

"There wasn't time."

"We weren't being fired upon. No state of emergency existed–"

"Are you *blind*, Atal? We're in a permanent state of emergency, since Fehajiq attacked!"

"May I assume, then, that you will continue to give orders on this mission without my knowledge or input?"

"I will do what I have to do," Fournier replied.

"Undercut me again, Georg–give another order without telling me, and I will assume I am relieved of command."

"You are not relieved!"

"Per regulations, I would be, if you continue to interfere. You would be creating a situation in which I am unable to command. I'd have to step down for the good of the mission."

Fournier swallowed. "You wouldn't."

Atal laughed coldly. "You know I would, Georg. I'll walk away and leave you holding the bag. I might even throw in with Metcalfe and his friends below."

"Damn you, Atal–!"

"All you have to do," the Captain interrupted, "is keep me in the loop.

It's not an unreasonable request, and it's in accordance with regulations."

Fournier sighed. "Very well."

"Good. Are there any other orders you need to tell me about?"

"Now that you mention it, I have a meeting with Colonel Druelinger in just a few minutes."

"The Marines? I thought you were about finished interrogating the civilians."

"Almost, yes. Now I need a force planet side. You see, I've decided it's time to evacuate everyone."

Metcalfe stood with Aronson, Elspeth and Icarus as the shuttle landed. Villagers gathered about them, curious. It was an unannounced visit, which couldn't be a good sign. Atal or any of the others would have notified him of their imminent arrival. His apprehension darkened to a simmering fear when the hatch opened and Fournier stepped out, flanked by Aer'La and Colonel Druelinger of the Marines.

After greetings were exchanged, including an uncomfortable hello between Metcalfe and Aer'la, Fournier said to Aronson, "Sir, I am here to advise you in person and in writing–" he motioned to Aer'La, who stepped forward and proffered a disposable data chip to Aronson, "–that this colony is to be evacuated. You will begin preparations to transfer your belongings immediately."

There was a suppressed gasp from the assembled Family members. Aronson spoke up, ignoring the chip in his hand as if it were of no consequence. "We will not, sir."

Fournier set his jaw. "You do not have a choice."

Aronson smiled and said gently, "God's children always have choices, Admiral. That is what being mortal is about. We show God's grace through our choices."

Druelinger stepped forward. He was a silver-haired man of average height, solidly muscled, a few extra pounds showing his age, cloaking the fact, known to Metcalfe, that he did not live a sedentary lifestyle.

"Sir," said the Marine Colonel, "my men and women do not like to use force against our own. It's the ugliest part of our job. I hope you won't push us to do it."

Unlike the Marines portrayed (unfairly, Metcalfe thought) in the popular holos, Druelinger was never arrogant, and always sought a diplomatic solution. He was, after all, senior officer representing his branch of service on the Confederacy's flagship.

"We will push you to do nothing, friend," said Aronson. "You will choose your own actions, as will we, based on our faith in God."

Druelinger shook his head sadly. "Our faith is in the orders of our superiors. When the order is given, we will come, and you will go."

It sounded nothing like a threat. It was a simple statement of the events the Colonel expected would occur.

"Four days," said Fournier. "Ninety-six hours from now," he keyed his implant, and the *Titan* ship's time appeared in the air, "the transports will land, and the Colonel's troops will take you aboard... with or without your cooperation."

Aronson nodded. "Without, regrettably. We will not use violence, but we will resist. I hope no one is injured."

"No promises," growled Aer'La.

"We are returning to our ship now," said Fournier. "You will be under continual surveillance from this point on."

"Of course," said Aronson.

Fournier and Druelinger turned to go. Aer'La hung back for a second, looking askance at Metcalfe, Elspeth and Icarus.

Metcalfe saw an opening, and took it. He took Aer'La gently by the arm and led her a few steps from their superiors. "You can't agree with this," he said.

"Look, Navy," she said, "I don't like the guy any better than you do. But he's right this time! These people are letting the Qraitians into our space! Innocent or not, they're wrong. You know what Qraitians can do."

Her eyes showed pain, but it was pain girded by anger. Fehajiq had nearly killed her. She hadn't forgotten.

"I do know, Aer'La," he agreed. "But we can't spend our whole lives seeking revenge. We can't let the actions of one lunatic turn us against the rest of the universe. We certainly shouldn't let them make us forget who our friends are."

"I haven't forgotten who my friends are, Metcalfe." She looked bitterly at Icarus, standing behind Metcalfe. "But I think maybe you've forgotten who your enemies are."

"I am not Terry's enemy," said the boy. "He is my brother."

"I wasn't talking to you, Qraitian! Keep your mouth shut, or I'll shut it for you!" She took a threatening step forward.

Metcalfe side-stepped between them. "You'll go through me," he said tonelessly.

"Yes," she said. "I will." She meant it, he knew, but there was the slightest quiver in her voice.

Aronson approached them, still peaceful, still smiling. "The Family will go into Communion now. We must seek the Lord's guidance."

Aer'La rolled her eyes. "Good-bye, *Brother* Metcalfe." She went to catch up with Fournier.

Seeing her, the Admiral turned and called, "Mister Metcalfe, I believe it's time for you to return as well."

Metcalfe held his place, gravely aware that this could be a decision point. In seconds he might no longer be an officer of the Navy. The life he had known would be left behind. Was he really ready?

"Admiral," he said, "I've been ordered to observe. Certainly there's benefit in seeing the Communion that's about to occur, in response to your orders. I believe Captain Atal should weigh in. Shall I contact him?"

Fournier's expression soured. "No. In a few days, it won't matter. When we come back, you'll return to the Navy, either as an officer, or a prisoner."

Metcalfe was well aware which outcome the Admiral preferred.

On any given day during the past year, Atal would have known where to find his Bos'n and midshipmen, with the exception of Sestus Blaurich. The list of possible locations was short: Smokin' Joe's on the Boulevard, Metcalfe's cabin, unless Metcalfe and Pallas had declared they wanted time alone, and, occasionally, floating prone in the Arch which held the great

Life Sphere captive. There they would look at the stars until all hours, passing around a bottle of whiskey.

Atal knew all these places and left them sacrosanct. He never disturbed his people, never watched their activities. He knew Metcalfe would keep them mostly legal, and Aer'La would keep them mostly unbroken.

Lately, they'd been none of these places. Perhaps conversely, lately, Atal had taken to breaking his own rule. He was watching and he was visiting, because he needed the company of his young proteges. Too much time spent with Fournier, perhaps; or was it too much talk of war, when he'd been through war enough in his life? Maybe he was getting old and wishing that he, like they, could be young and carefree and occasionally drunk beyond any imaginable excuse.

Whatever the reason, lately, he'd wanted to see them, and largely been unable to. Today, he needed to see them. He invoked Captain's privilege and had the ship's A.I. track them down. Strangely enough, he found Carson at a relaxed gentleperson's club on the Main Concourse. It wasn't his usual scene. Too quiet and reserved, too like a library. Refined men and women sitting about, sipping brandy and sherry, reading holos or playing very restrained card games. A few smoked safe synthetics in pipes. Quiet music played. It was not a place a young man came looking for action, and so it was the last place Kevin Carson would usually be found.

No, Atal corrected himself, the last place Kevin Carson would be found was *any* place that he would be sharing a drink with Sestus Blaurich. Yet here he was, in this quiet, snooty surrounding, drinking a swift half with his erstwhile enemy.

Atal quietly stepped up to their table. Before he could speak, a liveried gentleman server appeared at his elbow, decried that it was an honor to welcome the ship's Captain to their humble establishment, and offered him a drink on the house. Atal thanked him and requested Quintil Whiskey, neat. The server nodded smartly and started to ask if the Captain would also like an application for club membership, a mere formality, of course, when—

Atal held up his hand, smiled graciously and said, "Bad time. Perhaps you could have it sent to my A.I." He gestured that he wished to join the two young men who were now looking curiously in his direction. The attendant nodded and dashed away.

Atal gestured at an empty chair beside Carson and wondered, "May I?"

"Huh?" stammered Carson. "Of course, Captain! Please." He moved his chair over to make room.

"Thanks," said Atal, seating himself. His drink arrived, and he waved the server off before he could offer up a meal. Most likely he would have also offered up entertainment, a wide array of hallucinogenic drugs, and the virginity of the owner's daughter or son.

"I'm surprised to see you here, Captain," said Sestus Blaurich. "You're not known to frequent such establishments."

"Nor do I intend to be known for it, Mr. Blaurich. But I wanted to brief my officers on our current situation." He realized he probably should have said "junior" officers. Sestus would no doubt ask why Captain Darby wasn't included, and Atal didn't want to tread too far into that territory, lest he trip over the fact that he hadn't meant to include young Blaurich either.

"Shall we report to your Promenade, sir?" asked Blaurich. "At your convenience–"

"Not necessary, Mr. Blaurich. This is... informal. Ah," he held up one finger and gestured at someone by the door. "I hope you don't mind, I invited Cernaq and Aer'La to join us."

Blaurich looked non-plussed. Come to think of it, so did Carson. What the hell? Wondered Atal.

"That's fine, of course," Blaurich said. "We're happy to–"

"Don't be so obsequious, Sestus!" said Atal. "I'm intruding on your off-duty time, and I damned well know it."

"It's not like you do it every day, Captain," said Carson.

Cernaq and Aer'La approached. "You wished to see us, Captain?" asked the Phaetonian.

His manner was as calm as ever, but Atal sensed tension. Clearly the cohesion these young people had once shared was at a low ebb.

"Sit down, please," he said.

Aer'La drew up chairs for both of them and craned her neck, checking out the place. "Swank," she observed. "And stuffy. Looks like your kinda haunt, Five."

Sestus's answering smile was a taut, angry line.

"Let's keep the banter–and the insults–to a minimum," said Atal. "We've had a change in orders, and I wanted to tell you all personally."

"Where's Kaya?" asked Aer'La.

"She's ill," Atal lied. "Probably nothing, but Dr. Faulkner felt the symptoms bore observing. Until she's identified the infection, she's keeping Kaya confined to the infirmary and staying with her."

"She's in quarantine?" asked Carson.

"Not precisely. There's no cause for alarm. You know how cautious Dr. Faulkner is."

Atal did not look Cernaq's way. He knew that Cernaq knew he was lying. He hoped the boy wouldn't pry further. Fortunately, he kept his mouth shut.

"Now, as to the change in orders..." Atal contemplated his drink for a moment, then spread his hands on the table. "We're leaving Eleusis."

All eyebrows went up.

"Now?" asked Carson.

"Departure will occur during your next duty shifts. We've been ordered back to H.Q."

"Sir, may I ask–?" began Sestus.

"You may all ask anything. That's why I wanted to do this informally." He sighed and downed his drink in one gulp. It impacted the table with a sharp crack as he set it down harder than intended. "Look, people, this was not my decision. I doubt any of you are going to be happy with it, and I felt I owed... strike that... I never owe you an explanation. Let's just say I wanted you to have one anyway."

"So, why are we leaving?" said Carson. "I think that was Sestus's question."

"Admiral Fournier's orders," replied Atal. "As you're aware, a sizeable detachment of our fellow ships has arrived in the system. The Admiralty feels that there is sufficient force present to address both the Qraitian situation and the evacuation of Eleusis."

"So we are evacuating the colonists?" asked Carson.

Aer'La nodded. "Admiral Fournier visited them today. He gave them four days."

"It's not going to be a pleasant situation," said Cernaq.

"No," Atal agreed. "It's not."

"I'm guessing that our presence is desired closer to home," said Sestus. "To calm the current climate of fear?"

"That's the story," said Atal.

"But in fact," put in Cernaq, "you believe they just want us out of the way."

"Reading my mind, Cernaq?"

"No, Captain, but I do know how you think."

"Admiral Fournier and I... disagree on the best strategy for handling Eleusis."

"Then Fournier's wrong!" blurted Carson.

"Admiral Fournier is the Secretary, Carson," said Sestus with unusual forbearance. "He didn't get the job by always being wrong."

Carson downed the last of the beer in his glass. "That's a matter of opinion."

"Thank you for the vote of confidence, Mr. Carson," said Atal. "But I realize that I could be wrong in my approach to Eleusis."

"Yes, sir," said Aer'La. "I'm afraid you are."

Atal looked to her. She drew in her lip slightly, but held his gaze.

"Go on, Bos'n," he said. "As long as my officers follow my orders, I don't mind hearing when they disagree with me."

"Well, sir, it's just... I think having Qraitians in our space is too big a risk to take. I think we do need to tighten security. Otherwise, what's to stop another Fehajiq from coming in and trying another attack on us? And maybe succeeding this time?"

"We did only pull through by the skin of our teeth, sir," said Sestus.

"You may be right," said Atal thoughtfully.

Aer'La looked down at the table. "Five and I just agreed. I need a drink, now."

"Times change, Bos'n," said Sestus, pleased with himself. "Maybe this is the beginning of a beautiful friendship."

"Don't push it, Five," muttered Aer'La.

"Sir," Carson interrupted. "You haven't said–that is–what about Metcalfe? Is he coming back with us?"

Atal shook his head, noting the disappointment on Carson's face.

"I wish he were, but I've ordered him to detached duty, to observe the Family. Admiral Fournier has decided that he is to remain and... assist with the evacuation."

Carson swallowed, "And... if he doesn't?"

"You mean, if he disobeys a direct order from the Admiral?" asked Atal.

"Well, sir," said Carson, "from what I understand, Aronson's people aren't going to cooperate with the evacuation."

"Doubtless not."

"If Metcalfe takes their side..."

Atal said carefully, "Anyone who actively resists the evacuation order will be taken into custody... as an enemy of the state." As the words came out of his mouth, he found he needed to clear his throat.

For a moment, they were all silent. Carson stared into his glass.

"We're not leaving immediately," Atal said quietly. "Communications to the surface are open, and I'll approve shuttle usage for anyone who asks."

He did not say, "So get down there and convince that boy that he's about to ruin his damned life. Say something, say anything, to make sure that, when he comes back to Quintil, it's as part of Fournier's crew and not as a political prisoner."

He did not say, "I don't know how to fix this. I hope one of you does."

Nor did he point out to them, for he did not need to, that Metcalfe believed what Fournier was doing was wrong, and he might choose to be a political prisoner rather than participate in an immoral act.

What he finally said was, "If it's any comfort, Metcalfe is in a unique position to try and determine what the mystery of this planet is."

"Is there a mystery, sir?" asked Cernaq

"There's something down there," acknowledged Atal. "Something dangerous. I hope we can figure out what it is before... well, before something happens that we all regret."

"Metcalfe."

He turned at Pallas's call. He had been looking out across the lake when she came up behind him. Clearly, he was distracted.

"I thought you might be in Communion," she said, coming to stand beside him.

He shook his head. "The Captain radioed that you were coming down. I told the others I'd join them later." He gestured across the lake, toward the hills where the place of Communion was, where she had seen the Qraitian vanish into thin air. "I think it's going to be a very long vigil."

"Do you think they'll stay there all four days?"

He shrugged. "Maybe. What do you do, when you know armed forces are coming to take you away, and you've decided to just say 'no?'"

"Pray for patience and strength?" she offered.

"Exactly that," he agreed.

"I'm sorry if I called you away from it. If you want to go–"

He reached out and took her hand. "No. I'm glad you're here. It's... it's a confusing time. It must seem like I'm abandoning you."

"No," she said. "It seems as though you're conflicted about where you want to be right now. I don't see that as a personal reflection on me." She led him by the hand to a rough wooden bench where they could sit. "You need to be aware, however, that *Titan* is leaving. Within the next day cycle."

She felt his surprise, and perhaps a pang of fear. "Leaving? Before Fournier's deadline?"

"Captain Atal says that Fournier wants *Titan* 'out of his hair.'"

"I bet he does. Still–"

"He has brought in additional ships, a large detachment. I believe he means to keep the Marines here with him, to oversee the evacuation."

"To enforce it, you mean."

"Yes, I do. I also think..."

"What?"

"Metcalfe, Captain Atal believes himself to be the primary motivation behind this surprising order. I believe he's incorrect, at least in part. I think the Admiral is giving this order because of you."

"Because of me? How so?"

"Admiral Fournier does not know how you will respond if he uses force against the Family."

Metcalfe looked away. "I don't know myself."

"Yes, exactly. You are a formidable participant in this. If you stand with the Family against the Navy, the chances that the evacuation will become an embarrassing incident for the Admiralty increase greatly. Fournier wants to separate you from *Titan* in order to remove your support network."

His face darkened. "I'm not sure he need bother."

She studied him. "I know what you mean by that, of course. I think you should put it into words, though. You need to hear it yourself, and confront your own feelings."

"Well..." he considered it. "Aer'La seems to be diametrically opposed to me on this. Carson's angry at me."

"Carson does feel you've abandoned him. He began feeling that months ago."

"After the battle with Fehajiq, I know. I didn't mean to be distant. I just..."

"Suddenly feel very separated from everyone around you?"

He tweaked her nose. "I thought I was supposed to be putting it into words myself."

"You're a bit slow. You try my patience."

"Sorry."

"Ironic, isn't it? My people don't value spoken language, and yet we're more capable of putting thoughts into words. Thoughts, and especially feelings."

"It's that oh-so-ordered intellect of yours. It's one of the things I love about you."

As he said it, a sudden flash of awareness of what he was saying came to him. Then she saw the image of the girl, Elspeth in his mind. There was a sense memory, highly erotic, of her body warm against his. Pallas felt the extreme guilt wash over him, as he realized that he'd spoken of love for her, while the feeling of his night with Elspeth was still so fresh in his mind.

"She's very pretty," she said, not needing to specify to whom she referred.

"Yeah," he said without feeling.

"Why do you regret having sex with her?"

She felt from him a stab of irritation at her directness, followed by immediate self-reproach that there was nothing wrong with her candor and realization that he was just annoyed because she had touched the heart of his guilt.

"It's a Terran thing, I guess."

"Kaya tried to explain it to me–"

"You talked to Kaya about this?"

"Does that bother you?"

That my old girlfriend is talking to my new girlfriend about the girl I slept with the other night? She heard it clearly in his mind. He said, "No," out loud, but Pallas knew that was only because he felt it shouldn't bother him.

"'Girlfriend' is an interesting term," she observed. "Also Terran?"

"Yes. Why would InWorlders need a term to define a relationship that doesn't exist among them? If they want to form an attachment to someone and they're not sure it's going to work out, they just get married for a year or a month or five minutes." He sounded bitter.

"You disapprove of the transient nature of InWorlder relationships," she observed.

"I guess so. It's like they don't think there's anything worth committing to. No promise worth keeping, or even making."

"They get married."

He made a face. "Temporarily."

"They recognize that tastes and personal goals change. A lifetime contract for sharing of property and sexual fidelity is not something humans seem designed to maintain."

"Does that make it hurt less when the person who loved you yesterday doesn't love you today?"

"Does marriage prevent that from happening? Or calling each other boyfriend and girlfriend?"

"No. I guess it doesn't make a lot of sense, does it? Because all human love and marital customs are trying to deal with human emotion, and none of us really ever understand why we feel the way we feel. Our customs are irrational."

"That's true. And your feelings of guilt are irrational. You had a profoundly moving experience in the Communion with Elspeth. She is very attractive and seems to admire you a great deal. She offered herself to you and you have a healthy sexual response." She smiled and ruffled his hair. "A *very* healthy sexual response."

He reached his arms around her and pulled her close to his chest. He kissed her pale curls and whispered into them, "It's just that I love you so much, Pallas. I don't *want* to want anyone else. It scares me. In the last couple of months, everything has changed for me. I don't know if what I'm doing with my life is right. I think... I think I may want... need... to go and do something entirely different. What if... on the way... that means I leave you? What if... "

"What if you stop loving me?" she paraphrased.

He didn't answer. She knew he was afraid to say the words.

"Have you ever stopped loving anyone? Kaya? Kevin? Lydia?"

"No."

"I don't believe you're capable of it. But you're afraid, my love. Your deepest beliefs have been tested. All your feelings are changing. You faced death without flinching–"

He laughed. "I flinched. I covered it up by bullying Five."

"No you didn't. You did everything you knew you had to to keep us all safe and stop an attack. You never thought about fear, because there wasn't time. Now there *is* time. And the thought that your life's path, the things you need to do to fulfill your own happiness and your own personal sense of morality, might carry you away from the people you love... That terrifies you."

"Yes. Doesn't it bother you... that I might... not come back to you?"

"It bothers me that we might be separated for a time. I choose to believe you will always come back for me. If you don't... Well, that's the chance we take, loving someone, isn't it? There's always the possibility that one day they'll be taken from us. It would be easier and safer not to love. But we do it."

"Maybe... you could stay here with me?"

"I want to. I truly do. But I had to get personal approval from Admiral Fournier for this brief visit. I convinced him that there were additional interviews I needed to conduct in finalizing my report on the incident where the Qraitian was killed. He had one of the Marine pilots bring me here. If I don't return to the shuttle at the expected time, I'll be found and arrested. You have enough to think about right now, without having to worry about hiding me in a cave somewhere. Let's stay within the law, until we absolutely can't. Soon enough... no one will be allowed to live on this world."

"If Fournier has his way," he agreed.

"You don't believe he will."

"I don't."

"And you don't know why. You don't know how the Family will resist the armed might of the Navy and the Marines, but you believe something's going to happen when they try to evacuate the planet."

"I do. I think maybe the answer is locked in that Communion they practice. There is something up there, Pallas. You've seen it, I've... felt it."

"Is it God? Is that what you believe?"

"I don't know."

"But you're going to find out."

"Yes. I have to know what... who... is on this planet."

"Despite the danger," she said. "Your need to seek truth is the strongest I've ever encountered." She kissed him gently. "My fearless explorer."

She kissed him again, her mouth open, her arms enfolding him, one hand caught in his hair, the other stroking his back. He wasn't wearing his uniform jacket. She caught her hand on the hem of his shirt and pulled it up, then gathered it in both hands.

"What are you doing?" he asked.

"Undressing you. I want to see you naked. The sight of your body fills me with overwhelming sensations: admiration and arousal... it's... invigorating. It's like seeing the embodiment of everything I believe, everything good..."

"That Phaetonian moral ideal stuff, huh?" He grinned and kissed her nose. "What if the man who embodied all your favorite virtues were short, fat and had moles all over his face?"

She laughed. "'What if,' is a question that almost always brings unhappiness. Anyway, that's not what he looks like. The man who embodies all that I believe is perfect, and beautiful and... " She made a sudden grab again at his shirt and pulled it hard up over his head. "And I want to see all of him right now!"

They dissolved into laughter, falling against each other and then to the grass. Metcalfe discarded the shirt and rolled on top of her. "What if someone comes along?"

"I'll know. There's no one around. And I don't care!"

He shucked off his boots and pants, then began undressing her. She reveled in the feeling of his hands touching her, so gentle, so nurturing. She had been admired for her intellectual gifts growing up. She had felt strong friendship from Cernaq. Among the Inner Worlds, she often felt the lust of men who looked at her, and entertained blatant fantasies of sexual encounters with her. Their minds never impressed her, however, and so she never took any steps to fulfill their fantasies. When she'd first met Metcalfe, she had felt the same yearnings in him, seen the same sorts of graphic images of sexual congress in his mind, yet she'd also seen all that she saw now. His moral courage, his strength of conviction, the depth of his love when he did love.

No one had ever actually loved her. No one had ever actually put so much of his own energy into showing her how much she excited and aroused him. He did. The touch of his fingers on her skin, the kisses which brushed every part of her, his tongue exploring her... it electrified her. They'd done this so often, but the feeling now of the open air on their bodies, being naked with him under the setting sun of this world, and the caresses and attentions he was giving her. Her body rushed toward climax. She reached for him and whispered urgently, "Now!"

He was inside her, his body within hers, his mind within hers. His thoughts were as frantic and wordless as his actions. She felt him, though. His presence was alive in her mind, like a fire, burning. He was with her in every way. She was not alone. They were not alone. As their passion built, she realized they were truly not alone.

At first, she thought someone had approached them physically, outside, as it were, the boundaries of their minds and bodies and their lovemaking. But there was no one physically there. There was a presence *here*, in their minds, with them. She felt Metcalfe respond to it. It stimulated and excited him. It was a hint of the powerful god he had sought for so long.

God, yes. God was with him. She could feel that in his mind.

The presence was not welcoming to her, however. It was indifferent at first. It was cold to her. This... being... this intelligence, was drawn to Metcalfe. Perhaps it wasn't love. A strong attraction... moral... intellectual...? It wanted to be with him, it wanted to share the energy of this moment.

It was old and powerful. It was the being that Metcalfe had shared Communion with. She felt that it had been there as he'd taken Elspeth. She saw, as a third party might have seen, her lover's body entwined with the girl's. She was aroused by the image, and she felt... hunger? Yes, hunger. The creature in their minds was stimulated by the raw emotion, fed by the passion.

Metcalfe drove himself deeper into her, mind and body. His motions became desperate, rough. He needed her. He needed all of her. But the thing did not want her here. The mad thrusting of his body into hers brought pain. He had never hurt her before. Something must be wrong, and yet... she didn't want to stop. Even as she experienced pain, her passion grew. The thing's hunger grew. Her fear grew.

Whatever this was, it resented her presence, yet it would use this experience. It would use her, to be with him.

She was afraid. She wanted it gone. And yet she wanted to see it, to know it. There was a fascination which made her skin crawl, like the prey feels for the predator. It cannot look away. The fear makes every molecule of its body feel alive.

The pain grew. The pleasure grew more. As orgasm overtook her, she felt the powerful spirit that visited them surge. It shone like the sun. It sang with the voices of thousands. It consumed them and it fed them. It loved them, hated them and devoured them. In its passion, millions died in bursts of flame. Millions of beings like herself lived their lives and died their deaths, all for love of... who?

The world exploded, and everything went black.

Pallas awoke with Metcalfe gazing into her eyes intently, a look of concern on his face. It took her a moment to remember where she was. She reached out with her hands, and he was right there, his chest firm under one hand, his shoulder under the other. Still feeling as though she were falling, she reached out with her mind, and he was right there, worried, but warm, strong and reassuring.

He cradled her and stroked her hair. "My god, did I hurt you?"

It would be a lie to say he hadn't. She breathed, "I'm all right. It's just... it was... intense."

"Yeah," he agreed. "It was..."

She saw it in his mind. It was like it was with Elspeth. They hadn't been alone either. But the creature had not resented Elspeth's presence. She hugged him tight, pulling his head to her.

"Be careful, Metcalfe," she whispered. She knew there was no telling him to come back with her, to leave this place and this unknown entity. He had already formed some sort of bond with it. It was attracted to him, as she was. It resented her, and she...

She feared it.

"Don't worry," he assured her. "It's all going to work out, believe me."

She kissed him. "I believe you, my love," she said. But as they lay there, cuddling together for warmth in the cool of the growing dusk, she wondered, *for whom, exactly, it is all going to work out?*

CHAPTER ELEVEN

Sestus clinked his glass hard against Carson's, spilling beer on the table. "To the last of the civilian interviews!" he declared. He hefted the glass and drank deeply.

Beer spilled on the table only seemed proper, in this place. Unlike Sestus's stuffy club, where a spill no doubt resulted in a piece of furniture being immediately despatched for conversion to raw material, the Rendez-Vous, the ale house they were patronizing tonight, was one of those places where you could keep your feet on the ground in the event of gravity loss. The spilled liquor of past generations glued your boots to the floor. It was a favorite haunt of Carson and Aer'La.

Carson took a moderate sip and then added, "To the end of our time lashed to the mast."

The place was quiet tonight. Most of the bars and restaurants aboard were, since they'd begun their work. Carson couldn't be sure, but he thought there was more than a touch of resentment in the way the bartenders and the waiters behaved toward them. The easy camaraderie, the habit most of the locals on the Main Concourse had of calling out his name when he entered, were gone. Now they were formally polite, perhaps even deferential. Maybe it was having Sestus with him. Maybe it was that he had become 'the man,' and was held responsible for sending several of their fellows to the brig pending further questioning.

And why was he with Sestus? Granted, the guy had been less of an ass lately. He'd largely toned down his boasting, and he even seemed to be as impatient with Darby as Carson himself was. Of course, Metcalfe wasn't here. Metcalfe and Sestus seemed to bring out the worst in each other. Perhaps, with Metcalfe gone, he simply didn't have the triggers which tended to bring out his inner asshole.

Or maybe, with Metcalfe gone, Carson just needed someone... anyone... to talk to. It was a depressing thought.

Sestus slapped the table and shouted, "Barkeep! Another round!"

Okay, Carson reflected, he had become only partially civilized. He still treated most people like servants. It was amazing he didn't call the girl who was serving them 'wench,' or refer to their male hosts as "sirrah."

"Hadn't you better eat something?" Carson suggested, noting that there were already two empty glasses in front of Sestus; and they'd only been here about fifteen minutes.

Sestus waved him off. "We'll have time to eat. I'm gonna drink until I've wiped out the memory of every pleading, whining, inconsequential face I've had to look at this week!"

Now that sounded like the old Sestus. He was also inappropriately loud, and putting care into forming his consonants. It did not bode well for the evening, though idle curiosity made Carson wonder what the most privileged of their number looked like sloppy drunk.

Sestus reached out and took hold of Carson's half-full glass, banging it and sloshing more beer on both the table and his companion. "Fuck, Carson, keep up!"

Carson hesit. "I think one of us should keep a moderately clear head."

"Not tonight!" laughed Sestus. In fact, he practically giggled. "Tonight, we're going to forget every-damn thing!"

Two more glasses were placed in front of them. Sestus snatched his before it had been fully placed and downed half in two swallows, winking at Carson.

Carson shrugged, finished his first drink, pondered his too-jovial companion for a moment, and began on the second. It was going to be a long night.

"Kaya, you're skating on very thin ice," said Celia Faulkner.

Her young friend canted her head and asked, "What does that mean?"

"That you may be putting yourself in grave danger."

"No, I inferred that. I mean, how is that 'skating on thin ice?'"

"You don't know what skating is?"

"Of course I know what skating is! The last five Olympic Gold Medalists in figure skating were from Quintil! But how or why would anyone ever skate on thin ice? Does that mean the rink hasn't been serviced?"

"No, it means you might cut through the ice and fall into the icy water beneath and drown!"

"Why would there be water underneath the rink?"

Celia sighed. "On my world, we skate on frozen lakes in the winter."

"What an idiotic thing to do! You could be killed!"

Celia hung her head. "Oh, you poor, sheltered city girl!"

"I am *not* sheltered!" Kaya insisted.

"Sheltered," the Doctor confirmed. "And spoiled. But I mean that I'm very concerned that Ustenar is going to suspect you're not what you appear to be."

"That's my plan," said Kaya.

Faulkner's eyes went wide. "You *want* to get us killed?"

"No. I want to maintain an air of mystery. I want to fascinate her."

"Something of a snake charmer, eh?"

Kaya grinned an evil grin. "Doctor, that's downright racist!"

Celia shrugged. "If she wishes to call me a monkey, she's welcome."

Kaya's expression became serious. "The more I draw her attention to me, the less mental energy she has to focus on fighting with our side."

"With Fournier adding more fuel to the fire each passing second, I suppose that's not a bad idea," said Celia.

"And I hope to find out just how much they've learned about potential weaponry down below." Kaya finally commented on the Doctor's continual fiddling with a data display from her implant. Indeed, the older woman had not looked up from it once since Kaya had come into the room. "What are you doing?"

Celia grinned with one corner of her mouth. "Patching in to their data storage."

Kaya raised her eyebrows. "Now who's on thin ice? Maybe we should have brought Carson."

Celia looked up for the first time. "Young woman," she said with mock indignation, "just because I am in tune with the rhythms of nature, do not think I know nothing about technology! I was building and programming A.I. units before your father was born."

"I stand abashed."

"Don't. It's bad for the spine. At any rate, my time with the Qraitian prisoners gave me a glimpse into their shared psychology. Like us, they have no love of security. When it comes to encrypting and protecting personal data, their practices are slipshod. They have their own equivalent of using pet's names, family members names, significant dates, so they can remember the code sequences to access their information. The human–or Qraitian–element is always the weak link. Understanding psychology is the most important component of espionage."

"Are you finding anything?"

"Not yet. I'll let you know." She went back to work, asking idly, "You feel confident there's a spy among the Family?"

Kaya nodded. "Between those references to 'the source' by the dead officer, and Ustenar's comments about *her* sources, yes. And I think, before they move to take us home to die, dear old mother, they plan to smuggle additional forces in, to take over operations when all the humans are gone."

Celia leaned back against the bulkhead, wishing for some sort of cushion to sink into. Damn but these Qraitians lived uncomfortably! "Let's hope your father can change Fournier's course before any of us get whisked away from Eleusis."

It was early morning when Metcalfe joined the Family in Communion. He'd been told it was uncommon for all of them to gather like this and stay for more than an hour or two: uncommon, but not unheard of. There were contingencies in place. Now, they'd been in rapport for over twelve hours. Breaking physical contact, but apparently not breaking complete connection, Family members quietly distributed food which had been brought and set aside at the edge of the clearing for later use. Like a priest in Metcalfe's home church during silent prayer, they went from person to person, placing a sandwich or drink in each pair of hands, sometimes exchanging whispered instructions, never violating the sanctity of prayer. It seemed a good system.

Metcalfe scanned the faces, all serene, and wondered if any or all of them felt the sort of solid connection that he'd made that first time he had come here. He knew that, at home, prayer was, for some, an ecstatic experience. For others it was merely a marked period of time where they had to remain silent and try not to fidget or itch too much. Were any of these people actually wondering when the hell they could get up and leave, or trying not to think about how much their noses itched? It didn't look like it.

Few people stood. They'd been here quite a while. No one was asleep, however. That was surprising. He wondered if Communion could somehow relieve the body of the need for sleep. Or was religious devotion causing them to run on adrenaline?

He found Elspeth and Icarus. The boy lay prone, his body gently curved, reminding Metcalfe for all the world of a snake sunning itself on a hot day. And yet he did not feel the skin-crawling sense of revulsion snakes brought out in him. Nor, apparently, did Elspeth, for she lay on her back, knees up, eyes open and looking peacefully at the sky, with her head pillowed on the young Qraitian's belly.

She saw Metcalfe, and, not averting her gaze from the morning sky, held out one hand to beckon him. Having removed his clothes at the clearing edge, he came to her and sat, lotus fashion on the ground, taking her hand.

He closed his eyes and regulated his breathing, setting inhalations and exhalations to be equal. Faulkner had taught him meditative techniques years ago, and Pallas had reinforced his use of them. Phaetonians had taken meditation and bio-feedback to new heights, establishing an astounding level of control over their own bodies, and even the bodies of others. He wondered, idly, if the Family knew of or had experienced such control.

Relax, Terry Metcalfe.

The thought drifted in his mind. Was it "God?" Or was it his own subconscious voice, reprimanding him for thinking too much? No matter. He did need to relax and observe. He listened to his own breathing, then, expanding his field of focus, heard Elspeth's gentle exhalations, a soft hiss from Icarus. Around him, dozens, then hundreds, then hundreds upon hundreds breathed softly. All of the Family could be heard, he imagined. Some wheezed from asthma or age. Some sighed occasionally. All were peaceful, content.

It was almost palpable, the comfort they derived from this process. They were united. They had each other to care for and care for themselves in return. Powerful forces marshaled against them, yet, within this grotto, all was well. Nothing could hurt them. Fournier and all his weapons were of no consequence, for God was with them. He felt it, could almost hear it on each and every mind. Almost, almost, he could identify individual voices in the chorus of contentment and serenity.

Aronson was confident, strong. He would be what he needed to be. Elspeth was touched by the beauty of the feelings they shared, warmly happy that God was on their side. She saw the world radiating beauty as Metcalfe could not deny she herself radiated the same. From Icarus he felt excitement, a youthful, male edge of anticipation at the coming confrontation, and confidence that his faith would be proven true, his beliefs vindicated. All would be well.

Would it? Metcalfe could not suppress his fear. There were a dozen or more ships in the system now, each with the power to devastate this world. He knew the power of a warship, had commanded and used that power. How could these gentle people resist it?

He reminded himself that conscious thought was not the goal here. To meditate, to hear the voice within, required reaching past both reason and emotion. It required letting go. He wasn't good at letting go. He tried to blank his mind, tried not to think of the weaponry which might be brought against them.

Unbidden the image came to him of the Navy's forces coming here, armored, armed, heavy boots crunching through the forest. He saw the Family being herded into confinement, saw the Qraitians among them separated.

Then there was another image, one of the Qraitians, armed, about to fire a weapon; one of the Qraitians, vanishing. It was the image of the incident Pallas had witnessed, clear and accurate, because he had seen it in her mind. One moment he was there, threatening death to a family; then he was gone, as though he'd never existed.

It had happened here, in this place. It had happened right over there, right above the grotto. The father and his children... Metcalfe had seen them, seated together, when he'd arrived. They had stood here in the clearing, and the Qraitian had advanced on them, down the hill, death in his slitted eyes as he moved outward from the cave.

The cave.

Again, had something spoken in his mind?

He wondered about the cave. What was in it? What was the fascination the Qraitians had with it? Was it connected to the strange disappearance? Was it connected to this place, as a center of Communion?

Come to the cave.

Again, the voice that wasn't a voice.

He pushed a conscious question out with his mind, using the focused communication skills he'd learned from Pallas. *Is that you?*

I am I. Come to the cave.

Gently releasing Elspeth's hand, Metcalfe stood. The light of morning had grown in the few minutes he'd sat there. He could now see across the clearing easily, to the opening in the trees leading uphill, to the path beyond. He walked toward the cave. The path was well worn, and his lack of shoes didn't bother him. He wouldn't go far. He had walked barefoot outside so often as a child. It would be all right.

Where? asked the voice. *Where did you walk barefoot?*

He saw the farm in Virginia. The sun was bright, warm on his skin. The scent of blackberries drifted in the still air. Standing before the big house, they could look out and see countryside for miles around. They saw farmland, some worked and growing–their own–some wild and fallow. They saw ruins of buildings, burned out, crumbling, abandoned. Once, there had been villages and cities. Now, there was only the farm and its supporting village, the only thing for miles.

Lydia's hand was in his. They skipped out along the hillside, toward the trees which lined the yard and the road which led to adventures beyond. He felt the grass and dirt beneath his bare feet. He'd outgrown his last pair of shoes, or they'd fallen apart. New ones would be a while in coming.

Kevin ran ahead of them, exploring, looking for trouble, as always. Kevin turned to him, a crooked smile on his face, evil in his eyes, inviting. He held out tobacco he had smuggled, and paper he'd torn from books in the library. He invited Terry to smoke with him. He knew better than to invite Lydia. He wasn't afraid of Terry's temper, but he didn't want to provoke it, either.

Metcalfe remembered chastising his friend for tearing the books. Kevin had laughed in his face and rolled two cigarettes. They'd smoked. They'd gotten caught. So often, Kevin had led him to trouble, so often, they'd gotten caught. And then Terry had taken his ultimate revenge, leading Kevin into the biggest Trouble of all, out here in space.

Metcalfe suddenly realized that everything around him was dark. It wasn't a sunny day, and he wasn't in Virginia. Kevin and Lydia weren't here. He was on Eleusis. But...

Where am I? He asked the voice.

In the cave, was the reply.

He looked around. He had walked far, as he'd recollected those moments from his childhood, as he had fed them to the god of the cave.

Fed them? Was that right?

Not precisely, said the voice. *I do not feed on your memories, and yet they invigorate me. I am hungry for knowledge, Terry Metcalfe. Like you. I am hungry to know you.*

It's dark, he told it. *I can't see.*

Are you afraid? It asked.

No.

Good. There is nothing to fear. I am here. There is much to learn, and you want to learn, don't you?

I do.

Come, then, said the voice. *Come deeper into the cave, and I will show you what there is to be learned.*

He walked, sure of his steps, in blackness. The ground beneath him angled down. Somehow, no stones pricked his feet or tore at his flesh. Didn't caves always have loose stones? They fell from the walls, did they not? As he moved farther from the sunlight, the cave cooled. In a cave, it was often thirty degrees cooler than on the ground above. He was naked. Why was he not cold?

You need not be cold. I am here.

Where am I? Where am I going?

To a place unseen by most, Terry Metcalfe.

To the place where you keep the weapons?

Are you looking for weapons, Terry Metcalfe?

The Qraitians were looking for weapons. They came here.

I did not allow them to see this place.

What about the Family?

I do not want this place known, except to the few who are prepared.

How am I prepared?

Look within, said the voice.

Indeed, he could look nowhere else. It was still so dark. Cavern darkness, it was said, was the most complete, absorbing darkness known to humanity. Perhaps Qraitians were comfortable in the total blackness beneath the ground, but it had been known to drive humans mad. Idly he wondered if he was going mad.

Look within, it urged again.

He looked within. Without, he sensed it surrounding him, like the cool, gentle waters of the lake, enfolding him, covering him. Covering him? He was in over his head, but he wasn't drowning. He just had to remember not to breathe. It was easy.

He felt its power, overwhelming.

He'd felt power, alive around him, the greatest power ever harnessed, the might of the *Titan.* He had used it, commanded it, protected with it, killed with it.

This power was greater, this power in the darkness. This power could do anything. It could bring death. It could bring life. He tried to comprehend, but it was beyond understanding. Human thought could only limit it, set boundaries for it, not define it. Human thought was useless. Human thought was driven away. Without human thought came madness, but the power was still there.

Are you afraid of madness, Terry Metcalfe?

Was he afraid? Of madness? Of darkness? Of power? Which was which? Were they one? Power in the dark. It could create anything. It could bring light. Let there be Light. And there was Light, and it was good.

And darkness was good.

But light was there. It searched. It probed. It tickled him. He heard a laugh. He heard himself laughing. He laughed.

Darkness was everywhere.

The light played and danced. The light was–

"Terry!"

The voice was like a slap in the face.

No, wait... it was a slap in the face. Someone had slapped him. He shook his head, wondering–

Someone slapped him again.

"Terry!"

Who was this Terry and why did he keep slapping–?

"Terry Metcalfe, wake up!"

Somehow, he felt/saw the hand rear back again, and this time he grabbed it.

"I'm awake," he said, but he wasn't. He was happy in the dark, and the power, the dark which flowed around him and supported him like water–

Water?

He spluttered. Someone had thrown water in his face. It went into his nose and down his throat. He coughed, gagging as he inhaled some of it.

"What the hell?" he demanded, sitting up. When had he laid down?

"Are you okay?" It was Icarus, holding a lantern.

Where was–?

"Terry, why did you come down here?"

Elspeth. There she was. His head was cradled in her lap.

"I–" he started to say. He couldn't remember. Didn't know. "Where am I?"

"In the cave," said Icarus. "You wandered away from Communion, and we followed you."

"We were concerned about the depth of your rapport," said Elspeth, stroking his hair. "You were in really deep."

"It didn't feel like..." he stopped. What was the last thing he remembered? When had he slipped from wakefulness to full Communion with... whatever it was?

"That's what they all say," said Icarus. "No one realizes when it's overwhelming them. Then it does."

Metcalfe struggled to sit up. Elspeth supported his shoulders while Icarus reached out for his hand and levered him upright. "Thanks," he said. "I'm glad you came looking for me."

"We had to," said Elspeth. "When you wandered off... it's dangerous. People who've gone in that deep have died."

"I wish I'd known that before," said Metcalfe.

Elspeth shrugged. "It hasn't happened in Brother Aronson's time as minister. He's attentive to the ways of Communion and how it affects people."

Icarus craned his neck and shone his light against the cavern walls. "I've never been this far down in here before."

"I don't know what made me come here," said Metcalfe.

"You were in Communion," said Elspeth. "God made you come here."

He nodded. "Maybe."

"It's the only answer," she insisted.

Metcalfe got to his feet and accepted a lantern from Icarus. "As long as we're here, I guess we ought to have a look around. Or are the others expecting us back?"

Elspeth shook her head. "I don't think too many noticed we were gone. Everyone's still in Communion."

Metcalfe suddenly shivered and hugged himself. "Wow, it's cold down here."

Icarus laughed. "Of course it's cold, you idiot! You're naked."

"So are you," observed Metcalfe.

"That's different. My body adjusts to the ambient temperature. Yours doesn't."

"Cold-blooded, eh?" said Metcalfe. He noticed that Elspeth was, in fact, dressed. It was actually easy to overlook such details here, among the Family.

Icarus reached into a bag he carried and handed Metcalfe his clothes and boots. "Here. I grabbed these before we left. If you want to go exploring, you should keep warm."

After he had dressed, they started walking.

The place where they'd found Metcalfe had been moderately strewn with debris fallen from the ceiling of the cave. He must not have noticed, as he walked, that the floor had become less clear, the area more dilapidated. As they walked father down into the cavern, the path became even more strewn with rocks. They had to climb over some.

Elspeth cast her light over the walls and ceiling. "Has anyone ever been down this far?" she wondered.

Icarus answered her. "I'd say someone has. Look." He pointed his light.

It was a doorframe, set into the cavern wall. Though it was almost completely blocked now, they could still see the carved stone lintel set into the rock, about twenty feet off the ground. Coming down from it, on either side, there was evidence that the opening in the wall had been cut and shaped. Stray, fibrous formations in the rock lined what might have once framed an opening. These peeked out here and there amongst the other debris.

Metcalfe pointed. "Petrified wood," he said. "Someone built this a while ago."

"And then this had to have been under water," said Elspeth, "for the petrifaction to occur."

"So this area must have flooded at one point," said Metcalfe, shining his light along the ceiling. "We're near the lake. Maybe even under it."

"That's a big door," observed Icarus.

"Big enough to fly a shuttle through," said Metcalfe. "Must have taken a lot of work to carve out an opening that big. I can't imagine anyone would do that unless they really needed to."

"What do you mean?" asked Elspeth.

"I mean *that*," he pointed with his light, "was probably built by people who needed that big an opening."

She ran her eyes over it again and muttered, "Wow. They must have been huge."

"Big cave-dwelling monsters," suggested Icarus.

Metcalfe nodded and said, "Probably scaly and with venomous fangs."

"Now that was just rude," said Icarus.

Metcalfe chuckled and patted the boy's smooth shoulder. "Some of my best friends have scales and fangs."

"We'll never clear this to get through it," said Elspeth. "We'd need an earth mover."

"The passage curves around this way," said Icarus, gesturing and casting his light to his right. "Let's look."

Metcalfe started to caution the boy to take it slowly, but then decided there was no overwhelming reason not to keep looking. They were here already. If there was danger, they were as likely right on top of it now as they were if they went another few hundred feet. They followed the young Qraitian around the curve.

"Hey, look!" Icarus called out from ahead of them.

"What have you found?" asked Metcalfe. He and Elspeth jogged to catch up.

Icarus stood proudly before another doorway, once likely identical to the first they'd found. Unlike its twin, this one was partially clear.

"Why put two doors so close together?" Elspeth wondered out loud.

"Look at the curve of the wall," Metcalfe pointed out. "It comes around to this one in an arc from the other one. I wonder... " Casting his light ahead of him, he walked farther along. The pathway continued to curve gently. A short distance onward, however, stone blocked his way. If this had been a continuous, curved pathway, a large boulder must have fallen once, long ago. Around it, water had carried sediment and formed a cemented foundation of rock. Stalactites and stalagmites had formed all around.

Metcalfe crawled up onto a ledge formed by the boulder and brushed at the wall. He brought his light in close. "Here," he said. He pointed to a flat, striated area. "What's left of another wooden beam."

"A third door," said Icarus.

Metcalfe nodded. "And the same distance from the second as the second is from the first, along a curve. I think we're looking at points on a circle, or at least a partial one."

"Some kind of amphitheater?" wondered Elspeth.

"With many doors to allow maximum ingress and egress," agreed Metcalfe. "A lot of people... or... somethings... might have once gathered down here."

Elspeth shivered. "This is a sacred place. It feels a little like we're, I dunno..."

"Rifling through God's basement?" finished Metcalfe.

"A little."

"Hey, God led him here," protested Icarus.

"That's true," agreed Elspeth. "Don't you think so, Terry?"

"I'm not sure what I think," Metcalfe admitted. He jerked his head back the way they'd come. "C'mon, let's go check out that opening that's clear."

The doorway, however, did not admit them far into whatever this space had been. More debris and more formations from the ceiling blocked their way after about thirty feet. A shallow room was all they found.

"Looks like the ceiling collapsed," said Icarus.

Metcalfe cast his light upward, looking for openings in the rock.

"Yeah, but once upon a time this had to have been a huge room. Look at the way the wall curves upward, before the Stalactites obscure it. It's like there was a huge arch, or... "

"A domed ceiling?" suggested Elspeth.

"Maybe."

"What was that?" said Icarus.

"You hear something?" asked Metcalfe.

"Felt something. Like a footstep."

"Icarus's sense of vibrations is very keen," Elspeth explained. "He feels things before I hear them."

Then they all heard the splash of falling gravel, and footsteps, moving away.

"Someone followed us!" said Icarus.

"Hello?" called Metcalfe. He trotted quickly back out into the main passageway, shining his light. More footsteps sounded, quickening in pace.

"Whoever it is is running away," said Elspeth, following after.

They all three focused the beams of their lanterns along the pathway they'd follow here. Ahead of them, the footsteps grew fainter, moving away. They picked up their pace for a ways, jogging along the passage, but their pursuer had had a head start in doubling back.

"I wonder who–" Elspeth began.

"Look!" Icarus cut her off, pointing.

Ahead, on the cavern floor, a soft, blue glow pierced the darkness. Metcalfe stepped over to it, kneeling. "Radio of some kind," he said, holding the object in his hand.

Icarus looked over his shoulder at the object. "It's Qraitian," he said quietly.

"It wasn't here before. Whoever that was must have dropped it," said Elspeth.

Metcalfe checked the item over, showed it to Icarus. "You ever used one?"

"Sure," said Icarus. He looked at it. "It's got signal." He keyed the display and read a few indicators. "It's set for privacy, so we can't see who it's been in contact with."

Metcalfe let out a sardonic breath. "I'll give you three guesses."

"The log shows recent data flow, though. They were using it while they were following us."

"Reporting back to the ship in orbit," Metcalfe said.

"Reporting what?" asked Elspeth. "What were we doing that anyone would want to know about?"

"I don't know," said Metcalfe. "But Pallas said two of the Qraitian military were very interested in this cave. One of them died above. They must think the source of power they're seeking is down here, somewhere."

"Do you think it was someone from the outpost?" asked Icarus. "There's always an officer on duty, in case one of the Qraitian Family decides to return to the Empire."

Metcalfe shook his head. "The man who died here earlier was trying to kill members of the family. I'm guessing because he didn't want witnesses to his presence here. If so, I can't imagine any of his fellows coming back here when everyone's down in the grotto. He might be seen."

"Then... you think one of the family..." Elspeth didn't finish the thought.

"I'm afraid so," said Metcalfe.

"I don't believe it! Who could live among us, worship with us, and then–?"

"The same people," said Metcalfe, "who could try to kill a father and his two young children just for being in the wrong place at the wrong time."

They were silent for a moment. Metcalfe palmed the radio and shoved it into his pocket. "C'mon," he said. "We'd better get back.

Kevin Carson opened his eyes and searched blearily for his implant. Oh yeah... it was in his wrist. After a brief investigation, he also found his wrist, happily still attached to the rest of him, and tapped it twice. He was relieved when the time displayed revealed he had not slept into his duty shift.

His head throbbed, and even the faint light of the time display made him wince. He hadn't been this hung over in a while. He took inventory.

All his parts seemed to be there. He was in his own cabin... at least he thought so. His lips were tender and cracked, his mouth dry and sticky. His muscles ached, and he felt a dull pain characteristic of having been with a particularly enthusiastic lover. It wasn't his first experience with such sensations, not by a long shot. He usually remembered, though, if he'd gone out and gotten laid the night before.

He tried to remember the night before. Where...?

He decided he had better grab a hangover cure from the bathroom. He tried to sit up. His arm was asleep. Of course his arm was asleep, there was somebody on it. Must be the same guy who has his leg hooked around mine, Carson thought. Then the full impact of all these signs registered: he had gone out and gotten laid last night, he'd had very rough sex, and his partner was still here.

He reprimanded himself for sinking so low as to have forgotten, not only the encounter, but the identity of his lover. He could not turn on the light–could not face the possibility. Instead, he reached out and gently began a physical inspection with his hand. His partner was male, but then his specific symptoms suggested that; he felt a smooth, taut chest as he moved his hand up to find a face.

His subject groaned quietly and tightened the grip of his leg, snaking an arm around to pull Carson closer. The touch had made him stir. Was he awake?

"Morning," said a voice, which Carson was fairly confident was not his own.

Yes, his partner was awake, and Carson recognized the voice. For a moment, he didn't move, trying to decide what to say. He then frantically attempted to force himself to wake up. He closed his eyes tight and opened them again, hoping to reset reality by the gesture.

No change. He was not dreaming. He was in bed, naked and extremely post-coital, with Sestus.

Sestus raised up on one elbow and ran a finger gently down the line of Carson's breastbone. "You too hung over to talk? Do you need to throw up?"

Carson shook his head slowly.

"You all right?" Sestus wondered.

Carson finally found his voice. "How did we get here?"

"We walked," said Sestus. "Okay, we kinda staggered. It's possible we were carried part of the way by Marines. Not sure. It's a little fuzzy."

"My tongue's a little fuzzy."

Sestus laughed. "I'm not surprised. Although you weren't having any trouble using it last night."

"Oh my god," muttered Carson. "I don't remember anything after... I don't remember what I don't remember anything after."

"That's too bad, because we had a very good time. Well, I did. You sounded like you did."

"Just to be clear, your definition of sounding like it's a good time doesn't include your partner screaming, 'No, no, ow, stop that get off me,' does it?"

"It's been known to," Sestus admitted, "but not last night. You were pretty vocal that you wanted more and you wanted it harder."

Carson laid his head back and stared into the darkness. He tried to decide if he wanted to die, or if he wanted to kill Sestus and hide the body. And then die.

"You really don't remember?" Sestus asked, his hand now rubbing circles on Carson's chest.

"I really don't," said Carson tightly.

Sestus sat up, stretched luxuriously, winced once as he worked out a cramp in his shoulder, then flipped himself around on the bed. He ended up straddling Carson, one fist planted in the mattress on either side of Carson's shoulders.

"Then let's refresh your memory," he said.

"Sestus–" Carson began.

Sestus leaned in close and latched onto Carson's ear with his teeth.

Carson shoved him back. "Jesus Christ, you reek!"

"You didn't mind last night," Sestus observed. "But okay. We can do it in the shower."

"No," Carson replied coldly.

"But... Kevin, what–?"

Carson used one leg to lever Sestus off balance. He fell back onto the mattress. Retreating to the far corner of the bed, Carson said, "Sestus, this was a mistake. Please leave."

Disbelieving, Sestus said, "No! Fuck you!"

"You already did."

"And I told you, it was great! What's the problem?"

Carson stood and began feeling for his clothes. "Oh, am I supposed to be flattered? The great and powerful heir to Blaurich Industries found my services acceptable?"

"That's not what I mean!" Sestus shot back. "I meant I liked it! I like... being with you. I–"

"Get out, Sestus."

"No! I... What is this, is it a Terran thing? You feel guilty, because I'm a man? I thought you were okay with–"

"I'll never be okay with this," said Carson. "And not because you're a man, and not because I'm Terran. I shouldn't have... Look, Sestus, I'm sorry if I led you on or... I didn't want this."

"Why? I thought we were starting to get along."

"We were. That doesn't change who we are, Sestus. Jesus, you just published a book telling lies about my best friend. You made him look like–"

Sestus flopped back against the pillows. "Why is it always all about Metcalfe?" he moaned.

"Because he's my friend!"

"I don't see why. We're more alike, you know."

"We're nothing alike!"

"You're more open-minded than Metcalfe. You're more realistic, not so damned self-righteous." In the dim light, to which his eyes were adjusting, Carson saw Sestus smile. "You're a *much* better lover!"

For a moment, Carson considered jumping back on the bed and strangling Sestus. As he wrestled with the thought, his toe hit fabric, and he identified his pants on the floor. He pulled them on silently.

"Look, Carson," said Sestus quietly, "I won't say anything else about Metcalfe. I didn't mean to piss you off. I... I really do think we could be friends. Come back to bed. I'll take a shower and–"

"No," Carson cut him off. "No. You... stay here, that's fine. I'm going to go get cleaned up."

"Okay, you can have the bathroom first."

"No," said Carson. "I'm going to leave now. I need to get out of here."

"But–"

"If you need anything, the A.I.'s name is Galatea."

"Carson–?"

But Carson opened the door and left, not listening. He headed for Metcalfe's cabin. The door was programmed to admit him. He could use the shower there, and the A.I. would send him clothes.

Once in the room, however, its emptiness caught him off guard. Metcalfe was gone. About to be left behind on a planet which might be the first beachhead in the next Qraitian war. *Titan* would soon be speeding home without him.

Kevin Carson had always thought of himself as a loner. Now, he realized, despite that long-held self-image, he had spent most of his life not actually being alone. This morning, he felt as alone as he had since before he'd wandered into that farming village in Virginia as a boy of twelve.

His head still throbbed. Surrendering to impulse, he lay down on the bed. His friend's bed. Terry's bed. Suddenly cold, he pulled the covers over him and tried hard to summon a memory of thin, worn blankets, the chill of a Virginia morning in Spring, and two innocent children, just happy to be together.

He fell asleep and was an hour late for his duty shift.

CHAPTER TWELVE

Aer'La was back in her cargo bays and happy about it. While she had supported Admiral Fournier's plan to secure the ship by questioning all the civilians, she had to admit she hadn't enjoyed the work. Listening to the whining and pleading and outraged threats from those who felt their privacy was being violated was bad enough. Worse, though, was seeing the dead look in the eyes of those who accepted the treatment. They had learned over the courses of their lives that you couldn't argue with those in power, so you tolerate more than you probably should in an effort to not draw attention to yourself. If you were talented and lucky, you might even score a favor or become the favorite of an official who wasn't afraid to abuse his power to pay out special favors to his friends. In the eyes of these people there was always the same deadness, the same hopelessness, the same absence of any spark of rebellion.

It was the look of a slave's eyes. Aer'La had seen it too often in her short life. It was the look of the snitches and the masters' favorites who had gotten her in trouble, gotten her beaten, even gotten some of their fellows executed. Aer'La hated that look and hated those people. She hated weakness.

But right now, strength was an irritant. She thought of Metcalfe, who probably had the strongest personality among her friends. Because of Fournier's orders, their relationship had deteriorated almost to the depths it had been in when they first met, when he was the arrogant, schooled officer and she was the illiterate street trash who couldn't stand him. They'd won each others' respect over the course of months on *Arbiter*. Had they lost it again?

She hoped not. Still, she was angry with him. He didn't seem to get that you couldn't just let people who hadn't been vetted wander free among you, especially in a ship like *Titan*, where it would be so easy for one nutjob to kill everyone. He'd always been big on believing in the basic goodness of all people, and in trusting his fellows unless they gave him reason not to. Now he was taking it to extremes. She wondered if Sestus had something when he said that maybe the trauma of fighting Fehajiq had affected Metcalfe's mind.

She tried not to think about the fact that he was still on Eleusis, and they shipping out for Quintil. What if he decided to cast his lot with those pacifists in the Family, and never came back? Angry as she was, would she be okay with him being sent to Hydra Station?

She set a net of cargo crates in motion with a harder shove than she had intended and cursed as they rebounded off a bulkhead. Pushing off in freefall to catch them, she mentally kicked herself for getting distracted. She'd have chewed out any one of her crew who made such a mistake. As she reached out for the plastic net of the web, she heard a voice behind and below her.

"Bos'n!"

Hooking a leg around one of hundreds of anchor loops secured to the wall of the bay, she tightened her muscles and yanked the offending crates to a stop. Looking down, she saw Darby, floating awkwardly. How did a man float awkwardly in freefall after so many years in space? She supposed Darby was just uncomfortable wherever he went.

"Just a sec," she said. "Gotta secure this." She clipped the nearest titanium link from the net onto the same foothold she was anchored to, then kicked herself off in Darby's direction.

The idiot of course didn't have the sense to be near a wall or a handhold, like any intelligent spaceman. He'd just drifted in the hatch with barely enough inertia to move him at all. There was no way she could stop in front of him to talk. If she tried, she'd collide with him; so she set herself on course with him, took him gently by the arm, and let her momentum carry them both to the nearest handhold, where she could stop them. Darby, to his credit, was only moderately ruffled by this.

"What can I do for you, Captain Darby?" Her tone was neutral. They'd never been friends, but they had been forced to work together more closely than ever before through this crisis. They'd developed an uneasy truce.

"How many casual laborers are currently in your employ?" he asked.

She shrugged. "I'd have to check the log. Ceres keeps the numbers."

Indeed, her assistant managed all the reporting requirements of the cargo and maintenance operations at which the casuals labored. Aer'La didn't have the patience, and Ceres had a head for business like no exec at Atal Holdings could have matched. People often wondered why she was working as a casual aboard *Titan*. Aer'La fiercely discouraged speculation, and didn't ask any questions herself. A woman with a past that had caused her all too much trouble, Aer'La respected privacy... in those she felt she could trust.

"Estimate please," said Darby, rolling his eyes.

"Hundred twenty five, hundred fifty maybe."

He nodded. "Kindly have Ms. Smith provide the actual count by end of shift. We're scheduling interviews for them, beginning 0800 ship's time tomorrow. I suppose you'll want her to–"

"Uh, Captain Darby," she interrupted, "there's no need for interviews. My people are vetted."

His eyebrows raised. "What grounds do you have for making such a claim?"

"I vetted them," she said.

"Yes, well," he sniffed, "I'm sure you made a thorough job of it, no doubt you questioned them whilst they were shackled in your cabin–"

"Only the cute ones who smelled good," she corrected him.

His look of derision said that no games were going to be played today.

Aer'La sighed. "Look, Captain Darby, I promise you that I know more about my people than any background check could ever turn up."

"Bos'n, they are civilians. They are paid by the hour or the ton. They are not loyal to the Navy, or any other organization."

"They're loyal to me," said Aer'La, not trying to keep the edge out of her voice.

"They're afraid of you."

"Same thing, isn't it?" She didn't believe it was, but she enjoyed playing the part of the uncultured brute with him.

"It is not. While you have performed admirably during the course of our investigations thus far, your past record shows that you make, er, judgment calls which might not be in the best interests of the service. You've allowed contraband to be brought aboard, you've concealed evidence of criminal behavior–"

"I allowed contraband only when the rule that made it contraband was stupid," she replied.

"That isn't for you to say!"

"It damn well is. I'm in charge of these people! Does Captain Atal enforce every rule to the letter?"

He grimaced. "You're picking a poor example."

"You better watch it, Darby," she said quietly. She took a breath and continued. "As to covering for their pasts, well, if no one had done that for me, I wouldn't be here, would I?"

She knew he wanted to say that that was exactly the reason why he was in favor of questioning her people, but he seemed to have just enough brains to keep his mouth shut on that score.

"Bos'n," he said tightly, "this is not an option. The casuals *will* be questioned, beginning at 0800 tomorrow. This order comes from the Captain–"

"I doubt that!"

He cleared his throat. "Indirectly, then. The order was given by Admiral Fournier, before he transferred his flag to another ship in order to oversee the evacuation of Eleusis. Captain Atal is responsible for enforcing it, as am I, And we *will* enforce it. Clear?"

She set her jaw and stared at him for a moment. Finally she said, "I'll have Ceres schedule it. Now I have work to do." Turning, she kicked off and propelled herself away from him, as far and as fast as she could.

"I want to help you," said Ustenar.

Kaya was back in the Commander's lair, finishing the earlier, interrupted, conversation.

"You are helping me," Kaya replied in correct form. "You are taking me home."

Ustenar acknowledged the formality with a nod. "True, but let's be candid, shall we? I like you, Chhrrlk."

"I'm glad."

"You don't understand. I wouldn't like a traitor. I like warriors. You have too much of the warrior's nature to have ever wanted to join this despicable group of pacifist humans."

Kaya considered it. Was she being maneuvered into a trap? "It is my warrior's nature which caused me to realize the error of my ways."

For a few moments, Ustenar was silent. Kaya was no expert at reading Qraitian facial expressions or body language, but she believed the woman was becoming frustrated. The Commander confirmed her suspicions by slapping a claw hard against the stone on which she sat.   "I have closely studied the records of the others who betrayed us," she said. "There is a clear patten which you do not fit. They were outcasts, freaks, malcontents. Several of them have low aptitude scores. They were all incompetent warriors. Shirkers, slackers... Chhrrlk, you are none of these things!"

"You flatter me, Lady."

"And you insult my intelligence!" the other snapped, her voice raising.

Kaya was not sure what to say in answer. She decided silence was the best course of action.

The Commander went on, "If you are clever, and it is obvious you are, you will abandon pretense now. Tell me who sent you!"

Kaya felt a chill. Did she know? Had she discovered her "defectors" were human?

"Was it the Constrictors?"

Here Ustenar was using a term Kaya did not know at all, but she didn't think it referred to any group among the Confederacy. "The Constrictors..." she repeated. "No."

Ustenar made a sound of disgust which no human could have duplicated. "You say the term as if you'd never heard it, as if the Emperor's cousin and his machinations to claim the throne were not common knowledge!"

Qraitian court intrigue then. Political rivalry. Ustenar thought she was an agent of another party.

"I was merely... surprised," said Kaya. "That you would think that. The fact is that..." she took a deep breath to add emotional weight to one of the story points she and Doc Faulkner had rehearsed. "My mother was ill... dying, in fact. The elders of my family had asked her to accept suicide."

"As is proper," agreed Ustenar.

Kaya emulated a Qraitian nod. "Yes, but my mother is a healer. She believed that her case was not hopeless. She only wanted additional time to study–"

"Healers!" spat Ustenar. "Always wanting additional time. Fools! Does she want to risk the shame of a natural death? The death of a coward? Is she really willing to wait so long that she might not be able to end her own life with honor?"

"She felt the risk was worth taking, that she could learn of a cure, and add years of honorable life for others with her illness. We came here because of the stories we had heard of recovery from terrible illness."

"And you, warrior that you are, did not challenge her to battle?"

"I... she is my mother."

"Liar!" hissed the Commander. "As if any child raised within the bounds of civilization would allow its parent to proceed down a foolish course. I cannot believe that you refused to perform an honorable murder. In fact, I do not believe it."

"But–"

"Silence, Chhrrlk! You were sent by the Constrictors to disrupt this operation! Your faction wants to delay our expansion into human space and promote violence internally, so the Cousin may have his shot at the throne!"

"I don't know what you're talking about."

"Of course," said Ustenar with heavy sarcasm. "And you know nothing of the weapons systems discovered beneath the surface of Eleusis."

"I know only what you've told me," Kaya insisted. "I brought my mother here because I believed she could learn–"

"You believed she could learn how to thwart the Emperor's plan to control this world! Perhaps even to find a way to place the Eleusinian weaponry into the talons of the Constrictors! Yes, that would suit your band of vipers' needs admirably, wouldn't it? You know that our scans revealed a source of artificial, subterranean power on this world long before the humans ever came here! That the initial outpouring of Qraitian support for the human colony was a ruse, engineered to keep us on the planet, so we could monitor it. And now, as we're on the verge of claiming this power as our own, as we've learned to unleash its true, destructive potential, you think you're going to move in and take over! You want to use this power against your political enemies, instead of against the humans as the gods intended!"

"You are mistaken," said Kaya. "And I wonder... if you do suspect me, why are you telling me so much?"

"I tell you only what you already know. And I have no cause to fear, little Chhrrlk. If you step out of line, you'll simply die a little earlier than you otherwise would. You and your mother. She has already chosen to die with dishonor. Would you also choose that fate for yourself?"

Metcalfe sat alone by the lake. Upon their return from the caverns, they'd found that the Communion had ended, and everyone had returned to their homes. No one had questioned their absence from the service. Aronson had only suggested to Metcalfe that perhaps they should talk, when Metcalfe was ready.

He was not ready. Too much had happened that he did not understand. After the first Communion, and his passionate interlude with Elspeth, she'd explained to him that hearing the voice of God in one's mind was common, after Communion. Not clearly, and not in normal circumstance, of course, but the Family often heard god speak in dreams or during sex. After Communion, God's presence was ever in their minds, just below the surface. It wasn't a conversation, however. It was more of an overwhelming wash of emotion.

It was this which troubled Metcalfe. He'd forgotten most of what happened between his joining this latest Communion and the moment he had awoken in the caves with Icarus and Elspeth, but he did remember the voice in his mind. It had spoken clearly, in words, not in broad emotional strokes.

So now, while Elspeth and Icarus were finishing dinner, he had excused himself and come here alone, to pray. It was what he had done all his life when wrestling with a problem. He'd reached out to God, the one of the many gods his people believed in, the one who took special interest in him. He didn't know the god's name. That was a milestone on the walk of faith that he had not achieved. He did know that someone was listening to him, and it helped.

Sitting cross-legged before the expanse of still water, he closed his eyes and cleared his thoughts. Father Vaskis had taught him that it was best to try not to ask for things, or answers, or to pray for specific events to unfold a certain way. Still, he'd told his young charge, if you couldn't keep a pressing matter from your mind, then it was best to strip the question down to its simplest form and just focus on it.

Metcalfe had tried hard over the years to follow the old priest's advice. He wasn't good at it. His prayers tended toward monologue. He couldn't help but tell his god everything that was on his mind. What was a god, after all, if not a good listener? Now, of all times, Metcalfe needed a good listener. The thoughts and feelings which had assailed him since the battle to save Quintil were not ones he could easily share with his friends.

Tonight, however, he tried again to take Father Vaskis's advice. He framed the simple question, "What is happening to me?" and tried to focus on it.

Almost immediately, the reply came. *You are being chosen, Terry Metcalfe.*

He recognized the voice from Communion, the voice of the God of Eleusis. This was not the way prayer was supposed to work!

Are you sure? Asked the voice. *Perhaps this was always the way prayer was supposed to work, and somehow humanity fell out of practice. Come, Terry Metcalfe. Come to the cavern and talk to me.*

Can't I just talk to you here? he asked it.

There are things I want you to see.

He rose and walked. As he went, he asked, *Do you speak to others this way?*

I try, said the voice. **Few are willing or able to listen.**

And I am?

You are looking for answers. You came to this world seeking your purpose, questioning your path. You came prepared to listen.

That can't be all. Surely many others ask those same questions, seek those same things.

Very true. There is more–much more!–to you than being a humble seeker.

How much more? he wondered as he scrambled up the hill to the place of Communion. *What is it that You see in me?*

I see the One, the voice replied.

The One?

The One who is best-suited to serve and be served by this world. You are heir to the secrets of this planet you call Eleusis, Terry Metcalfe. You are chosen the be the recipient of its power.

Me? Why me? Has anyone else ever been chosen?

Many have come close, but no; no other has ever been chosen.

Then why me? Metcalfe asked again. *I just got here. I don't even know if I believe all of what the Family believes.*

I am not the God of the Family. I am... Eleusis. Call me that.

The significance of the statement was not lost on Metcalfe. For a Terran, the naming of a god was a sacred thing. For a god to come out and tell him its name...

I did not say I am a god, said Eleusis. **I am Eleusis.**

Metcalfe had now passed through the clearing and stood at the mouth of the cave. It was bathed in moonslight, but it was dark within. He hesitated.

Come inside, Terry Metcalfe. There is no danger.

Elspeth told me that those in deep communion–

You are not in a state of ecstasy. You are completely lucid and conscious. Our last contact cemented a bond between us. Come in–

Behind him, Metcalfe heard the snap of a twig and the brief scramble of brush which suggested that someone had jumped for cover beyond the edge of the path.

Someone's followed me!

He retraced his steps, searching the darkness.

It is the one who followed you earlier, said Eleusis.

The one who was reporting back to Ustenar, thought Metcalfe. An enemy agent.

Again he heard a telltale snap. Before he could fully turn in its direction, however, a weight greater than his own struck him at speed, someone had flung themselves at him from the brush. He went down hard, taking the impact in a shoulder roll. His attacker grappled with him, serpentine phalanges reaching for his throat. It was a Qraitian, as he expected.

Against the alien's superior strength, Metcalfe could do little. Talons dug into his flesh. He grasped the wrists of his opponent with both his own hands and kicked out furiously, trying to inflict as much damage as possible. Where the hell was the weak spot on a Qraitian, anyway? He had seen Icarus sheathe his penises. He knew the reproductive organs were well protected, so there was no kicking this guy in the balls.

Do not struggle so, Terry Metcalfe, said the voice of Eleusis. ***You waste energy. I will assist you.***

Suddenly, the Qraitian's grip relaxed. Metcalfe could breath again. The body on top of him went limp, and he easily rolled it off him. Standing, he stepped back to allow the light of the moons to reveal the face of his attacker. Sadly he recognized Daedalus, the father of his young friend Icarus.

Carson was on duty in the radio room when Sestus caught up with him later that shift. Carson tried to ignore him and focus on work, but Sestus was determined not to be ignored. He'd probably never been ignored in his life, and he clearly wasn't about to let Carson be the first to break his streak.

"Come on, Kevin, you've avoided me all day! "

Carson spun on him. "Why in hell do you care? We've had a few drinks, and we slept together! So what? Okay, I was a great shag, but–"

"You say that with such confidence."

Carson rolled his eyes. "Confidence hell–I'm the best shag in the Inner Worlds and you damn well know it!"

"I don't know it. I'm pretty sure I'm the best shag in the Inner Worlds. But I can't confirm since I haven't actually had sex with me."

"Not for lack of trying, I'm sure."

"Funny," scoffed Sestus. "You didn't have any complaints last night."

"I don't remember last night! Was I even conscious?"

Sestus drifted toward him, smiling despite the venom in Carson's tone. He leaned in close to his ear and whispered, "I don't know, do you usually beg for more in your sleep?"

The warm breath on his flesh sent a shiver through him. He couldn't help it. Sestus was drop dead gorgeous; but what of it? He was designed to be that way. It meant nothing. He was still an arrogant prick...

Who was now nibbling on Carson's ear.

He raised his hand and slapped Sestus on the back of the head. "Knock it off!"

"Ow!" Sestus giggled. "Why?"

"Because, dammit, Sestus I *don't like you!*"

Sestus shrugged. "Does that have to be a barrier? I've had sex with lots of people who didn't like me."

"I'm sure."

He reached for Carson again, but Carson kicked away.

Sestus grinned. "Hard-to-get turns me on, you know."

"I know. You did time for rape last year, remember?"

The grin faded. "That was Aer'La's fault."

"No, that was *your* fault. You forced yourself on someone."

"I got rough with a girl who liked it rough," said Sestus defensively. Clearly, the subject was one of the few which could make him lose his cool. "She even said so."

"She said you forced her!"

"And then she said she didn't hold it against me. It was a misunderstanding."

"How is a girl saying, 'no, stop, don't' while you try to feed her your cock a misunderstanding?"

"Because she always said that! It's part of the game! How am I to know the difference when I'm dealing with someone who usually means 'yes' when she says 'no?' How do I know this time it really means 'no?'"

"Well I really mean 'no,'" snapped Carson. "My god, Sestus, what makes you think I would even consider being your lover? You're the one who went on a holo interview and told the universe I like men!"

"You do like men. I only told the truth."

"But that's my business! It's my truth, and I didn't want it told!"

"Why?"

"Because I'm Terran, you idiot! And Terrans aren't... comfortable with that side of sexuality."

"You mean Terrans are all bigots."

"Not all... but yes, a lot of us are."

"So you wanted me to keep your secret, because you want to pander to bigots."

"No! I didn't want you to keep my secret! I didn't know you knew my secret! How was I supposed to know you'd hire the same call boy I did at the same club I go to and that he'd have no discretion?"

"Well, the call boy you hired was on Quintil, Kevin. And he's expensive. I've had every courtesan on Quintil who's expensive, boy or girl. So I was going to have yours. And Quintils don't believe in discretion about sex, because we don't think sex is a crime, like your people do."

"My people do not think sex is a crime!"

"As long as it's always with the same partner, that partner is of the opposite gender, and the match is a permanent one blessed by the Church," Sestus pointed out.

Carson sighed. "Okay. *I* don't think sex is a crime. But I am Terran, and so to me it's personal. It's not a party game, unless it's a very exclusive party. Dammit, Sestus, you invaded my privacy!"

"I did you a favor. Now you don't have to hide."

"You're a twisted fuck, Blaurich!"

"Now, Kevin–"

"A twisted fuck who commits sex crimes and pays to have them covered up, who sells other people's secrets to gossip mongers, who bullies my friends–"

"I bully your friends?"

"The first week we came aboard, you hired goons to have Metcalfe beat up!"

"He was coming on too strong. He didn't understand the way things work on a real Navy ship. He needed a lesson, and I figured a good thrashing was the only thing a Terran would understand."

"Oh, now it all makes sense! Now that you've explained the rational reasons behind your violent and bigoted behavior, I see that you're a wonderful human being! Of course I'll have sex with you!"

"Great!" Sestus began unfastening the clasps on his jacket.

"That was sarcasm, asshole."

"Was it sarcasm last night, when you told me you'd wanted me since the first moment you saw me?"

"No, it was liquor. And how do I even know I said that?"

"Ask your A.I."

"Galatea? You let Galatea *watch*?"

"Why not? I like to have a record of my sexual encounters. Gives me something to watch during quiet moments alone."

"Fine. I'll send you a copy of the file. Happy masturbating."

"In vino veritas, Carson. You told me you wanted me. You know it's true."

"Get out."

"It's true."

"I said–"

"Why can't you admit you find me attractive? Are you afraid of what Metcalfe might think?"

Carson didn't actually realize that he'd launched himself at Sestus until their bodies collided and he had the other man by his collar. He vaguely heard a voice call someone a son of a bitch, and he recognized the voice as his own. Blinded with rage, he tried to slam Sestus's head against the wall, but his anger caused him to miscalculate the force and trajectory of his attack in zero-G. They both rebounded off the wall and went careening, grappling with each other, about the small cabin.

He held on to Sestus's coat fiercely with one hand, flailing with the other, trying to strike his opponent anywhere he could. He wanted Sestus bloodied. He wanted to beat him until he could no longer move. The bastard!

Sestus eluded his blows, then levered himself up and seized Carson by his own collar with both hands. Carson attempted a head butt, but his quarry twisted, then ducked back toward him and, unexpectedly, kissed him full on his open mouth. Carson cried out, but the cry was strangled. Sestus's tongue danced against his, insistent and wanting. Carson's own tongue responded, unbidden. Then so did the rest of his body. He wanted to beat the shit out of Sestus, but this felt so *good*. He had been so busy with the battle at Quintil and the refit of *Titan* that had followed, that it had been a while.

Sestus had wrestled Carson's pants off and was floating under him, doing incredible things with his tongue, when the hatch alarm sounded, indicating that someone was trying to enter, but the mechanical lock was set.

"What the hell?" panted Carson.

"I locked the door, idiot! I came here to have sex!"

Carson pulled away from him and made a mad grab for his pants, floating just out of reach. He only managed to brush them and send them flying farther away.

"Now whoever's out there knows there's something up!"

Indeed, there was a knock at the hatch.

"It's probably no one," Sestus laughed. He called out to the A.I. to identify the visitor.

He went pale when the mechanized voice (the Radio Room A.I. was not set with a humanized persona) replied, "Fournier, Admiral G."

"Oh, sure! It's nobody!" hissed Carson.

A muffled voice called out, annoyed. "Mister Blaurich? What the devil's the matter with this lock?"

"He knows you're here!"

"Fine! Maybe he doesn't know you are!" He called out loudly, "One moment, sir! It appears to have jammed!"

"But—"

Carson's protest was lost as Sestus snatched him by the back of his coat and, with the reflexes of trained aerialist, pitched him toward an open storage closet. Grabbing his free-floating pants, Sestus tossed them in behind him, and, with a well-placed slap on Carson's bare ass, closed the door. Carson barely heard him mutter, "Now keep your talented lips shut!"

In the darkness, Carson tried to wriggle back into his pants. The space was entirely too small. Oh well, if Fournier happened to open the door and find a midshipman stuffed into a storage cubicle, would the presence or absence of pants make that much difference?

The hatch cycled open outside. He pressed his ear against the closet door and listened, hoping that the Admiral would not suspect what he had actually interrupted.

"What happened?" he heard Fournier demand.

"This was caught in the actuator. Carson must have left it out."

Carson didn't know what object was being credited with jamming the hatch, but he nonetheless made plans to insert it, unlubed, into his ardent would-be lover when he escaped his confinement.

Fournier muttered something uncomplimentary, then asked Sestus what he was doing here.

"Covering for Carson for a few minutes," was the answer. "The Captain gave him permission to send a last message to Metcalfe before we left orbit."

"Wouldn't it have made sense to send that from the radio room?"

"Er—it would. Carson needed more privacy. Um... Terran religious thing."

Carson couldn't hear a head shake, of course, but he knew Fournier's was doing just that.

"Well, I'm glad the ship's computer was able to locate you quickly. I need you to get packed and transfer to the *Henley* as soon as possible."

"Sir?"

"You're taking command for the duration of this mission."

"Thank you, sir! May I ask why?"

"Because I need someone I can trust keeping an eye on that Qraitian ship while I go to Eleusis and oversee the evacuation. We're going to take the colonists by force in–"

"–Seventy-two hours, yes."

"No. In twenty-four hours."

"But the announced deadline–"

"Would give them time to prepare some sort of idiotic protest, possibly to hide the Qraitians among them, or lose themselves in those caves near the settlement. I'm not going to give them that chance. We're taking them early."

"Strategically sound, sir."

"Qraitians are to be separated and imprisoned, as are known Qraitian sympathizers. I understand your colleague Mr. Metcalfe may have placed himself in the latter category. This might prove an interesting assignment."

Carson swore despite himself. There must be some way to get word to Metcalfe, but he didn't dare send a standard radio signal. And it would be contrary to orders, downright treasonous. If he were caught, he might even be executed.

"You are not to breathe a word to Atal. Clear?"

"Clear, sir."

"Good. You'll be in command of the operation, Sestus. It'll be good publicity for you. I had thought about sending the Atal girl as well, but she's apparently under some ridiculous quarantine. Never mind. You leading the mission alone is better. Do you understand the opportunity I'm offering you?"

"Yes sir. Thank you!"

"Good. Gather your things and than report to me aboard the *Henley*."

Carson heard the hatch close again. A few seconds later, the door opened and light bathed him. Sestus, smirking, offered him a hand. Carson knocked it aside and, grabbing the door frame, hefted himself out.

"Hear that?" Sestus asked. "He's going to make me a Captain!"

"I doubt it. Seeing you as a Captain takes a lot of imagination, and he has none."

Carson, out of confinement, moved to get dressed again. What had Sestus been thinking, anyway, seducing him while they were both on duty?

Whatever it was, he was apparently still thinking it, for he blocked Carson's attempts to reclothe himself, and his hands resumed their interrupted work. Carson wanted him to stop, truly he did.

Sestus nuzzled his cheek and whispered. "I'll request you aboard my first command."

"I'll already be dead and cracking ice in hell," Carson replied, but he stopped fighting Sestus's efforts and pulled him closer.

"You're an ungrateful bastard, Carson."

"Shut up and get your clothes off."

CHAPTER THIRTEEN

"I've got something," said Celia Faulkner when Kaya returned to the lair they shared. She was still hunched over her implant.

"What were you going to say if someone found you doing that?"

Celia shrugged. "That I was corrupted by my time among humans, that they gave me an implant, and that I was studying the death rituals so as not to bring disgrace on my family."

"You're good."

"Kid, you have no idea."

"What have you found?"

"Collected intel on the... whatever it is on Eleusis. Watch."

She tapped the virtual keyboard before her, and a holo appeared between them. The scene was a forested hillside on Eleusis, probably near the Communion grotto Kaya and Pallas had explored. Several young people, boys and girls, walked ahead of the unidentified person recording the scene. They carried backpacks and water bottles, as though out for a day trip at least. A few of them were Qraitian. Kaya also recognized Brock Aronson from briefing images. She'd met none of the Family in person while she was there.

"See that? The bright red thing?" Faulkner pointed. Along the path hikers followed, a small mammal was curled up, apparently dead, near a clump of foliage.

"Some kind of animal," said Kaya. "Eleusis's answer to a squirrel? It's cute."

"Well, if you see one, don't pick it up and give it a cuddle. It's an evil squirrel from hell. The species is native to Eleusis, and was catalogued by the first exploratory ships. They're carnivorous, and eat larger fauna. Their fangs inject a venom similar to a cobra's. It can paralyze a creature up to the size of a horse. If not treated immediately, it's fatal to humans."

"Oh no!" Kaya cried. The boy in the lead of the procession had stepped on the creature's tail. The resulting shriek caused him to leap into the air, away from his would-be attacker, and caused the others in the party to scatter. The small creature, angered, hesitated only a moment before pouncing at its frightened quarry, fangs bared, ready to strike. All the humans and Qraitians screamed. Then, in mid leap, the predator vanished.

"Just like the Qraitian soldier!" said Kaya in amazement.

"There are more clips. Apparently recorded by their agent below and transmitted to Ustenar. That's why your pair was nosing around the cave. It seems to be the center of activity. Watch this one."

Two humans this time, an adult male and female, were at the cavern entrance where Kaya had seen the first disappearance. The vantage point was not close by. Whoever recorded this was following at a distance, observing stealthily, even as Kaya and Pallas had just a short time ago.

The pair started to enter, and a fall of rocks suddenly cut loose from the ceiling just inside the mouth of the cave. They both scampered back, miraculously unhurt. The fall had done its work on them, however. They quickly left the area.

"They were lucky," said Kaya.

"Not at all," Faulkner countered. "Watch it again, slowed down."

She repeated the holo clip, beginning at the moment the rocks first fell. This time, Kaya could see that several larger chunks were on a trajectory for the intruding couple. As each came within inches of its target, however, it vanished. Dozens, hundreds of others fell unhindered.

"Something didn't want them hurt," observed Kaya.

Faulkner nodded. "And yet something also appears to have triggered the falling rock. It came from nowhere. It's as if this was a gentle, harmless warning. Now, look at this last one."

Children played on the lake, swimming and happily splashing each other. Kaya smiled. It really was a beautiful place, and such a peaceful life! Suddenly, one small, red-headed girl, looking to be about eight, waved an arm as though in distress. Kaya could see from the expression on her face that the child was in pain. She called out to her fellows that she had a cramp, and begged for help.

"I'll spare you the ensuing drama," said Celia. "It's hard to watch. The poor thing was in deep water, and her playmates were not strong enough swimmers. The bastard recording this was close enough to help, but apparently wanted to wait and see what would happen."

"How did he... or she... happen to catch this incident in particular?" asked Kaya as the image faded and Faulkner searched for her next reference.

"He... she... didn't," explained Faulkner. "You've no idea how many thousands of hours of records there are. Someone's watching every damned thing the Family does. But these entries were flagged. Here we are."

The red-headed girl was out of the water now, but not out of danger. Kaya felt herself flinch at the blueish tinge of her skin. Brock Aronson hunched over her, his hands moving frantically over her limbs, attempting to restore circulation. After a few moments with no sign of improvement, he performed mouth to mouth. Still the child did not respond.

"The girl was dead," said Faulkner cooly. "The other children hadn't gotten her out in time. It was too many minutes before Aronson or any other adult was fetched. Saved alongside the holo records were her vitals. Cardiopulmonary resuscitation would not have revived her alone. Defibrillation likewise. If I had her in a hospital, I might–might!–have brought her back. As a vegetable, most likely. But watch..."

As Aronson, despair creeping onto his face, slowed his efforts and looked sadly at the pathetic, lifeless little form, the girl began to cough. The elder's eyes wide, he reached to check her pulse. His astonished smile confirmed it was present.

Celia stopped the image.

"The damned thing... whatever it was... brought a dead child back to life."

Kaya shook her head. "You'll forgive me if I can't get past the fact that someone recorded that incident, and just let it play out. Someone who could have saved the girl long before miracle cures were necessary."

"True," agreed Celia. "I suppose we must remember that this... someone... had every reason to suspect that events would transpire the way they did."

"That's no excuse," said Kaya. "Letting a child die..."

"Warriors throughout our history have justified letting children die. Need I remind you that you're but a child to me, and yet, here you are, by my side in mortal danger."

"I made my own choice, Doc. That little girl didn't."

"I sympathize, Kaya, but please focus on the bigger issue at hand. There's a force on that planet with the power of life and death. We've seen it in action repeatedly now. Whenever the family is in danger, the threat just disappears. And it's so powerful it can restore the dead. Imagine what it might do to a ship that tries to attack Eleusis. Or to troops who attempt to use violence against the family. It had no compunctions about killing that Qraitian."

Kaya triggered her own implant to life. "We have to warn the Captain."

"It's risky," said Celia.

Kaya did not look up from her work, manipulating the small communications booster she had smuggled within her suit to allow her implant to encrypt and transmit a signal to *Titan*. "It is," she agreed. "But they have to know."

"The Captain is already aware that there are weapons down there, Kaya. It's why we're here."

"He doesn't know that the Qraitians have been aware of this weaponry for years, that they've been studying it all along, and that many of their people who have come here were undercover agents. They have likely now identified the method for triggering the power of Eleusis. Violence directed at the Family seems to be the key."

"All you have to do is anger the Eleusinian god," agreed Celia. "Trying to enlist the gods in your battles is a dangerous business."

"I don't believe this... whatever it is... is a god, Doc. I think there's an intelligence there, directing a lot of power."

"Sentient?"

"I don't know about sentience. It may only be some kind of automatic system. If it's got any decision making capability, though... well, the most troublesome aspect of any system designed to make decisions is that it can be outsmarted."

"They've got to know, you're right. Before they do something stupid."

Kaya made a final adjustment to the encryption routine and said, with satisfaction, "There. That should do it." She keyed her implant to begin uploading her prepared message.

As a graphic appeared in the air, showing the upload progress, Celia asked, "Do you think all the Qraitians below are really just masquerading as members of the Family?"

"Ustenar doesn't seem to believe that, no. She–"

The door to the corridor suddenly dilated open. Kaya quickly killed her implant's holo signal as Ustenar and two guards entered the room.

"Well," said the Commander. "Sending letters home, are we?"

Kaya was silent. There was nothing to say now.

Ustenar sighed. "Did you really think a signal could leave this ship without being noticed?" She turned to one of her guards. "Where was it going, Legionnaire?"

"To the Confederate vessel," the Qraitian male who had been guarding them announced. "To the *Titan*."

The Commander nodded. "Can we decode it?"

"Doubtful."

"Of course." She looked to Kaya. "Not satisfied to merely monitor our progress then, are you, Constrictor? You would actually ally yourselves with the humans? Try to enlist them to your cause? No doubt you intend to foment battle between us, in hopes that we might all be destroyed and leave this planet's secrets ripe for your party's picking."

When Kaya did not answer, the Qraitian woman advanced on her.

"Well?" Ustenar demanded.

"You seem to have it all figured out," said Kaya.

Ustenar spat in her face. Kaya ignored the gesture and resolutely held the Commander's eyes.

Turning back to the guard, Ustenar said, "Bring them both on deck. Order all personnel to report and witness the execution."

Ceres approached Aer'La in the office they shared. Aer'La didn't care for offices, but was entitled to one. She'd largely signed it over to Ceres, visiting only when reports absolutely had to be reviewed. 'Reviewing,' for Aer'La, meant putting her sig on the work Ceres had done, usually without reading it at all. Ceres had a head for the petty details and never failed to tell Aer'La about the important things.

"You'd better look at this one," she said, frowning. "First round of questioning. Twelve people missing an entire shift."

Aer'La rolled her eyes. "This is so stupid!"

Ceres watched her carefully. Aer'La could tell she wanted to say something, but wasn't sure she should. "Spill it," she finally told her assistant.

"You were in favor of these interrogations before."

"When they were of civilians, yeah."

"Our people are all civilians, technically."

"Our people are better screened than any snots out of the Academy!" Aer'La shot back. When Ceres said nothing, she asked, "Do you think I'm wrong to be annoyed?"

Ceres shook her head. "No. I guess I was just... surprised... that you weren't annoyed before this."

"Meaning?"

"Meaning it's not like you, Aer'La. You don't usually go along with policies which lock down people's ability to come and go as they please. I thought authoritarian measures went against your grain."

"Now you sound like Metcalfe!"

"Is he wrong?"

Aer'La whirled furiously, causing Ceres to back up. She was immediately sorry she had done it. Ceres was the last person she wanted to scare. She couldn't do her job without Ceres. Forcing herself to be calm, she said, "Yes, he's wrong. At least about the civilians. The Qraitians are a threat, Ceres, a real one. It may not seem like a nice thing to do, but... tightening security will keep us all safe."

"Will it?"

Aer'La shook her head. "I don't know. I just know... we have to do *something*. We have to be able to protect ourselves."

It was only an hour or so after their passionate encounter that Sestus re-appeared in the radio room, his bag strapped to his shoulders, obviously ready to depart. "I came to say goodbye."

"Okay," Carson acknowledged, only barely looking up at him, "goodbye."

"That's it?"

"What do you want?" asked Carson, "my goddamned scarf to carry with you on the crusades?"

"You're still mad at me?"

"I don't know what I am."

"You know," said Sestus with an edge of concern in his voice, "that you can't tell anyone what you overheard."

"I know. I don't like it, but I know. What did you tell Captain Atal?"

"Only that I've been asked to remain and assist the Admiral. He wished me luck."

"I bet."

"So... we're going to leave it this way?"

Carson blew out a hard breath. "There's no 'it' to leave, Sestus. There's nothing between us, all right? Just some crazy physical attraction that I don't even understand. Thanks for the sex, now go be the Military Prince of Industry, bring civilization to the savages, drive off the invading lizard hordes, and, while you're at it, be sure to tell my best friend I said 'hi' before you lock him in his cell and throw away the key."

"I won't–" Sestus began. He fumbled for words. "If Metcalfe cooperates, he won't be arrested."

"Metcalfe and 'cooperate' are not two words which go together."

"So why are you so hung up on him?"

"I'm not. We grew up together. He was the only friend available."

"Well, in case you haven't noticed, he's not available any more. And I am."

"You're leaving too."

"Yes, but... I'll be back.:"

"And Metcalfe will rot in jail."

"I... I hope he doesn't."

"Be better for your career if he does."

"Do you really think I'm that shallow? Why did you sleep with me then?"

Carson spun and said coldly, "Because I'm a whore, Sestus, just like you. Both of us, whores, just looking for a free drink and a good time, and whatever else we can get. Don't look for loyalty, because people like us don't have any."

Sestus swallowed. He stared at Carson until the other, fed up, said, "You have a mission, Blaurich. Don't keep the Admiral waiting."

Daedalus walked ahead of Metcalfe, the Lieutenant's gun pressed firmly against his spine. "You don't have to do that," said the elder Qraitian. "I promised you I wouldn't resist any further."

"And I'm supposed to trust the word of an admitted spy?"

"I may be a spy, and so deception is a necessary part of my job. I am still a Qraitian, however. We take our word of honor very seriously. As I recall," he said, narrowing his already slitted eyes, "it is you, Mr. Metcalfe, who have proven yourself deserving of the label 'trickster.'"

"We don't trust each other. Let's just leave it at that. If you could, you'd kill me, so no one in the Family would know you're a spy."

"Very true. I would consider it a signal honor to kill you."

"Is there a price on my head because I killed so many of your people?"

"Certainly not! Among Qraitians, such things as bounties don't exist. There are far greater benefits to be gained from a fortuitous killing. When we kill one of our own, we assume all that is his: his property, his family, his wealth... or his debts. In addition, a killer also earns his quarry's status."

"But I'm not one of your people."

"Quite the contrary, Mr. Metcalfe. On the day you took thirty-eight Qraitian lives, you became a member of Qraitian civil society. Your status is not grand, but it is above that of all of those who defected to join the Family, as well as that of prisoners, the menial classes, and the enlisted ranks of our military."

"I don't understand."

"You eliminated thirty-eight embarrassing non-conformists from our midst. You did so by displaying superior strategic skill and cunning. You served our Empire, and admirably."

"I would have thought letting all of Quintil die would serve your Empire."

"To kill by deception, and leave us a once-valuable resource, worthless, bombarded with poisonous Senterium-K? If ever we conquer your home world–"

"Not my home world."

"Just the same, if ever we conquer any of your worlds, we will do so in honorable battle, leaving as many of your people as possible alive to serve us, and leaving your resources intact. There is no honor in simply killing."

"Fehajiq didn't see it that way."

"Fehajiq is an extremist and a mental defective!" hissed Daedalus. "I know, for I taught him when he was young. As the warrior who defeated him, you are highly regarded in Qraitian society."

"I suppose I could walk right into the Emperor's palace and demand an audience."

"Certainly you could!"

"Really?"

"Absolutely! He would be delighted to speak with you. He might even offer you a meal of the tenderest rodents before your death."

"Death? I knew there'd be a catch."

"Oh, he'd put you to death, of course. But, as a Qraitian of status and a guest of the Emperor, none other would dare touch you, except by his direct command."

"But if you kill me here–"

"My own status would be elevated."

"Sorry, but that won't be happening."

"I agree with you, sad to say. The creature, whatever it is, will protect you."

"Creature?" asked Metcalfe.

"The one they call 'God.' It has bonded with you, perhaps even more so than it has with the rest of the Family. It will kill anyone who threatens them, or you."

"As it killed your legionnaire the other day?"

"Yes. We had suspected it from observation already. We'd seen predators–mammals and reptiles as well–simply disappear when a member of the Family was in danger. Our man, the one who tried to silence the father and his children, only proved our suspicions."

"I'm still keeping the gun at ready," said Metcalfe. Just for safety's sake, he also verified that Daedalus's weapon was still holstered on his own hip, where he had secured it after divesting his opponent of it. It had surprised him, at first, when he'd not been asked to remove his sidearm as a guest of the Family. He'd thought that pacifists would naturally eschew arms. Aronson had explained that it was standard practice for the colonists to go armed, both for purposes of hunting meat to eat and for protection from wildlife. If what Daedalus claimed was true, of course, this second reason did not stand. Still, Aronson had pointed out that his spiritual ancestors had been armed as they'd pioneered North America on Terra. Eleusis was not a very different environment.

Daedalus continued to lead the way in the direction they had started out an hour ago. The Voice of Eleusis had guided them–or guided Metcalfe, rather–into a hitherto unseen offshoot in the numerous tunnels beneath the lake. It led rather far away from the cathedral which he, Elspeth and Icarus had found, wandering on their own.

Cathedral. The word pricked at his subconscious. When had he started to think of the domed opening in that sense?

Since they'd started on their journey, the Voice had been silent. There had been no choice to make, except to keep going or turn back. No guidance was required. The Voice wanted him to see something, Metcalfe knew, and it was up here, further along.

"It ends here," announced Daedalus as their lanterns illuminated the space ahead. Accustomed to darkness, the Qraitian's eyes picked up more quickly than Metcalfe's on the sights which were to be seen.

Metcalfe stepped forward, inspecting the walls. Indeed, they seemed to draw together. Had the voice led them to a dead end? Or had he missed an instruction? The slightest anxiety crept over Metcalfe, as well as a mild claustrophobia. He hated being lost, and to be lost in a cave where the tunnel opening suddenly dwindled down to nothing was too much like nightmares he'd had. He turned and shone his light back in the direction they'd come, half expecting to see that there, too was a solid wall. He was relieved to see that nothing had changed, and reprimanded himself for being foolishly emotional.

Daedalus inspected the closed-off end of the tunnel. "There's a flat place here. It's not a natural formation."

"Are you sure?" wondered Metcalfe.

"Friend Metcalfe, my people are born and bred beneath our worlds' surfaces. We know the characteristics of tunnels, I assure you. This has been sealed artificially."

Metcalfe studied what he now saw was a squared-off section of the cave wall. In the low light, he could see little, and so used his hands to get a sense of it. It occurred to him that, in the dark, he might drag his fingers across something alive, a "creepy crawly," Lydia would have called it. Then he reflected that his companion in exploration was more closely related to a snake than he was to a human, and that one of his dearest wishes was to kill Metcalfe. Creepy crawlies suddenly seemed benign. There was peace of mind in putting the threats in your surroundings into perspective in relation to each other.

This peace of mind did not prevent him from jumping backward and having to cut off a yelp of surprise when, in response to his probing fingers, the wall suddenly opened. He stumbled over his own feet, and Daedalus steadied him, a taloned "hand" on his shoulder.

"Thanks," said Metcalfe. Then, realizing that he had neglected to keep the gun on his opponent for some moments, he decided the whole "at gunpoint" business was silly and crammed the sidearm into his belt.

"A door," observed Daedalus. "Mechanized."

"And powered," agreed Metcalfe. "But powered by what? This place... " He craned his neck and looked into the darkness beyond the opening, saw the rubble at his feet, where the door had cleaned itself of scale and dust as it retracted into the wall. "It's old as hell."

"How old is hell?" asked Daedalus seriously.

Metcalfe shook his head. It was just an expression. "Ever so much more than twenty," he muttered.

"Shall we go in?" Daedalus wondered.

"It would seem to be the plan," said Metcalfe. The voice had told him to follow the path, and answers would be his. He wasn't sure just what the voice was, but he did want answers. "Here goes," he said, and took a step inside.

Immediately, light flared in the opening beyond the door. Metcalfe suppressed any reaction this time, and kept up his pace.

Daedalus, following him, said, "Automatic lights. As if they were expecting someone."

"Or just waiting for the next visitor. Maybe it's even on a motion sensor."

They were in another tunnel, or corridor, more aptly. In this one, the walls of the cavern were carefully shaped. Flat sections could be seen where outcrops of rock had been trimmed away and smoothed down. It was only a small chamber, but clean. Rocks did not litter the floor, only dust. Ahead was another door, metallic this time, or perhaps the last one was metallic too, and twin to this one. The outer one had been exposed to the elements for... how long? This one had not.

"Another door," said Daedalus. "I wonder if it opens–"

Before he could say, "The same way," or "as easily," Metcalfe had proven both conditions held. The second door flashed into the wall. Beyond, a second set of lights activated at their presence.

Both men gasped.

They had seen a ruined cathedral. They had seen a millennia-old mechanism function under power to open a door. Now they saw a city which rivaled any metropolis on either of their worlds, stretching out before them for miles, here beneath the ground. For Metcalfe, it was like discovering fabled Atlantis or Manhattan, both mythical cities long ago sunk beneath the sea. One might never have existed at all. The other was the subject of too many incredible stories for all of them to be true. Here on Eleusis was another mythical, lost city. Dead. Buried. Yet still intact and amazing.

Neither led the way now. They walked side by side, marveling at their find. That a past civilization had thrived and died here, no one doubted. Yet none suspected that beneath the lush surface of beautiful Eleusis was this magnificent achievement. Spires climbed so high they actually touched the sky, for the sky in this place was the roof of the cavern. Sweeping, elevated roadways hinted at powered transportation. Few windows were in evidence, for there was no sunlight to illuminate a landscape. Artificial light glowed all around, making this a city of lights in the midst of darkness. On Terra, Paris still existed, despite the destruction around it. Metcalfe had never been there, but he knew it, too was called a city of lights. He imagined it must look a great deal like this.

Paris, however, was alive, inhabited. Despite the overwhelming sense of wonder he felt, Metcalfe had to admit that this place felt... haunted.

"Where does the light come from?" Daedalus wondered aloud. "What power source could last this long?"

"Geo-thermal, maybe?" Metcalfe suggested. He did not stop to wonder how the term would translate into the Qraitian's tongue, or if Daedalus would recognize the Terran standard. He looked around. "This must be where they lived, the people who used the Cathedral. I wonder what they looked like. We know they weren't human, or even humanoid. Judging by their architecture, they were a lot bigger."

Daedalus pointed to his right. "Metcalfe, that structure has windows."

Indeed, squatting just off the raised stone walkway on which they'd traveled into the edge of the city, a geodesic dome structure was coming to life at their approach. Lights flared on within, revealed through floor-to-ceiling windows on every side. It looked like a giant's gazebo. Within were curved structures which might have served the function of chairs for whatever beings once lived on Eleusis. They were arranged in a ring, facing the center of the dome. In front of each was a circular disk, suspended by a cable.

"Data terminals, I'm sure," said Daedalus.

Metcalfe nodded. "Given the proximity to the city's entrance, and the fact that it's one of the few buildings you can see into, probably a welcome center of some sort. Visitors would see that this was where they could come for information."

"And it did light up in welcome," said the Qraitian.

"Okay. Let's accept some hospitality." Metcalfe strode to the building's nearest entrance. There were four, situated ninety degrees apart along its perimeter. He completely forgot any threat Daedalus might offer. It seemed that Daedalus had also forgotten that he might wish to be threatening. He followed the human's lead into the building.

The door they approached opened even more readily than had the tunnel doors. As far as the facilities here were concerned, it might have been yesterday, or just minutes ago, when the last inhabitants walked the city byways.

Within, the air smelled of age, the stagnant mustiness of rooms long unused. Everything was in good condition, however, if dusty. Metcalfe approached one of the stations and slid into the large seat.

"Do you think it will still work?" asked Daedalus.

"If we can figure out how to activate it. The doors responded to motion or touch–" With his fingers, he brushed the disk before him, having to stretch to reach its surface. It flared obediently to life, displaying symbols and glowing, alien characters.

"Now if only we could read it," the Qraitian said.

Metcalfe studied the display. "This," he pointed at a small pictogram, a circle containing lines, "could be a map."

He touched it. A diagram filled the screen.

"It is a map," said Daedalus. "Of this city, it looks like."

"Could be," agreed Metcalfe.

At the bottom of the map, at four and seven o'clock on the circle, were two symbols which Metcalfe took to be previous and next indicators. He pressed the four o'clock one. The image changed. A new map appeared.

Daedalus leaned in over his shoulder. "Another city?"

"Or a view of this city at a different time?"

"I don't think so," said Daedalus.

Another touch of the same button produced a third, similar map. He then touched on of a series of circles, graduated by size, along the top 90 degrees of the map. The map zoomed in, focusing on the center of the city.

"I think I'm getting the hang of this," he said. He touched another circle and the view zoomed out. The city shrank to the center of the image. On either side were the lines which logically represented tunnels. They seemed to lead to other diagramed developments. "Wow," Metcalfe muttered. He touched another circle, zooming the map out as far as it would go.

"Multiple cities," observed Daedalus. "Ringing this central area."

"That must be the cathedral," said Metcalfe.

"Cathedral?"

"It's a... gathering place, we think. We found it earlier, Icarus and Elspeth and I." He wondered if Daedalus would react to the mention of his son's name. He did not.

"So this was only a single warren. An amazing complex!"

"I wonder if any of the other cities are still intact," said Metcalfe. "Or what happened to the inhabitants." He started to lean back, realized that there was no support behind him, balanced and crossed his arms. "Do you think it only has maps? How do you suppose we ask it for more information?"

A voice rang out in the air. "Additional information is available. Please provide a specific question or subject area."

Metcalfe felt his eyes go wide. He knew that voice, though he had not heard it aloud. It was the Voice of Eleusis, the voice of God.

"Qraitian," said Daedalus.

"What?" muttered Metcalfe, then realized what Daedalus meant. "No. I heard it in Confederate Standard."

"Interesting. Telepathy?"

"That wasn't telepathy. It spoke aloud."

"This station," said the voice, "is capable of communicating in any language of the user's choice, or of directing multiple languages to multiple users on tightly focused, localized audio transmissions."

"It can create sound right in our ears," said Metcalfe.

"That is correct," said the Voice.

"Have I spoken to you before?" asked Metcalfe. "Do you know who I am?"

"This station is intended for information and referral only. A list of services provided is available upon request. It does not have access to personal data on any citizen, for security and privacy reasons. To maintain a list of secured nodes, please specify the service desired."

"That's okay," said Metcalfe.

Daedalus studied him. "What is wrong, Mr. Metcalfe? Why did you ask if it knew you?"

"It's just... I know that voice. That's the voice that's been speaking to me. Only here it's, it's just an A.I., a computer of some sort."

"You've been hearing voices?" asked the Qraitian.

"Just one voice. Since the first Communion I had. It was unreal, at first, like a dream, but then... right before I found you, it was starting to become outright chatty."

"And it stopped when I appeared?"

"Just after. The last instruction was to follow the tunnel that brought us here."

"But that voice was inside your head?"

"Yes. Like telepathy. But it was this same voice. I recognized it immediately."

"Metcalfe, this appears to be a simple civic administration A.I."

Metcalfe looked at the screen before him, shaking his head. "Not simple. There's nothing simple about it. Whatever this is, it's survived the destruction of an entire civilization, and it's still operating, still waiting for someone to interact. These units have limited functionality, but they're all part of a network." He tapped the screen, as a child tapped a parent for attention. "Is that correct?"

The Voice of Eleusis, or a flat, emotionless copy of it, answered, "This station is a node in the comprehensive data network. That is correct."

"And there are nodes with higher levels of access, correct?"

"That is correct. For a list of—"

"That's not necessary. Is there a node which has access to all the stored information in the comprehensive network?"

"You are referring to a supernode."

"Can you give me a list of supernodes?"

"I cannot. Supernodes are restricted to access by Program Engineers. No citizen or visitor may access a supernode, for security reasons."

"Do supernodes control all other functions of this network?"

The answer chilled him. "Supernodes control all that is."

"Wow," said Metcalfe, wonderingly.

"Mr. Metcalfe?" prompted Daedalus. "What are you thinking?"

"I'm thinking, Daedalus that we've found 'God.' He—it—is an artificial intelligence, part of a network which once controlled these cities. This workstation was limited to pedestrian use, but the network itself was so powerful that—"

Metcalfe stopped, realizing that Daedalus was silent. Of course he was silent, Metcalfe was in the middle of a sentence, but... something was different. He eyed the Qraitian, reached out and took his arm. Daedalus did not respond. He did not move at all. Leaning in close, Metcalfe could not even hear the sound of breath, and yet he did not think Daedalus was dead.

"What the hell—?" he said out loud.

I have stopped the Qraitian's mind temporarily, Terry Metcalfe.

It was the Voice again, but this time inside his head, this time the full, rich, Voice of Eleusis. Within its tones lay intelligence and passion, not like the audio of this computer terminal in front of Metcalfe. This was... God.

"Why have you... stopped him?"

Because I do not wish him to attempt to escape, or to harm you. We need time. We need to talk. You came seeking truth. Open your mind. Here it is.

On this day, my friend, you shall become immortal...

CHAPTER FOURTEEN

Aer'La was eating alone in the mess hall. Everyone was so busy lately that she rarely saw any of the others, except occasionally Cernaq. This morning she was just coming off a double shift, the result of Darby's pulling all her people in for questioning and leaving her short. She had cleaned her plate and was about to return for her traditional second helping of bacon when she realized that someone was standing over her, looking down. It was a woman, not unattractive, well-dressed, obviously a Quintil. She had that oh-so-educated, oh-so-cultured air about her.

"Bos'n Aer'La?" she asked.

Aer'La sniffed. She wore too much perfume. "Yeah?"

The woman put out her hand. "I'm Lucinda Grae."

Aer'La didn't take the hand. "Metcalfe's shrink."

Grae looked uncomfortable, but nodded. "I'm providing him with counseling, yes. We don't care for the term–"

"What do you want?"

Grae cleared her throat. "Uh... may I sit down?"

Aer'La shrugged. "Navy's chairs, not mine. Can't promise I'm staying, though. Got work to do."

"You just came off a double shift."

Aer'La glared at her. "You know that how?"

Grae smiled professionally. "I was assigned to monitor the crew following the Fehajiq incident. I have access to the schedules—"

"Stay out of mine."

"Aer'La, I only want to talk."

"About what?"

"I thought... maybe if there's anything on your mind—"

"Metcalfe's gone, so you're bored? Drumming up business?"

"Actually, my sessions with Mr. Metcalfe—I can't really discuss them, of course—but they've led me to believe that perhaps you... that is—"

"He told you I'm nuts?"

"I don't like that word."

"Then you'd hate what I'm thinking."

"I'm sorry if I've upset you. I just wanted to let you know I'm available if you need to talk."

"Because Metcalfe said I'm losing it."

"He didn't, no."

"What did he say?"

"I can't tell you specifically. I drew the conclusion that you suffered some emotional trauma—"

Aer'La laughed coldly. "I've been suffering emotional trauma my whole life. I don't need anyone poking around inside my head. I can deal with it."

"Deal with what?"

"With—I don't—why am I talking to you?"

"Maybe you need someone to talk to."

"I don't!"

"You seem very hostile. Is there a reason?"

"Yeah! I hate people who don't mind their own business!"

Grae sat for a moment, looking at the table. She said quietly, "I didn't mean to upset you. I'll leave you alone—" She started to get up.

"He's pissed at me for helping Fournier, isn't he?" said Aer'La suddenly.

"He... didn't say."

She nodded. "That's what it is. He can't stand the thought that Fournier might be right for once. Well he is right. And... " she sighed, a low growl, really. "Maybe you're right, too. I almost died out in space when Fehajiq attacked. It... it was rough. I'm dealing with it! But it reminded me how easy any of us could go. I'm just doing everything I can to keep the people I love safe. Even Metcalfe. Even when he's being an asshole."

"You're dealing with it?"

"Don't start!"

"I just mean... any nightmares, or–?"

"It's none of your damn business!" said Aer'La. She stood and moved to leave.

"Aer'La, if you change your mind..." Grae called after her.

Over her shoulder, Aer'La snapped, "Leave me alone!"

She left the mess hall and headed to her cabin. It was an hour before she realized she'd forgotten to get her damned second helping of bacon.

When Metcalfe returned, once again leading Daedalus and holding a gun on him, Icarus was the first to see them walk into the clearing at the center of the Family's village.

"Terry?" the boy asked in surprise. Then, with dread in his voice, "Father?"

Daedalus held his pose, a serene captive. "It seems the time for truth has arrived."

"What do you mean?" asked Icarus.

"Icarus–" Metcalfe began.

The boy cut him off. "What do you mean, Father?"

Metcalfe was silent. He had no idea how to break the news. He believed Daedalus's earlier assurances that Icarus was innocent of any knowledge of his father's espionage. He wished fervently that he could spare the boy pain, and yet there was no way to do so. "Tell him, Daedalus," he said.

"I came here to investigate the weaponry of the original inhabitants of Eleusis. I came at the order of the Emperor."

"But... we came here to escape the mindless violence of the Empire!" squeaked Icarus, his voice shaking. "You believed–"

"*You* believed!" his father hissed. "I am a Qraitian, and loyal to my family and my Emperor. Your... deviance... was a convenient excuse. It made my coming here more believable."

"You used me as a cover story?"

"And why not?" demanded Daedalus. "You owed me something, after the shame your beliefs brought upon me!"

"Shame?"

"Do you know what it was like, when you sang your un-warriorly pacifist beliefs to the four winds, being identified as the father of a freak? A coward? They knew all about you, from your earliest days at school! Why do you think I was chosen for this mission? I welcomed this chance to redeem the family honor! Short of wishing you had died in the egg, it is all I can do!"

Icarus reeled as through struck. His throat heaved and pulsed, and a sound like an antique air compressor, spitting from a leaking hose, escaped.

"Stop that idiotic sobbing!" barked Daedalus. He turned to the gathering crowd, which included Brock Aronson and Elspeth. Apparently for their benefit, he said, "A lifetime it seems I've listened to such noise! Too sensitive to contain his emotions!" He looked at the boy, who back-pedaled away from him until Elspeth caught him gently by the shoulders and cradled him in her arms. "Didn't you wonder why it was so easy for us to escape and come here? Did you really think that I could have just left without the Emperor's knowledge?"

Gulping back sobs, Icarus said, "I thought you could do anything." He looked at Elspeth, at Aronson, at Metcalfe. "I didn't know," he insisted, hysterical. "I - I believe in the way of the Family! I thought my–I thought Daedalus did too." He stared long and hard at his father, perhaps working up the courage to say more. He could only manage a feeble, "I didn't know"

"Of course you didn't," said Aronson soothingly. He looked at Daedalus. "Are there more? Like you? Sent here to spy?"

"Perhaps," said Daedalus, defiant.

"And will you reveal them to us?"

"Never."

"Pallas could find their names," suggested Metcalfe.

Aronson shook his head. "Dr. Pallas is far too high-minded for such tactics. Nor will we attempt to learn who they are. They will reveal themselves, in time."

"What do you want to do with him?" asked Metcalfe.

"You'll kill me, I suppose," said Daedalus.

"Of course not," said Aronson, disgusted. "Though it is a puzzle, what to do with you."

"Send me home," said Daedalus with sudden passion. "Take me to the intake office! I wish to go home and be executed, die like a Qraitian!"

"What do you mean 'executed?'" asked Metcalfe.

"I have dishonored my family," said Daedalus without any real feeling. "I must die."

"But you were doing the Emperor's bidding."

"And I did so gladly, knowing that I would end my life on the floor of the execution hall, if I was lucky."

"I don't understand."

"Because you are a *human*!" Daedalus spat the word. "You and your kind have no morality! Appearances are what matter–all that truly matter. Qraitians understand that, truth or lie, a besmirched reputation must be absolved. That can be accomplished only by the death of the disgraced, even if his sin is but a fabrication." He turned to Icarus. "I will go, and I will surrender my life with pride, to redeem our honor." He held out his hand. "Come, son. Join me in death. I will kill you myself. It is permitted! If you honor me, as your father–"

Again, Icarus's throat heaved. "I'm sorry Father," he choked out. "I love you. But I do not honor you. I cannot." He pulled himself from Elspeth's grasp and walked away.

Watching him, Metcalfe said to Daedalus, "I wonder...which is the greater dishonor: to be held in contempt by your society? Or by your son?"

"So," said Brock Aronson, "you know the truth."

The man's face was an impassive mask. Aronson had one of those faces which looked the same from the final setting of its features in young adulthood until its owner was well past middle age. Added to that was the deep, timeless quality his eyes possessed. He evoked wisdom and serenity. In his presence, one felt absolute confidence that all would be well. Metcalfe reflected that he had once felt the same way upon meeting Jan Atal, but Atal was not serene. Determined, competent, unyielding, but never serene.

They had retired to Aronson's private study. Metcalfe sat opposite the elder at Aronson's desk. It was a privilege he got the impression few were granted.

"I suppose I do know the truth," Metcalfe agreed. "I'm surprised to learn that you do, though I shouldn't be."

Aronson smiled. "The Voice of Eleusis has spoken to us all, on some level. It long ago called me into the caverns. I saw the lost city. I learned of the massive, artificial intelligence which once ran this world."

"And yet you didn't tell your people they're worshiping a false god."

Aronson considered the question while he took a sip of coffee. "Tell me, Terry, do you believe every word in the Book of Heroes?"

"Of course not. They're fables."

"And yet, do you not believe that within their fanciful lies there is truth?"

"Yes," admitted Metcalfe.

"Then you understand that, though their belief that this ancient network is a god is mistaken, our people have nonetheless found true faith? Many religions are rooted in some fallacy or myth. That doesn't weaken their power to do good. And our religion is not rooted in this deception. It is merely energized by it. Or do you think that the existence of this machine somehow negates the existence of a divine spark in every man and woman?"

"Certainly not," said Metcalfe quietly.

"For that matter," Aronson went on, "who is to say that an artificial intelligence could not also be a tool of the Almighty? Perhaps even a machine, if it is intelligent, might have a spark of the divine."

Now Metcalfe smiled. "Are you suggesting computers have souls?"

"Is it so ridiculous?"

Metcalfe shrugged. "I've constructed rudimentary A.I. systems with my own hands. Every student at the Academy has. You're suggesting that I created life?"

"No," said Aronson. "Just as, had you impregnated Elspeth the other night—"

Metcalfe had been taking a sip of coffee. He stopped and held the cup away from his lips, regarding Aronson with self-conscious amusement. "You're certainly... well informed."

"I am sorry," said Aronson quietly. "You assumed your liaison was a secret."

"Well..."

"Do not think, please, that the child sang of your exploits to the four winds. Actually, it was Icarus who told me he'd seen you, and I cautioned him on his need for discretion."

"I appreciate that."

"Though there is nothing shameful about celebrating god's love physically. We long ago abandoned such taboos when we left earth. The only crime associated with sex is the use of it to manipulate others, or the creation of a child for which you cannot or will not provide. But I did not mean to make you uncomfortable. I merely meant to draw an example. Had you impregnated Elspeth, would you, in fact, have created the soul of the resulting child?"

"No," said Metcalfe. "I'd merely be participating in a process already set in motion long ago."

"As you were when you assembled component parts into a complete A.I. You did not pioneer the concepts of artificial intelligence. While I'm sure you have an excellent grounding in them, you probably could not, with no previous training or knowledge, create such an intelligence out of nothing."

"I couldn't, no."

"So, in creating a human to someone else's ancient plan, or in creating an A.I. to someone else's newer, but still pre-existing plan, you do not actually bring the intelligence to life. If a brain, biological or artificial, attains sentience, it has gone beyond your original participation in its design, even if you happen to be the most skilled gengineer on Quintil."

"I... suppose that's true."

"And I believe, as a member of the Church of Terra, you still subscribe to the orthodoxy which states that God or one of the gods is responsible for causing sentience–creating souls in humans."

"Yes."

"So why couldn't God–any god–create a soul and put it into an intelligence which is designed to mimic our own in so many ways?"

"I... I hadn't thought about it."

"The Voice of Eleusis might very well be as much a part of God as you or I."

"The Voice," said Metcalfe slowly, "seems to believe that it and I together might be more than just a part of God."

Aronson set down his cup and looked meaningfully at Metcalfe. "So, as I suspected, you are the One." He said it without surprise, but he said it carefully. Almost with... reverence?

"That's what it told me. That it had waited for the One."

Aronson said, "Eleusis has waited a long time for you... for the One."

"It told you that?"

"It told... someone that." Aronson looked away for a moment.

Metcalfe did not speak, waiting for an answer. If he waited long enough, he was confident the other man would offer one.

He was correct. "You are not the first I've known who received Eleusis's offer."

"You?" asked Metcalfe.

Aronson shook his head.

"My late wife. She was made the offer."

"It told me others had come close, but there had never been another One in all this time. So... Mrs. Aronson..."

"Leah... was ill. Terminally ill. The Voice..." He closed his eyes for a moment, a painful memory settling over him.

Metcalfe allowed him his time to process whatever he was remembering. He could see in Aronson's face that he did not battle the sadness remembering brought; he simply let it rest upon his mind.

"The Voice offered her a cure," Aronson continued. "In exchange for her becoming the One it needed, it would restore her health, give her her full life span."

"What happened?" Metcalfe asked gently.

"After experiencing its memories... seeing the power at its disposal... power to destroy as well as create... Leah feared she could not control such power. She also would not agree to a bond which she felt contravened the one she shared with me. To maintain the sanctity of our marriage, to prevent the misuse of the voice's power in the hands of a mortal, Leah chose to let her disease run its course. She died a month after her encounter in the cavern."

Aronson's eyes, haunted, turned to Metcalfe's again.

"I'm sorry," Metcalfe said quietly.

But Brock Aronson smiled gently. "So was I, to lose my love. But the bravery she displayed then... and always... none was more suited to be God's instrument in the world."

"Do you think she made the wrong choice?"

"It was not for me to think. Had she chosen the cure and become the One... that would have been the right choice too, for her. Leah always made the right choices."

"Then maybe she could have handled the power."

"We'll never know." He leveled his eyes on Metcalfe. "Can you handle the power, Terry?"

"Friend Aronson–"

"Brock, Terry. No need to be formal. We have shared secrets, after all."

"Brock, then. Why are the Qraitians here?"

Aronson raised an eyebrow. "Because they know that the Voice controls great power. It can be used as a dreadful weapon, if they can learn to both trigger and focus it."

"If what Daedalus said is true, none of them gives a damn about faith. Except possibly Icarus."

"Do you doubt the boy's faith as well?"

Metcalfe considered it, shook his head. "No. He's sincere. But I don't think any of the others are."

Aronson nodded. "It's very likely you're correct. And what would you have us do about it?"

"You mean would I round them all up and put them in custody, like Fournier wants to do?"

"It's a rational plan."

"Yes," agreed Metcalfe, "it is. If your only goal is to protect yourself and those you trust absolutely. But that isn't the only goal, Brock. Not of the military, not of the government, and surely not of God's people. Any god."

"And what is our goal?" Aronson asked like a teacher leading a student.

"To offer everyone a chance at the best life they can have, free of interference by others."

"An adequate summary. And if there's a very real possibility that the Qraitian members of the Family are here to interfere–to take that chance from the rest of us? Is protecting that chance not the first goal? Must not the rights of the few take the inferior position to the good of the many?"

"No," said Metcalfe. "Because the first goal is giving *everyone* that chance. The minute we deny it to someone, we fail."

"And what of those who attack us directly? Can we not deny them, in order to protect ourselves?"

"Only for our immediate protection may we act against them. And we're not denying them their chance, at any rate. It's not ours to deny them. The chance to follow God's path is always there. No, Brock, I can't see casting out members of the Family based on suspicion, any more than I can countenance what Fournier is doing back on *Titan*–questioning and detaining the innocent in order to appear effective."

"And who are the innocent?"

"Anyone who's not been proved guilty," Metcalfe replied.

"You know your beliefs well."

Metcalfe grinned. "I've had some of them drilled into me since I was a toddler. Some I discovered through painful experience."

Aronson lifted his cup to take another swallow of coffee, found it empty, frowned, and set it down. "What do you intend to do, Terry, when Admiral Fournier comes for us? He will, you know."

"I know."

"It would be safest for you if you simply returned to your ship with him, assisted him in arresting us–"

"I won't do that."

"Can you stand against your friends? Can you go to jail? Possibly lose your life in the name of our cause? All these things may happen. Where will you stand, Terry?"

"On the side I think is the right one."

Aronson studied him. "For someone who's faced with the choices which confront you, you seem very calm and decisive. Far moreso than when you arrived."

Metcalfe smiled. "Do I?"

Cernaq felt the man's fear through the closed door.

He had come to the interrogation room on the Main Concourse, answering Darby's summons. The Deputy Captain had said it was urgent. When Cernaq arrived and felt the fear, which for him was like hearing screams of terror through the closed door, he had burst in at a dead run, afraid someone was injured.

Darby, startled by his entrance, had whirled, his body partially hiding the other man. Cernaq recognized him as a cook who was always visible behind the counter at Smokin' Joe's. He didn't know the man's name. They'd never had occasion to speak. Guiltily, he thought that Carson would probably know it. Carson seemed to learn everyone's name and use it. It was a strength of his and made him popular. On Phaeton, you didn't ask someone's name unless you had business with them, and something to offer them for the trouble of answering your question. And then you asked telepathically, which was far easier.

Now the cook was too upset to answer questions. Reflexively, Cernaq attempted to send thoughts of reassurance to him. Not knowing the situation, however, it was hard to know what to reassure him about. Besides, those InWorlders who were not used to dealing with telepaths couldn't easily receive telepathic transmission. One had to know it was coming, and exert effort to filter out the other mental noise and make sense of it. It was a bit like learning to speak all over again, realizing that the patterns of sounds those around you were making represented concepts and could be pieced together into a message. It had taken his fellow Arbiters some months to learn. Indeed, it had taken Cernaq a great deal of exposure to InWorlders, and some coaching from Pallas, to learn to broadcast his thoughts in a manner even the most adept non-telepaths could receive.

"Captain Darby," Cernaq asked, "what's happened to this man?"

"I'm questioning him," snapped Darby with disgust.

"I thought you'd completed the questioning of the civilian populace."

"The first phase, yes," sniffed Darby. "Some were held over for further investigation." He gestured at the table and the disheveled man, still in white t-shirt and slacks, as though he'd been pulled right from his work place. "In his case, we learned nothing during the first phase, because he doesn't speak Standard."

"So... despite a lack of evidence of any wrongdoing, you brought him in and kept him?"

"Correct."

"For how long?" asked Cernaq.

"Three days," Darby said. He then took a severe tone. "You are not here to ask me questions, Midshipman!"

"My apologies, sir. What do you require?"

"We need to interrogate him before he can be released, but no one else aboard speaks this... " he paused and looked at the display from his implant. "Franch."

"French," corrected Cernaq.

"French, then. It's a dead language."

Cernaq nodded. "Almost dead, yes; spoken only in one city on Terra. It dates back to a time before the last major Terran war. It was the language of a small nation which was essentially obliterated."

"But a group of refugees banded together, left Terra and formed the colony of..." Darby checked his display again. "Elba. A colony dangerously close to Qraitian space, where they speak nothing but French."

"Metcalfe has mentioned the French to me. Apparently, they were very loyal to their language."

"A likely story," said Darby. "What planet in the Confederacy doesn't teach its children Standard as a first language?"

Cernaq shrugged. "Phaeton." It was true. Standard was taught, but as an elective. Many natives of his world never had cause to speak aloud, and so learned no traditional language. One was adopted readily enough, if need be. Telepathic learning was much faster than the educational practices of other InWorlders.

"And, apparently," added Cernaq, "Elba."

"Well then, all the more reason to suspect he's a spy. Your people don't learn the language because so few of you leave your world. If this Elba also doesn't prepare its people to join mainstream society, why would he come to the most powerful ship in the Confederacy? Why would leave he leave his backwater planet in the first place?"

"Because 95 percent of the population is starving after solar activity changed their climate and they lost their crops?" asks Cernaq.

Darby's eyes narrowed. "You read that in his mind?"

"In the news, last year. Elba was declared a level three disaster world. Its residents are seeking any job they can off world, in order to send money home to their families. No doubt this man... have you learned his name?"

"Hawkins."

"No doubt Hawkins shipped out with one of the smaller relief ships, and hired on aboard *Titan* at one of our ports of call. Don't we have records which would reflect his employment?"

"We do not," Darby said irritably. "That is precisely my point, and the Admiral's. No thought has been given to security! We've allowed free access to this ship for years now. We don't know who we're carrying!"

"And how may I assist you with Mr. Hawkins?" asked Cernaq, already knowing and fearing Darby's answer.

"I want you to probe his mind!"

"I believe Dr. Pallas and I already addressed–"

"I don't care what you addressed! I need this man interrogated!" He softened his tone. "If you can provide us with answers, Mr. Cernaq, and they clear Hawkins, we can release him. It would be the humane thing to do."

Cernaq paused. Darby was right about that. Hawkins was terrified. Stray images of torture, malnourishment and lifelong imprisonment flashed at the periphery of his consciousness, where Cernaq could not help but pick them up. The name of Hydra Station, a notorious holding facility for prisoners deemed too dangerous for the general correction system, or even for standard military detention, loomed like a viper in his thoughts. It was whispered that no one had left Hydra Station alive. No doubt, he'd been told such tales by his compatriots. Rumors of people "just disappearing" were rife in the Confederacy since the battle at Quintil and the resulting security crackdown.

It then occurred to Cernaq that, for him to have heard rumors, he had to be communicating with someone. "Doesn't Mr. Saunders speak French?" he asked Darby.

"He does, somewhat, I believe. But I can hardly let a man who's being detained himself serve as an interrogator."

"And why have you not simply employed a translation program? French is in the database."

"I tried that. He ignores me. Keeps gesturing with his hands."

Cernaq looked into the eyes of Hawkins. The man was still afraid, though Cernaq's own arrival seemed to have calmed him somewhat. Likely just having someone to distract Darby's attentions had helped.

Gently, Cernaq reached out with his mind. *May I read your thoughts?* he asked.

Hawkins cocked his head, apparently having received the transmission. He made no response, mentally or verbally. Cernaq couldn't know whether he was refusing to answer, or whether he simply did not understand. He could receive no sense of whether or not Hawkins would allow him to breech the barriers of his mind.

Curious, Cernaq performed a scan of Hawkins's brain functions. This was permissible, by Phaetonian law, since it did not tap into the conscious mind. It simply verified the operation of certain autonomic functions: respiration, muscular control, nerve inputs.

Cernaq frowned and looked up at Darby. "This man is mute, Captain Darby."

Darby's eyes widened, only briefly. "The hell you say!"

"Hasn't he been seen by a doctor?"

"No," said Darby, "why should he?"

Cernaq sighed and worked hard to keep his tone respectful. "As I'm sure the Captain is aware, regulations require the medical examination of prisoners held for more than a ship's day."

Darby inhaled sharply, started to speak, inhaled again. Finally he said, "Regulations are... relaxed... for the duration of this investigation."

"That's unfortunate," said Cernaq. "It would have saved you time. He cannot answer your questions verbally."

"And he doesn't have an implant!" barked Darby. "So he can't file his answers."

"Implants are expensive," Cernaq reminded him. "He could key them into a terminal."

Darby shook his head. "Probably doesn't know how to type. See here, Cernaq, we've wasted enough time. I need you to probe his mind and determine his status."

"I asked permission to access his thoughts. He did not answer."

"You asked?"

"Of course. As you said, it would be easier on him if he and I could communicate. But he did not reply to my telepathic inquiry. It's very likely, in his agitated state, that he could not discern it."

"I've heard enough speculation! I don't care what's likely and what isn't." Darby punched up a display from his implant. "Here are the questions we need answered. Pull the answers from his mind."

Cernaq crossed his arms and straightened. "I've told you, sir, my principles do not allow—"

"Your principles be damned! Loyalty to the Confederacy comes before the customs of anyone's home planet. You are an officer under my command! I gave you a direct order! Carry it out, or you will be disciplined!"

Cernaq's reply was immediate and cold. "No."

Darby's face turned purple. "You are on report!"

Cernaq nodded. "In fact, I intend to report my actions to the Captain immediately."

"I will report them! You are denied access to the Captain!" Darby whirled, heading for the door. "You will remain here until I return!"

When the Deputy Captain had left, Cernaq turned to Hawkins, who now looked puzzled as much as afraid. "Je m'appelle Cernaq," he said to the prisoner. "Je vous promets vous ne serez pas lésés."

Aer'La emitted a low growl as the safety strap pulled free at her sharp tug. It should have held rigid, clipped securely in place to a hook extruded from the bulkhead. Instead, only partially closed, the latch slipped free at her tug and hundreds of cubic feet of cargo spilled from the restraining net.

She swore out loud, causing Ceres Smith, floating behind her and to the left, to start. Ceres was accustomed to Aer'La's outbursts. They rarely caused her to bat an eyelash. It had been a bad week, however. Aer'La's fits of temper came more and more often, with even less warning than usual, and they were more fueled by rage than her mate had ever seen.

"Who the hell was responsible for this section?" she demanded.

"Goyer," said Ceres. "The new kid."

Her eyes smouldered. "This time I'm gonna do it, Ceres. This time I'm gonna snap one of his arms! Where is he?"

"Bos'n," said Ceres slowly, "he's not here."

Ceres calling her by her title was a warning sign, Aer'La knew. She'd long ago given her mate permission to address her informally when they were alone. She liked the older woman, and found her to be above reproach when it came to doing her job. Ceres only called Aer'La "Bos'n" when Aer'La was being unreasonable and Ceres thought she was so far gone that she might even lash out at a trusted ally.

"Where is he?" Aer'La asked tightly.

"Questioning," said Ceres. "They pulled him in an hour ago."

"If he's lucky, they'll send him off to life imprisonment."

"You joke," said Ceres, "but the fact is that his latches weren't double-checked because his spotter *was* held over for additional questioning. And that means additional questioning back at HQ, not here on *Titan*. So we won't be seeing the spotter, or about a dozen others they've kept, before next planetfall, if ever again."

Aer'La spat out a breath. "How the hell are we supposed to run this operation if they keep taking away my people?"

"I don't think they're particularly interested."

"They'll be interested when the perishables are allowed to spoil, and the fragile items arrive broken! Darby may not like to admit it, but the private shipping we take care of pays more than half of this ship's operating budget!"

"Aer'La," said Ceres in that motherly tone that annoyed the Bos'n about half the time she used it, "maybe you need to take a break. This whole business is getting to you. I can cover–"

"No!" Aer'La blurted. "The last thing I'm going to do is desert you when we're down so many people."

A brief tingle in her wrist indicated an incoming message for Aer'La. She keyed a visual display. The face of one of the ship's security team appeared. She didn't remember his name. Ordinarily, security was a slight concern aboard the *Titan*. The team charged with overseeing it was mostly concerned with handling police duties among the civilian passengers and residents, and so were confined largely to the Life Sphere. Aer'La met with them occasionally, but their services tended to be self-regulating. They knew their jobs and so she didn't bother them.

In the past week, however, she was hearing from them more and more as Darby pressed them into service to "plan accommodations" for his victims.

"What is it?" she demanded.

"I'm required to advise you, Bos's: we just escorted a prisoner to the brig."

Aer'La smacked her forehead. "Why? We don't have room for detainees in the brig! It's for–"

"It's for military prisoners, ma'am. I understand that. This isn't a detainee. Captain Darby ordered one of the officers arrested for insubordination."

"Please tell me it was Blaurich."

"Midshipman Blaurich has already shipped out, Ma'am. It was Midshipman Cernaq."

The words hung in the air. Ceres's face went pale as she watched Aer'La slowly build towards a meltdown. She didn't even bother to end the transmission from her implant. After a few seconds of free-floating, letting the words sink in, she balled her fists, threw back her head, and screamed.

Ceres slowly backed away. Aer'La absently registered that that was a good idea.

She needed to hit something. She needed to hurt something. She needed to destroy something. Enraged, she kicked off from the wall, flinging herself at the loose cargo net and its slowly escaping contents. She struck full-on against a crate larger than she was, but not so large that she couldn't grasp its corner handholds. In zero-g it was no trouble to lift it over her head. She reared back and brought it down hard, crashing against the other crates.

Dissatisfied with the impact of the bulky object, she shoved it away and seized a smaller one, easier to handle and swing. This she used to pummel the larger crates and the bulkhead to which the net was secured. Once, the crate caught in the net, she pulled viciously and the net tore. In the back of her mind, she registered the amount of force it took to tear a cargo net. She was in danger of tearing her own muscles, straining that hard.

She didn't care.

She grunted in satisfaction as one of the larger cases cracked when she struck it again. She brought the small crate down for another blow. Contents began to spill from the ruined container. Textiles, she noted. Fabric from some distant planet.

She heard Ceres below and about her, quietly ushering her people out of the hold. Smart girl, Aer'La thought. They're not safe here. No one's safe here. She swung the crate harder. As she beat it until it splintered against the casings of its fellows, its contents, too, escaped. Glassware. Good, she thought. She hung onto the largest shard of the crate and began batting at the glass pieces, closing her eyes to protect them from fragments. It became a game, lashing out blindly, finding out what she could hit.

As she continued her rhythmic destruction of property, the last coherent thought she'd had echoed in her mind. *No one's safe here.* It shot back and forth inside her skull, rebounding. *No one's safe here.* It swung back and forth, like the pendulum in the antique clock Carson had bought in a junk shop on their last planetfall. (He loved that stupid thing. What was it with boys and machines?) Her arms swung the improvised bat in the same pendulum swing. *No one's safe here.*

It became a chant, a mantra. (Cernaq had taught her meditation.) She recited it once for each swing, each burst of broken glass. *No one's safe here.* The swings began to connect less often, the sounds of shattering coming less and less. The glasses and mugs were drifting away, or she had destroyed them all. Her swings slowed, became less regular. Still, she recited the phrase. She found she was saying it aloud now. How many times had she said it?

"No one's safe here," she heard her own voice advise, and the truth of the words struck her.

No. No one was safe here. Not around her. Not aboard *Titan.* Not in space, damn it all. No one was safe.

Aer'La released the last piece of the crate and floated, spent. She hugged herself, and realized she was trembling. Drawing up her legs, she pulled into a fetal position and floated. She didn't know for how long.

Arms enfolded her. She flinched, but realized they were gentle, not threatening. She allowed herself to be pulled into an embrace. Breathing raggedly, she let someone smooth her hair and stroke her back and arms.

Ceres. Ceres had stayed.

She looked up into her mate's eyes and saw profound sadness. "I'm sorry," whispered Ceres. She laid a hand gently on Aer'La's cheek.

The touch of kindness after her blood had surged in rage overwhelmed Aer'La. Her chest heaved. She could not stop her chin from quivering. Despite her, the tears came.

Ceres tightened her embrace and brought her hand to the back of Aer'La's neck, weaving fingers in her hair and drawing her closer. "It's okay," she whispered.

Aer'La buried her face in the older woman's shoulder and sobbed. She couldn't help herself. She had no strength left. She'd spent it all. She could only cry as Ceres stroked her hair and rubbed her back.

"Shhhh," Ceres whispered against her ear. "It's okay, baby. It's going to be okay."

CHAPTER FIFTEEN

She had calmed herself by the time she arrived at the brig. Cernaq sat calmly in the cell, as if he were waiting for a business meeting in the lobby of an office building. The only thing missing were the marketing holos an office would display in a maddening loop. When he saw her, he stood and smiled weakly.

"Sorry to pull you away from work."

"Oh, don't be an idiot!" she reprimanded him. "Like I wouldn't have come!" She took his hands. Being Bos'n carried privileges. She was allowed to be in the cell with a prisoner, as long as she didn't rough him up too much. "What happened?" she asked.

"The same argument as before. Darby wanted me to probe the mind of a detainee."

"And you wouldn't?"

"I couldn't."

"Dammit, Cernaq, why not? It wouldn't hurt him!"

"It's an invasion of privacy," Cernaq said slowly. "To enter a mind uninvited, putting what's mine, my thoughts, into his most personal space. It's rape, Aer'La. Nothing less."

She grimaced. "Rape hurts a lot more." She knew.

"Physically, yes; but an invasion of the mind can cause psychic damage which takes a great deal longer to heal than physical wounds, if it heals at all." He took his hand from hers. His expression went cold. "Darby has gone too far in his quest for security. It's all gone too far. Someone has to stand up and try to stop it."

That he had pulled away both physically and emotionally was not lost on her.

"You think I've gone too far?"

He hesitated before replying. "When I answered Darby's call, he had a man–Hawkins–in for questioning. He couldn't speak, and he wouldn't answer me telepathically. But I felt his fear. And I saw his fear. Aer'La... he was afraid of you."

She shook her head quickly, angry, confused. "I don't even know any Hawkins!"

"Everyone aboard this ship knows you. There's always been a sense of caution, a belief that you might snap and attack someone–"

"Only if they deserve it!"

He smiled thinly. "Even so. Now, however, at least in Hawkins, that fear has... deepened. Become exaggerated. There are... rumors, Aer'La. Stories of torture. Of people being taken away and never seen again. Fournier and Darby have established a climate of intense fear. You've become the instrument of that fear, the focal point."

Aer'La felt her anger creeping back up. She'd been so angry that he had been arrested. She'd wanted to snap Darby's neck. Now, here was Cernaq, blaming her for his capture.

"I came here to help you," she said shakily.

"I know. The trouble is, Aer'La, I'm not the one who needs help."

"You're in the brig, dummy! Did you notice? Darby will have you shipped off to hard labor, if he can! And you don't need help?"

"I'm not worried. Captain Atal and Professor Mors will see to it that my case is defended. They can't force a telepath to do something morally wrong, just because he's in the military. Darby's just angry, and showing off his power. In doing that, though, he's going to hurt a lot of people who can't defend themselves, people who don't have the law on their side. But they haven't done anything wrong. They're just here, and so they're in his sites. His... and yours."

"I can't believe you're blaming me! For everything that—"

"I'm not blaming you for everything."

"I hope not!"

"Just for your part in it."

For just a moment, she thought about hitting him. He'd never made her that angry before. Metcalfe had. Carson had. Never Cernaq. Cernaq she had always trusted. He would never hurt her, never betray her. He was too pure and good and innocent. He'd always been there for her. When they'd tried to send her off to slavery again. When she had almost died in the shuttle explosion... adrift in space... no air... vacuum... blackness... her lungs burning... Even once she'd gotten suited up, the air had nearly run out... enclosed in the suit... the heat of battle around her... soundless bursts of light and debris...trapped in her plastic coffin... trying to hold her breath... her lungs burning...

Aer'La!

Something was hurting her hand. She lashed out and slapped it away, then drew the wounded hand to her, nursing it.

Aer'La! Look at me!

She looked at her hand. Crescent marks pocked light blue flesh. Four of them, making a larger crescent. Fingernails.

"Aer'La?"

Cernaq. Cernaq had dug his nails into her hand, bringing her back.

"Breathe, Aer'La."

She did, and realized it had been some time since she had. She gasped, gulping air.

"That's it. Slowly. Take a deep breath and hold it. The air's not going anywhere."

She inhaled, trying to do it slowly. He was holding her hand again.

"You can hear my voice, right?"

She nodded.

"And you can feel my hand. You felt pain when I grabbed you."

"Pain," she repeated.

"Where are you sitting?"

"On a bench. In the brig."

"How many people are in the room?"

"Two." She looked up into his golden eyes. "And one of them's an asshole."

Cernaq shrugged. "Fair enough. Are you with me?"

She nodded again.

"You were back there."

"Back out in space, yes."

"Sorry I hurt your hand. You needed a sudden stimulus. I could trigger the pain receptors in your brain directly, but I was afraid that might just play into whatever you were experiencing."

"S'okay."

"Aer'La, this isn't going to get better on its own."

She leaned back against the bulkhead and crossed her arms, hugging herself. "So now I'm to blame and I'm crazy?"

"You're not crazy. You're traumatized. You almost died."

"Not the first time."

"No. But it was the first time it was like this. In battle—"

"With Qraitians!" she shot back. "In battle with Qraitians! Qraitians almost killed me! They almost killed ten billion people!"

"And you think frightening everyone on *Titan* to death will prevent that happening again?"

She shrieked at him. "You don't know what it's like! You don't know how it felt!"

"No one knows that as well as you, no; but I've been there for every nightmare, every flashback, every sense memory that triggered—"

"Get out of my head!" she screamed. Immediately, she regretted it. She hadn't meant it.

"All right," said Cernaq. He wasn't angry. He wasn't hurt. He held her gaze, his face betraying nothing.

"I didn't mean—"

"What did you mean?" he asked gently.

"I don't know!" she said. "I don't know what I'm feeling or thinking or... "

"Maybe you need to figure that out," he said impassively.

"Dammit!" she hissed. "Dammit and damn you! Stop being so... Phaetonian!"

"It's what I am."

"Yes! It's what you are! A damned, mind-reading, smarter-than-everyone Phaetonian! And right now you're reminding me why everyone hates you people so much! You're acting just like Pallas!"

"Am I?"

For the second time, she felt the impulse to hit him, punch him in the face, make him bleed. She got up and left, silently, before the impulse won.

"Let him go, Darby!"

"Sir, I will not," said the Deputy Captain evenly. "He has deliberately refused a direct order. There is no room for lenience."

They'd been arguing for some time. Darby had come to Atal's promenade after ordering Cernaq arrested.

"I'll make that call, Mister! And I'm making it."

"If you overrule me, Captain, you're breaking the back of the chain of command! I would have to demand to formal investigation–!"

"And you're dangerously close to–"

The door chime sounded, and the door opened immediately, without Atal's invitation. Carson strode in as though on a mission.

"Sorry, Captain, I–"

"What do you mean, barging in here uninvited?" demanded Darby.

"I've received a transmission–" Carson began.

"There is no transmission which relieves you of the need to be courteous–" interrupted Darby.

"I think the Captain should be the judge–"

"Well, obviously you've decided to judge–"

"Both of you *shut up*!" barked Atal.

The two men stepped back, startled. Atal did not often raise his voice. It wasn't usually necessary. People listened to him.

"All right, Mr. Carson, what have you got?"

"Transmission from Kaya, sir. It was interrupted. I think she's in trouble."

"Let's have it."

"It was encoded. Text only." Carson keyed his implant, and the words appeared in the air before them. Only a handful, and the thought was not complete. "She confirms there are spies on Eleusis," Carson summarized. "And she starts to say something about weapons systems, capable of matching any force brought against them with greater force. She says 'Do not attempt–' and then stops." Carson waited a moment and, receiving no reaction, said, "Pardon me for asking, sir, but... where is Kaya?"

Atal sighed. "Sit down, gentlemen."

They sat, Darby, for his part, seeming to have forgotten all about the earlier argument. His eyes showed intense curiosity.

"Kaya and Dr. Faulkner have gone undercover. They're aboard Commander Ustenar's ship, disguised as defecting Qraitians. You see, Kaya was investigating these... supernatural claims of the Family's. She saw a Qraitian, apparently vaporized by an unknown force, when he threatened members of the Family. We concluded that there was a power here that might be used against us, and that the Qraitians knew about it. We had to know how much they knew about it."

"Why didn't you contact Confederate Intelligence?" demanded Darby. "Certainly Admiral Fournier could have authorized–"

"Admiral Fournier wanted to act immediately," said Atal.

"You didn't approve, did you?" asked Carson.

It was a breach of etiquette, and they all knew it, for a junior officer to ask such a question about a Captain's opinion of an Admiral's order; but Atal only shook his head.

"It's a terrible risk," said Darby quietly. "They could be killed!"

Atal nodded. "They could be."

Carson swallowed. "Sir... how do we get Kaya and the Doc out?"

"Did you even have a plan for that?" demanded Darby.

"Captain Darby, I have one daughter. Do you think I would send her–not to mention the ship's physician–into harm's way with no plan to retrieve them?"

Darby was chastened. "I wouldn't think so, sir, but–"

Atal nodded. "But it looks pretty bleak. Not to worry. I know Qraitians. If Kaya's in trouble, she reveals her identity as an officer. They won't kill her. They can't. She's too valuable. Especially when she promises to deliver Fehajiq to them."

"What?" Darby demanded.

Carson nodded, seeing Atal's point. "They'd do anything to bring Fehajiq and his rogues back home to die."

"B-b-but you don't have the authority!" stammered Darby. "You don't have access to the prisoners–"

"Admiral Fournier does. And that was his... reason..." Carson knew Atal wanted to say 'excuse.' "...For sending us home. We're to collect Fehajiq from Hydra Station."

Darby's eyes went wide.

"Well... I suppose the plan has yielded valuable information." Darby admitted.

"Indeed so," said Atal. "Fortunately, we've got some time to contact Fournier and convince him to take no action against Eleusis."

Carson started to speak. Whatever it was, the boy looked guilty as hell. He was wrestling with his conscience.

"Something to say, Carson?"

"Sir," Darby interrupted, "there are some things you don't know. I was ordered to keep silent, but–"

"What is it, Mr. Darby?"

"Sir, Admiral Fournier briefed me on his intentions before he left us."

"And?"

"And he plans to take the colonists before the deadline, so they don't have time to prepare."

"Shit," whispered Atal.

"If there is any truth to the Qraitian intelligence–"

"Then Fournier and all the people he's got with him could be wiped out," Atal finished the thought.

Darby went pale. Carson, too, was profoundly bothered. "He put Sestus in charge of the evacuation force," the boy said quietly.

"He would," said Atal. "Good for his career."

"His career may be over," said Carson with more glumness than Atal would have expected.

"We won't let that happen, Carson. Mr. Darby, full speed to Eleusis."

"Sir," asked Darby, and for once his tone was not belligerent when questioning Atal, "what about Fehajiq?"

"For now... the offer will have to suffice. He's not going anywhere... and we have to. Snap to, Mr. Darby."

Darby leapt to his feet. "Right away, Captain." He practically marched from the room.

As the door closed behind him, Atal turned to Carson. "I need you to get me a priority encrypted channel. We need to alert Admiral Fournier, if we can."

"If he'll listen," added Carson.

"A very big if," agreed Atal.

"Sir," Carson wondered, "what about Cernaq? I couldn't help but overhear–"

"My hands are tied, Carson, unfortunately. All that's in me wants to override Darby's order. But releasing a man from custody when he admits he's disobeyed an order–that's stepping farther outside the bounds than even I've ever done. Cernaq is making a stand for what he believes in, and he knows what he's doing... I hope. For now..." He gazed momentarily into the empty space visible beyond the bulkheads. "He's as safe as any of us."

Metcalfe was finishing breakfast in Aronson's kitchen when a voice called out from the front porch. He recognized it as belonging to Colonel Druelinger. It was a simple "hello," rather than the sometimes-hysterical outbursts others under the Colonel's command were given to. Metcalfe had occasionally been embarrassed when accompanied by Marines, brandishing guns in the faces of civilians and shrieking, "Confederate Marines! Stand down! Place all appendages where they can be seen!"

"We're in the back," called out Aronson. He looked to Metcalfe, setting down his fresh cup of coffee with mild annoyance. Metcalfe was gathering that Aronson relished nothing so much as a cup of coffee, and the only thing in the universe which annoyed him was being denied one. "I suppose we must receive guests."

"It's Colonel Druelinger," said Metcalfe. "He won't be alone."

Indeed, he was not. When they entered the front room–the house had only four rooms, apart from the kitchen–Druelinger stood, armored but with his rifle at rest, flanked by Sestus and Fournier. Sestus smirked when he saw Metcalfe. Fournier, as always, looked sour. Beyond them, through the screen door, Metcalfe could see several dozen Marines, all armed and armored like their leader, some on the porch, the rest lined up in the yard.

"Friend Druelinger," acknowledged Aronson, "and Friend Fournier." He turned to Sestus. "I do not know you, young man."

Sestus rolled his eyes. "Is this sham necessary?"

"Politeness is always necessary," said Aronson.

"This isn't a social call," replied Sestus.

"That will do, Mr. Blaurich," said Fournier. "Mr. Aronson, as leader of this colony–"

"I am not," said Aronson quietly. "God leads here."

"The Confederacy has designated you as the leader and representative," Fournier informed him. "We do not recognize governance by supernatural beings, or any other form of anarchy. As said designated representative, you are hereby ordered to instruct your fellow colonists to cooperate in an immediate evacuation–"

"We were told we had four days to decide," said Aronson.

"There is no decision to make, sir. This is a military action. You are leaving, freely or in military custody; but you are leaving. Today. Certain developments have accelerated our schedule."

"And if we refuse to cooperate?" asked Aronson.

Fournier nodded toward the Marines outside. "You will be conveyed to your destination. For your own safety, and the safety of the Confederacy, you will leave this planet."

There was a clatter of footsteps on the porch, and Metcalfe heard Elspeth's voice demanding that the Marines let her through. Obviously, they had no orders to the contrary, for she rushed in the door seconds later,

Icarus in tow, letting the screen door bang shut behind her. She looked rumpled–probably having just woken up. Her tone was urgent, alarmed. "Brock, what's going on?"

Metcalfe was impressed by her complete indifference to the display of military force all about her. Despite their lack of threatening gesture or word, the Marines were an intimidating presence who tended to make those around them nervous. Elspeth, raised to peace and having probably never witnessed violence, didn't have it in her catalog of fears that a human being, one of God's creatures, would raise a hand or weapon against her. Was it simply innocence that made her so confident? No, Metcalfe decided as she turned flashing eyes on Fournier and Druelinger, there was no denying that this girl possessed raw bravery in its purest form. Unbidden, the memory of her scent, her silky flesh, her warmth in his arms came back to him. He felt a surge of pride that she had chosen him.

"We are being required to leave this planet," said Aronson calmly.

"What?" she demanded.

"The Admiral has moved up his deadline," said Metcalfe as neutrally as he could. He had expected this, but still it angered him.

"You will all be escorted to a holding area," said Fournier, "where you will be kept under guard pending transport. I believe there is a large, single-room structure a short walk from this building?"

"Correct sir," said Druelinger. "Large enough to accommodate the entire populace."

"The meeting house," said Elspeth. "You'd defile our place of worship with a military presence?"

"Miss," Druelinger said politely, "pardon me, but the building looks unused."

Aronson nodded. "Meetings have been held at the place of Communion for so long, the meeting house has been idle."

"That's not the point!" snapped Elspeth. "It's still a house of God!"

"The Confederacy recognizes no special status for such buildings," said Fournier. "Religion does not legally exist in the Inner Worlds."

Elspeth's voice was dry. "I'm sure God will be amused to hear that."

The Admiral ignored her. "Colonel, have your people distributed at strategic points throughout the village. Station enough personnel on the...

meeting house... to ensure no one escapes. Take these two young people there now."

"This has been our home for generations!" cried Elspeth. "Where will we go?"

"The Navy will provide relocation services," said Fournier. He cast a disapproving glance at Icarus. "The Qraitians, of course, will be detained and questioned. Arrangements have been made for final transport to Hydra Station."

Metcalfe flinched. Were the words "final transport" accidental, or were they carefully chosen to remind Fournier's audience that prisoners did not leave Hydra Station?

Whatever their intent, the grimness of their meaning was not lost on Icarus. He let out a ragged hiss of anxiety and took a step back from the Confederate men. "No," he pleaded, "no, let me stay with my family!"

Elspeth reached out a protective arm to him and gathered him to her, stroking his glistening neck with her free hand and making clucking noises over him.

Fournier could not contain his look of disgust at the display of affection. Druelinger maintained an impassive face, but Metcalfe could tell that a human embracing a Qraitian made him uncomfortable, at the very least. Sestus made a noise of contempt and looked away.

"We can't separate them now," said Fournier, his tone making it clear he wished he could. "Take Aronson with you on your rounds," he instructed Druelinger. "Mr. Aronson, you will encourage your people to cooperate–"

"I will not," said Aronson sadly.

"Brock," said Metcalfe, "it's futile to resist them. I know none of the Family will fight, but even trying to escape, someone might be hurt. It's best if you encourage them to follow instructions. Colonel Druelinger's people will do their utmost to avoid injury, but they're also very deadly if they need to be."

Fournier's face registered his surprise. "Thank you, Mr. Metcalfe. I'm aware of your sympathy for the views of these people. I'm glad to see that you remember you're an officer first."

Metcalfe remained silent. Let Fournier think what he would.

"How soon do you intend to take us from here?" asked Aronson.

"That will depend on the condition of your ships," Fournier replied.

"Our ships? We have few ships here. The original colony transport ship was cannibalized long ago for raw materials. What small craft we have—"

"Will be pressed into service for the purpose of evacuating you from this world. We don't have room for all of you. Metcalfe, assist Blaurich in assessing the condition of their vessels and preparing them for flight. Report back to me with an estimated departure time."

"Will we at least be allowed to gather our belongings?" asked Aronson.

"As time allows, we will escort your people from detention... from the waiting area... and supervise the collection of necessary personal items. Colonel Druelinger's men will see to it, and their power of veto will be absolute."

"Why bother?" wondered Elspeth bitterly.

"Young lady," replied Fournier, "whether you believe it or not, we're doing everything we can to protect you." He nodded to Druelinger. "Have these two taken to the meeting house."

Before Druelinger could speak, Metcalfe stepped forward. "May I escort them, Admiral?"

"I don't see why not."

"I'll come along," said Sestus.

Metcalfe gave a mirthless smile. "Don't trust me, Blaurich?"

"Not one bit, Metcalfe."

Metcalfe placed an arm gently around Elspeth's shoulders, and clasped Icarus's arm. "Come on, you two. We'll—"

A frantic bleeping rent the air. Fournier, startled, pulled his portable radio from its clip. Ship to surface communications required more power than was safe for an implant to handle. He keyed up, and a voice from his ship in orbit began speaking even before he could identify himself.

"It's the Qraitian ship, Admiral! Coming abroad, weapons armed."

Fournier swore. "Why?" he demanded. "Why now?"

"Sir," replied the voice, "they're claiming they've caught Confederate spies aboard their ship. They're planning to execute them."

Stripped of their disguises, Kaya and Faulkner, under guard, watched from the command deck of the Qraitian ship as a holo formed in the open space before Ustenar. The Qraitians kept even the operational areas of their ships under gravity, perhaps, as a race, feeling more bound to the rock of their home world than humans did. Humans had spent their history attempting to defy gravity. The Qraitians seemed to resent having to leave its comforting restraint.

Ustenar perched on an elevated stone dais, looking for all the world like a cobra, curled but at ready to strike. The holo coalesced into an image of Fournier, and the Commander hissed at him.

"What is the meaning of this?" Fournier demanded. In the image, Kaya could see he was on the command deck of a ship not the *Titan*. "How dare you train weapons on–"

"Spare me your outrage, Fournier! How dare you place human spies on my ship? I should kill you right now. I may not have the chance again."

Fournier did not flinch. "You should probably give some thought to the odds you're facing, Commander. We've over a dozen ships against your one."

"But we," Ustenar gestured to the guards to come forward, "have your spies, Admiral."

Kaya was shoved roughly into what she assumed was the pickup area for a holo camera. Why did the Qraitians not simply use floaters? Or was Ustenar going for the psychological advantage of shoving them around in view of the Admiral?

Seeing her, Fournier shook his head.

Kaya nodded. "Admiral."

At least he had the sense not to call her by name, thought Kaya.

"I see you know each other. Good. Humans are so stupidly sentimental about each others' lives. I would imagine you'd like to see them spared."

"Killing them accomplishes nothing."

"Not true," said Ustenar. "It prevents them from telling you any more of what they've learned. I don't know what was contained in this one's transmission–" From the dais, she kicked the back of Kaya's head. It didn't particularly hurt. It was merely intended as an insult. "–but I don't want you learning anything more."

Fournier held his face impassive, but Kaya could read that he knew nothing of her transmission.

"This needn't result in open hostility," Fournier said.

"It already has. You've taken hostile action by sending spies–!"

"As if you didn't have spies on the planet below!"

Good, thought Kaya. Perhaps he knew nothing. Perhaps he was fishing. Still, it was the right thing to say.

"All Qraitians on Eleusis are invited guests. Defectors, lured here by your extremist cult. They did not infiltrate a military vessel, sacred territory of your government."

Fournier crossed his arms and set his jaw. "We'll offer you an exchange. The two humans for all the Qraitians below."

"Why would I trade spies, from whom valuable information could be extracted, for excrement, which is only suitable for use as fertilizer? No, Admiral. I do not wish to trade. Before I kill them, I am going to interrogate them. Perhaps they will answer questions for me, such as... where is Captain Atal? Where has he taken his great ship? Why would your finest warrior leave the field of battle?"

"This is not a battlefield," said Fournier. "At least it doesn't have to be."

"That will depend upon what I learn from your spies, Admiral. Now, if you wish me to spare them... that is, if you wish me to return to you whatever is left when I'm done with them... your ships will maintain position outside attack radius."

Ustenar snapped a command, and Fournier's image winked out. She turned to the two human women. "We'll see what you're worth to your comrades, I suppose. And we'll see what you know." She gestured to the guards, who pulled Kaya back and led them from the room.

Metcalfe found Icarus in a small anteroom by the entrance to the meeting house. Druelinger's Marines had begun bringing in members of the Family in the past few minutes, and the young Qraitian had disappeared. The boy had been silent since the revelation of his father's true purpose in coming here. Now that he was also fearful of the threat of Hydra Station, Metcalfe was especially concerned about his state of mind. He'd left Sestus reviewing the specs on the family's meager fleet of space ships and come to check on him.

Icarus stared out one of the two large windows in the room, a shiny blue flask clasped in one hand.

"Drinking?" asked Metcalfe.

Icarus regarded him sullenly.

Metcalfe wasn't going to be deterred. "Want to share?"

"It'd kill you," the boy said thickly.

"Really?"

"Yeah. Poisonous to humans. Well, in quantity. A drop would make you sleep all night." He held the flask out and stared at it. "I stole it from my father."

"How much have you had?"

Icarus shrugged. "Doesn't matter."

Metcalfe laid a hand on his shoulder as he slid into lotus position next to Icarus. "It does to me. I can't blame you for getting drunk, but it won't make the problem go away. And it won't leave you in any condition to help–"

"To help what? To help them drag me off to die? Just because I was born Qraitian?"

"Don't lose hope, Icarus," said Metcalfe quietly.

"Hope. What's hope? I've lost my birth family. They're going to take away my new family."

"Trust me, Icarus, nothing... *nothing* can take family from you."

The boy looked at him, his eye membranes, transparent, but visible in the strong sunlight, drifting lazily instead of flicking quickly open and shut as they normally would. "Who's your family, Metcalfe?"

"I had a sister. Lydia. She's dead."

"Something took her from you, then."

Metcalfe shook his head. "She's always with me. And I have a friends, back on my ship. They've been with me for a few years." He settled farther down, arching his back and leaning against the wall. "Of course some of them are a bit angry at me right now, for being here."

"Then why are you here? Why are you thinking of leaving them, if nothing can tear families apart?"

Metcalfe sighed. "I didn't say nothing could tear them apart. I said nothing could take them from you. You can give them up yourself."

"Is that what you're doing? Giving up you family?"

"Maybe... maybe I'm just growing away from them a little. Maybe I'm finding a bigger family, or a different one. People do that, you know. You don't necessarily stay with the family you were born into."

"I didn't," said Icarus.

"No. And you chose that. You chose to be part of this family. I don't know what's going to happen to me, Icarus, but I'm going to choose, too. I won't let circumstances do it for me. I won't let them do it to you, either. I promise you, I won't let the Navy take you from your new family."

Icarus laughed.

"What's funny?"

"You. Going out of your way to help me. I'm a reject. A miserable excuse for a Qraitian. And you're a human that my people respect as an enemy."

"I'm not proud of that."

"My... Daedalus... says that when you pass on from this life, those you killed will be waiting to serve you in the afterlife. Their souls honor you."

"I don't want servants. Even though I guess they were crazed murderers, I didn't want to kill them. For all I know, they were bullied or threatened into serving Fehajiq."

"No," said Icarus. "The extremists go into battle for the glory, and to advance their families' status. Fehajiq has lost his status entirely. His family is on the streets now, but the ones you killed? They're honored. Do your people do anything like that?"

Metcalfe rested the back of his head against the wall, closed his eyes. "Not as directly. We honor our dead, yes. We had a funeral you know, for Fehajiq's casualties."

Icarus, taking a drink, sputtered and almost choked.

"You *what?*"

"I guess it was kind of... informal," explained Metcalfe, a little taken aback by his friend's reaction. "We read the names of the dead. Fehajiq gave them to me. We prayed, at least I did, for their souls to be received with–"

Icarus laughed out loud, a throaty, hissing sound.

"What?" Metcalfe demanded.

"If you told anyone that, anyone back in the Empire, they would kill you where you stand and defile your body!"

"They would?"

"Terry, that's the ultimate insult! To be prayed for, memorialized by the person who killed you?"

"I thought your people respected their enemies!"

"No! We–they–Qraitians–hold enemies in contempt. They're lesser people. Lesser in the eyes of the gods. That's why it's okay to kill them. The only enemy you respect is the enemy who defeats you, who kills you."

"Is that why Fehajiq wanted me to kill him, after the battle?"

"Absolutely! You insulted him by leaving him alive. And then you..." Icarus giggled and rolled his body into Metcalfe's. "You prayed for them!"

"I... I thought it was gracious!"

"Qraitians don't recognize grace. If someone who's defeated us is kind to us, it can only be because he's showing contempt, treating us like dumb animals, not worth the honor of death. To not wish torture and punishment on your dead enemy is like saying they were too stupid to be expected to atone for their actions! You've dishonored their memories for all eternity. If their spirits could return to this plane, they'd rend you limb from limb."

Shocked, Metcalfe could only offer, "I tried to do the right thing."

Icarus continued to laugh and beat his head against Metcalfe's shoulder.

Despite himself, Metcalfe smiled. "Stop that!"

The boy was beyond speech. Watching him dissolve into a fit of hilarity, Metcalfe could only laugh himself. When Icarus finally recovered his voice, he looked up into his friend's eyes, but that only made him laugh again. "You're one of a kind, my friend," he stammered.

"Seriously, it's not funny," Metcalfe protested; but once again, Icarus was overwhelmed by the intoxicant and by what was probably a burst of hysterical mirth brought on by fear of what was coming next.

Metcalfe put an arm around him, felt his body continue to shake with quiet laughter. Actually, when he thought about it, it was probably the funniest damn thing in the universe.

CHAPTER SIXTEEN

"Communion? What the hell is that?"

"It's a kind of worship service," Metcalfe explained.

Sestus lowered his head into his hands. "Do you ever just stop? Can't you act like a civilized man, instead of a savage dancing in the jungle?"

"It will keep them calm, Sestus. When the Family is upset, they pray. Don't you want your prisoners to be calm?"

"They're not prisoners. We're just keeping them here for their own safety, because they're uncooperative by their own admission. But yes, I guess we want them calm. I thought they could only do this..."

"Communion."

"Right. I thought it had to be up at the caves."

Metcalfe shrugged. "That just makes them feel closer to nature. God is everywhere. And it's not like we're going to let them leave, is it?"

"And why do you have to be part of it?"

"They trust me, don't they? My taking part in their services got you that."

"I guess you did talk them out of running for the hills when the Admiral gave his order."

"There you go." Metcalfe grinned. "Want to join us?"

"Take off my clothes and sit chanting nonsense with a bunch of fanatics? No thank you."

"You're right, there won't be any cameras to broadcast your glorious body to the universe."

"And I've got ships to inspect. And so do you," he stabbed Metcalfe with a finger.

"Don't touch me, Five."

"I'll be..." he pulled a map from his implant, targeted the holo to appear in front of Metcalfe. "Here's two of the ships. I'll start there. Join me in an hour, or I'll send Druelinger to hunt you down. You've delayed long enough."

Metcalfe smiled confidently. "Not delaying, Five. Just making sure everything goes smoothly."

Metcalfe clapped his hands, and a tiny image from his implant exploded to the size of a shuttle's nose and jumped into the air over the heads of the assembled Marines. They were seated, cross-legged or standing, leaning on their rifles, in what amounted to a town square. Charred ends of logs and a ring of stones evidenced that many bonfires had burned on the spot around which they gathered.

In the fading heat of the evening, it was still warm enough that several of their number had loosened or removed parts of their armor. The residents of the Eleusis Colony all being secured within the meeting house, they felt a measure of relative safety.

"We have these five ships," said Metcalfe. "There are three others, but they weren't serviceable at all."

"Second-hand crap," muttered Sestus.

Metcalfe grinned. "And despite the generous offer from Blaurich Industries to supply new ships, we have to make do with what's on hand. These ships, combined, will hold 850 residents, approximately. We'll have to calculate payload on the fly. Colonel Druelinger, we'll need your troop transport to make space for about 500 colonists. Doing that, we can handle the evac in relays of two flights, assuming the ships Mr. Blaurich and I serviced survive the trips."

"I thought this was my operation," Sestus said quietly at his ear.

Metcalfe turned and smiled pleasantly. "By all means, take over." He cleared his throat and announced, "Mr. Blaurich will now complete the briefing."

Sestus stepped up to take Metcalfe's place at the center of the gathering. "We'll place a small contingent on each ship, including a pilot and armed escort."

"Metcalfe and I will pilot the large ships. The civilians will be made aware that we will not hesitate to fire at the first sign of trouble. A ship not conforming to the flight plan will be destroyed. That should discourage any attempted uprisings aboard the transporting ships."

Metcalfe cleared his throat. "That's not going to be an issue. The Family has agreed to come peacefully, and pursue their grievance with the Confederacy through the legal system."

"So they say," countered Sestus. "Every group has its rogues."

"Not this one," maintained Metcalfe pleasantly. "I can vouch for them."

Sestus almost shrugged. "It's been a long day's preparation. We leave at first light. That's all."

Druelinger stepped up to dismiss his people. Metcalfe held up a hand to him and said quietly, "If I may, Colonel, Mr. Aronson has asked me to offer you and your troops a gift in gratitude for your peaceful handling of the evacuation."

The man cocked his head, surprised. "Really."

"It's their way," Metcalfe explained. "Grace under fire. There's a large quantity of corn whiskey that would go to waste otherwise. I've tried it. Pretty smooth."

Druelinger grinned appreciatively. "I think I see why you've taken to these extremists, Metcalfe."

The men and women cheered and whistled appreciatively as Druelinger made the announcement, and Metcalfe led a small group to one of the barns to collect the casks. He oversaw their setup as a meal was prepared, and, personally distributed a portion of the first cask to all, insisting everyone participate in a toast to a successful mission. No one declined. *Titan's* Marines never declined when he bought them a round of drinks.

Later, as a fire blazed in the square against the cool of evening, and metal camp cups clanked in additional toasts, Druelinger sat with Metcalfe. He was glad of the Colonel's company, already tired of arguing with Sestus after only a few hours together.

"I'm glad to see," said the elder officer, "that the rumors about you going soft aren't true. I was afraid we had lost the man who saved our asses from Fehajiq." He lifted his cup with a nod. "It's clearly not the case."

"Thanks, Colonel. I can assure you that I'm very clear on what my duty is now."

He lifted his own cup and took a sip, regretting, after all, that it contained only water.

Metcalfe led Sestus, one arm under his shoulders, the other on his elbow for steering, into one of the prayer lodges. Sestus's weight was heavy against him, and, for the last few steps, his feet dragged more than they walked.

How much had the idiot drunk? He'd never known Sestus to get sloppy, but then he avoided socializing with him whenever possible. Idly, he wished a network holo camera were here to see this particular interaction.

"Time to sleep it off, Five," he said as he dumped his charge onto an unoccupied bed.

Sprawled awkwardly on his stomach, Sestus bawled out, "'Nother 'round!"

"Another round would kill you," said Metcalfe, holding Sestus's shoulders in place so he couldn't get up.

"Don't wanna lay down! The room spins if I lay down!"

"I imagine."

"Metcalfe?"

"Yes?"

"Turn off the room."

"Can't," said Metcalfe. "It's on a timer. Computer-controlled."

"Shit."

"Do you need to throw up?"

"No. Not yet."

"Okay, well," Metcalfe started to rise. "Sleep well."

Sestus grabbed his arm. It took him two tries, and even then he continued to flex his fingers against Metcalfe's forearm, as if unsure he actually had hold of him.

"Undress me?"

"Not on a bet."

"I can't sleep in my clothes."

Metcalfe sighed. "I'll take off your boots."

Sestus giggled. "You're a good friend, Metcalfe."

"I'm not your friend, Sestus."

Sestus made a noise that was half dismissive growl and half hiccup. "Well... y'could be. I'm not such a bad guy... y'know."

"And still I hate you." He finished removing the second boot, despite Sestus's random struggles, and tossed both to the floor.

"Yer just... sayin' that."

"No. I hate you. You're a despicable human being."

Sestus giggled again and rolled onto his back, staring stupidly up at him. "Don't leave. Stay with me."

"No."

"Please?" Sestus whined. "It'll be fun. I'm a level eight sex partner. Certified. Got awards."

"But you're drunk and you smell and there's still that whole I hate you thing."

Sestus's face seemed to slide downward in a grimace, as though it perhaps had lost its characteristic attachment to his skull. "I don't wanna sleep alone!"

"Oh, god, you're gonna cry."

"My head hurts, and the room's spinning, and..."

"Please don't cry."

"Why don't you like me, Metcalfe?"

"You've physically assaulted me on several occasions."

"You were the new guy. It was... y'know... hazing."

"You wrote a book trashing me as an incompetent token."

"My comp'ny's Public Info... mation Officer wrote that, ack'shly."

"And you're a rapist."

"Matter of opinion."

"Oh, and you once took advantage of a discriminatory order from the Admiralty to force me to have public sex with you."

"Bu' aside from that..."

"We could definitely hook up. If I liked boys and you were the last human being in the universe, I might consider it."

"It's not fair... You like everyone."

"Hardly."

"Everyone likes you."

"Double hardly."

"An' you don't even hafta try! I took classes! Didja know? I took classes in how to make people like me!" Sestus's lip quivered. An abortive sob turned into a belch.

"Oh, Jesus," muttered Metcalfe.

"An' it doesn't work! They like ta look at me! They like ta have me at their parties. No one really likes me."

Metcalfe sighed again, sat back against the foot board of the bed and almost (almost!) considered placing a friendly hand on Sestus's leg.

"Sestus... you try too hard. You collect endorsements and lines for your resume and... you think of friends in terms of what they can do for you. You only have time for people who've got some sort of power. People who can advance your station. You only had time for me once I started getting attention from the Admiralty and the media. Now you want to be friends. But you don't want to be friends with me, Terry Metcalfe, a person. You want to be friends with the hero of Quintil.

"And the ironic thing is that there is no hero of Quintil. There's just a guy who got put in charge for a little while for purposes of taking a test; and he happened to be sitting there when we got attacked. And then he couldn't notice that he was scared to death, because everything was going

to hell around him. So he stopped breathing for a few minutes, realized he
was probably going to die right there and right then; he tried to follow the
book and took the only options available to him. Somehow, through sheer,
dumb luck, he didn't die and he didn't let all of Quintil get killed. That's
not heroism. That's blind desperation and a few lucky breaks.

"Stop looking for opportunities to advance, Sestus, and you'll find they
show up anyway. Stop looking at what people can do for you, and start
looking at who they are. You'll find they're pretty interesting. A lot of
them are worth knowing and worth having as friends. Stop collecting
sound bytes, and start collecting experience. People will like you. Probably
not me, but... someone will see that there's good in you. Somewhere. Deep,
down, under all the certifications of merit and all the training in being swell.
And there is good in you, Sestus. There is in all of us. I... dammit, I guess
I don't really hate you, Okay? Do you think you can sleep now?"

Sestus snored loudly, waking himself up just in time to prevent him
choking on the copious amount of vomit he then deposited on the bed
spread.

He was glad to close his eyes for a moment.

Hadn't someone just been here?

Metcalfe. Yes, Metcalfe, sitting on the edge of the bed.

He was talking... saying something.

Oh hell, he was always talking.

Still, it was odd... Sestus in bed... Metcalfe, sitting with him in the
darkened room...

But it wasn't dark, it was bright, like a summer's day. Yes, it had to be
Summer. Everything was so green on the lawn, and the children were
barefoot.

Children? Yes, children, dozens of them, hungry-looking things.
Barefoot and dressed in rags. That one looked a bit like Metcalfe. Did
Metcalfe have a kid? Surely not one that old! This boy was almost a
teenager; scrawny, short, but still approaching puberty, if not there already.

The boy stood before a small girl with the same coloring. Did Metcalfe have two kids? A secret family? Who knew? There were bigger kids, better-fed kids, advancing on the little girl. The Metcalfe-boy spread his arms, trying to make himself as wide as possible to block their path to her, a pathetic attempt.

They shoved him, knocking him to the dirt. He shouted for the girl to run, but she scrambled to help him stand. One of the large boys kicked him in the ribs and she charged forward to kick the assailant's shins. Another boy scooped up the Metcalfe-boy and held him by his ragged collar only long enough to deliver a hammer blow into his jaw. Then the girl's would-be defender went down again. He coughed and spit. Blood flew from his lips to the ground.

Stop it! Sestus tried to call out. *You children behave!* They couldn't hear him. He couldn't hear him. He was sure he had shouted, but no sound came out. The bullies moved in on the boy, leering, hatred and bloodlust in their eyes.

He had to help. There had to be some way. The boy could be killed, and–

Sestus awoke in the midst of an earthquake. The floor tumbled and lurched. Gravity went wild, became homicidal, in fact, reaching out and taking hold of him like a pair of strong hands, trying to seize him and fling him from his perch. The ceiling was caving in. Huge chunks of debris fell, each one striking him in the head. His skull rung with bout after bout of blinding pain. How was he staying conscious? How could he even be still alive? How could a human body withstand so much damage? Reality itself had come unhinged.

"Mister Blaurich! You've got to wake up!"

How did an earthquake know his name?

"Take cover!" Sestus screamed, wondering if anyone was still alive to hear him.

"Mister Blaurich!" the voice called, louder now.

Sharp pain exploded in his right cheek. Someone had slapped him. It was more immediate, hurt worse than the tons of rubble which had fallen on his head. How was that possible?

Another slap, this time on his left cheek. Again someone called his name.

A third slap. Sestus reached out instinctively, grabbed his attacker's hand. "Stop it! That fucking hurts!"

"Sorry, Mr. Blaurich, but you need to open your eyes."

He did so. Then he closed them.

"No. No I really don't. It's bright in here, and my head hurts. Did you not notice that the ceiling fell on it?"

"What?"

"We're having an earthquake, you moron!"

"Mr. Blaurich! Snap to!"

What? Who was this idiot, spouting military jargon like some empty-headed drill sergeant when they were all about to die? He opened his eyes again. If he only had seconds left before the whole building fell, at least he could kill this idiot and make those seconds quieter. First, though, he needed to know the identity of his victim.

"Colonel Druelinger?" he registered. He barely recognized his own voice as he said it, and he doubted Druelinger understood it. His mouth was completely dry. And his breath was foul. He could taste it. Had he thrown up?

"What's this about an earthquake?" the Colonel demanded, standing in the midst of a very intact room in a log cabin on... what was the name of the planet? Eleusis, right.

"Uh..." grunted Sestus, looking around him, processing his surroundings as he came awake. "I thought the ceiling was falling on my head." He rubbed the back of his neck. "I still think it did."

Druelinger nodded, smiling grimly. "I imagine it feels that way. You threw back a good deal of whiskey last night, and the first round was spiked."

"Spiked? What–?"

Druelinger held up a small flask, blue and shiny. "I found this in the barn where Metcalfe got the casks."

Sestus took the proffered flask and sniffed it. A bitter scent assailed his nostrils. "What the hell is that?"

"Careful! Don't taste it! I can pull the name for you from the chemical analysis, but I can't begin to pronounce it. A Qraitian intoxicant. Highly toxic to humans. Less than half the capacity of that flask, poured into one of those barrels of whiskey, would be powerful enough that a shot from the barrel would knock out a healthy man for ten hours."

Sestus shook his head, regretted it. "But Metcalfe handed out the first round. I remember, he gave everyone a shot before the toast, then said that the barrel was bad and..." He trailed off, realizing what had happened.

"And dumped the first barrel, after every single one of us had a drink from it, so that no one could have two shots of the compromised whiskey. He didn't want to kill us, just knock us out while he and the Family took to their ships and went off-planet."

"But there wasn't enough room in the ships for all of them," protested Sestus. "Their largest transport was beyond repair–"

"Because the primary inertial guidance node had been removed."

"Metcalfe said they must have cannibalized it."

"And used it for what, a paperweight? No offense, Blaurich, but I can't believe you fell for that. One critical part without which a ship can't be launched turns up missing–the one part for which there are no spares, because they so rarely fail." He shook his head. "Metcalfe must have hidden it earlier. Once we were all passed out, all he had to do was replace it, and he had enough carrying capacity to take everyone we'd been holding into space."

Sestus buried his face in his hands. "Dammit! That traitorous son of a bitch!"

"Don't feel too bad. We all fell for it. Shoulda realized the stubborn bastard gave in to the whole evac plan too easily. Metcalfe never gives in without an argument."

"Tell me about it."

Druelinger held out a hand. "Come on. You've got to get up–" He surveyed Sestus's overall condition as he hauled him to his feet. "Get cleaned up too. We need to rejoin the fleet."

Sestus, now showered, reassembled and, thankfully, without a hangover since the Marines never traveled without doses of the finest treatments Quintil credits could buy, had made contacting Fournier his first priority.

"Yes, we've spotted them," said the Admiral's frowning image, miniaturized and standing, for all intents and purposes, on Sestus's lap. "At first, we thought you'd simply neglected to transmit voice confirmation, since all the identification data being auto-transmitted was accurate."

"Well, it would be," said Sestus. Of course it would be, since Metcalfe was providing it.

"Then I contacted Colonel Druelinger, after you failed to answer me."

"My apologies, Admiral," said Sestus with no small amount of guilt. "I was a bit under the weather."

"I quite understand the situation," said Fournier. "Druelinger explained. What I don't understand is how you failed to double-check behind Metcalfe when he said those ships were inoperable, and why in the hell you let him serve everyone drinks!"

"I wasn't thinking, sir."

"You damned well were not! But none of that is relevant at the moment. Now we need to be prepared for whatever they're planning. An attack, most likely."

"I disagree, sir. Non-violent resistance is the Family's hallmark. Besides, if they wanted to battle us, they'd have minimized our forces in space by disabling the Marines' transports. Clearly, they aren't trying to keep us grounded."

"Then what the hell are they planning?"

"I wish I knew, Admiral. They planned the escape so carefully, I can't imagine their plan ends with all of us hanging there in space, staring each other down."

Fournier shook his head. "It may end with them being blown out of space, however. Contact me when you've assumed command of your ship. I'm going to try to get those idiots to respond."

The holo winked out, the tiny figure disappearing from its place in front of him. Sestus felt relieved not to have the Admiral, albeit a tiny version of him, standing on his crotch. He leaned his head against the bulkhead. He had been lucky enough to score an inner end seat in the row on the transport. Beside him in that row sat eleven Marines, and their row was one of a dozen or more.

A blast of voice from nearby caught Sestus's attention. One of the Marines' radios was on and tuned to pick up intership traffic.

"Signal acknowledged," said an automated voice. Sestus recognized it as the A.I. from Fournier's ship, the automated harbinger of an incoming transmission. "Commander, Eleusis Colonial Evac, hails Commander, *CNV Lindstrom Douglas.*"

In response, he heard a demand from a live voice, Fournier's voice. "This is Admiral Fournier. How dare you declare yourself a force in opposition to the Confederate Navy? Who the hell is commanding?"

"We're not in opposition, we're simply a private vessel," came the answer.

But the speaker did not have to give his name to be recognized. Sestus muttered it disgustedly aloud before he'd heard the second syllable:

"Metcalfe."

Sestus was on the command deck of his ship, the *Henley*, before Fournier accepted Metcalfe's request to confer. In the interim, the Admiral had accepted a call from Captain Atal, en route back to Eleusis, quite against orders.

"I didn't have much choice, Georg," Atal had said, "since you've been ignoring my priority call for hours now."

Fournier had sent Sestus a private message while his ship docked, saying he needed all available intel on Metcalfe's ship, an antique passenger liner they'd thought disabled. While Sestus was working up a response, he'd heard another voice on the radio, which he had borrowed from the Marine for the duration.

"Fournier!" Ustenar barked over the channel, "there are unidentified ships from the planet's surface encroaching on us! They are to withdraw immediately, and assume a neutral posture, or we will fire on all available targets!"

"Not a good day to be the Admiral," Sestus muttered to himself as he entered *Henley's* command deck hatch and kicked himself toward the tactical console. The junior officer he'd left in charge saluted and cleared out of his way.

Fournier's response was tight. "I assure you, Commander Ustenar, that the ships in question are not authorized by me. They are rogues, launched without permission, and include renegades from both our side and your own."

"Then you will not mind if I fire on them?" asked Ustenar.

"I think it would be wise to speak to them first," admitted Fournier. "Their... commander... has a channel open."

"And why have you not asked him to state his business?"

"I was gathering intelligence first on their capabilities."

"Indeed. I would request that all communications between this... rogue force and your ship be made open to me. Flatly, Fournier, I do not trust you."

"The feeling is mutual, madame. Very well. Please do listen in." On the holo feed which Sestus had punched up, he saw Fournier turn to one of his officers. He ordered the channel to Metcalfe opened.

In front of Fournier, a hologram of Metcalfe appeared, arms crossed, relaxed, perfectly calm. "Admiral, I take it you've studied our ships' capabilities. You're aware that were not armed. The Family presents no danger to the Naval or Qraitian forces–"

"And you speak for the Family?"

"For the moment, I do."

"Where's Aronson?"

The elder of the family appeared next to Metcalfe. "I am here, Friend Fournier, but Terry Metcalfe speaks on our behalf."

"Metcalfe will speak on no one's behalf!" Fournier shot back. "He is a criminal, a deserter. Our first order of business will be your surrender of him to–"

"I am sorry, Fournier. That will not be happening. Metcalfe will explain."

"No! You will speak for your people! I will not negotiate with a criminal!"

Aronson inclined his head slowly. "Among the Family, only he who is moved by the Spirit must speak. The rest are to observe a contemplative silence. I will be silent now." He stepped out of the pickup and vanished.

Fournier's image shook its head. "You've made a real mess of things this time, Metcalfe, not that I'm surprised."

"Admiral," said Metcalfe, "I assure you I have not deserted, nor is my intent to disobey your orders."

"You drugged our troops and stole ships from under our noses!"

"The ships were not stolen, sir. They belong to the individual members of the Family, and are being used with their permission."

"They were commandeered! Even the owner of a ship is subject to criminal charges if he attempts to reclaim it from authorized military use. And you poisoned the men and women who were there to supervise the evacuation!"

"I did what I had to do to protect everyone involved, sir."

"What the hell does that mean?"

"I ask to meet with you in person," said Metcalfe. "You and Commander Ustenar. There is vital information I must share with you. I can explain everything when we meet."

"We will not meet with you," said Ustenar. "I am not satisfied, despite your staged performance, that you, Metcalfe, are not merely in league with Fournier. Your people's attempts to infiltrate us have been sloppy thus far, but it is clear your intentions are hostile. The spies are going to be executed–"

"Spies?" asked Metcalfe, surprised. "What spies?"

"What spies indeed?" mocked Ustenar. "They will be questioned again, before their sentence is carried out, to determine what they know of your motives, Metcalfe. If they are what I suspect, I will respond with the full force of my ship's weapons–"

"Commander," said Metcalfe evenly, "I have to caution you not to attack the Family's vessels, or the Navy's for that matter. It could easily result in your immediate destruction."

"Is that a threat, Metcalfe?" demanded Fournier.

"Absolutely not, Admiral. It's a fact."

"You said you were not armed!" responded Ustenar.

"Our ships are not. We are not. But there are forces at work here which you do not understand. You're aware of what happened to one of your own people on Eleusis."

"He was assassinated by the Family," said Ustenar.

"He was not. He initiated violence, and was neutralized. The same thing will happen to you now, on a much larger scale, if you do not–"

"Metcalfe, if you are in control of weapons on the planet's surface–" Fournier began.

"I am in control of nothing," said Metcalfe. "And there aren't any weapons, as we understand weapons, sir. There are... forces, however."

Fournier nodded and said sarcastically, "The God of Eleusis, I suppose."

"That's what it's been called, yes," said Metcalfe. "I assure you it's very real."

"Superstitious nonsense!" barked Fournier. "And I'll listen to no more of it. Mr. Metcalfe, you will surrender yourself immediately, and allow Colonel Druelinger to board and assume command of that ship. His vessel is maneuvering into position now, and–"

"Do not approach this ship!" Metcalfe warned urgently. "Warn him off, Admiral!"

"You are not giving orders here!"

But Sestus could read in Metcalfe's tone that giving orders was the last thing on his mind. When Fournier had mentioned Druelinger, Sestus had seen something in Metcalfe eyes that he had not seen often: fear. Metcalfe had not been afraid when he'd nearly committed suicide by ramming the *Titan* into a captured freighter. His damned faith kept him from fearing for himself. He feared for others, though, when they were threatened. Right now, Sestus could tell, Metcalfe was worried for Druelinger and his troops. Sestus started to contact Fournier on a private channel, but things were moving too fast.

"Fournier," said Ustenar, "I will give you only moments more to assume control of those vessels. If your Marines cannot do it, I will take action."

"Admiral, Commander, please," said Metcalfe, "let's meet in a neutral location, and I'll explain–"

Fournier wasn't listening. "Druelinger!" he called out. "Move in! Take that vessel! Bring Metcalfe to me immediately!"

On his tactical display, Sestus watched the green color-coded outline of the Marine troop transport, the one he'd ridden to his own ship and which had since undocked and set course for Metcalfe's vessel. It inched forward at Fournier's command, approaching the unarmed passenger liner from which Metcalfe spoke for the family.

He heard Metcalfe call out on another channel, "Colonel Druelinger, this is Metcalfe. I have intelligence to which the Admiral is not privy. It is urgent that you not engage this vessel."

"Sorry, Metcalfe," said Druelinger's voice through the radio.

In the holo display before him, Sestus saw Metcalfe close his eyes. He said quietly. "I'm sorry." He reached his hand out for something nearby, and his image winked out.

"Metcalfe!" Fournier ordered. "Re-open this channel!"

He was met with only silence. Moments later, the green avatar of the Marine vessel came so close to the red of the passenger liner that they almost touched. Then the green shape simply vanished.

"What the hell?" muttered Sestus. For a moment, he suspected a malfunction, but the other ships all showed on his display. "Where's the transport?" he demanded of his junior officer.

The woman shook her head. "No reading, Mr. Blaurich. And nothing on visual. Colonel Druelinger's ship is gone."

Emerging from an L-space conjugate, *Titan* was just coming into communications range of the Eleusis system when the radio channels exploded with chatter about the vanished Marine transport. Kevin Carson, supervising ship's communications from the Command Deck, signaled Atal over.

"What now?" the Captain asked grimly.

The channel to Fournier had been open before, and re-established when they emerged from their travel in L-Space. Neither the Admiral nor any of his crew were responding directly, however. They simply left the line open. Carson had heard the tail-end of a conversation between Fournier, Metcalfe and the Qraitian Commander.

"Colonel Druelinger and a Marine transport were attempting to dock with the Family's ship. I think... I think they've been destroyed, sir."

Atal's eyebrows shot up. "Who? The Marines or the Family?"

"The Marines, sir. Their ship dropped off tracking. Telemetry just ceased. Eyewitnesses say it just... disappeared from space." He searched his Captain's face, looking for any trace of relief or other emotion at the news that Metcalfe wasn't gone. Druelinger was a shipmate too, of course, and all his people.

Atal maintained a poker face. "Explosion?"

Carson shook his head. "There one second, gone the next."

Atal swore and muttered, "Like the Qraitians Kaya saw." He asked, "There was no hostile action from the Family ship?"

"No sir. I caught the last bit of traffic, right before it happened. It sounds like they warned the Marines off."

"Who did? Who's in command of the Family ship, Aronson?"

Carson swallowed. "Metcalfe, sir?"

The Captain closed his eyes and took two precise, deep breaths. "Get Fournier's attention, and put me through."

Carson nodded, and turned to key in a priority alert across the open channel. They had ignored all vocal requests for attention, so floating there saying "hello? hello?" would be a little silly. But a priority alert would flash a glowing, chiming avatar in someone's face aboard Fournier's ship.

After fifteen seconds, he shook his head. "They're too wrapped up in what's happened, sir."

"Patch us in to what they're saying, then."

At Carson's request, the audio traffic from the three ships filled the air.

Fournier was shouting. "–Tell me it's beyond your control! You just killed hundreds of people, Metcalfe!"

Metcalfe's voice was strained. "This ship took no action, sir. Colonel Druelinger's ship was identified as a threat and... eliminated." He sounded... uncertain.

Metcalfe never sounded uncertain.

Atal whispered to Carson. "Get me visual as soon as we come into range."

"And who identified it as a threat?" Ustenar's voice this time, laced with fury.

"That's what I'm trying to tell you," said Metcalfe.

Atal turned to the helm. "Full speed. Let's get in on this."

"That they were killed by a myth and it's beyond your control? I won't buy it. This has gone from a case of cultural tolerance, taken to ludicrous extreme, to a verifiable threat to Confederate interests. Primitive superstitions don't cloak your real motives, Metcalfe. You've snapped under the pressure of the battle with Fehajiq, and you're lashing out at us out of some twisted desire for revenge or absolution for your sins."

"Admiral, I'm saner than I've ever been in my life. And there's nothing primitive about rational people observing an unexplained phenomenon. There's more to reason than blind devotion to scientific orthodoxy!"

The holo grid in front of Carson lit, indicating a lock on an active signal. He'd had it set to pick up visual from Eleusis.

"Metcalfe," said Fournier, "you will stand down. Now. You will surrender that vessel and yourself, or—"

"I can't do that, Admiral," Metcalfe barely whispered.

"Enough!" shrieked Ustenar. "Fournier, you engineered this! It's a deception to drive us away!"

"I assure you Commander—"

"I believe not a word you say, human!"

"Metcalfe is acting against my orders!" Fournier finished.

Ustenar paused, as if considering it. Calmly, she said, "Fine. Prove it."

"What?" asked Fournier. "How?"

"Destroy the liner. Kill this Metcalfe, and I'll accept that you wish to negotiate a cease fire."

"Commander, you will not dictate—"

"Otherwise, I will open fire on your ship, Admiral. You may take us down, but we will die in honorable battle, and you will simply die."

Atal called out, trying to get his superior's attention. "Georg, don't! We're coming into–"

Fournier's voice cut him off. "Mister Blaurich! Your ship is closest. Move into position!"

In the space above the grid, images shimmered into being. The passenger liner that must be the family ship floated at a distance from the squatting, hideous bulk of the Qraitian vessel. Off on the extreme edge, completing a narrow triangle, was a small Confederate frigate. Sestus's ship, it had to be. The image must be coming from *Douglas's* camera.

"Don't do it, Blaurich," muttered Atal at Carson's shoulder; but the frigate *Henley* inched forward.

"Target the liner," said Fournier's voice. "Destroy that ship, before they kill anyone else!"

"Admiral, no!" came Metcalfe's voice. "I'm not asking for myself, or even for the others. Sestus," he implored his fellow officer, "think! You saw what happened to Druelinger! If you attack us, you could all be killed! Please, let me–"

"Cut that damned channel!" barked Fournier.

Metcalfe's voice went quiet in mid-sentence.

As the frigate came around, Carson dug his fingernails into the handholds of his retaining harness. "Sestus, no..." he whispered. He wanted to leap from his seat, to rush to a shuttle. Ridiculous. They were still out of range. *Titan* would get there the fastest, and she would be too late to help.

"Weapons at ready," said Sestus.

Carson wanted to hide his eyes, but couldn't look away. This was it, he thought. Sestus was about to fire. Would his shot destroy Metcalfe's ship? Or would the mysterious unknown force swallow the frigate whole? Who was he about to lose, his best friend or his latest lover? His anger over his last words with Metcalfe came back to him, as did the bitterness of his parting with Sestus. Dammit, he couldn't lost either of them now!

Behind him, Atal drew in his breath, his own frustration almost palpable. Like Carson, he knew they couldn't get there in time, they could not save whoever was about to die. Helplessness settled on the command deck like a radiation blanket, heavy and smothering.

"Sestus please," Carson whispered. "Please, please, please oh god, please..."

He was still chanting his mantra all unawares when Sestus's weapons flared, particle beams lashed out angrily, and the engine module of Fournier's ship detonated in a blaze of silent fire.

CHAPTER SEVENTEEN

He couldn't have explained it if anyone had asked why he'd done it. Sestus had taken control of the main cannon, personally firing the shot Fournier had ordered. Ostensibly, he hadn't wanted any of his junior officers to fire the shot which destroyed a ship and killed hundreds of people. What had made him deliberately target Fournier's ship, dealing it a crippling blow without actually (he hoped) injuring anyone, he couldn't possibly have put into words. As he had targeted the shot, the image of a scrawny boy standing up to bullies, a little girl cowering behind him, was all his mind's eye could see.

"Damn," he said tonelessly as he watched the incandescence of the blast fade, saw the blast damage to the ship he had just fired on, "my shot went wild."

His junior looked at him in disbelief. "Sir?"

"Perhaps it was the same force which destroyed the Marine transport," he said. "We can't risk using weapons until we know what the hell is going on here." This last he said with authority, as his confidence grew in his story. "Can we raise the Admiral?"

She shook her head. "Communications went out. You must have–that is, the blast must have taken out their antenna array."

"Damn," he said again. "So the Admiral's out of the loop for the time being." He chewed his lip for a moment, realizing that, without Fournier, he was in command of the operation. The thought frightened him, but, at the same time, relieved him. Fournier was being too aggressive. Ordering the Marines in had been one thing, but ordering an attack on a ship which, apparently, had just vaporized the transport. Too risky. Perhaps he could manage the situation without getting anyone else killed. "Get me Metcalfe," he told the young woman.

Within seconds, his rival's face appeared before him, an ironic smile showing. "I suppose I should thank you for our lives."

"I believe the expression is 'oops,'" Sestus replied.

"It was a lucky mistake then," Metcalfe conceded. "The blast would not have hit us. I believe your ship would have followed Druelinger's if you'd fired on us."

He said it so casually... Metcalfe and Sestus had never been friends, it was true. But Metcalfe was so the stalwart, upstanding type–the "violence is the last refuge of the incompetent" type. How could he speak so easily about the deaths of dozens of their colleagues? Men they'd only hours before gotten drunk with! Still, Sestus had to think about what the official account of this incident would say.

"Perhaps... whatever it was... the thing which killed Druelinger and the rest, diverted my shot."

Metcalfe merely shook his head.

"Sir," the junior officer said quietly, "Commander Ustenar is demanding to know what's going on. She wants to speak to the Admiral."

"Tell her we're attempting to ascertain his status," Sestus ordered. It occurred to him only then that he should be trying to do just that. He needed to reach an understanding with Metcalfe first, though.

"Fournier's off line," Sestus told him. "Communications knocked out by the blast."

"Seems you're in charge."

"So it seems, and I have to go with the Admiral's last order, Metcalfe; you've got to stand down. Turn that ship–all those ships–over to Naval authority."

"Actually, Fournier's last order was to destroy us."

"I think we've established that would be suicide."

"You're right. And I can't stand down, Sestus, for the same reason you can't fire on me. The Family must not be taken from this world. I should say no one must make the attempt. They can't be taken. Anyone who tries to force the issue will be destroyed. And that's not a threat. I'm not the one pulling the strings here, nor are Aronson or any of his people."

"I don't know why, but I believe you."

"Probably because I'm telling the truth. Sestus, you've got to make Fournier see reason."

"That's the trouble. From his perspective, he does."

"He doesn't know what I know."

"And what do you know?"

Metcalfe hesitated. "Unfortunately, Sestus, not enough to explain it to you. Let's just say that the Voice of Eleusis is an old and powerful entity. It protects what it considers to be its own, and it considers the Family its own."

"You are kind of pushing the envelope to trust, here."

"I know."

"So what's your end game, Metcalfe? What has to happen so that we can all leave here alive?"

"The Family must be left in peace, by both sides. Any of the military forces can stay, as long as they don't act."

"I don't see that happening."

"It has to. The danger, otherwise, is too great for everyone involved."

At his elbow, the junior office gently cleared her throat. "Sir, the Qraitian Commander is becoming belligerent."

Sestus sighed. "Stand by, Metcalfe."

"I'm not going anywhere."

Sestus nodded, and Ustenar's image flashed into being before him. He gently shunted Metcalfe's holo out of the pickup, not wanting to incite the Qraitian any further.

"Fournier isn't responding!" she blurted. "Is he dead? Who in the names of the Forgotten are you?"

"Sestus Blaurich, ma'am, commanding the relocation forces. Admiral Fournier is–"

"Blaurich? Never heard of you. Are you a captain? Your facial skin is smooth and taut. In a human, that means you're young, since you do not shed old skins."

"Correct, Commander; and no, I'm not a captain. I'm... " he cringed inwardly. "A midshipman."

"I see," she hissed in a tone which suggested Sestus had been judged and sentenced.

"Admiral Fournier is very much alive, I'm certain. An... accident has damaged his communications array. I've no doubt he'll be in touch with you as soon as possible. In the meantime–"

"In the meantime, while I'm delighted to see that you've taken to firing on each other–"

"It was a misfire, Commander."

"Which delights me even more. An enemy who can't hit a target is certainly a hazard, but not a credible threat. Your incompetence will make my job that much easier."

Sestus ground his teeth, realized he was doing it, stopped. "And what is your job at this juncture, Commander, if I may ask?"

"To collect all Qraitian nationals and leave this system immediately. The situation here has become too unstable. I cannot risk my ship and crew any longer."

"Very well," said Sestus. "I trust you won't object to our continued presence here... in our own space."

"I do, in fact. I object very strongly. It has been demonstrated, Midshipman, that there is a formidable power at work on and around the planet Eleusis. Whether or not that power is subject to the control of intelligences human or Qraitian remains to be seen. Its very existence, however, is a threat to the security of the Qraitian Empire. We cannot allow your forces to remain. This planet needs to be quarantined."

"All due respect, Commander, you can't tell us what to do in our own space."

"I can, Mr. Blaurich; I must. What's allowed under treaty, and what additional treaties need to be established, these things are for the diplomats to decide. But here, today, I must act in my Empire's interests as I understand them. Leave this space, or I will be forced to take decisive action."

"Commander, I believe you saw the results of my people's attempts to take action."

"I did. I attribute them to incompetence. Or trickery. We are dealing with the trickster Metcalfe, after all."

At any other time during his association with Metcalfe, Sestus would have conceded that point. Metcalfe could be devious, for all his holier-than-thou pretensions; but, though he didn't know why, Sestus believed Metcalfe's assertion that what was happening here was beyond human control.

"I assure you, Commander, there is no trickery here, just a great big unknown."

"I want the Family ships to leave the system," said Ustenar.

"That's our plan too, ma'am." Indeed, Sestus reflected, what she was proposing wasn't really a bad plan at all. If people died en masse just by coming to this place, it was best to stay away from it. But the Qraitians hadn't been afraid to explore it before, possessing more knowledge about its destructive potential than the Confederacy had. Why would they suddenly fear it now? Probably they wouldn't, and Ustenar just wanted to be free to figure out a way to harness the massive destructive forces to which Eleusis was home.

"And I want all Qraitians in their custody brought to my ship, immediately," pressed Ustenar.

"That's a different story," said Sestus. "Let me re-establish communication with the Admiral–"

"Quickly, then!" she snapped. "If I don't soon have my people, I will take them, with all the weapons at my disposal."

"Of course it's out of the question," said Aronson, strapped into the co-pilot's seat aboard the Family's liner. "I can't believe she expects us to hand over members of our Family, whatever their background."

"She doesn't expect it," said Metcalfe. "It's just an excuse to fire on us."

"They won't be able to kill us, nor would the power of Eleusis be of any benefit to them," said Aronson. "You know that better than anyone."

Metcalfe nodded. He had closed the channel to Sestus on the frigate, wanting to confer privately with Aronson. "Actually, I think Ustenar also knows it, knows it very well. She's trying to keep things unstable, hoping to goad the Navy's forces into launching an attack that will get them all killed."

"It might work," said Aronson. "That young man," he meant Blaurich, "seems inexperienced and scared. Your Admiral Fournier seems to have a hair trigger as well. If they attack–"

"They will," said Metcalfe with conviction. "Someone will attack."

"Then they'll die. We can't allow–"

"No one will die," interrupted Metcalfe.

Aronson looked at him, astounded. "Terry, people have already died! Friends of yours!"

Metcalfe hesitated. "I know," he said darkly. "It... They moved in when I told them not to–"

"And Blaurich or Fournier may fire on you, despite your sincere advice against it," said Aronson. "And they will die!"

"They won't. Druelinger moved before I was ready. It couldn't be helped."

Aronson shook his head sadly, never taking his eyes off Metcalfe. "Is this the same man who came to my world, seeking peace? Is this that same man I'm talking to, telling me now about unavoidable losses like the coolest military strategist? You're speaking of human lives–God's children!–not chess pieces."

"I know," said Metcalfe. "I promise you, Brock, no one–no more–will die. I... we... have a plan."

"You and Eleusis?"

"Yes."

"All right. Tell me the plan."

"I can't. Not all of it, anyway."

"Why not?"

"Because you'd feel honor-bound to share it with others. That would defeat its purpose."

"So you don't trust me."

"On the contrary," said Metcalfe, "I trust you implicitly. It's because I know how strong your morals are that I know you would take steps I'm not ready for you to take."

"If I'm behaving morally, and yet I'm acting against the best interests of your plan, Terry... how moral can your plan be?"

Metcalfe took a breath and considered it. While he did, the control room hatch opened. He heard someone enter behind him. Undeterred, he answered Brock's challenge. "Our plan is neither moral nor immoral. It simply will work."

"Terry," said a nervous voice behind him. It was Elspeth's. She had been the one who came in. "You're frightening me. You don't sound like yourself."

"You haven't known me that long," he said, even he thought a bit coldly.

She floated around and settled in front of him, anchoring himself on the armrests of his couch. "But I have known you, and you're a warm, loving, *human* man. Now you sound like a machine."

Metcalfe reached out and took her hand gently, starting to speak.

Aronson cut him off. "Is that it, Terry? Are you being influenced by Eleusis? Is it changing the way you think?"

Elspeth looked from one to the other. "I don't understand," she said. "Influenced by Eleusis? I–"

"Eleusis is a machine," said Metcalfe. "The intelligence you feel when you Commune is an ages-old computer. It has chosen me as its human... agent, I suppose."

She shook her head. "This isn't possible. Brock, you knew about this?"

"I did, child. For a long time."

"Why didn't you tell us?"

"It didn't matter. As I told Terry when he learned the truth, all intelligence can speak for God. It doesn't matter if it's machine or human. Our Communions with Eleusis truly bring us closer to the Lord."

"Then why don't you trust Eleusis now?" asked Metcalfe. "Why are you suddenly afraid that it's influencing me in the wrong direction?"

Aronson sighed. "Because I fear, I suppose, the influence of human weakness. Eleusis has harmed no one in millenia... now it is causing harm again. I wonder if it is not best left to find its fate... and seek God's will... by itself."

Metcalfe tightened his grip on Elspeth's shoulder, squeezing affectionately as he reached out and clasped Aronson's hand. "Both of you... trust me. Please. Everything's going to be fine."

They are frightened. Are they frightened of me?
No, Eleusis. Of both of us.
But our plan is to protect them all.
Yes. Unfortunately their fear is part of the plan.
What if they become too afraid?
We can't let that happen. We won't.
Something's wrong...
It's happening again. I'm separated again, asking people to trust me, making the decisions without them. It's not what I want.
Then why do you keep letting it happen?

Kaya leaned, shoulder to shoulder with Faulkner, against the rear bulkhead on the command deck of Ustenar's ship. She was relieved, she realized, to be rid of that damned Qraitian skin suit. Yes, the loss of it meant her life was in grave danger, but still, it was good to be in one's own skin.

The Commander reared up on her dais, ready to strike, as Sestus's hologram reappeared before her.

"Well?" she demanded.

"I've still no communication with the Admiral," said Sestus. "If you can just–"

"And the Family? Are they sending us their Qraitians?"

Sestus shook his head. "No, Commander. They will not surrender those they consider to be members of their own family. I'm afraid–"

"I'm afraid I can wait no longer, Midshipman. Unpredictable as events have become, I may not have another chance. I'm sure you understand that my first priority is to work the will of the gods."

"Metcalfe would understand," said Sestus. "I don't believe in gods."

"I'm sure they'll find that amusing when you stand before them. I wonder if they'll laugh as they sentence you to the eternal waking death?" She chuckled, a sound like dry leaves in a burning desert wind. "No matter. I know what the gods would have me do. I must eliminate the threat to my people, and all who would perpetuate it. I will begin by eliminating your ships." She turned to her officer. "Target the *Douglas!*"

"Fire on that ship, and I'll have to—" Sestus began.

"No, Midshipman... You cannot prevent your Admiral's destruction. Our ship outguns yours severely. Fight us and you die... and then he dies. I'll pick you off one by one." She turned to her crew and issued orders to each in turn. "Bring us around, attack speed! Lively, now! The first to shoot is heir to the warrior of Quintil!"

Kaya leaned her head in close to Celia's. "Whatever it was that took Druelinger... will it hit us too?"

Celia replied, "I don't know. Does the entity—whatever it is—care about violence that isn't directed at the Family? Or do you believe them that it's a trick of Metcalfe's. That he destroyed the transport?"

"Terry kill a hundred of our own shipmates? I don't believe that for a minute. I saw his eyes. I know him. He was horrified, and as surprised as anyone. Well, maybe not surprised. I think... he knew it was going to happen."

"He tried to warn them off."

Kaya watched as the crew busied themselves, fulfilling Ustenar's urgent commands. She felt the ship pivot, inertial dampers not keeping up with the sudden acceleration. On the tactical display, she saw the growing image that represented Terry and the Family, a target for every weapon on this war ship.

"If it happens... if we... vanish... Will it hurt, do you think?" she asked the Doctor.

"Are you afraid, Kaya?" said Celia.

She shook her head. She thought of Dad, of Yank, of Cernaq, Carson and Aer'la. "Just wish I could say goodbye." She looked up into the ancient eyes of her companion. "It's been an honor, Doctor."

Celia smiled, crinkling her eyes and mouth and bathing Kaya in an affection she'd rarely felt from anyone. To her surprise, the Doctor cradled her head with one hand and kissed her gently on the lips. "It's been an adventure, little one."

Ustenar screamed for the weapons to fire. Kaya heard the insistent hum of power building to release. She counted down, knowing the cycle of the weapons all too well. She picked the predicted point in time and, despite herself, counted down to it.

Four... three... two...

There was a blast of impact as something struck the ship starboard. Was this it? Was this what it had been like for the others? Not a peaceful, sudden end, but a detonation not witnessed by outsiders? Like being on the event horizon of a singularity, from the inside, it lasted forever?

She squeezed Celia's hand.

Ustenar swore, threw back her head and hissed at the ceiling.

"Particle beam strike," reported one of the crew. "Starboard, just aft of—"

Another impact rocked them.

"Names of the Forgotten!" shrieked Ustenar.

"Commander!" called the crewman, pointing, drawing her attention to the holo display of space beyond.

Kaya followed his gesture and fully yelped an exclamation of glee.

There, coming around again, preposterously massive yet agile as any vessel in space, coming in hard, guns blazing, was *CNV Titan*.

"Commander Ustenar, this is Atal. Stand down. Any attempt to fire on Confederate vessels, military or civilian, will result in the destruction of your ship."

Atal crossed his arms and waited tensely for a response. The Qraitian wasn't stupid or insane, unlike the terrorist Fehajiq. She had to know that

Titan was too much for her. He was rewarded with Ustenar's image blazing into existence before him.

"You attacked us, Captain!"

"A warning shot only. You'll find I struck heavily armored areas. No significant damage." The ship to ship equivalent of a slap on the ass, he thought to himself; but she wouldn't have understood the reference. "I am requesting a cease fire while I assess the situation."

Her slitted eyes widened. "Shouldn't that come from Admiral Fournier?"

"It should, but I am unable to contact him. You may assume that I command the Confederate forces until you hear otherwise from the Admiral or myself."

She smiled and assumed a relaxed posture. "Very well. I grant a temporary cease fire. It will give me the time I need to execute two spies."

Atal forced his expression to remain neutral. He was not a nervous parent, and had accepted long ago that his daughter's life was one comprised of the same level of danger that had defined his own. He didn't believe she would kill Kaya and Celia, not while there was value in them as hostages. Still, any threat against his child made his blood boil.

"You've caught spies?" he asked casually.

Ustenar gestured, and Kaya and Faulkner were pushed into the holo pickup.

Atal nodded. "Ladies."

"Captain," said Kaya. "Good to see you."

"You're aware of their presence?" asked Ustenar.

"I sent them," Atal replied. It was only half a lie.

"You baldly admit to committing an act of espionage? I would execute you as well, if I could, Captain, and be well within my rights!"

"Every Qraitian alive would execute me, Commander. Many have tried. I believe my head mounted on the wall of the den would be the key to infinite wealth and power in the Empire. You won't be getting the chance to execute me, Commander, and you'd be a fool to harm these two."

"Spies forfeit their lives, Captain. It's even admitted in the treaty. How dare you spy on–?"

"My Terran allies have a saying, commander. Something about a speaking pot calling a kettle black."

"I don't–"

"It means that you're just as guilty as I am, and more. You may have the invitation of the residents of Eleusis to keep a ship in orbit here, but you're still in Confederate space, in violation of treaty. And your people placed spies among the Family long before I sent those two in. Kill those two, and I have no reason to allow your ship to leave this system intact. Clear?"

"Nothing is clear, Captain! We have a standoff. What do you propose to do?"

Atal sighed. "Give me ten minutes, Commander. I just got here and I have no idea what the hell's going on. Ten minutes. No firing of weapons, no executions."

"Agreed. Ten minutes."

Atal turned to Carson. "Cut the channel. Get me Blaurich."

When the young midshipman appeared, he looked haunted. Impeccably groomed as ever, but with a care-worn expression in his eyes. "Captain? Relieved to see you."

"I imagine you are, with your weapons malfunctioning as they are." Atal worked hard to keep the amusement out of his tone. He had never liked Sestus Blaurich, all through the years the boy had been (unwillingly, from Kaya's end) part of his daughter's social circle. The heir to Blaurich Industries had never given him cause to feel the satisfaction or pride a Captain wants to feel in his officers. Today, though, he wondered if perhaps there was a shred of hope for the boy.   "An unfortunate accident, sir."

"It will be so logged, Mr. Blaurich."

"I appreciate that, Captain."

A pity, thought Atal, that the first-ever alliance between their rival families couldn't be written up in a press release. His father's team of toadies would have drooled over the opportunity.

"Drop back and hold a defensive position with the Family ships, Mr. Blaurich. Any word from the Admiral?"

"None, sir. I assume they're repairing communications."

"Very good. Atal out."

Carson called out, "Sir, I've run a visual check on the *Douglas's* comm array. It's a total loss. I believe we have the necessary replacement parts aboard. Shall I arrange a repair team?"

Atal considered it. If he didn't send someone immediately, he'd catch hell. On the other hand, as soon as Fournier was back in the loop, he'd catch hell. "Never do today what you can put off until tomorrow," he muttered.

"Sir?" wondered Carson.

"Not, uh... not until I'm completely up to speed on the situation, eh Carson? Would hate to deploy resources prematurely."

Carson grinned. "Yes sir."

"But keep an eye on them for me, would you? If they're in trouble I need to know." *If Georg Fournier is going to burn alive,* he thought, *I at least want to be there to watch.* He reprimanded himself for unprofessional thinking, then realized that such a reprimand mattered as little to him as it would to one of his midshipmen.

Carson monitored the silent hulk of Fournier's ship, glad of an excuse to look busy and not interact with others. He wasn't up for having to entertain just now, and that's what all social or work occasions with other people were to him, gigs where he had to entertain.

An introvert by nature, Carson had been told he had a way with people. He supposed it must be true, given the number of attractive girls and women, and, more recently since his friends had learned of his primary gender preference, boys and men, he'd lured into beds... and bathroom stalls, alleys, communication booths, spaces under tables in crowded restaurants... Not that he had suppressed his preferences before they'd found out... before Sestus had revealed them... He'd just been more circumspect, picking up male partners only when off ship and alone.

Sestus... The twinge of anger he felt at remembering Sestus's sharing of his private life on a holo documentary faded, replaced by confusion and anxiety.

At first, it had taken him some time to come down from the emotional peak of anger and fear he had reached when he'd thought Sestus was going to blow his best friend–and hundreds of others–out of space. Now, grateful though he was, he just wanted to know why Sestus had taken the awful chance, speaking career-wise, of attacking Fournier's ship. And he had no doubt that a deliberate attack was what it was. Despite Sestus's discretion in speaking of it, and despite the suggestion that perhaps Metcalfe or some alien power had sent the shot wild, he was fully confident that Sestus had, in fact, acted decisively to save the lives of either Metcalfe and the Family, or himself and his shipmates, if, as expected, the attack would have been neutralized and the attacker destroyed.

What did this mean? Was Sestus now an ally–god help him, even a *friend?* If so, there would be the advantage of being able to have Sestus as a lover, openly, without the awkwardness of having to admit that he was sleeping with his best friend's mortal enemy. Of course, Metcalfe didn't seem to be flustered that Aer'La considered Pallas, his own lover, to be her mortal enemy.

The thought struck Carson then that he didn't know if he *wanted* an above-board relationship with Sestus. Why wouldn't he? Was it just that he had grown accustomed to keeping his sex life secret, and derived pleasure from the masquerade? Or was it that he'd just, well, expected this... whatever it was... to *end?*

He felt a bit guilty. Was he using Sestus?

He told himself to stop being silly. He hadn't strung Sestus along. For heaven's sake, he'd told him at each encounter that he despised him and wanted to end it! And Sestus was known as a love-them-and-leave-them artist himself. Why should Carson feel guilty?

Because, perhaps, Sestus had just saved his best friend's life? At the risk of his own career? And part of Carson was confident... afraid... that Sestus had done it as a favor to him.

"Well, Mr. Metcalfe?"

Since his experience in the caverns, through his decision to lead the

Family in peaceful resistance against the very Navy in which he served, even through confronting Fournier and Ustenar, being called a traitor, being attacked–well, having someone attempt to attack him–Metcalfe had felt calm. For the first time in his life, he'd felt completely at peace with the decisions he had made and the plans he'd laid out before him. He'd felt the most sublime confidence a human being could feel.

Until this moment.

Now, with Jan Atal's ice-blue eyes piercing him, bringing the sensation of final judgment right over the data network and into a holo re-creation, Metcalfe asked himself just what the hell he'd gone and done now.

"Well, sir... we seem to have a situation."

"At your trial, I'll be sure to testify to your gift for understatement."

"Sir... we can't take these people away from here."

"'We,' Mr. Metcalfe? You're going to have to forgive me if I ask you to clarify just who you're including when you use the pronoun 'we.'"

"Okay... that was fair, I guess. Believe me, Captain, I'm not here trying to stand against you, or even against Fournier. In fact, I'm trying to keep you all alive. Another attack on the Family would be–"

"What happened to Colonel Druelinger's people?"

"I honestly can't explain, sir."

"Meaning you don't know?"

"Meaning I don't understand it. The power of Eleusis caused–"

"But you knew it was going to happen."

"I knew Eleusis... wouldn't let us be taken by force."

"And now 'us' is you and the Family?"

"Of necessity, Captain, yes. You see... it's bonded... to me."

"It? Eleusis?"

"The... god of Eleusis."

Atal almost rolled his eyes. "Metcalfe, dammit! Do you know how that sounds?"

"Yes, I do, but... Captain, it's real."

"I understand how you feel about these things, but–"

"No, sir! I mean it's verifiably, objectively real. I could take you to it and show it to you."

"A god?"

"An artificial intelligence more sophisticated than any developed by the Confederacy. It controls the planetary weapons grid. It's responsible–that is, it was used to bring about–the death of the original inhabitants of Eleusis."

"Millennia ago?" Atal was skeptical.

"Yes."

"And it's still operational."

"You saw what happened to Druelinger's ship."

"I didn't see it, but I follow." Atal took a deep breath. "Metcalfe... please answer this next question very carefully: are you in control of this... intelligence?"

"No, sir. No more than I could be in control of you or any other intelligent being."

"But you say it's bonded to you."

Metcalfe nodded. "Yes. It's been searching for a long time for someone like me, to help it find a focus for its powers. A human focus. No, I suppose that's a bit racist. A *mortal* focus."

"Why? What does it need?"

"The same thing any of us need, Captain. Why do we seek out contact with other people?"

Atal ignored the question. "Are the Qraitians correct? Is there a... a doomsday weapon down there?"

"Yes," admitted Metcalfe. "One capable of wiping out everyone in this system. Possibly its scope is even broader than that. I don't know. But the Qraitians will never control it. It's... adopted the Family. It will act to protect them. That's why Ustenar was trying to bully Five–Sestus–into firing on us. She believed that Eleusis would be spurred to destroy him. "

Atal straightened, crossed his arms. "Your recommendation, Mr. Metcalfe?"

"Withdraw, Captain. Leave the Family in peace. Make it clear to both sides that interference with this planet will only lead to more deaths."

"Admiral Fournier will never accept that."

"Captain, I'm afraid he doesn't have any choice. This planet... belongs to this intelligence. We accept its domain over its own world... we come and go in peace... or we die."

CHAPTER EIGHTEEN

Georg Fournier fidgeted in his acceleration couch and blew out a heavy breath between his teeth. He'd already counted to 100 forwards and backwards, trying to maintain patience. It had been nearly an hour, now, since that snot-nose Blaurich had fired on his ship.

What had the boy been thinking?

It didn't matter. Time to deal with that later. For now, he had to get back in the loop.

The communications officer turned to him, his face impassive, but strained.

"Well?" demanded Fournier.

"No progress, sir. We've tried improvising a new array out of–"

"I don't want excuses, dammit! I want communications online, now!"

"I understand that, Admiral, but the blast took out our antenna array. Without it–"

"What about the portables? I've tried mine, and it's dead! If it can reach the ship from a planet's surface–"

The man shook his head. "On board ship, the portables can't get through the radiation shielding to transmit out. It's also a security feature–"

"Then *bypass* it!"

"Sir, you have to understand–wait –!" The man looked at the display before him, puzzled.

"What is it?"

"We've been monitoring the surface of the planet, the area where that apparently artificial lake formed."

"And?"

"Well, Admiral, if you look here–" He gestured, and a topographical image of the planet appeared, with the lake highlighted. "This is the planet Eleusis."

"Obviously."

"We were still scanning and recording up until the moment of the blast. We were looking for radiation, electromagnetic activity, anything suggesting weaponry."

"Yes," said Fournier impatiently.

The officer gestured again, and graphics of the Family's liner and the Marine transport appeared. The transport's image was in motion, recreating the moment when it attempted to dock with the Liner. "Here," the man said. "As the transport moves in, watch the planet."

Just as the ship's image vanished, In and around the lake, Fournier saw a patch of glowing blue, warming to green.

"See that? It lasted for several minutes. Now watch as the transport is destroyed."

The green flared to yellow, then quickly faded out.

"What the hell was that?"

"A massive electro-magnetic surge, Admiral. It built, then suddenly flared. After the ship disappeared, all activity ceased."

"Was there a beam or any sort of discharge?"

"None. No apparent conduit or transference of the energy to the ship. Just the buildup, surge and disappearance as the ship was... attacked."

"So it's not a weapon firing."

"No, sir. Whatever it was, it's as though... as though something was building up to the act of destroying the ship, but did it with no visible contact with the ship."

Fournier nodded. "Good catch, mister. But why are you looking at it right now?"

"Because, sir... the same buildup of E.M. is occurring again right now."

"So... it's about to destroy something else."

"We don't have a lot of data to go on, sir, but..."

"But the last time that buildup occurred, we lost hundreds of men and women. We can't just sit here and wait to see who its next target is, us, the *Titan* or the Qraitians."

"Or perhaps the frigate, sir. Eliminating the last ship to threaten the liner."

"Whatever it is... we've got to destroy it."

"Sir? Our guns are offline."

"So they are. Nor do we know what they'd do against an unidentified E.M. source. But we do know what will create an E.M. pulse sufficient to neutralize any power source in the area, and enough structural damage to collapse the caverns underneath that lake. Ready two missiles and nuclear warheads."

The man's eyes went wide.

"Do it," said Fournier. "I don't know what it is, but we can't control it. We're going to take it out of action permanently."

In the main cargo hold, Aer'La was alone, cleaning up the wreckage of her earlier outburst. It was a self-imposed penance. Work. Work was all that could keep her mind off all that had been going wrong in her life. Cernaq was in jail. Metcalfe was probably going to be shipped off to a relocation center or Hydra Station.

She was pretty sure Carson was sleeping with Five. They'd been spending entirely too much time together lately, and she'd seen them together a few nights ago on the Boulevard, very drunk, Carson's hands all over Five in that way that suggests a man is interested in one thing. Aer'La suppressed a shudder. Good looks aside, Sestus Blaurich was a low-life. How could Carson do that to himself?

She surveyed the damage she'd done, in just seconds, to her own domain. Why had she done it? Because she was angry and felt helpless. Because she felt cut off from the people she loved. Because she was lonely. She had done something that hurt her as much as–more than–it hurt anyone else. Was that what Carson was doing?

Somewhere, someone called her name.

She stopped, putting down the broken crate she'd been moving, and looked around. She was sure the hold was empty of others. Ceres knew she needed time alone, and would have seen to it. Her implant hadn't activated. She was sure, however, that someone had called to her.

She heard it again. She pricked her ears and looked around. There was no one here, and it had not been a sound. Telepathy? It had to be. Thinking about it, she recognized the voice she'd heard, but not heard. It was Cernaq. Yes, Cernaq was calling to her. That had to be it.
He was projecting his thoughts to her.

She attempted to answer him, calling out his name with her mind; but there was no response. There was only the continued sensation that he was calling to her, that he was in trouble.

Well, of course he was in trouble! He'd been stubborn about his damned Phaetonian principles, and gotten arrested! What did he expect her to do? Break him out?

He broke you out, when you were arrested.

What the hell, she wondered. A voice, but not a voice. Words, but not words. Someone... something... had spoken to her. Voices in her head...

Great, she thought. First she was having nightmares, then waking flashbacks, now voices in her head? Was she cracking up completely? Her experience in space, when she'd almost died... No, dammit! She had been through so much in her life, how could that be the thing that broke her? Was it because before, she'd had nothing to lose, and now she had friends, family almost?

Family, she reflected bitterly. Where was this 'family' now? You've just gone soft, she told herself. You've let them make you soft, and that allowed your close call in space to scramble your brains.

She wished Celia were here. More than anyone, even Cernaq, Celia could help her make sense of the craziness when it overwhelmed her.

So why hadn't she told Celia anything about the nightmares, the flashbacks? Why had she tried to keep it all to herself, even forbidding Cernaq to tell anyone? At least, she thought, Cernaq had been decent enough to keep her secret. He could have revealed the things he knew because he was a telepath, and because she let him be close to her. He hadn't. His principles, his Phaetonian upbringing, forbade it.

His principles. The same principles that put him in a cell. An image came to her... Cernaq in his cell, alone, calling to her... an earlier image filled her mind... the ceiling of her cabin, dark, a guard at the door. She'd been arrested. The Varthan slaver Harl had had her drugged... Cernaq was there, too... He'd reach into her mind, reached through the fog of drugs, found her where they'd tried to hide her away.

She'd begged him to kill her. He had refused.

And then... Metcalfe... given a direct order to reveal her location... he'd also refused... He had been arrested, too, almost blown his career. He'd led the search parties to a fake corpse, cobbled together by Celia. All a ruse. All to throw the Varthans off the trail and send them home, so Aer'La could live in peace.

So Aer'La could be free.

Cernaq... Metcalfe... so brave in the face of overwhelming odds. When she herself had given up, begged for death. She, who held herself above everyone as the strongest person in the universe, had been ready to quit. Her friends hadn't let her, and now they were in trouble. Now Cernaq was calling to her.

She would go to him.

Cernaq looked up as she approached his cell. Before she could speak, he said, "I'm glad to see you. I was surprised when you contacted me."

Aer'La was brought up short. "I contacted you?"

"Yes," he said, a puzzled grimace on his face. "I must admit I was astonished to receive telepathic contact from you–"

"Cernaq, I wouldn't know how to contact you telepathically!"

"Well, of course, it wasn't the sort of coherent broadcast a trained telepath would–"

She put up a hand. "Don't be a snob."

"Sorry." He grinned. "I mean it was mostly just an emotional impression that you wanted to talk to me. No, stronger than wanted–needed."

"I got the same thing!" she replied, relieved. "I thought it was–"

"–More psychological fallout from your ordeal?"

"A snob *or* a know-it-all!" she pressed.

"Sorry again. I don't mean to be either, Aer'La."

"I hope not. *You're* the one who needs *my* help right now, after all."

"It's funny you should mention that. When I felt you... what I thought was you... trying to contact me, I had these... "

"Flashbacks?"

"I was trying to stay away from that word."

"It's okay. I had them too, only they weren't, I dunno, *threatening* like the ones I had about being exposed in space. They didn't scare me or make me panic, they just... reminded me."

"Of what?"

"Of when I was under arrest, like you are now. And you and Metcalfe broke me out and kept me safe."

Cernaq nodded. "We do seem to spend an inordinate amount of time incarcerated, don't we?"

She shrugged. "Just troublemakers, I guess. What was your... flashback?"

"You remember Danvard, of course?"

She shivered and hugged herself. "How could I forget that psycho? You killed him to save Metcalfe, and then his ghost took over your mind."

"It wasn't his ghost," said Cernaq, straining for patience. "I absorbed his personality and memories."

"His ghost."

"It's not a supernatural phenomenon."

"A dead guy took over your mind."

Cernaq softened his voice. "And you... all of you... found a way to link your minds to mine and drive his dominant personality back into my long term memories, putting me back in control." He reached out a hand towards her, unable to touch her through the barrier of transparent alloy between them. "I was a prisoner in my own mind, a scared, crying child. I was lost, Aer'La... and you found me."

"We all found you."

"You comforted me, reminded me I had friends."

"Yeah, well," she said, uncomfortable with his evident gratitude, "it was Metcalfe who drove Danvard away."

"It was Metcalfe and I, together. Only after my psychic strength was bolstered by your friendship, yours and the others."

She laughed. "It's funny, y'know. You say we spend a lot of time in–"

"Incarcerated," he prompted her.

"Right, that. I guess it's a good thing we're all so good at busting each other out."

"I guess it is."

"So," she said, keying the lock release sequence–the Bos'n's authorized security override, which opened all cells, "C'mon. Let's get out of here."

The door retracted, but Cernaq did not move. "What are you doing?" he asked.

"Read my mind, dummy. I'm busting you out. Weren't you listening?"

"But–"

"It's wrong, what Fournier and Darby were doing. Locking people up and prying into their personal business for no good reason. All it does it scare people. It doesn't keep anyone safe. I never should have gone along with it. I should have had guts like you."

He shook his head. "I thought it made sense to you. You said you agreed–"

"It did, but... dammit I don't like it! Once I saw how it affected my boys and girls below decks, and you... "

"Once it was happening to you, you saw it was wrong." He came forward to the door where she was, looked into her eyes, his gaze flinty and unswerving. "You are a completely selfish individual," he said bluntly.

She started to respond, but he put his fingers to her lips and stopped her.

He smiled, his feline eyes taking on a predatory gleam. "You have no idea how much that turns me on."

"So where are we going?" asked Cernaq. They were headed towards the boat deck, Aer'La pulling herself frantically along. Each hefted over their shoulders a small bag Aer'la had packed with essentials.

"Shuttle?" she said.

"Shuttle to where?"

He reached to grab her hand, missed, caught an ankle. Any port in a storm, he decided, and pull himself up, face to face with her. Reluctantly, she halted. "What?" she demanded.

"Aer'La... I understand you're trying to get me to safety." He spread his hands in a seeking gesture. "Where, amidst all that is happening, is a safe place?"

"Metcalfe's ship?" she suggested.

"That would be pragmatic. It's the least likely to be destroyed."

"On the other hand," admitted Aer'La, "any ship approaching it might be destroyed, either by that... thing... whatever it is, or by the Qraitians. Or Five."

"Not to mention that Metcalfe is courting a charge of treason." He considered his words and then muttered, "Again."

"What difference does it make? The way Fournier's stacked the deck, anyone can be locked up for treason. This is a great chance for him to get us all out of his hair. For life."

"Our stealing a shuttle and taking off without a flight plan is not going to add points to our defense attorney's argument."

"We could go to the planet, to Eleusis. We could just... colonize."

"Colonize a world controlled by a mysterious intelligence of undefinable destructive potential?" asked Cernaq.

"Sounds a lot like us–a mysterious intelligence and an undefinable destructive potential."

He smiled. "Seriously, Aer'La. Stop and think this through. Eleusis is the center of controversy. If we go there, we might–"

After a few seconds of silence, she motioned for him to continue. When he still did not, she jabbed his shoulder with her palm. "Cernaq! What is it?"

"I've just received another... broadcast."

"Who was it?"

"No idea, but... Something is very wrong, and we are going to need help."

"Captain!" Carson called out. "Fournier's ship is opening missile bays!"

Atal bolted from his acceleration couch too quickly, only a spaceman's experience in zero-G allowing him to catch himself and check his inertia as he reached the Midshipman's side.

"What the hell?" he demanded.

"I guess we weren't moving fast enough for him."

"Any idea what he's getting ready to launch?"

"Attempting to scan, sir, but without telemetry–"

"Any idea where Pallas is?" the Captain asked.

"No idea, sir. I haven't seen her since we left for Quintil."

"I don't know if a telepath's abilities would help, but..."

Unspoken in Atal's musing, Carson suspected, was that the Captain didn't completely trust Pallas. Unlike Cernaq, who, ironically for a telepath, had a face one could read like a book, Pallas was an unknown quantity. More than once, she'd taken actions that rankled both the Admiralty and *Titan's* own Captain. Carson often wondered if, were she not both a protégé of the respected Professor Mors and Metcalfe's lover, Pallas might have been long ago removed from her position of civilian observer aboard *Titan*.

Hell, he reflected, after the incident on Procyon, a lot of people thought she should be off-loaded, if not locked away as a threat to society. A more powerful telepath than Cernaq, Pallas also possessed a limited power of telekinesis. It had been a valuable asset on occasion, but on Procyon, she'd fallen under the influence of ancient native technology which had forced her into a never-ending dream state. Still conscious of her surroundings in a way no psi-blind person could ever be, she'd known when Metcalfe had deliberately put his life on the line in an attempt to save her and dozens of other victims of the dream generator. She had lost control and lashed out with her mind, giving Cernaq quite a bump on the head with a piece of flying debris, knocking him unconscious. A lot of people had asked, was she too powerful, too unstable to be on *Titan*? A lot of people were still asking.

Memories of Procyon weren't pleasant ones for Carson. The dream generator, created by the native race of Procyon A-F to allow the last of the race to sleep through the final cataclysm which destroyed them, had long survived the death of its makers. Still active, it held in thrall the archaeological team who came to explore the ruins. Unchecked, it would have held them in dream-state until they died, and their deaths would have come quickly. Everyone who came within range of it for more than a brief span of hours would succumb. Pallas, in an attempt to control the device, had fallen victim to it. Before she'd gone under, she'd revealed that the device could be deactivated, but only via direct interface with a sentient mind, and that mind would be burned out, killing the person who initiated the sequence.

Metcalfe had overheard conversations in which Darby and *Titan's* then-Ship's Physician, Romney Flynn, had suggested that Carson was the most expendable among them. They were going to recommend that Atal order him to deactivate the device. While everyone knew the Captain would never give such an order, would first have given his own life to switch the thing off, Metcalfe feared for Carson, as he already feared for Pallas. He'd snuck off to deactivate the dream generator himself.

Carson still remembered confronting Metcalfe that night, in the ruins of the Procyon hospital, where the last of the race had gone to dream themselves into eternity...

The harsh glare from lamps floating near the ceiling bit the soft darkness of the Procyon night, piercing the cloak of ebony which suited and respected this place. It was as though some predator's claws had torn gouges out of black velvet, leaving holes through which unwelcome light poured in like acid, eating away at a world where it didn't belong.

The hospital–the tomb, Doc Faulkner had first believed it to be–had an acrid smell of age which enhanced the illusion. Carson's footfalls echoed about him in the huge chamber as he cast his lantern's beam, searching. In the far corner, a figure was silhouetted in the glow of one of the team's lights, kneeling over the harmless-seeming, vaguely cubical shape of the generator. It might have been mistaken for any other appliance–a holo field transmitter, a power unit, a dishwasher; but it was a method of execution more deadly than any Carson had seen in a museum of Terra's history. The electric chair, the gallows, the gas chamber, each had killed a single victim, or, at their worst, the number of occupants who could be crowded into a room. The dream generator could quietly snuff out every life for miles.

Carson raised his sidearm, taking a bead on his best friend's back.

"Get away from that thing," his voice rang off the crumbling walls. "Now."

Not looking up, Metcalfe asked, "Or what, you'll shoot me? Kinda counterproductive, if you're trying to save my life."

"I'll stun you."

Calmly, Metcalfe tapped the top of the device's casing. "I've already setup the sequence. I only have to trigger it by touching this panel–" He reached out for a glowing, square grid.

"No!"

Now he looked up, his black eyes cold, hard, determined. "You can't fire fast enough to stop me." A glint of softness appeared in his face. "Kevin, this has to be done. All these people are going to die, unless I do this."

"Listen to yourself–'unless *I* do it!' You've got a messiah complex the size of this planet. I'll bet you've dreamed about pulling a stunt like this." Carson's voice sounded shrill to his own ears, it trembled like a rock on a precipice, about to plunge into the abyss. Why was he lashing out in anger? He didn't want to be angry. He wanted–

"I don't want to die," said Metcalfe quietly. "But I'm not afraid of it, either. I know it's not the end. Don't you see, Kevin, someone has to decide which one dies to save the rest? I led this mission. I'm supposed to make that call."

"The Captain is here," Carson argued desperately. "He's in charge now." He held the pistol steady, even as he felt his whole body shake. He shivered as though the air were suddenly an arctic blast, but it wasn't. In fact, when he'd come in, it had been uncomfortably hot in here.

"I haven't seen him, so I haven't been relieved," said Metcalfe.

Ever the comeback, ever the clever argument, right unto death. *But you can't die, Terry,* Carson's mind shrieked out. *You can't!*

"You bastard. Fine then, you call the shots. Order me to do it."

Metcalfe shook his head. "You haven't been exposed long enough. I'm already under a death sentence. You're not. Besides, you don't know how."

Tears began to sting Carson's eyes. He was losing this argument, as he lost every argument with Terry; and he couldn't. He couldn't! "I can read the same files you did. I'll stun you and take your A.I. unit –"

"I deleted everything. I won't let you do it."

"But you're–no!" Carson sputtered. Christ, he was fucking sobbing! What the hell was wrong with him? How could a spaz like Metcalfe, the boy who cried at the drop of a hint, stay so calm, while Carson, the strong one, the stoic, came apart at the seams?

His mind raced. What to say, what the hell to say! *You stupid bastard, you're fucking this up! Stop him! Do anything! Save him!* "You're worth more... to the ship. The others–they need you! They don't need me!"

Metcalfe's face became gentle. "Of course they do."

Damn him! Winning the argument, tearing his opponent to shreds, but still giving that "I care about you" face. Asshole! Condescending–Metcalfe was reaching for the panel.

"No–wait! You don't–" Carson babbled. "I haven't told you–dammit! Terry, don't do this!"

Metcalfe smiled at him. "It'll be okay, Kevin."

Carson screamed. Every fear he'd known–the greatest fear he had ever known–about to come to life before his eyes, and he, powerless to stop it.. "No, you won't! You're not gonna die! You're–!" He tightened his finger on the trigger. Could he fire in time? If not, he'd set the damn thing to kill and stick it in his own wretched mouth.

And then Atal's voice, firm and commanding, "Mister Carson... stand down."

Carson whirled. "Captain! Don't let him –"

Atal nodded calmly. "I have no intention of it." He reached out his hand to Carson. "Here... give me that gun before you hurt someone." One huge hand closed gently over Carson's own, urging his clenched fingers off the butt of the pistol, allowing it to slip from his grasp and into Atal's other hand.

And then, while Metcalfe was distracted by the presence of his Captain, it was Romney Flynn himself who stunned him. It was Romney Flynn who slipped behind them as they carried the unconscious Metcalfe out. It was Romney Flynn who died, triggering the deactivation sequence and saving them all.

Carson's sobs had quieted, his tears had dried and he'd come back to himself. By the time Metcalfe had awoken to see his best friend looking down at him, Carson had been able to resume insulting him for all he was worth.

Metcalfe, as usual, had found a way to play the superior role. Lying on the ground, his head pillowed on a backpack which Carson had placed there, he had listened quietly as Carson called him an egotist, a hothead, an arrogant glory hound. At a break in the stream of invective, he'd asked "Are you all right? I was worried about you back there."

"Fuck you!" snapped Carson. "I wasn't the asshole with his hand on a suicide switch!"

"No, but you were pretty torn up."

"I was *pissed*, you jackass! You were pissing me off! You always piss me off!"

"I see," said Metcalfe quietly. "Of course, that was my plan. I did the whole thing to piss you off." His dark eyes gleamed with laughter.

"Fuck you, fuck you, *fuck you!*" Carson had said again, and he snapped up one hand as though about to backhand Metcalfe in the mouth.

Metcalfe, unflinching, reached out and took hold of the hand, squeezed it. "Thanks, Kevin, for trying to save me."

"What do you mean trying? I did save you, shithead! I kept you talking–your favorite thing to do–while the Captain and Flynn got you out of there."

Metcalfe nodded gravely. "Well, thanks then."

"And don't you *ever* pull a stunt like that again, or the pistol won't be set on stun! I'll blow your fucking head off and put an end to all my misery!" This time he did lash out his raised hand and strike Metcalfe, but only on the shoulder.

Still, Metcalfe said, "Ow!" as he laughed.

"That's for panicking! And losing your head over a girl! Everyone was about to die, not just your latest crush, Romeo! But you lost it and went charging in there, handling equipment you know nothing about! Fuck getting yourself killed, you could have got everyone killed! It's a good thing the rest of us stayed calm!"

"I guess so," said Metcalfe.

"So the next time, remember to *think*. Display some of that damned leadership you're supposed to have so much of. Stay *calm* and don't showboat when everyone's about to die."

Everyone's about to die.

Carson jolted back to reality with that phrase echoing in his mind.

Where? Of course, he was on *Titan's* command deck. What the hell was he doing? Daydreaming? He had been thinking about Procyon, and then suddenly today was gone and it was as if yesterday was just happening now. It was almost like he'd fallen asleep on duty, but a quick inventory told him he hadn't been asleep. He'd just... slipped into full recall.

"Everyone's about to die," he heard himself say again.

And, indeed, everyone was about to die. Here. Now.

"Sir!" he blurted out. It occurred to him immediately that Atal was right next to him, and the raised voice had been unnecessary.

"You all right, Carson?"

"Fine sir, but... we've got to stop Fournier."

"Probably true, but why the sudden conviction?"

"I - I can't really explain, I... sir, Metcalfe said any attack on the Family could result in all our deaths. I believe him."

"So do I."

"Fournier won't. He'll try to act himself, bypassing Metcalfe's warning. He'll want to eliminate the source of the threat."

Atal raised an eyebrow. "Eleusis?"

Carson swallowed. "I think he's loading nukes. He's going to try and wipe out the... Entity. And we've got to stop him!"

"So? You want to commit mutiny based on speculation?"

"Well, sir, put that way... I guess I do."

"Put that way, Mr. Carson, I'm afraid you're right. But we have no communications, and Pallas is not responding to my calls. She's most likely trying to reach Metcalfe. We'll send a ship, but I'd like to talk to Fournier now. Get me Cernaq."

"In the brig, sir?"

"Where else?"

"The security firewall will block his implant."

"Use the intercom, then."

Carson paged the guard station in the ship's detention area, but received no answer. Baffled, he signaled for the next manned security checkpoint and asked them for a status. While he waited, a telltale flash caught his eye from the status panel for the boat deck. Inner airlock sealed, hold depressurizing... A ship was preparing to launch. He started to alert Atal–surely no ship could be authorized for space under current conditions. He was interrupted by a call from Security.

"Mister Carson? Sir, the guard on duty was asleep. Shall I put him on report?"

"Uh... " Carson hesitated. "First get back to the cell block and bring out Midshipman Cernaq. He's needed on the command deck."

Carson waited again, his apprehension growing. A sleeping guard in an area where Cernaq was being held? Coincidence? The Phaetonian's control of the metabolic and autonomic systems of others made it easy for him to put someone to sleep, even at a moderate distance. Cernaq would never... but a ship was getting ready to launch.

Following this train of thought, he was unsurprised when the guard came back to report in a much-flustered tone that the prisoner had apparently escaped.

Carson cut the channel without another word, then turned to Atal.

The Captain immediately said, "Something's wrong."

"It... could be nothing, Captain. A... bookkeeping error."

"Where's Cernaq?" Atal pressed him.

"I'm... not sure."

"Carson–"

"Captain, I believe I can find him. Permission to leave my station?"

Atal chewed his lip for a moment. "I should call Security."

Carson shrugged. "Why go to the trouble, sir? I really think it could be a mistake. Let me investigate."

"Five minutes," said the Captain. "Cernaq. On the command deck. Five minutes. No questions asked. After that–"

But Carson didn't hear the rest. With a relieved, "Thank you, Captain!" he was out of his couch and through the hatch. He hoped he could make the boat deck in time.

"Atal!"

"Commander Ustenar?"

"Your ten minutes are up. Don't try to convince me they're not. I'm quite familiar with time conversions to your system."

"I'm sure you are, Commander. Yes, the ten minutes has passed."

"Further, we note activity aboard Fournier's ship. What exactly is he planning?"

"A tactical nuclear strike against the planet," said Atal easily.

Ustenar sputtered. "I cannot allow that!"

"Because the weapon you so desperately wish to control would be destroyed?"

"I will not allow the use of such weapons in proximity to my own people."

"Good comeback. In fact, I happen to agree with you, Commander. I'm working right now to convince the Admiral to change his plans."

"I could convince him of that with a well-placed missile, Atal. Can you think of a reason I shouldn't?"

"Because I'd blow you out of space?"

Ustenar snorted with laughter. "I doubt it. Not while I hold two hostages."

"Don't try me, Commander. I will convince Admiral Fournier."

"And what of the Family? Have you convinced them to surrender their Qraitian members and withdraw?"

"They seem to be holding all the cards at the moment," said Atal.

"Cards? What cards?"

"An expression, Commander, nothing more. It means that the balance of power is weighted in their direction right now. All we can do is practice diplomacy."

"I have no patience with diplomacy, Captain!" She stopped, her image looking at something beyond the pickup. "Atal!" she demanded. "Why are you launching a vessel from your ship?"

Atal bit his cheek in frustration, but kept surprise off his face. After a moment, during which he glanced at a status readout at Carson's station and confirmed that a shuttle was launching, he said, "Communications to the *Douglas* are out, Commander. I'm... sending a delegation. I'll keep you advised. Atal out."

He killed the channel to Ustenar and counted to ten backwards as he hailed the departing shuttle.

Still wedged into a cramped corner of Ustenar's command deck, Kaya watched with sympathy as her father tried to keep the Qraitian calm. When he switched off, she demanded that the channel be re-opened. Kaya thought for a moment that Ustenar might actually lash out and strike her watch officer when the man couldn't comply.

"We cannot risk the destruction of the planet, though with any luck, the missiles would do no damage and Fournier would be destroyed." Ustenar said when she had managed to calm herself. "Prepare to fire on the *Douglas* on my order. Atal's diplomacy, weak as it is, will no doubt fail. We will have to destroy Fournier."

"Atal's diplomacy doesn't have a high failure rate," said Celia from next to Kaya.

Ustenar's deadly gaze warned that the Doctor's opinion was not invited.

"Still," said the Qraitian, "perhaps there are better ways to eliminate the human threat than by destroying it ourselves. That would draw Atal's attention to us instead of the family. I wonder... our agent, the one they call 'Daedalus'... is his communicator still active?"

The watch officer sent a transmission and received a signal which seemed to satisfy him. "It is. I imagine they did not have time to search him."

"Good," said Ustenar. "See if he's free to speak to me."

CHAPTER NINETEEN

"Atal on *Titan* to Shuttle Bravo! Carson, that better not be you, but I know it is–"

Carson, in the pilot's couch, nodded to Cernaq to acknowledge the signal. As he did so, "Bravo" cleared the hatch opening, dropping out of its slip and into open space. Carson engaged engines and swung away from *Titan* fast.

"Cernaq here, Captain."

Atal swore under his breath in a language Carson didn't know. "I wish I were surprised. What the hell are you three up to?"

"Three sir?" asked Cernaq mildly. "Why do you say–?"

"Because I know it can't be five! Kaya and Metcalfe are off-ship! Cernaq, Carson and Aer'La. If you're not all three aboard that shuttle, I'll turn in my membership chip in the know-it-alls' union."

"You got us, Captain," said Carson.

"Dead to rights," Aer'La admitted.

"Carson, I sent you to retrieve Cernaq to the command deck!"

"So that he could try to communicate with Admiral Fournier, prior to our launching a ship carrying a delegation to the Admiral," said Carson. "Well, Cernaq is already trying to communicate with Fournier–"

"Pointless, sir," reported Cernaq. "The Admiral's psi-index may actually be negative. I can't even sense him."

"There you have it, Captain. We have to get Cernaq closer, and now we've launched the delegation–"

"You weren't going to be the delegates, Carson," said Atal. "In fact, you three would probably be among my last choices for the job."

"Sir," Carson said, all lightness now gone from his tone, "I know that. I figured you were planning to go yourself."

"You figure correctly, now–"

"Captain, this ship could very well be destroyed by the Qraitians, or... wiped out of existence by the Entity on Eleusis. The odds we'll survive the next few minutes aren't ones I'd bet on, and I'm a known sucker."

"He is, Captain," confirmed Cernaq.

"Now he tells us the odds!" muttered Aer'La.

"We can't let that happen to you, Captain. Whatever you may think of us at the moment–"

"The words 'mutinous dogs,' come to mind."

"Yeah, I figured it would be something like that. But we're loyal to you, really. Look, once we get there, do you think we'll be able to convince Fournier not to launch his missiles?"

"Not a chance in hell," said Atal. "Which is why I wasn't going to send you."

"And, with all due respect, your chances, sir?"

Atal was silent a moment. "Forget what I said about turning in the know-it-all card, Carson. I'm giving it to you."

"Let's hope you don't bury me with it," Carson said quietly. "Although, if all this goes wrong, I don't think there'll be anything to bury. And, Captain, one more thing: what were you going to do if Fournier refused to back off? Given the choice between mutiny and certain death for all of us?"

"I'm not as certain about the certainty as you apparently are, Carson, but... I'd probably do whatever it took to stop those missiles."

"And, again, don't you think it's a lower price for the Confederacy to pay if the three of us get sent up for mutiny, instead of you?"

"You had no right to make that decision for me, Mister! In fact, making it *was* mutiny."

"Conceded, Captain."

"E.T.A. to rendez-vous with *CNV Linstrom Douglas*, nine minutes," Cernaq announced. "Still no success with telepathic contact."

"Shall we turn back, Captain?" asked Carson.

"You wouldn't if I ordered you to," said Atal impatiently.

"I would, if I believed you thought it was the right thing to do, but I don't. Nor would you order me to do it, because it's not the right thing to do."

"Thank you, Carson," Atal said quietly.

"Any time, sir."

"And if you survive this, I am going to kick your ass so hard you'll beg for a court martial."

"I promise you can kick whatever's left of it, sir."

"All right, dammit, what's your proposed plan of action?"

"We dock, offering assistance; we meet with the Admiral, bearing a message from you, asking him to stand down and await restoration of communications or a face-to-face conference. Then, when he refuses, we sabotage the missiles."

"A message from me? Please tell me you don't already have it!"

"Naturally I do, sir. But I'd appreciated it if you'd record a genuine one. My forgery skills are not at their best on such a tight deadline."

Georg Fournier himself met them on the ship's small boat deck. He did not look pleased. "I would have expected Atal to come personally."

"Captain Atal felt his attentions were better placed in calming the Qraitian Commander, Admiral," said Carson. "I hope we will serve satisfactorily in his stead."

Fournier grunted, but his expression suggested they didn't even come close. "What was the delay? *Titan* arrived in the system some time ago. Has Blaurich been taken into custody?"

"We believe the stray shot which struck your ship was, in fact, diverted by the Entity," Carson lied easily.

"Entity? What entity? Don't tell me Metcalfe has you believing–"

Cernaq interrupted. "He has us all believing, Admiral, that there is a powerful artificial intelligence which still functions beneath the surface of Eleusis, a remnant of the civilization which was destroyed so long ago." Cernaq told the tale as if he'd known it all his life, a by-product, Carson supposed, of his allowing his Phaetonian friend to speed-read it directly from his own mind. "This intelligence single-handedly controls an arsenal of weapons designed to protect the planet from any and all attackers."

"Then why," scoffed Fournier, "didn't it do so, so long ago? Why didn't it protect the inhabitants of Eleusis? Why aren't they still here?"

"Unknown. Though Dr. Faulkner and Midshipman Atal speculate that the Entity, what the Family of God calls 'the God of Eleusis,' destroyed the original inhabitants itself."

"I am aware of those speculations," said Fournier.

"The Entity destroys anything it considers a threat to itself, or to anyone with whom it has bonded," explained Carson.

"And it's bonded with Metcalfe," said Aer'La.

"Of course it has," said Fournier, giving a slight roll of his eyes.

"Then you understand how vital it is that you take no action against the Family or the planet itself," said Carson. "We observed from *Titan* that you were readying missiles."

"So I am. And they'll be launched as planned."

"But sir–" Carson began.

Fournier nodded impatiently. "I know. You hoped to convince me to take no action, because your Captain wants to take no action. Well, children, it's time you learned that your Captain isn't infallible. Now, more than ever, I'm convinced that your... Entity... is a threat to the safety of anyone who comes within its range; and we do not know its range. The only sensible course of action is to neutralize it as quickly and as fully as possible."

Carson nodded. "I was afraid you'd say that."

"Your personal fears do not interest me, Mr. Carson. My orders stand. Now," he looked to Aer'La and Cernaq. "If the two of you would join the crew attempting to restore our communications?"

Aer'La nodded slowly. "Parts are in the shuttle."

Carson said quickly, "I can retrieve them, if you want to go ahead. I believe we've wasted enough of the Admiral's time, don't you?"

As Aer'La and Cernaq drifted for the hatchway into the ship proper, Fournier turned to Carson with the hint of a satisfied smile. "Mr. Carson, I must say your attitude has improved. Between your work on the background investigations and this, I believe we may–"

The rest of his words were lost in a gasp as Aer'La caught him from behind in a choke-hold. "Don't struggle, Admiral," she said crisply. "A human windpipe is way too easy to crush."

"Wha–" he tried to say.

Aer'La tightened her hold. "Stubborn, isn't he?"

"Don't damage his voice, Aer'La," said Cernaq. "We're going to need it."

Fournier's eyes widened in fear.

"He's thinking," announced Cernaq, "that I'm going to pry into his brain, force him to act according to our wishes, make him give the orders we want him to give, and then leave him a babbling, drooling, empty shell. The images are quite detailed and graphic." Cernaq used Aer'La's shoulder as a fulcrum to lever himself to eye level with the Admiral. "You needn't fear, Admiral... I promise not to make you drool." He closed his eyes, and Fournier's own eyes went blank.

"Command deck, this is Fournier."

"Command deck, Admiral, this is Gregson."

"Gregson... the missiles..."

"Ready for launch on your order, Admiral."

"Disarm them. Stand down."

"... Say again, sir?"

"Do not launch. I repeat, do not launch. We've received... new intelligence."

"As you say sir. I must confess it's a relief. Captain Atal was able to neutralize the threat, then?"

"It's... too early to tell."

"Yes sir. Sir?"

"Eh? Yes?"

"Are you... feeling well, sir? You sound -- "

"Tired is all, Gregson. Tired and... relieved."

"Yes sir."

"Fournier out."

On *Titan's* command deck, Jan Atal looked over the holographic images of the several ships that concerned him: the liner, the frigate *Henley*, the battleship *Douglas* and the Qraitian. He'd looked back and forth between them too many times in the past few minutes, each time wondering just when the hell he'd become the guy who sat and watched things happening.

His hands were tied, as were everyone's. The Entity, the Voice of Eleusis, called the shots, and it was only speaking through Metcalfe. Fournier was out of touch and taking drastic, inadvisable action, with only Carson, Cernaq and Aer'La to stop him. Kaya and Faulkner were prisoners aboard a ship whose commander wanted nothing short of the destruction of everyone else.

A tone signaled an incoming transmission, and Sestus Blaurich's image appeared before him.

"Status, Mr. Blaurich?" he asked.

"Holding position, sir. The Qraitians don't appear to be making hostile moves. Yet. Have you had word from the team you sent to the *Douglas*, sir?"

"Not while the main antennas are down. And their first order of business was to carry my recommendation to the Admiral that he not fire those missiles he's prepped."

"Sir," said Blaurich slowly, "what if he's right? What if a tactical strike is the only way to stop that thing?"

"I don't believe it can stop that thing, Blaurich. I–"

"I'm picking up something on visual from his missile bays, sir..."

"What's–I see it too."

"Looks like they're standing down."

"Then the Admiral listened to reason."

"I suppose he did. How else would..." Sestus trailed off.

"Something on your mind, Mr. Blaurich?"

"Just... wondering, sir... wondering who you sent?"

"In fact Mr. Carson led the team."

Sestus looked troubled.

"Well?" asked Atal.

"Just wondering what Carson would do, sir, if the Admiral didn't 'listen to reason.'"

The wait was wearing on Kaya. Ustenar had, fortunately, not so far been prompted to attack. Why Fournier had stepped back from firing the missiles she didn't know, but he had. Hopefully that gave Ustenar at least grudging confidence in her father's diplomatic skills. Kaya dreaded to think what might happen if violence erupted. They might all be wiped out in an instant, and yet sitting and waiting for something to happen was exhausting.

Her eyes drifted shut for the third time in as many minutes, and it occurred to Kaya that she didn't know when she'd last slept. It might have been more than a day. Celia, too, appeared to be tiring. Somehow the Doctor, though over a century old, seemed to be able to go on for days without sleep. Perhaps it was her alleged supernatural powers, but Celia Faulkner was indomitable. A force of nature unto herself. Kaya knew she was human, but couldn't imagine her dropping from exhaustion or succumbing to illness.

Kaya, on the other hand, was about to succumb. Perhaps if she just closed her eyes for a moment...

Kaya opened her eyes, wondering how long she'd been asleep. She stretched and reveled in the warmth which surrounded her. Beyond the thick blankets she kept on her bed, she knew that the climate control was set to keep the room cold. It helped her sleep, and so she had the A.I. cycle her cabin a third below body temperature during her sleep shift. She liked the contrast of a very warm bed in a fairly cold room.

And it was a very warm bed just now. Snuggled against her, his arm draped about her and gently cupping one of her breasts, Yank snored gently into his pillow. Her pillow, actually, but the one he'd used after last night.

Last night had been amazing!

After years of his following her around like a puppy dog, declaring his old-fashioned, Terran-inspired love for her, she'd allowed him into her bed. Honestly, she would have allowed him into her bed at any time since the day they'd met at the Academy. She particularly remembered the encounter in the showers that first day, he flustered at realizing that male and female cadets shared a locker room. Silly Terran! He had expected the customs of his home to be replicated in space. What would have been the point of keeping genders separate? In the Inner Worlds, it was understood that a naked body was just a naked body. It wasn't an invitation to copulate. And why keep a student from seeing only half the population naked, when she might choose from all of the population to find a lover?

She still remembered him, striding out of the showers, naked and dripping, casually drying his hair with a towel. Were she honest, she'd have to admit her breath had caught. She wanted him immediately. Had he been any other cadet, she would have had him that very night. Academy regs forbade cadets sleeping together during basic, but it was done. She certainly hadn't remained celibate all those weeks.

Terry Metcalfe wasn't any other cadet, however. That was apparent from his reaction when she had spoken to him, complimenting him on his endowments. Seeing a nude woman before him, in what he'd considered an exclusively male domain, he'd dropped his towel, covered his crotch with one hand, turned to scoop up the towel, exposing other bare assets that she appreciated just as much, and turned crimson all over.

Kaya had rarely seen an embarrassed blush, Quintils were so well trained in controlling their bodies. Right from the start, she'd picked up that Terry Metcalfe was different, special, even. She wasn't going to have him in her bed the first night. Later, she realized, she didn't want him in her bed. Beautiful to look at he was, those eyes so dark and intense, that skin so pale and prone to blush; but he had the most perverted ideas about sex! He expected any partner he took on to agree to an exclusive contract with him.

It was sick, and Kaya wanted no part of it.

As she'd grown to know him, she realized it was just the norm for his world. Carson had adjusted all right to the free and easy ways of the Inner Worlds, sleeping with every girl he could find. In those days, Carson's own Terran-inspired perversions kept him from admitting he also liked boys, even preferred them. Metcalfe, however, wanted a girl, and just one. The girl he wanted was Kaya, and his devotion smothered her.

What had changed her mind, she wondered idly as she turned now to gaze on him, smiling in his sleep, naked, warm and peaceful in her bed? Of course, she knew what had changed her mind. It was the strength he'd displayed on the mission he had just completed. That had to be it.

He'd gone undercover, he and Aer'La, to break up a slaver ring. Hugo Roloff, a highly placed Admiral in the Navy, was running an operation which kidnaped young people from all over the Confederacy, brainwashed them, altered them to look like Varthan Ferals, Aer'La's race, and then shipped from out of Confederate space.

Disguised as teenage runaways, Metcalfe and Aer'La had gone to the popular youth hangouts on the planet Den, a world on the border which was a seat of much of the criminal activity in the Confederacy. Roloff's goons had picked them up, drugged them, and taken them to his private estate to be "conditioned." He didn't know they were wearing wires and being monitored by a local journalist.

It was a messy mission, which had ended in Roloff's death at the hands of one of his young victims. It hadn't ended, however, before Metcalfe and Aer'La had spent a day in Roloff's clutches. In order to save unknown hundreds, possibly thousands, of children, the two officers of the *CNV Arbiter* had had to put themselves in harm's way. "Harm," in Roloff's case meaning being used for sexual gratification.

Kaya didn't know what he'd gone through, but she knew it had to have been humiliating, painful, degrading... and yet he had returned the same

Terry Metcalfe, angry young man, going toe to toe with her father to convince him to protect the boy who'd murdered Roloff. She'd seen then that this young man had reserves of strength the depth of which could not be guessed. She, Kaya, had decided he deserved a hero's welcome home. She'd given him one. A nagging part of her hoped he wouldn't go from here and make her feel like property, but she suppressed it. This man was worthy of her love.

She turned to face him, keeping his arm around her. His eyes opened, and, seeing her, his smile grew. "Morning," he said.

She stroked his hair, found it damp from a hard sleep. "Morning. Breakfast?"

He stretched and made a contented sound. "Maybe not yet." He rolled closer and kissed her, his tongue gently separating her lips.

She smiled as they broke the kiss. "Again? I thought I wore you out."

"Yeah, kinda," he grinned.

"Seriously," she said, bringing her fingers up to trace the outline of his collar bone. "Was it... okay?"

He thought for a moment. "No," he said finally.

"No?"

"No. I wouldn't describe the fulfillment of all my fantasies as being 'okay.'" He kissed her again. "It was incredible."

She pulled away slightly. "That's not what I meant. I know the sex was good. I was top of my class as a sex partner."

"And modest, too."

"Modesty is a public relations ploy," she said. "It has no place in honest, intellectual discourse."

He laughed. "I see. Sorry."

"I'm serious, Yank... Terry..." The moment seemed to call for more than a caustic nickname. "I'm not asking for feedback on technique. I need to know if you were... comfortable, after..." She didn't know how to finish the sentence.

His face reflected recognition. "Oh. That."

"Yeah. I know you're handling it well, but... sex is a little close to home after... whatever happened."

"You want to know what happened?"

"No, of course not! I just... okay, dammit, I'm curious."

"It's okay."

"No! It isn't! Please don't tell me anything you don't want to. I just... if you need to talk..."

He lay on his back and adjusted the pillows behind his head. "I... was drugged most of the time."

"So you don't remember?" she asked hopefully.

He shook his head. "No, I do. It's... kind of like... foggy, but he made sure we were awake when he was... doing things. I remember getting slapped awake several times." He rubbed his jaw. "Still kinda sore. He threw ice water on us too, and used some sort of shock device."

Kaya swore under her breath.

"He talked... a lot. I think hearing himself talk about what he was doing aroused him, y'know? He was proud of it, that he... initiated... each new arrival personally."

"Initiated?"

"Um... fucked."

The word jarred her. Metcalfe didn't swear as often as many people. More when Carson was around, but rarely when alone with her. She realized it wasn't an expletive in this case, just a description of what happened.

He continued. "He had a couple of his goons hold me down –"

"Terry–"

"And he... forced it in–"

"Don't! You don't have to tell me–"

But Metcalfe didn't seem able to stop. His eyes looked as if focused on something far away. He spoke as though by remote control, automatically. "He did it dry. It was weird. I heard somebody screaming. I thought it sounded familiar, and maybe I'd better do something about it. Better help. Then I realized it was me screaming. It was only after that that I felt the pain." He laughed coldly. "Isn't that funny?"

She threw her arms out impulsively and pulled him to her. "There's nothing funny about it," she whispered into his hair, kissing it and stroking his back. "I wish I could bring him back and kill him all over again." She realized she was crying. She'd never let him see her cry.

He settled his arm around her shoulders, comforting her now. "Well... he's dead. He can't hurt any of those kids any more."

She looked into his eyes. "Was I wrong, though? To ask you here last night? After what you'd just gone through, to let our first time be something you'll remember right alongside–"

"Kaya," he smiled gently. "This... here... has nothing to do with Roloff."

"But, Terry... he raped you!"

Metcalfe nodded. "I suppose he did; but, after all, I knew going in that that's what would probably happen."

"You did?"

"Aer'La was pretty blunt about it. She told me that she was prepared for what she needed to do. She'd been trained for it, after all, all her life. She wanted to make sure I was ready."

"Who could be ready for that?" Kaya wondered.

He hugged her close. "I'm here. I'm not hurt. Okay, I'm a little sore, but the Doc helped with that. There's no lasting damage, and the bastard who did it is dead and I'm glad."

"And... being with me... doesn't make you remember...?"

"Being with you makes me think about being with you. Kaya, rape is violence, not sex. You could carry out the same physical actions with me, but it would be an entirely different act. I wanted this. I've wanted it... forever."

"That's an easy intellectual distinction to make, Yank, but... are your emotions in sync with it? Does it really feel completely different to be touched by me?"

"Completely. Being with you is what I want. What happened back there... that was just doing the job... using any weapon at my disposal, though I'll admit it's not the kind of weapon I ever expected to use. I did what I had to do, to save all those kids. I'd do it again. I bet you would too."

"I don't know about that."

"Well..." he rolled her onto her back and arched himself above her, smiling down, "maybe you could at least give me another reminder of what good sex feels like?"

"Human!"

Kaya sat up, startled by the Qraitian's call. Had she been asleep, or...?

Next to her, Celia whispered, "Are you all right?"

"I asked you," said Ustenar, glaring down on her from the dais, "if you know the nuclear capability of that class of Confederate battleship."

"Uh... the *Douglas?*" Kaya faltered, "I think so. Give me a moment." To Celia's worried gaze, she said, "I guess I just dozed off."

Celia clucked her tongue. "You did nothing of the kind. Your eyes closed for a moment, and then you went into some sort of trance. If I didn't know better, I'd say you were spellcasting."

"Later, Doc." Kaya stood, and moved to stand close to Ustenar's watch officer. She squinted at the display, partially reminding herself of the specs of the *Douglas,* and partially trying to puzzle out what the hell had just happened to her. That she was a horny little bitch she'd known since puberty, but to slip off into a stupor of sexual fantasy in the middle of a mission, when everyone was about to die? Something else had to be going on here. It wasn't like she was pining away, nostalgic for her brief fling with Yank. She still loved him, yes, but as a brother. He was with Pallas now, primarily. He was happy, and she was content.

"Well, human?" Ustenar prodded her. "I want to know the weapons capability of that ship. Tell me, or your friend," she pointed to Faulkner, "dies."

Weapons. The word touched a trigger point in Kaya's mind. All those months ago, Yank had talked about all the weapons at his disposal, about using sex as a weapon.

"*Montague* class," Kaya said to the Commander. "Standard array of cannons, eight batteries; a bomb bay on the belly of the ship, for low orbit attacks; and missiles. Four launch bays, probably a hundred missiles on board, capable of bearing both offensive and exploratory payloads; and a stockpile of chemical explosives, plus probably six nuclear warheads."

Ustenar had been attracted to her as a Qraitian...

"Good," said the Commander. "What do you suppose are the odds they were going to launch the nuclear payload?"

"It's what I'd do," replied Kaya, "if I were stupid enough to attack an enemy that powerful. It's the only chance I'd have of wiping it out, but it's not much of a chance."

Was it possible...?

"And Fournier. Is he stupid?"

What a question! Of course she thought he was, but, if she were honest? "No," she told the Qraitian.

Ustenar nodded.

"But he may be desperate."

"Desperate enough that, although he appears to have withdrawn, he may yet launch the weapons?"

"It's... possible."

She hoped she wasn't saying too much. She wasn't even sure what she was saying as she tried to process, placate, and hold the Commander's interest, all at the same time. In minutes, they might be in battle.

"Very well," sighed Ustenar. She turned away. She was talking to someone–who? Of course, the spy, Daedalus. She'd been placing the call, when... When Kaya had suddenly and inappropriately begun reminiscing. The more she thought about it, the more she was convinced it was not happenstance. Someone was trying to communicate with her. Was it Metcalfe?

"It's time to act," Ustenar was saying to Daedalus. "Stay on this channel. I shall move to," she cast a glance at Kaya and Faulkner, "a more secure location."

As the Commander left, her words rung in Kaya's mind. It might, indeed, be time to act. She muttered to Faulkner, "I wish we knew what the hell she and Daedalus were planning."

Faulkner did not respond. Her eyes were focused on something, something far away, perhaps not even in the room with them.

"Doc?" she said.

The Doctor's eyes widened. "I think," she said slowly, "that I may know what they're planning..."

Aer'La set Fournier into an alcove designed as a quick resting place for boat deck hands to ride out sudden accelerations. Cernaq gently fastened the harness about his unconscious form.

"Now what do we do with him?" asked Aer'La.

Carson shrugged. "Leave him here?"

Cernaq said, "I've calmed his sleep centers to the point that he'll be out for hours. Long enough for us to return to Titan, I suppose."

"Which begs the question, Cernaq," Carson challenged him. "You were too morally conflicted to probe the minds of detainees on Titan, even to keep yourself out of jail. Why is this okay?"

"Because Fournier is a direct, identified threat, whereas all those civilians were not," explained Cernaq. "I'm not some starry-eyed idealist, Carson. Do you think I never come down out of my ivory tower?" He looked disdainfully at the inert figure before them. "Besides. I don't like Fournier."

Carson chuckled. For a moment, Aer'La stared, her mouth open. She then launched herself at the Phaetonian, impacting his upper torso with her breasts, catching him up in her arms and sending him flying backwards several yards. His own arms could not return the embrace, for he needed them to slow their backward flight before he cracked his skull on the wall of the boat deck.

Aer'La didn't seem to care that his arms weren't also around her. She kissed him hard and didn't release him for some time.

Celia Faulkner was quite accustomed to having visions. It was part of the life of one who followed the traditions of Wicca. Or perhaps it would be more accurate to say that it was part of the life of one who followed and understood those traditions. Plenty of amateurs mouthed words about the Goddess and spiritual energies, but hadn't a clue as to what the Craft was all about. Their minds were not open, hadn't been trained, and couldn't actually see the supernatural in the natural world around them. Their blindness was similar to that of a feral child who hadn't learned language skills. Not knowing what spoken language was, all that noise would only frighten and confuse her, if she noticed it at all. For someone who knew the language, however, the message couldn't be missed. Above all, the Craft was a discipline.

The vision she was experiencing at this moment was foreign to her experience, however. Its clarity, its immediacy... the way it seemed to show her events that were happening in a concrete way, right *now*. It was more like receiving a holo transmission than having a supernatural experience.

She saw the Qraitian Daedalus, whom she hadn't even met. She recognized him, though. He was on a ship, most likely the liner the Family had used to escape the Marines. He was speaking quietly, secluded in what looked like a small stateroom. In holo before him was Ustenar. Faulkner could tell that she was in her lair on this very ship. Yes. The conversation was happening now, it had to be.

"We have seen time and again that it is impossible to harm the Family," Ustenar was saying.

"Indeed," agreed Daedalus. "It will make it difficult to secure control of the machine."

"Difficult," said Ustenar, "but not impossible. First we must eliminate all other threats."

"Metcalfe controls all communication with the Voice," said Daedalus. "I believe he can also direct its action, or at least appeal to it to act. If you attack the Confederates–"

"I'm not going to attack the Confederates, my friend. You are."

"I don't understand. The Family would never let me–"

"They are pacifists! Kill some of them, if you must. Kill all of them!"

"They cannot be killed. Eleusis–"

"They cannot be killed, but neither will they fight," growled Ustenar. "They told me you were a master of deception! Deceive them! Find a way to launch an attack on the *Titan*, and the rest will take care of itself! The Confederates will return fire, and Eleusis will destroy them, as it did the Marines."

"But this is a passenger liner! It carries no weapons!"

"It carries life boats, does it not?"

"It does," admitted Daedalus.

"Be creative, then. But launch an attack on the *Titan*. It need not be successful. It need only provoke a response. You will be perfectly safe, but our enemies will be eliminated."

Daedalus said gravely, "It shall be done, Commander."

The vision faded as Ustenar closed the transmission. Celia, still shaken by the abruptness of the experience, leaned in close to Kaya.

"Daedalus... the spy... he's planning to attack the *Titan*."

"What?" Kaya demanded. "How do you know?"

The watch officer turned and looked at them. They were silent for a moment. When he looked away again, Celia said, "I'm... not sure. I somehow received a vision of what Ustenar and Daedalus were saying. They're hoping to provoke the Captain and Sestus into attacking the Family."

"They'd be destroyed!"

"That's the plan," said Faulkner. "I don't know that your father will fall for it, but–"

"Celia, we've got to warn *Titan*."

"I'm open to suggestions as to how."

"You and Cernaq have sometimes been able to communicate across great distances..."

Celia shook her head. "I've thought of that, and tried. He's either out of range or he's unconscious. Pallas is also unresponsive."

Kaya considered it. "If we could reach their radio room..."

"Do you think you could distract Ustenar? Get her out of here? The others are so cowed by her, in her absence I know how I might be able to slip away. I came prepared for that."

"I think I know a way to get her attention," said Kaya. "But I'm afraid it would blow our ticket out of here."

Celia nodded, understanding. "Then I'll work on alternate transportation." Quietly, leaning in closer to Kaya to cloak her movements, she triggered her implant and opened a saved program.

The hatch opened, and Ustenar strode in. Celia and Kaya made eye contact, the Doctor silently acknowledging that now was the time to act. Kaya smiled apologetically, then grabbed Celia by the shoulders and hauled her to her feet, shoving her roughly against the bulkhead.

"You traitor! You wouldn't dare! Just to save your worthless life?"

Not knowing what it was she would dare, Celia said defiantly, "I would!"

"What in the Names is going on?" demanded Ustenar.

Kaya released Celia and turned to face the Commander. "My... colleague..." she almost spat the word, "wants to trade certain information for her freedom."

"Commander," Celia begain, "I can tell you–"

"Shut up! If we're going to die, at least face it like a grown-up!" barked Kaya, raising one hand as if to cuff Celia in the mouth. She turned back to Ustenar. "I'll tell you myself. It won't make any difference. I am an officer of the *Titan*. I was on board during the battle with Fehajiq. I–" she glanced over her shoulder at Celia, prepping her for the lie with her eyes. "I led the raiding party which captured him." In fact, Celia had done so.

"Really?" asked Ustenar, coldly. "Well, anyone can claim–"

"And," Kaya said, wavering internally, but hesitating in speech not at all, "I am Terrence Metcalfe's lover."

"Okay," sighed Aer'La, still keeping her eyes happily on Cernaq. "We stopped the missiles. Now?"

"The communications array," said Carson. "We really do need it working again, so we can talk to the Captain."

Cernaq shook his head, distracted. "I'm trying to reach Pallas. I should be able to, but–"

Aer'La ran her fingernails through the hair at the back of his neck. "Do we have to talk about her right now?"

Cernaq turned to her, a patient smile on his face, then went limp, shut his eyes, and floated free like a leaf fallen to the surface of a pond.

"Cernaq?" Aer'La cried out.

"Don't move!" a voice called. From around a bend in the corridor, a young man in a lieutenant's uniform sailed forward, a pulse gun leveled at Aer'La.

Carson recognized the voice as that of the man Fournier had called on the command deck. "Gregson, isn't it?"

"It is," said the officer coldly. He looked to where Fournier was secured and nodded. "As I figured. I thought the Admiral sounded a little off, besides his order being completely unexpected. Then I saw the I.D. data from your shuttle, and realized you'd brought a telepath. Our internal systems are working just fine, thank you very much, Mr. Carson. All three of you were scanned and identified upon entry. You're all under arrest for mutiny. I'd advise you not to resist. In an attack on a flag officer, lethal force is authorized. I'll kill you all if you take a step out of place."

"I don't doubt it," said Carson. "But Gregson, you've got to understand the stakes here."

"I understand that you allowed a telepath to violate the mind of the Secretary of the Navy, not to mention physically assaulting him."

"Captain Atal can explain–"

Gregson snorted dismissively. "I know you people put a lot of stock in what you think Atal will do to protect you. He may be a troublemaker, Carson, but Jan Atal is loyal to the Navy. If he were here, he'd be doing just what I'm going to do."

"And what's that?" asked Aer'La, who had reached out one arm to cradle Cernaq's limp body. Carson was relieved to see he was still breathing. Gregson had only stunned him.

Gregson held the pulse gun up for them to see, thumbed the safety lock and slid its selector switch to lethal intensity. "I'm going to fire those missiles," he said. "Now."

CHAPTER TWENTY

I'm not comfortable with what's happening...

Why not? All is going according to plan. We knew that an attack would be made upon me, that the Qraitians would attempt to foment violence against the Family–

I didn't know my friends would be involved!

How could they not be? They are here, after all.

Yes, but... I thought the... the violence... I thought Ustenar would be a player. Certainly Fournier, maybe Sestus–

You thought your friends would be safe in the background? You thought you could stage a war and your loved ones would not be drawn into it?

Ouch.

That is very like many of the leaders of wars in the history of Eleusis, Terry. It's an extremely irrational belief, isn't it? And immoral. You told me that the root of what is called moral is the simple statement "Do unto others as you would have them do unto you."

It is.

But then, is not sending others off to war, while keeping yourself and those you love protected from war, a violation of that principle? You would have others not make war with you, so–

I get it. It sounds hypocritical.

Our dialogue is not spoken, Terry. It does not "sound" hypocritical. It simply is.

Except that I'm not staging a war, dammit! I was... engineering a demonstration. I was showing potential enemies the consquences of their projected actions. Enemies like Fournier and Ustenar. I–we–were going to let them attempt their violent solutions, and then show them how pointless they were.

That is what we're doing. It's going very well.

Except that... Kaya's identified herself as someone that Ustenar has no choice but to kill, Daedalus is about to stage an attack on Titan, Cernaq's been shot, Aer'La and Carson are at gunpoint...

Are these not the consequences of violence you intended to show them?

Not exactly. I hadn't expected...

Expected what?

Heroism, dammit! I hadn't expected my friends to go charging into the line of fire, putting themselves in danger, trying to save the day!

Then, my love, I believe I would have to classify you as a "slow learner."

Eleusis?

I didn't say that.

Hello, Metcalfe.

Pallas?

Who else?

Here?

Where else? By your side. So to speak.

But you're on Titan!

Physically I am. Psychically, I am here with you. Now. And always.

But... Eleusis... could you excuse us?

I cannot, no. But I will be silent.

Pallas, this is...

A surprise?

Yes. It's like... when we've been psychically joined, those other couple of times...

It's exactly like that. You recall I asked for a permanent bond?

Yes.

This... is it. And I assure you, I didn't force this on you.

How -- ?

During intercourse the other day.

I thought it had to be voluntary.

Metcalfe, it was. You wanted it.

I...

Oh, not consciously, perhaps. But your inner mind–your soul, if you will, though I don't recognize such unscientific terms–knew what it wanted. It reached out to mine, and mine answered. The link was established.

But... you didn't say anything!

I said quite a bit, most of it begging.

I meant–

I know. My point is I was caught up in the throes of orgasm–an incredible orgasm, thank you–and unable to articulate that the bond was forming.

And then you hid it from me.

To avoid pressuring you, yes. But now you're in danger, as are we all. And whatever happens, this time I will be with you.

Well... that's good; but I'm not making much progress here.

Why do you say that?

Because I had a plan. We did. Eleusis and I. We would bring the Family into space, and then the Qraitians and the Navy would posture and threaten and become violent.

Congratulations. You've succeeded.

But... no! I didn't expect the others to do all these things! Spying on the Qraitian ship, attacking Fournier...

Which bothers you more? That they attacked Fournier, or that Sestus was one of the attackers?

Don't get me started.

Did you expect your friends to sit idle?

I... I thought everyone would be left guessing. How did Celia know what Daedalus was planning? How did Cernaq know something was up with Fournier? How did Carson know that–?

342	Steven H. Wilson

You're asking how each of your friends obtained information about the emergency which should not have been available to them? That's obvious. You told them.

I what now?

Well, I told them, relaying your information. Metcalfe, we're joined. Our minds are together. When you want something, I work for it. You wanted each of them to know–

I didn't! I did not say, "Hey, Pallas, tell Aer'La to release Cernaq."

No, I suppose you didn't. But you wanted me to do just that.

Okay, this mind-reading thing is all well and good until you start reading thoughts I didn't think!

We often think thoughts we're not aware of.

We do?

No, I don't. You do. You can't help it. Your mind is untrained.

Pardon me!

I do try. The human subconscious is a vast and unexplored area for most. We have desires we never realize as coherent thoughts, unless we take the time to analyze them. For instance, you're aware that Aer'La has been unusually angry of late, even for Aer'La.

I am.

You must know that she's even been distant with Cernaq, damaging their personal relationship.

I know.

Well, then, if you had time, what would you tell them?

I... I'd tell them they need to trust each other! To talk! That it's okay to ask for help...

So is it surprising that you relayed to them, through me, images that caused them to think about friendship and trust?

But–

And Carson? The two of you have been distant, fighting. If you weren't afraid of his anger, of being rejected, what would you say to him?

That... I'll always be here for him.

Precisely. As you always have been. To show him the extent of your devotion, you need only cause him to reflect on your past together, and all the times you've been there for each other.

Okay, well–

And Kaya. As she's concerned about you, as she wonders what affect Eleusis has had upon you, as she's watching violence erupt around her, and wondering if you're behind it–

She's got to know that there's no length I wouldn't go to to keep everyone safe!

Which is just the message I relayed to her, by reminding her of your shared experiences together.

Oh... Damn...

Just as I showed Sestus that, no matter the situation, you're always doing what it takes to protect your charges.

You could have left him off the list.

Sestus believes in you.

I do not want to know that.

Neither does he. But he does.

Well... your messages went a bit far, Pallas. They all took them and... got stupid...

Meaning they put their lives on the line, trying to make a difference.

Yes!

Just as you would!

Whose side are you on?

Yours, always, my love; but you must be honest. Your friends are not chess pieces. They are people. You cannot expect them to be less noble than you would be. You cannot expect to make a plan for them to follow if it involves them being less than what they are. That was the flaw in your plan. You forgot to account for your friends. For that matter, you forgot to account for your own expectations of them, expectations that, whether you believe it or not, they want very much to fulfill.

So now what?

You tell me. You can keep them all safe.

Yes, I can. Well, Eleusis can. Only...

Only what?

Only if they find out that the real prime mover behind all that went wrong was actually me, will they ever forgive me?

Kaya had to admit that, despite the unimaginable danger in which she'd just placed herself, she was enjoying the look of utter shock on Ustenar's face. The final, calculated blow had been delivered. Would it be enough? Surely no Qraitian could resist the bait of a lover of the leader who'd brought down Fehajiq. Even if they never tracked down Yank, there would be status in killing her.

"If what you say is true," said Ustenar slowly.

"I assure you it is. My... mother can confirm."

Ustenar looked to Celia, who shook her head. "I told her that boy would bring her to no good. But who listens to their mother anymore?"

"Silence!" snapped Ustenar. "None should listen to you. You would have bartered the secret of her identity to me, in hopes of currying favor?"

Celia, looking abashed, nodded.

"I would have killed you immediately. Out the airlock, I think." She turned to Kaya. "Should I kill her now?"

Kaya tried to sound as contemptuous as she could. "Let her instead live to see my dead body, and see the way a brave woman dies."

Ustenar cocked her head. "You accept that you must die?"

She leaned in close to Ustenar. "I know there's no way out of this. I've botched my mission. I've brought disgrace on my family, on the man I love. You're going to execute me, I understand that; but let me die the death I've earned, as someone with rank in Qraitian society." She clasped the taloned appendage near her in both her own hands and breathed quite deliberate into the Commander's face, whispering, "Ustenar, I want it to be you. I've never met a woman of such strength. I know you feel it too. I want to die by your hand. I petition for the Right of Choice!"

The Qraitian woman stopped, impressed. "You've done your research, human."

"Human, yes," agreed Kaya. "But to be accorded Qraitian honors as one who has defeated Qraitians in battle."

Ustenar pulled back and stared. Kaya wondered if she had gone too far. Then the Commander turned to her watch officer and said tersely, "I'm taking this prisoner to my lair for questioning."

She led Kaya to the rear hatch. Celia watched sadly after them until they were obscured from view. Then, assured that all the remaining Qraitians would be too sickened by her cowardice to look upon her, she turned back to her implant and set to work.

For the first time in an hour, Metcalfe looked up from his couch in the control cabin and spoke. "Everything's about to happen very quickly."

Aronson studied him. "You do not seem as confident as you did earlier."

"I'm fine," said Metcalfe.

"Something has happened," the elder man maintained. "Something has changed. Is it merely that you do not like seeing your friends in danger, despite the ability of Eleusis to protect them? Or is it something more?"

Metcalfe ignored him.

Behind them were Daedalus and Icarus. Elspeth, at Aronson's insistence, had gone to a stateroom to rest. Daedalus said, "Perhaps friend Metcalfe does not like the callousness with which the machine treats other beings?"

"Why are you still here?" Metcalfe asked coldly.

"Am I not one of the Family?"

"You are a spy," said Metcalfe. "You came here to uncover the secrets of Eleusis and use them for war."

"And how are you using them?" asked Daedalus. "It looks to me as though quite a few people are about to die."

"They're not," said Metcalfe quietly.

"Indeed," said Daedalus. "It is easy to live peacefully, is it not, when you command the greatest weapon in the universe?" He leaned in close. "But do you command it, friend Metcalfe?"

The Qraitian waited, when there was no answer, he said, "You're right, Aronson. His confidence is shaken. Something has changed."

"You need to leave," said Metcalfe.

"Indeed? Where would I go? If I am not one of you, may I return to the Qraitians, as Ustenar has requested?"

"They would kill you," said Aronson.

Daedalus held his head high. "I would die willingly. It's a choice I made before I came to your blighted world."

Aronson shrugged. "I stand in the way of no man's free will."

Daedalus nodded. "That is your folly, but still, I am grateful. Perhaps my son would go as well."

He looked to the boy, who simply stared back, mute and uncertain. Could he be considering it? wondered Metcalfe. Had his father's betrayal so dispirited him?

"No," said Metcalfe sharply. "Icarus stays here, and so do you."

"It is my right–" began Daedalus.

"To hell with your rights."

"Terry!" protested Aronson.

"I'm sorry, Brock, but you wanted me to lead your people in this, and you're getting my leadership. I'd go a long way to ensure that everyone enjoys his free will, and I'd sooner live with a live rattlesnake than keep this reptile in our midst." Metcalfe saw Icarus cringe at the word "reptile," and the way he uttered it. He pressed on. "But all hell is about to break loose, and we need him where we can keep an eye on him."

Daedalus nodded. "As I thought. Your principles are not what you pretend they are. You are still a warrior, and this is still a battle." He turned to his son. "Come, Icarus. Let us prepare to meet the new era of peace."

When they were gone, Aronson held his eyes fixed on Metcalfe for a long time.

"What?" Metcalfe asked.

"Your way is not the Family way."

Metcalfe nodded. "Perhaps not, but I couldn't let Daedalus have what he was asking for. In truth, he didn't want it either. He's under orders to stay here."

"He is?"

"From Ustenar. He's planning to betray us. That's why he put on that show for Icarus's benefit. He's asking him for help even now."

"How can you know that? Eleusis?"

"Not only Eleusis. You see... Pallas is in contact with me. Phaetonians can establish permanent mental bonds."

Aronson nodded understanding. "She explained that to me. And you accepted such a bond with her?"

"Apparently."

"She confers you quite an honor."

"Yes, I know. And, with her, with Eleusis, I know, well, everything that's going on around us."

"Omniscience?"

"Limited, maybe, but... I don't know another word for it. And right now Daedalus is telling Icarus his plan."

"Lifeboats? Father, I don't understand."

"Not just lifeboats, Icarus. Missiles. Launched on the right course, with proper speed—"

"Launched at what?"

"The *Titan*."

"But why would we attack—?"

"We are not attacking. We are causing them to believe that we are attacking. They will attack us—"

"Father, is this part of your plan to end your life?"

"Certainly not! Think, my son! No harm can come to us."

"But the humans! Father, I know you do not accept it, but I do embrace the ways of the Family. I cannot allow anyone to be harmed as a result of my actions!"

"No one will be harmed, Icarus. You heard Metcalfe before. He is in control now. The entity—the Voice of Eleusis—will not cause harm."

"Then why—?"

"Son, you want to help Metcalfe, don't you?"

"He's my friend. Of course I do."

"Then help me put together this sham attack. It will prompt action. That is the basis of Metcalfe's plan, made with Eleusis. They plan to allow the threat of violence to build to a crescendo, then they will show everyone how easy it is for Eleusis to thwart that violence. But Metcalfe is losing confidence. He doesn't like seeing his friends threatened, even in a war game. We need to help him carry out his plan."

"But I thought... It sounded like, maybe, Metcalfe and Eleusis were disagreeing. Remember, Eleusis killed all those Marines. What if–?"

"Icarus! Do you trust your friend?"

"I do!"

"You don't act like it. I thought you believed in faith."

"I do believe."

"Then have faith in God, and have faith in your friend. And help me to help them."

"Well–"

"It will be easy, Icarus; and I assure you that no one will be harmed."

It was amazing, Kaya reflected, the kinds of things that sexually aroused some people. Granted, Ustenar wasn't human, but she was a sentient being. While no human research on Qraitian sexuality had ever been performed, Kaya believed it likely that sentient beings experienced sexual desire in basically the same way, no matter their origins.

Ustenar seemed to have a death fetish. The more Kaya talked about dying at the Commander's hands, the more flustered the Qraitian became. Kaya encouraged every bit of it, drew her out wherever possible. She refused no advance, and did her best not to look askance at anything Ustenar said or did.

Would Ustenar even know if a human looked askance? This was all new territory. Kaya might be the first human in history to attempt to use seduction against a Qraitian opponent. She thought ruefully that that, at least, was some sort of legacy, if this was the mission that ended her career and her life.

"You humans have such delicate skin," Ustenar observed, stroking Kaya's thigh, scratching lightly with her talons. "It's not a good design."

Kaya was nude, of course. There had been no room for clothing beneath the false skins they'd donned to impersonate Qraitians. Since those had been taken away, and Qraitian ships naturally did not stock human clothing, she and Celia had nothing to wear.

"That's why we usually wear more clothing than your people do. Our hides aren't as tough."

Ustenar looked at her quizzically. "We don't have fur at all," she said.

Fur? Kaya wondered. She realized something had been lost in translation. They weren't speaking directly, of course, but were using the translation tech which had been built into her implant. They'd let them keep their implants for the very reason that they allowed the humans to communicate. Kaya had used the word "hides," which probably translated into a Qraitian term for a mammal's skin, which probably equated to a skin covered in fur, mammals having never evolved as far on Ustenar's home world as they had on Terra and elsewhere.

Ustenar dug in with a talon, causing Kaya to wince and drawing blood. "It cuts so easily," she observed. "I could tear you apart with little exertion."

Clearly, the thought excited her. Kaya kept her expression neutral as Ustenar stared at the droplet of blood oozing from the wound. Her eyes were as close to round as Kaya had seen them.

"Human blood," the Qraitian nearly purred, "is not toxic to us." Her eyes gleamed horribly, and her tongue danced and flickered out of her mouth. "We learned that during the last war." She brought her head to Kaya's thigh and buzzed her tongue over it, collecting blood which she then tasted by snapping her tongue back in.

It was like watching a frog eat an insect. Kaya suppressed revulsion. If Ustenar wanted to further employ her tongue in this game, she was afraid she might vomit.

The Qraitian hovered closer. Kaya leaned back against the stone on which they reclined. "Your skin will separate so beautifully," said the Qraitian, "when I execute you. I wonder where I will begin." She caressed Kaya's chin with her talons.

Swallowing, Kaya said, as clinically as possible, "The jugular vein in the neck will be quickest." She felt suddenly cold. This woman was going to kill her! It was becoming a reality in her mind. She would die soon, at the talons of Ustenar. If she had a chance of survival, it lay in prolonging the seduction.

"I'm not sure I want it to be quick," Ustenar whispered. "I want us to enjoy it. Do you think it's possible to derive pleasure from one's own death?"

"I–I suppose it could happen," Kaya breathed. What the hell was the Qraitian doing? Her talons were dragging downward, making trails over Kaya's breasts, her belly... going lower.

She told herself to hold it together. This was the goal, after all, to get the Qraitian horny. Drag it out, make–ugh!–*love* to her.

To keep her focus, she reviewed in her mind the five vulnerable spots along the Qraitian spine which Faulkner had taught her. The exercise helped her maintain calm, and she would need the information soon. Not soon enough, she reflected sourly.

"Well," said Ustenar, "we –" She stopped, looked around. Was something wrong? "It's very warm in here," she observed.

"Perhaps you're flushed from the enjoyment," said Kaya. She immediately realized her mistake.

Ustenar looked at her as though she were a simpleton. "Qraitians do not 'flush,' human. Our bodies adapt to the ambient temperature. If I say it is getting warm, that is objective fact." The Commander stood and went to the wall to check the temperature settings. Qraitians did not make the extensive use of holo technology for interface that humans did. "It says it is set correctly," she said disapprovingly, "but I still feel warm."

"Perhaps you should check the one in the next room," Kaya suggested helpfully, hoping it wasn't too leading.

Ustenar didn't seem suspicious. Clearly she was too aroused to focus much attention on practical matters. She dilated the door into her inner lair and stepped through.

Kaya jumped quietly to her feet. There might not be another opportunity to act. Next to the climate controls on the wall was the comm panel. That was another relative crudity of the Qraitian military: they didn't bother with personal implants for communications. Kaya easily keyed the privacy setting, preventing the command deck from calling in. When and if Daedalus launched his attack, it might buy her father some precious seconds of confusion if Daedalus couldn't ask for further instructions.

She returned to the stone couch just as Ustenar returned, saying, "I've lowered this room's temperature and ordered a full system diagnostic routine. Some idiot is not paying attention. He will pay in other ways." She raked her eyes over Kaya's prone form and said appreciatively, "Later."

Celia Faulkner opened one eye discretely and observed the Qraitians on the command deck. Nearly half an hour ago, she'd pretended to drift off to sleep, assuming that the sight of an old woman napping would strike not even a Qraitian as suspicious. Indeed, coupled with the show of defamation Kaya had put on earlier, it should serve to relax them, suggesting that their remaining prisoner was not a credible threat.

She'd had to discipline herself to not actually fall asleep. It was tempting, after all they had been through; but Kaya was counting on her to do her part.

The Qraitians were no longer moving. Celia keyed her implant to display the true temperature, and found it sufficient. Torpidity would have set in some time ago. She had seen it often among the prisoners she'd tended decades ago. She'd even induced their torpid state to promote more rapid healing. Often, because they were stubborn and proud, she'd had to sneak it on them, as she had done here and now.

Having used her implant to interface with the ship's climate control system, something she'd come prepared to do, she had programmed their ship's thermometers to show the expected temperature for active Qraitians. In fact, she'd forced the heating system to go so high that, being cold blooded and driven by external conditions, the Qraitians would sleep while she continued her mission.

Making a series of increasingly loud sounds to test her work, and getting no response, she was satisfied it was safe to leave the command deck. Ships schematics, studiously committed to memory, told her where the boat deck would be. She would ready a launch, then return to Ustenar's lair to collect Kaya. By that time, the girl should have the Qraitian Commander incapacitated, if not actually dead.

She did not notice, in her hurry to escape and her wariness to avoid any active Qraitians in the corridors, that her implant showed a system diagnostic had killed her interface process. Nor did she register, as she ran, that the ship was becoming colder.

Elspeth had returned to the liner's control cabin and was attempting to alleviate the tense silence between Metcalfe and Aronson. Still in constant touch with Pallas and Eleusis mentally, Metcalfe knew he must seem distracted to the others. It was difficult to compartmentalize a telepathic conversation, a "real" one (although that conversation was currently sparse) and his concern for his friends as events unfolded. Pallas had promised to tutor him on the discipline required.

"Metcalfe," Aronson called out suddenly. His voice was still calm, and yet one could see that, for him, this was a peak moment of stress. "I show that life boats have been launched from our vessel."

Metcalfe nodded. "I told you he planned to betray us."

Elspeth stepped forward and watched the images of dozens of tiny craft, fanning out from the liner like tadpoles dispersing after a stone hits the surface of a pond.

"He left?"

"No," said Metcalfe. "He's still here. It's a ruse. He and Ustenar want to turn us against each other."

"Stop him!" cried Elspeth. "Someone might be hurt!"

"No one will be hurt," said Metcalfe. "Eleusis... predicted this."

"And you agreed?" asked Elspeth.

Metcalfe didn't answer.

"Terry?"

"Eleusis," he said slowly, "thinks it's best not to interfere. Not yet."

"I wonder," said Aronson, "given its history... will it interfere before or after more of your friends are killed?"

Atal was on his promenade, fingering an otherwise untouched mug of coffee, as he stared, quite literally, into space at the Qraitian ship, when Darby called. It had only been minutes since he had left the Deputy Captain on watch.

Darby's tone was urgent. "Sir, the liner–"

"What is it?"

"She's launching life boats, bound for *Titan.*"

"What the hell? I thought–"

His implant pinged with a call from Sestus Blaurich. The Midshipman's image appeared before him, fatigue beginning to show. "Captain–"

"I see it, Mr. Blaurich," said Atal tightly.

"Sir, the *Douglas*–"

"Eh? What about the *Douglas*?"

"She's re-armed missiles, Captain, preparing to fire."

Atal slammed down his coffee cup and made his way to the door, talking as he moved. "Can we raise Carson or the others on *Douglas*?"

"To whom are you speaking?" asked Darby.

"Either of you, dammit!"

"My readings show their communications array's still out," said Sestus. "Portables can't function, and–"

"How many on the lifeboats?" Atal demanded. "Darby?"

"Captain, it doesn't make sense."

"What doesn't make sense?"

"They're empty, sir!"

"Then why," asked Atal as he jumped into a bounce tube and drifted upward towards the command deck, "are they attempting to dock with us."

"Respectfully, Captain," said Sestus, "I don't think they are attempting to dock with you. Their trajectory and acceleration are all wrong. They'd be braking by now if–"

"Make it march, Mr. Blaurich!"

"The life boats are on a collision course, sir. I think they're being used as missiles."

"That's ridiculous!" barked Darby.

"It's not, actually," said Sestus. "With the motors set on overdrive, and on a collision course, those boats could do a hell of a lot of damage to *Titan*. I estimate severe structural compromise and high potential for loss of life. A third of them are on course for the Life Sphere, Captain."

Atal swore. What the hell was the Family up to? He didn't allow himself to wonder what Metcalfe might be up to. "Prepare to engage, Mr. Blaurich. Take out as many as you can."

"And the missiles, Captain?" asked Darby.

"I'll be on the Command Deck any second now, Mr. Darby. Bring us aft of the *Douglas* and about. Target the missile bays. We're going to pick them off as they launch."

Kaya was bleeding. Ustenar had opened a vein in her wrist. Not a life-threatening injury. On its own, the blood would coagulate and the wound would begin to heal. Ustenar was not allowing that. She held the wrist, flicking at the wound occasionally, scraping gently to keep up the flow, sometimes squeezing to coax more blood out. She waved the arm over Kaya's naked form, splattering her.

Kaya reckoned that she needed to act within a minute. She'd have to lure the Qraitian into an embrace, confess some deep secret. In that moment, she would use the training Celia and her father had given her. She'd decided not to incapacitate. She would kill Ustenar. Kaya had particapted in more types of sexual congress than most people could imagine. She'd committed acts which, on old Terra, would have gotten her burned at the stake or broken on the rack. She'd enjoyed them all and didn't believe in perversion. The Qraitian Commander, however, was the sickest, most loathsome creature she had ever encountered. Kaya wanted her dead, soon and forever.

There was a knock at the door. An angry, persistent pounding, really.

Ustenar reared up her head and shrieked, "What is it?"

The door dilated, and Ustenar's watch officer stepped in slowly, struggling with someone outside whom he was dragging by the shoulders. There was a familiar cry as he yanked the shoulders hard, and Celia Faulkner stumbled into the room.

"We've had a... disturbance, ma'am, with this one. There have also been–"

"Why didn't you call me?" demanded Ustenar, standing and, thankfully, removing her offending phalanges from Kaya.

He regarded her darkly. "Your comm unit was refusing calls." He nodded at Kaya, then went on, grabbing Faulkner by her short, gray hair and wrenching her chin up. "This one tampered with the climate control systems. We were rendered torpid. The ship must have corrected–"

"It did. I ordered a full diagnostic, you incompetent fool! Why did you not detect–"

"Much was happening. Commander, the situation is deteriorating rapidly. As I stopped the human from readying a launch, *Douglas* was beginning a launch sequence on its missiles."

"They had disarmed!" protested Ustenar.

"They've re-armed them, Commander."

"Destroy them!"

"We cannot. The frigate and *Titan* are in defensive posture."

"Well–"

"There's more," he told her. "The liner has sent its lifeboats, set to detonate, on a collision course with *Titan*. The frigate is engaging those while *Titan* has moved into position to destroy the missiles. Commander, if I may–"

"You may not!"

"Commander," he snapped. "The young human female–I've been monitoring their news broadcasts–"

"I did not order–"

"I thought she looked familiar. Commander, she is the daughter of Atal, and she has distracted you. I must report that you have failed, and–"

Ustenar spun on Kaya, her mouth open, fangs bared.

"Atal's daughter?"

"At your service," said Kaya.

"Return to the command deck! Destroy the frigate! And broadcast this image to the *Titan*!" Ustenar snapped at the watch officer. "Atal will watch as his daughter dies." She raised her arm, extending her talons. She smiled. "The jugular vein, is it? I trust it will open when I tear you head from your body?"

Metcalfe, the machine has too much influence over you.

That is not fair, Pallas. This is a partnership. Metcalfe is the One I have chosen to guide my actions. I am no more influencing him than he is influencing me.

No balance of power is ever perfect, Eleusis. It is always weighted to one side, yours, in this case. Metcalfe has told you he is not comfortable with the actions you have chosen. Our friends are in great danger. They are suffering. No matter that you may save them at any moment, their pain and fear cannot be discounted.

She is right, Eleusis. I don't like this.

You are losing confidence in our plan, Terry. That is all. You are mortal, and your emotions confuse you. You cannot be at peace in the perfection of the plan.

What if we make a mistake? What if we miscalculate?

I do not make mistakes. I merely follow my directives and produce results you did not expect.

And if the result I did not expect is the death of dozens of people? Or hundreds?

Have you considered that, perhaps, some of them must die in order to protect untold millions at a later time?

I have not.

Be careful, Metcalfe! This intellect is not what you think it is.

Pallas, your input is becoming damaging. Your presence is unwelcome.

You want Metcalfe to yourself, you mean.

That statement leads to the same desired result, yes. I would like you to... go away.

She's not going anywhere!

Terry, she is upsetting you. You and I were in agreement, until she forced herself into your mind.

I did not force myself into his mind. He invited me. You, Eleusis, want Metcalfe to be separate from everyone else, everyone he has come to depend on, everyone he loves.

He does not need them.

You see everyone here—me, the Qraitians, the Family— as statistics. We're pieces in a game, automatons on your playing field. You had Metcalfe thinking that way, too, as your perfect plan moved forward. He was so adapted to your central planning philosophy that it actually surprised him when his friends behaved exactly as they've always behaved.

It did not surprise me! I had calculated their actions, and they do not affect the plan. Indeed, they serve to enhance its desired effect. Their deaths will have tremendous emotional significance to the other mortals.

Deaths? What deaths?

I have recalculated the plan.

No one's going to die.

It is for the good of the greater number that they do. The fear which will be produced will secure our safety.

Since when do you understand fear, Eleusis? Since when do you manipulate emotion this way?

Since we became One, Terry. That is why I needed a mortal companion. I must understand mortals, if I am to control them. My previous companion did not understand them, and that is what led to the need to eliminate all that threatened us. This time, it will be different. Most will be saved.

You... you're going to let them die! Kaya, Carson, Aer'La and Cernaq.

It is best.

I won't let you.

Think, Terry. Don't just feel. You were the one who first recognized that their actions surprised you. They are unpredictable. Outside your control. They create emotional turmoil in you which endangers the plan.

They are more important than the plan!

Nothing is more important than the plan.

They are my friends. I love them.

It was Metcalfe's subconscious desires which prompted their actions. He needs them. He counts on them. If you destroy them, or let them die, he will be your enemy.

Metcalfe is the One. He will not be my enemy, but you distract him, Pallas. You must go away.

I will not.

Eleusis, don't hurt her!

I won't hurt her, but she cannot stay.

Pallas!

She is gone. You and I are alone now, Terry; and everything is going to be all right.

Watching Gregson one-handedly re-key the launch sequence as he held the gun on them with the other, Aer'La felt Carson's arm slip around her. She didn't resist as he gathered her close to him.

"Security will be here any second," he breathed into her ear.

She nodded, understanding that, if they were going to stop Gregson, it would have to be now.

Gregson saw the gesture and grinned. "You don't have to say your goodbyes just yet. I'll allow the three of you to share a cell. It's a small ship, after all." He continued his work.

Aer'La heard the motors engage in the missile bays, the launch cradles being restored to ready position. It would only be a matter of seconds before they could be fired.

"Release Cernaq now," whispered Carson. "When I let you go, be ready to kick off. He won't have time for a second shot before you get to him. Don't waste time. If you have to kill him... "

He left the thought unfinished. She looked into his eyes with meaning, making sure he meant what she understood him to mean. Carson was going to rush Gregson, let him fire, let himself be killed, so Aer'La could take him.

She shook her head gently. Carson kissed her forehead. "No other way, love," he whispered. He nodded to Cernaq. "Take care of him. Tell him..." he took a deep breath. "Tell him it's all right to tell Metcalfe everything."

Again she shook her head, rapidly to signal that she didn't understand.

"I hate to be callous," said Gregson, watching them, "but I think you two should separate. You can exchange regrets when I'm finished and I have you safely in custody."

"If you say so," muttered Carson. He looked to Aer'La, smiled sadly and mouthed the word "'Bye." Then he released her, kicked hard against the bulkhead and sailed forward.

Gregson shouted, "Fuck!" and took aim.

Aer'La tensed, letting Cernaq float free and preparing to launch herself at Gregson. Carson would be avenged. She could already feel the Lieutenant's neck snapping in her grasp.

The pulse gun fired. Beyond the bulkhead, Aer'La heard the rocket motors engage and the missiles streaked out of the ship towards Eleusis.

"Atal! I have something to show you!"

Ustenar's voice clipped and sputtered as her shrieks exceeded the specified range of the audio signal. Atal didn't look to see her face on the holo.

"I'm a bit busy, Commander, trying to intercept some missiles."

"Spare me your lies. I have your daughter, Atal!"

His blood ran cold. It had only been a matter of time, he knew, before the Qraitians put two and two together. The holo showed Kaya, stripped of her clothing and struggling in Ustenar's grip.

"Her sole purpose was to distract me while you and Fournier destroyed the secrets of Eleusis! I told you I would not allow that to happen, Atal. Your attempts to shield Fournier will not work. I will destroy the frigate, and the missiles. But first," she raised her hand to strike. Grasping Kaya's hair, she yanked the girl's head back, exposing her throat.

"Say goodbye, Atal," Ustenar snarled.

"No!" Atal shouted, moving as though to grab hold of the hologram and stop its movements. "Wait–!"

Ustenar brought down her arm. Kaya screamed.

"Enemy coming around, Captain," reported the *Henley's* gunner. "Targeting."

Captain. How long he had waited to be called that. He'd have traded all his wealth not to carry the title just now. "Fire all batteries," snapped Sestus. "Drive them off! We have to stop those life boats!"

He heard the staccato pulses of his ship's cannons, lashing out. He looked to the gunner, but she shook her head. "Got a few, sir, but not enough. We'll need–Captain! Look!"

Sestus's eyes went wide as he saw before him the Qraitian ship's starboard missile bay opening. "They're preparing to fire. Take evasive action!" he ordered.

The Qraitian ship lurched and surged forward, right at them. A suicide run? No. He saw the glint of sunlight on a silvery casing as a missile tore out from the Qraitian's belly.

By the time Ustenar's ship reached his, there would be nothing left of the frigate but debris.

Under his breath, he muttered, "See you in Valhalla, Metcalfe."

CHAPTER TWENTY ONE

No! Eleusis, stop now!

This is what must be, Terry. It is all according to the plan. It would be better for you if you stopped your emotional processes, at least while the plan is completed.

You will not kill them, Eleusis.

I will not. They will kill each other.

I will not allow them to.

You must not interfere! You told me that they must be free to choose their own actions!

But their choices are being made because you exist. You... I... We have a responsibility to prevent harm that results because of our actions.

Terry, what are you doing? You're overriding my programming? You're using the weaponry of Eleusis.

I'm stopping this.

Terry, no. The plan must continue. I will continue the plan!

No, Eleusis! You must–

"Stop!" Terry Metcalfe screamed. In the control cabin of the Family's liner, Aronson, Elspeth, Daedalus and Icarus reacted in surprise at the sudden outburst. Metcalfe had been so quiet after the life boats launched, and while the *Douglas* had fired its missiles, while the Qraitians had turned on the *Henley*. Now he was red in the face, breathing hard, and he lurched against the straps of his couch as though, under normal gravity, he were trying to jump to his feet. He cast his eyes about like a madman.

"Terry!" cried Elspeth, "what's wrong?"

Metcalfe took a ragged breath, but did not answer. Instead, he checked the readouts before him and punched up several views of the space surrounding them. When he'd examined several displays, he seemed satisfied, and slumped back against the couch, relieved.

"What has happened, Terry?" asked Aronson.

"Nothing," breathed Metcalfe. "I stopped it."

Celia Faulkner wanted to close her eyes as the Qraitian Commander reared to strike Kaya. She didn't want to see the girl die so long before her time. She knew that she could not look away, though. There had to be some way she could help, some way to stop Ustenar, or die trying.

She struggled in the grasp of the watch officer. He easily held her arms in check. She lashed out with her feet, conscious that Qraitian feet were so heavily muscled and armor plated that she could do little damage. She must have annoyed him, at least, for he spun her body, driving her out the door of the lair, where she struck the bulkhead opposite.

She heard a scream, Kaya's scream. She'd never felt so helpless. How to help Kaya, when she was out-muscled, naked and alone? And beyond that, how to stop missiles which may have already fired? How to cease this ship's headlong plunge into battle? Goddess!

"Listen to me," she said to the watch officer. "I know your Commander believes that she can control this... weapon. She can't! You've all got to see reason. If we continue this violence, that thing on Eleusis will kill us all!"

He looked coldly at her, seizing her again by the hair on the back of her head and wrenching her neck. "Be silent!" he hissed.

The impulse to spit in his slitted eye hit Celia. What more harm could it do? They were all dead anyway. She looked up, scowling... and her gaze met empty air. The hand on her neck was gone. Unsupported, she slumped backwards, banging her shoulder.

Kaya had stopped screaming.

Out of the corner of her eye, through the open door, she saw on Ustenar's holo display three angry lightning bolts issue forth from Fournier's ship. The missiles had launched, she registered, but there was more pressing danger.

"Kaya!" she called out, and, rising to her feet, charged through the door.

The room was empty. A trace of Kaya's blood on the stone couch displayed the only evidence anyone had been there at all.

The holo still displayed. She confirmed that the *Henley* had not been destroyed by the missile which the command deck had fired on Ustenar's order. Nor was there any evidence of life boats about to collide with the *Titan*.

She spun the holo to see the image of Eleusis, fearing she would see flashes of nuclear fire; but Eleusis remained, stalwart, untouched.

She reached up and ran her fingers over the comm controls. She had seen them used often enough in the past hours. She stabbed the transmit control to signal *Titan*. Obediently, Jan Atal shimmered into being before her. On his face was a mask of shock.

"Celia?" he said absently, his eyes still fixed elsewhere.

"Jan," she gasped out, "the Qraitians have vanished. I think all the missiles did too."

"Confirmed," said Atal. "All at once." Still distracted, he asked, "Are you all right?"

"Fine, Captain, but you look like hell."

Now he met her eyes. "I was just communicating with Ustenar," he said, his voice dead. "She was... she was going to kill Kaya; and then they both... they both disappeared. I don't know what the hell it all means."

"I believe it means," said Celia, "that the Voice of Eleusis has at last spoken."

"I don't understand," said Darby, floating next to Atal on the command deck of the *Titan*. "Where did the Qraitians go? And Midshipman Atal?"

"I don't know," said Atal. "They just... vanished."

"Sir," said Darby, his face suddenly pale, "you don't suppose... That is to say, Colonel Druelinger and his people also just vanished."

"I don't even want to think that way, Darby. Whatever just happened, it caused the missiles from *Douglas* to disappear off our instruments, as well as the missile that was about to destroy *Henley*. The life boats are gone... I'd say there was intent to prevent harm. I'm going to believe that Kaya's alive... somewhere. Raise Blaurich and get me a status report."

Darby turned away to signal the *Henley*. Behind them, the entry hatch opened and a voice called out, "Captain Atal!"

He spun, surprised. "Pallas?"

She floated toward him, pale, eyes bloodshot. She looked like she had the mother of all hangovers.

"What happened?" he asked, taking her hand and guiding her into a couch.

"I was in my cabin. I was in communication with Metcalfe. And with Eleusis."

"Eleusis? You were able to speak to the entity?"

"The machine, Captain. A very powerful, sentient machine, but with a machine's single-minded determination to fulfill its programming."

"But does Metcalfe have control of it?" wondered Darby.

"A fair question, Captain," said Pallas, her voice weary. "I believe he had... programmed it... to eschew violence. It and he had together developed a plan for a peaceful demonstration, one which would convince the Confederacy and the Qraitian Empire of the power of Eleusis. The end result, they calculated, would have been a truce, with the Family left unmolested."

"You're speaking entirely in the past tense," noted Atal.

"I am. Eleusis... did not know how to account for my participation in its mental link with Metcalfe."

"It resented you?" asked Atal.

"Were it human, that is how I would describe its behavior, as jealousy. Metcalfe, for his part, became increasingly uncomfortable with the emotional cost of their plan as it progressed."

"He lost his nerve," quipped Darby.

Pallas leveled her gaze at him and said tightly, "Captain Darby, you and I have always maintained a cordial working relationship. If you wish to keep it thus, you will not insult Mr. Metcalfe again. He does not 'lose his nerve.' He wanted to act earlier and more directly to spare his friends the terror that they were experiencing as a result of the planned demonstration."

"I'm guessing he didn't succeed," said Atal.

"Worse," Pallas replied. "Destabilized by my presence, and baffled by Metcalfe's request to alter their course of action, Eleusis... reevaluated. It decided that there was a flaw in their plan, not because it caused harm to humans, but because Metcalfe was compromised by human emotion when he developed it. It was proposing to override the moral and ethical programming Metcalfe had instilled in it." She closed her eyes for a moment, as if overwhelmed by the memory. "A few moments ago," she continued, "the lives of all of Titan's junior officers were directly threatened, each by different perils. Eleusis intended to let them die, and prevent Metcalfe from helping them."

"What happened?" asked Atal.

She shook her head, and, for the first time, appeared as close to tears as Atal had ever seen her. Whether they were tears of grief or frustration, he wasn't sure. "I don't know," she said pathetically. "Eleusis forced me out of rapport I shared with Metcalfe. I'm cut off from communication with either of them. Captain... I don't even know if Metcalfe... or any of them... are dead or alive."

"You stopped what?" Aronson demanded.

Metcalfe, visibly shaken, groped for words. Finding none suitable, he said, "Everything. All of Eleusis and everyone else's plans. The missiles, the lifeboats, the... Ustenar was about to slash Kaya's throat... Carson was about to be shot... I stopped it all."

Daedalus held up his communicator. "Ustenar is not answering," he said.

"Where did you get that?" asked Aronson.

"I knew he had it," said Metcalfe.

"You knew...?" Aronson whispered, amazed. "What game exactly are you playing?"

"A war game," said Daedalus. "A war game which is no game. What has happened to my countrymen, Metcalfe?"

"They're gone," said Metcalfe. "All of them. Anyone who was in danger, anyone who was a direct threat. They're gone."

"Gone where?" asked Aronson.

Metcalfe shook his head.

"Eleusis sent them away."

"I sent them away," Metcalfe corrected him. "It was Eleusis's power that did it, but under my control. Eleusis wanted to let a lot of people die. I forced its hand."

"But you don't know where you sent them?" demanded Daedalus. "You wield power you do not understand, power which can stop armies, trump all our weapons." He looked to Aronson. "Before, at least, the power of Eleusis was a threat, but one we could live with. Now it is under the control of one human who doesn't even understand it."

"You wanted it under Qraitian control," observed Aronson.

"I wanted it under military control," Daedalus corrected him. "Under proper authority. Now... we're at the mercy of one person." He glared at Metcalfe. "One person who must be stopped, before he loses control and destroys us all."

Daedalus lurched forward toward Metcalfe. Aronson caught him by the shoulder. "Don't be a fool, Daedalus! Eleusis won't allow you to harm the boy, and neither will I!"

Daedalus lashed out with one arm, backhanding Aronson in the gut. Caught off guard, the elder human sailed backward and struck his head on the edge of a couch. "I may die," Daedalus said quietly, "but I will die protecting my people."

Icarus, who had remained so strangely silent, called out, "Father—"

Daedalus looked at him, for the first time since he'd been revealed as a spy without contempt. "I protect you as well, my son. You are Qraitian. Do not forget."

"No!" shouted Icarus. He kicked forward, trying to collide with Daedalus. Inexperienced in zero-G, he sailed uselessly past, while his father kicked off an launched himself at Metcalfe.

Daedalus's target said softly, "Daedalus, you fool," raised his hand and gestured. Daedalus lurched and peeled suddenly away, as if struck by a blow from an invisible hand, a very powerful hand at that.

"Father!" cried Icarus, only now catching himself on the edge of a console and righting his orientation to look in Daedalus's direction. The elder Qraitian floated opposite Metcalfe, his head hanging, unsupported by his prodigious neck muscles, lifeless.

Aronson rushed to his side, but his face held no hope. It was obvious that the unseen force had snapped Daedalus's neck. He felt fruitlessly for a pulse, then looked to Icarus. "I'm sorry, Icarus," he said.

"No!" screamed the boy. He spun awkwardly, leveling an angry gaze at Metcalfe. "You killed him! I'll–" he sputtered, not knowing how to complete the threat. When he moved as if to attack Metcalfe himself, Elspeth shot her arms out and held him.

"Icarus, don't!" she cried. "You'll be killed!"

"He won't," said Metcalfe, his voice raw. "Eleusis... would not hurt Icarus."

"Then why," demanded the boy through his sobs, "did it kill my father? Why did *you* kill my father?"

"Because your father wasn't really one of the family, Icarus; and because he actually sought death. He intended to die, killing me. Eleusis could not process the subtleties of mortal motivations. It saw that Daedalus wanted to die, and it granted him death. I... I'm too weak to stop it... I'm... sorry."

"Sorry?" the boy shrieked. "You're *sorry*? You're a murderer! My father was right! With you controlling all this power, lives will be destroyed by the millions! I wish he'd killed you!"

Icarus buried his face in Elspeth's shoulder and sobbed.

"Terry," she said weakly, "he doesn't mean it. He–"

She didn't finish her sentence. Metcalfe had vanished.

"Captain Atal," said Aronson, "I believe it's time we talked."

"Past time," agreed the Captain. "I've lost a lot of people, Aronson, and I'd like to know where they are."

"As would I, Captain. Your young friend Metcalfe just vanished."

"Like the others?"

"I don't believe so. It was after the... event... which eliminated the missiles and left the Qraitian ship empty."

"Almost empty," piped up Celia Faulkner, who holo appeared beside Aronson's on *Titan's* command deck.

"I'm pleased to hear that you're well, Doctor."

"'Well' is a relative term, Mr. Aronson," she replied, "but I'm alive, and I'm here. I can't say either with certainty about the other occupants of the ship."

Atal winced, the thought that Kaya might be dead disrupting his efforts to maintain confidence that she could survive anything thrown at her. "From the accounts we're getting, it seems those who vanished were either in danger or putting others in danger."

Aronson nodded. "That is how Terry explained it."

"So he was around long enough to explain the... event."

"He says he caused it, Captain. He used his influence to redirect Eleusis's power, sending those who were threatened... elsewhere."

"And where is elsewhere?"

"That's just it, Captain. He didn't know. He only knew that his intent was to save them. I hope that means they were merely transported, and not destroyed."

"There's an old saying about good intentions, Aronson," said Atal bitterly.

"I'm aware of that, Captain; but hope is my stock in trade."

"Can you tell me the circumstances of Metcalfe's disappearance?"

"One of our people, the Qraitian Daedalus, was a spy."

"'Was?'"

"He is dead now. He attacked Metcalfe, thinking, if he killed Eleusis's human interface, it would protect the rest of us. Metcalfe merely gestured..."

"The Qraitian vanished like the others?"

"No. That's the odd thing. His corpse was left behind."

"Sir," interrupted Darby. "I've made every attempt to reach the *Henley*. Their systems are functioning, but there's no answer."

Atal had a sinking feeling. What if the missile or debris had breeched the hull? Was *Henley* a floating coffin?

"I ran an inventory of data implants, Captain," Darby went on. "As far as I can tell, the ship is empty."

"And we still have no word from Admiral Fournier. Nor can we expect to. Aronson," Atal asked, "would you agree that the most likely place for the missing to have been transported, if indeed they're alive, is the planet below?"

"I would, Captain. Several of my people have proposed that we return."

"I agree with them. We've readied a transport. I could use an escort from your group to show what's what down there."

"We would be happy to do so, Captain. Hopefully the presence of members of the Family will also keep you safe."

"Hopefully," agreed Atal. "In any event, if Mr. Metcalfe has paved the road to hell for us, it seems only considerate that we travel it."

Carson landed, hard and unexpectedly, on dirt and stone. The landing was unexpected on several counts. For one thing, when he'd begun his leap, there had been no gravity, making it not so much a leap as a guided flight in freefall. For another, he hadn't expected to impact any sort of surface, when his target had been Gregson. Finally, he hadn't expected to be alive for the impact.

Behind him, Aer'La called his name, it was half a cry of concern, half one of puzzlement. Carson stood, dusted himself off, and turned to her.

She and Cernaq stood as he had seen them seconds ago, with her arm around the Phaetonian; only now Cernaq was awake and they were all standing in a cave. Carson started to voice a very profane exclamation of dismay, but he was interrupted by a scream.

Kaya's scream.

All three spun, prepared for combat with whatever threat lurked in the shadows from whence her call of alarm came. There was no threat, however, only Kaya, reclining nude on the cavern floor, one arm outstretched as though to wield off a blow. As the echo of the scream died, she seemed to realize that whatever or whoever she was defending herself against was no longer present. She looked around self-consciously, recognized with wide eyes where she was and that her friends were with her, and stood.

Carson reached her first, shucking off his duty jacket and offering it to her.

"Do I look that bad?" she wondered.

"No," said Carson, "Well, you're bleeding. It's also that cold in here. How are you not shivering?"

"It's warmer than the Qraitian ship was, especially toward the end, and I've been without clothes there for hours." She looked around. "Where the hell are we?"

"We were just aboard Fournier's ship," said Aer'La. "I was getting ready to kill his lieutenant."

"And I was getting ready to be shot," supplied Carson.

"Commander Ustenar was about to rip out my throat," said Kaya.

"I should say," observed Cernaq, "that we've changed our situations for the better."

"We haven't changed them," said Carson, also looking around to scan the area," but someone has."

There was a footfall from deeper within the cavern, down one of the tunnels which led away from the gallery where they'd found themselves. It suddenly occurred to Carson that they could see, and there should be no natural light within a cave. Patches of a phosphorescent substance on the wall answered his unstated question. It was painted, apparently, in regular patterns. Not a natural phenomenon.

The footsteps drew closer, stopped, and a figure emerged. A male, familiar in shape, and yet the walk and the carriage of the body were not familiar. "Hello friends," said a voice also familiar and not.

"Metcalfe!" Aer'La exclaimed. She started forward.

Cernaq restrained her. "That's not Metcalfe."

"We are Metcalfe," said the figure, stepping into the light. "We are the Voice of Eleusis."

"Cernaq?" asked Carson.

"Metcalfe is within that mind, but he is not in control."

"Did you bring us here?" asked Kaya.

"We did," said the voice, Metcalfe's but not Metcalfe's: richer, stronger, manipulating the vocal instrument with a machine's precision.

"Then you saved our lives," said Aer'La. "But what about the missiles?"

"Gone," said Metcalfe.

"Gone where?"

"Nonexistence."

"Matter cannot cease to exist," countered Cernaq.

"Correct," agreed Metcalfe. "But it can be converted to forms so different that it is unrecognizable. The missiles are now hydrogen, fueling the sun of this world."

"So... no one was killed?" asked Aer'La. "You stopped... everything?"

"We did."

"Where's everyone else?" asked Kaya. "Where's Dr. Faulkner?"

"Where you left her."

"With the Qraitians?"

"They are not where you left them. Your friend is safe. Everyone is safe. Metcalfe used our power to protect them."

"Then... why are we here?" asked Cernaq.

"You are Metcalfe's friends. He has made it clear to us that you are necessary to our continued existence together."

"Existence... as what?" asked Kaya. "What have you done to him?"

"His emotions overwhelmed him, even as he saved your lives. He is not functioning within optimal parameters. Human minds require rest. His is resting. As to what our existence shall be, it is quite simple... We are God."

"How did I know that someday those words would come out of his mouth?" wondered Carson.

"We are God," he repeated. "You are God's reflections. Like the story Metcalfe knew as a child, the Blind Men and the Elephant."

"Each 'saw' a different part of the Elephant, and mistook it for the whole," said Carson. "Only together could they understand the totality. Is that it?"

"Yes. We need you. You each have a different view of the world. You each seek your own self-interest. Through your differences, you educate us."

"If you're god," asked Cernaq, "why do you need to be educated. Are you not omniscient?"

"You make fun of us, Cernaq. Metcalfe remembers that you always deliberately misunderstood God. The idea that any being could know all things is ludicrous."

"Then are you omnipotent?"

"We do not know. It is possible. We can do much that no other known being can do. We command energy beyond the imagining of any single one of you. That is why we must have you. We must direct this energy to better purpose. We need Metcalfe to do that, and he needs you."

"Let us speak to Metcalfe," demanded Carson.

"He is not ready. Nor are you. If you are to be the first of our priests–"

"Oh, give me a break!" muttered Aer'La.

"–you must know our history."

Metcalfe gestured, pointing to the space behind them. At first, no one turned, confused as to what this strange Metcalfe/Eleusis hybrid wanted of them. Then, from one of several entrances to the chamber, in the direction which Metcalfe indicated, a voice spoke.

"I am Eumolpus," it said. It was a dry voice, aged and brittle. It sounded weary, unsure of itself. "I have been dead for many, many thousands of your lifespans."

Carson turned to its source and saw what was clearly a hologram of an old man. He was nondescript, somewhat disheveled. He looked like one of the math professors from their days at the Academy.

"He was the First One," said Metcalfe.

"The first what?" wondered Aer'La.

"I think he means the first human with which Eleusis interfaced," suggested Carson. He looked to Metcalfe. "Is that right?"

Metcalfe nodded. "He was the First One, the first living being with whom I could communicate directly, the first to pay attention to me. He was not human, though we make him appear so in this construct. This is an approximation of how you would see such a person, were he one of your own. We draw from Metcalfe's memories. Listen to him. Speak to him. He will explain to you what it is I was, what it is we are, what it is all of us will be."

"When originally constructed," said Eumolpus, "the thing you call Eleusis was only an artificial intelligence, intended to oversee this world's weaponry. I... I was its... keeper, I suppose. A humble programmer, charged with keeping it maintained and ready to defend us."

The image heaved a sigh. "Once, this world was a paradise. I believe its surface is now much as it was when my ancestors roamed it freely. They lived in peace, lived off the land as simple hunters and gatherers. Eleusis–the world of Eleusis–provided for all of their needs. Their way of life was too innocent, too perfect to last in a universe unfortunately riddled with envy. Our nearest neighbors, from a star system but a few light-years distant, possessed a civilization technologically developed far in excess of our own. They saw that our world was rich in natural resources. They came. They took this world from my ancestors.

"For generations, my people lived as slaves under their conquerors. Aliens ruled our world, using it as they saw fit. We began to adapt to their civilization. We were children, living under the guidance of the most malevolent of foster parents. We became so acclimated, indeed, that an occupation force was unnecessary. We ruled ourselves to suit their whims. Our leaders were all native-born Eleusinians, trained on their planet as governors and military leaders.

"But every child grows up. In adolescence, he becomes hostile to his parent; and so it was with us. When I was but a young student, the revolution occurred. We threw off our bonds, cut ties to the conquerors' world, declared ourselves free. During this initiative we built the intelligence which now rules this world, the heart of a planetary defense network. I was an apprentice at the time, and as I grew, so did the machine. I became, in what should have been my middle years, its primary programmer. No other seemed to be able to communicate with it as effectively as I could.

"The machine-driven war was a success. We fought our opponents to standstill, and then we negotiated a treaty. They would leave our planet in peace, if we would but send them, each year, seven thousand of our young people to serve as their labor force. Our opponents had become so dependent upon their technology that they could not or would not be reduced to manual labor. Our children were to fill that need, as indentured servants. I am ashamed to admit that this arrangement was amicable to us.

"Perhaps there is some sort of cosmic justice, then, in the fact that the first ship never departed. Our enemy had negotiated only to gain time. They returned, in force, and decimated us. They laid waste the surface of this world. We were driven underground. Under the machine's direction, we again drove the enemy away, for a time. The cost of our respite, however, was unthinkable. Our once paradisiacal world was now not only stripped of resources, but unlivable. We took up permanent residence in the caverns, and our remaining leaders decided that organization must be imposed, some sort of rigid order, an emergency government.

"The machine was upgraded, expanded. It now served two purposes: it ran our defenses still, but it also oversaw our survivors, who were now resource-poor and unable to care for themselves. I was in... a unique position of power, for only I knew how to control that which controlled all.

"But... I was never... comfortable... with people. I enjoyed the quiet efficiency of machines. I preferred the company of an artificial intelligence, always rational, always predictable. I had accepted, early in adulthood, that I would never mate, never sire children, never have a family to ease my path into old age. This made me separate from my fellows. It made me different. And when I was left alone as the One who could speak for the Machine... it made me come to see my people as little more than animals. I grew comfortable in my solitude, alone with my job of programming their daily lives, of improving the Machine.

"Until one day... my Machine... my child... awoke."

There was the slightest trace of moisture evident at the corners of the old, flat eyes. Of course, whatever kind of creature Eumolpus had been, he probably didn't show sentiment in this way.   Eleusis... or Metcalfe... possibly both, were putting on a show.

"The Voice of Eleusis spoke for the first time, to me. At first I thought it was an anomaly, a stray error I'd made in programming. I was getting old by this time, after all. My mind was failing me. I realized, however, as it continued to communicate, that this was no freak occurrence.   In continuing to improve and expand my creation–for so I now thought of it–I had given it such capacity that it gained sentience. For the first time in my life, a living being recognized me, reached out to me, depended on me... *chose* me. It *was* Eleusis now, and I was its First One.

"Each citizen of our underground community was mentally tied into the computer in an interface, so that they could communicate, learn and be part of civil society.   In the beginning, we had envisioned that this interconnection would allow our people to develop and learn, become self-sufficient, become leaders; but the leaders we had grew old and died. No new ones emerged to replace them. The survivors and their children, born to a lightless world, were content to have their needs met, their lives directed, by the Voice of Eleusis. My machine and I became rulers of the world.

"We calculated that it could not be long before the enemy returned to battle us again. We crafted a plan to prepare for that eventuality. We would marshal every resource, including our people, to defend this world. We built a new way of living, centered upon preparation for war. With less and less of my involvement as we went along, the Machine directed them to become the perfect warrior culture. They spent all their lives in games of war, fighting, injuring, killing each other. The deaths we realized were a waste of resources, and so the Machine studied, tested and developed ways to repair nearly any injury a mortal body could withstand. It could stave off aging. It could raise the recently dead. In time, we delivered to our people immortality.

"I, of course, was prime beneficiary of this new technology, this new, magic-seeming power of the Machine. I no longer aged. I need never die, my companion told me. I would be its First One, its Eternal One, its Only One. That was fortunate, for no other was found among the populace, over more than a hundred generations in which I lived, who could communicate directly, using his mind, with the Machine. All could feel its presence, and it could feel theirs, but only as raw, emotional impulses.

"The Machine relished our companionship but... I came to see that it also thrived on the emotions of the people. At first, it was just curious about mortal emotion. The intellects of my countrymen were childlike and reactionary. As the Machine became sentient, it grew almost to depend on high emotion, as though it were a flesh and blood sentient, addicted to a drug. On pedestrian matters, it supplied my people with data, but in what we came to call communion...it only gave emotional stimuli, feeding their passions so it could experience their emotion in return. They did not converse with it. They did not recognize it as an intelligence. Only I saw it as an equal.

"And so It and I were alone amongst a growing population. We decided to interact with the others–I no longer thought of them as my kind–as different, higher beings... as gods. We founded a religion, and to worship us, to pray to us, to serve us, was to learn the craft of war." He stopped and hung his head. "An entire civilization, existing only to protect the lives of one man and one machine. As the surface of our world recovered, we let them go above, as a reward, for recreation. All else they knew was training for combat, and death and rebirth."

"Death and rebirth," muttered Kaya. "That... that was my vision! I was–"

"You were one of our... subjects. The Machine sensed your interest, even across the gulf of stars. It sent you an emotional experience, laced with some information, hoping to lure you closer."

"It worked," said Kaya.

"What happened to you?" asked Carson. "That is," he corrected himself, realizing he was addressing a hologram, "what happened to Eumolpus?"

The hologram shrugged, looking, perhaps, a bit self-conscious. "I died," it said, with an attitude a man might assume when confessing that he, too, went to the bathroom, or was otherwise prey to the weaknesses of the flesh. "All mortal things do."

"But," Carson protested, "you... Eleusis... had such power. It could stave off aging, you said."

"The Qraitian intel show it healing open wounds, reversing fatal diseases, rasing the dead!" added Kaya. "Why did it let you die?"

"In the end," Eumolpus said slowly, "the choice was... beyond its control. Eleusis was my child. My only child. My only legacy. In some ways, it is still a child, searching for a parent. It has searched a long time, and now it has found Metcalfe. Now all can be as it was." The image of the old man began to fade. It said, "Goodbye," and was gone.

"Now you know all," said Metcalfe.

"Now we don't know a damn thing!" countered Aer'La. "Some old guy lived a long time, built a freaking monster computer, and then died! What does that have to do with us?"

"You are the heirs to the First One—all of you."

"I thought Metcalfe was the heir," said Carson.

"You are my friends. Eleusis has realized that I cannot... function optimally without you."

"We are not your friends," said Cernaq. "For you are not Terry Metcalfe. You are Eleusis, interfaced with his mind, controlling his body. Terry is so far suppressed beneath your control that I cannot find him."

"He is here, nonetheless. When he is well again–"

"What does that mean?" Kaya demanded. "How is he unwell? What are you doing to heal him? How do we know you're not controlling his mind, indoctrinating him, the way you did all your subjects so long ago?"

Metcalfe's face registered surprise. "Controlling *him*? He is the One. It would be blasphemy to exert control over him."

"And speaking of your subjects," Kaya pressed, "I saw them destroyed. I saw this whole complex," she gestured to the chamber around her, "collapse under an attack from 'the gods.' I saw the people slaughtered... by you, I can only guess."

"We... Eleusis and the First One... were flawed," said Metcalfe sadly. "The Machine saw only pure logic and reason, bereft of morality. The Man... the Man lacked any sense of connection to his fellow creatures. He could not temper the harsh logic of the Machine."

"Morality is pure reason," said Cernaq. "Your argument does not hold together. It sounds to me as though you were both immature and irrational."

"No time for philosophy, Cernaq," said Carson.

"There is always time for philosophy," replied the Phaetonian.

"There will be time for all of you to teach me all that you know," said Metcalfe. "You will stay here."

"We're not staying anywhere!" snapped Aer'La."

"You have no choice. Metcalfe needs you. You will make him whole, and I will care for you."

"So you're making us slaves?" asked Cernaq.

"Metcalfe needs you to be happy. I will keep you here, for his sake. I will build a paradise again on this world. I will drive away all who would do harm."

"And if we would do harm?" asked Carson.

Metcalfe only smiled. "Metcalfe loves you. You will stay."

Footsteps sounded in the chamber, coming from far away.

"Someone's coming," said Aer'La.

Metcalfe nodded. "More of your friends have arrived."

Atal entered the cavern chamber, a pulse gun in his hand, leading Aronson, Elspeth, Icarus, Pallas and Celia Faulkner. Pallas and Elspeth both rushed forward to Metcalfe, Celia to the four others.

"What have you naughty children been up to?" she asked, unable to manage her accustomed tone of arch disapproval. She gave each a quick visual check, fussed over Kaya's wounds.

"It would appear we've been kidnapped," said Carson.

Pallas stood at arm's length from Metcalfe, hesitating to touch him, although Elspeth had no such compunctions. She placed one arm around his shoulders and asked, "Is he all right?"

Pallas shook her head. "This... is not Metcalfe. It is his body, but... What have you done with him?" she demanded, suddenly and sharply.

"He is unharmed," said Metcalfe. "No one will be harmed, if they do not threaten Eleusis. But you must all leave us."

"I want to speak to Metcalfe," said Atal.

"He is not ready."

"And when will he be ready?" asked Pallas. "When you have worn down his resistance and convinced him to allow you to enslave everyone within reach?"

Metcalfe looked coldly at her. "Metcalfe loves you," he said, "but I see that you are a threat."

Cernaq stepped forward protectively, taking a place beside Pallas. "If she is a threat to you," he said quietly, "then so am I."

Atal placed himself between the two and Metcalfe. He placed a hand on Metcalfe's shoulder and said quietly, "No one is here to threaten you, Eleusis. We are here because our people may be in danger. You've caused a lot of people to disappear."

"They are unharmed," said Metcalfe.

"I'm glad. But now you propose to keep several of us here against their will."

"It is for the best. It will make Metcalfe happy."

Carson started to speak. Atal shushed him with a raised hand.

"Perhaps it will," he conceded. "I'd like to hear that from him. Will you let him speak to us?"

Behind Atal, Pallas quietly slipped her hand into Cernaq's. Their eyes closed.

"He is not ready," said Metcalfe again. "He does not wish to speak to you."

"In all the years I've known Metcalfe," said Atal gently, "there was never a time I can think of when he didn't have something to say."

"The ordeal of saving you from your own violence has tired him," said Metcalfe. "He–" He broke off, looked suddenly startled, then confused.

"No," he said to no one in particular, "that isn't true. It–" He leveled his gaze at Pallas and Cernaq, pointed. "Those two are prying within our mind!"

"It isn't your mind," said Carson. "It's Metcalfe's."

"He does not wish..." Metcalfe began. His face contorted, an expression of sudden pain coming to it. "No!" he gasped. "I want to... I want to talk to..."

"Eleusis," said Atal, "let him speak to us. You have no right to hide him from us!"

Metcalfe winced and reacted as though punched in the gut. He stumbled, steadying himself against Atal's shoulder.

"Keep it up, you two," Carson said the Phaetonians. "I think you're getting to him."

Elspeth stepped next to Carson and took his hand. "You all need to join us," she nodded toward Aronson and Icarus, "in Communion."

"You want us to join with that machine?" Carson whispered?

"Metcalfe is joined with it already," said Elspeth. "Together, we all might reach him."

Carson looked at Kaya and Aer'La. Kaya nodded. Aer'La asked, "Does it hurt?"

Elspeth smiled and shook her head. She reach out her other hand to Aer'La, who reluctantly took it, muttering, "Freakin' mind games. Show me where the computer is, and I'll make it let us go!"

Atal was now supporting Metcalfe's limp form. The eyes stared vacantly. Sweat began to bead on his face. Atal took hold of his shoulders and drew him up roughly until they were eye to eye. "Mister Metcalfe!" he snapped in his best voice of command.

Blearily, Metcalfe muttered, "Captain?"

"Mister Metcalfe, stand to attention," said Atal. "That's an order!" Slowly he released Metcalfe's shoulders and stepped back from him.

After a few halting steps back and forth, Metcalfe stood on his own, faced Atal and said raggedly, "Reporting for duty, sir."

Atal grinned, but Pallas said, her eyes still closed, "Be careful, Captain. Eleusis is still with us."

"She's right," agreed Metcalfe. "It... isn't very happy with any of you."

"Can you control it?" asked Atal.

"I don't control it," said Metcalfe. "It chose to... bond with me, I guess. I have some influence, but we're not exactly seeing eye to eye right now. I think maybe you should all get out of here, and let me talk to it."

"I think that's a very good idea," said a voice from one of the chamber's entrances. "Metcalfe and I have a lot to talk about, including the fact that Eleusis may not have made the best choice in picking the One."

There was no need to turn to identify the speaker. They all knew the voice.

A grin on his face, two pulse guns in his hand and pointed at Metcalfe and Atal, Sestus Blaurich said, "After all, why wouldn't such a perfect machine want to choose the best design available?"

CHAPTER TWENTY TWO

"Mr. Blaurich," demanded Atal, "what are you doing here?"

"I thought we'd decided everyone on the Henley had been... taken," said Aronson.

"So they had," said Sestus. "But I brought this one," he gestured to himself, "here. I find him interesting for many reasons."

"It's not Sestus," said Metcalfe, "it's Eleusis."

"When did Sestus enter into a rapport with the machine?" asked Pallas. "I don't believe he had the opportunity."

"Sestus did not," said Eleusis in Sestus's voice. "I learned from my contact with you, Pallas, how to breach the human mind without the consent of the owner of that mind. Is that not what you did to Metcalfe?"

Pallas stiffened. "It is not. He invited me—"

"Then why was he surprised when you appeared in our rapport?" asked Sestus.

"He didn't realize, consciously, what his desire was. Had you not forced the issue, I would have taken the time—"

"—To explain that you'd forced yourself on him?" Sestus grinned a leering grin.

Metcalfe stepped forward, still unsteady on his feet, but determined. "Leave her alone. Your quarrel isn't with her."

"But it is, Terry," said Sestus. His tone was not combative. It might even have been called plaintive. "My quarrel is with anyone who tries to influence you."

"Because only you should be allowed to influence him?" asked Pallas.

"Because he must decide for himself what he wants. I don't object to keeping his friends here, but Terry is the One."

"It sounds as though you think perhaps Sestus could be the One," muttered Atal.

"He is more practical than Terry. He understands people as well, but he's not afraid to use force when it's called for. Perhaps I could reconsider–"

Celia Faulkner sniffed. "Congratulations, Eleusis. You've learned the fine art of playing one of us against the other. 'Do what I want, or I won't be your friend anymore.'"

Sestus nodded. "As I said, this human is more practical."

"Leave it to Sestus to teach a computer bad habits," said Kaya. Carson shot her a dirty look.

"Eleusis," said Metcalfe loudly, "let Blaurich go. You and I can work this out."

"We can indeed, Terry. I'm not ready to release this one yet. We will need help deciding on a course of action, deciding the fate of your friends, and all those who've come to my world. We will need Sestus Blaurich."

"Why?" asked Atal.

Eleusis ignored him. "We will also need you," he pointed to Carson, "and you," he pointed to Elspeth. "The rest of you," he added suddenly, "must leave now."

"We won't," said Atal.

"Then you will die. All of you."

Metcalfe stepped up to Atal and gripped his arm. "It can do it, Captain. It can wipe out all of you with a thought. It's so unstable right now, I couldn't stop it."

"We can't just leave!" blurted Aer'La.

Atal looked at Metcalfe for a long moment, then surveyed the faces of the others. "I'm afraid we have little choice," he said.

"No!" Aer'La shouted. Her face deepened nearly indigo with anger. "Dammit, I've had enough!"

"Aer'La," Metcalfe said in warning.

Aer'La had already thrown herself at Sestus, however. "It's in a human body, and I can hurt it!" She took Sestus by the lapels of his jacket and threw him against the cavern wall. He reeled from the impact, but did not lose his balance. He lifted one arm, gesturing at Aer'La.

Metcalfe jumped in front of her. "Don't!" he said to Sestus. "You will not harm her!"

"Get out of the way, Metcalfe!" Aer'La ordered him. "I'll—"

Sestus smiled disarmingly, and, behind Metcalfe, Aer'La coughed. As he whirled, she grabbed her throat and tried to gasp for air. Her eyes grew wide and one arm flailed wildly.

Cernaq rushed to her, attempting to offer aid. "She can't breathe!" he called out.

Watching with amusement, Sestus said, "I am not hurting her, Terry. I have simply caused her bronchial tubes to close. She cannot take in oxygen."

"She'll die!" said Metcalfe.

"She'll remember what dying feels like, and she'll pass out. She won't be hurt. It's only a warning."

"Stop it, Eleusis!" said Metcalfe savagely. "I'll stay and talk... or whatever it is you want, but stop this!"

Sestus shrugged. Aer'La gasped, taking in a huge breath, and collapsed against Cernaq.

"Captain, you will take them all out of her now," Sestus said to Atal.

Atal crossed to Aer'La and took her arm, helping her stand. "If we go to the surface, you won't harm anyone?"

"I will leave you undisturbed until I reach a decision," said Sestus.

"Eleusis," said Metcalfe, "let them all go. Let them take their ships and leave the system. You don't need—"

"No one leaves, Terry. Their fates will be in your hands."

"No," said Metcalfe. "Eleusis, that's wrong, to make one person responsible for the lives of so many others. If you won't let them go, at least let Aronson and the Captain stay. You can learn from their wisdom. They–"

"They exert far too much control over you. They must go, or I will kill them first."

Atal clasped Metcalfe's shoulder. "Terry... I've left all our lives in your hands before. You didn't let me down. You won't now."

Metcalfe swallowed and whispered, "No, sir. I... I won't."

"All right, Eleusis. We're going. I can't stop you, but I can say... you chose Metcalfe for a reason. I believe... it was a good reason. I believe you made the right choice. Now follow that choice to its logical conclusion, and listen to him."

"Go," said Sestus stonily.

Atal gestured for the others to precede him, and they left the chamber, leaving Metcalfe, Carson and Elspeth alone with the possessed Sestus.

When the sound of footsteps had begun to fade, Metcalfe asked, "Why did you ask for Carson and Elspeth to remain?"

"Because," said Sestus, "there are three roles that other mortals may play in a life: friend, lover, or enemy. As we decide how we shall deal with other beings, you must evaluate each type of relationship. Pallas is not an appropriate lover, for she leads you astray. Elspeth believes she is falling in love with you."

Metcalfe looked briefly at the girl, self conscious. She cast her eyes at the ground.

"Carson is your oldest friend. He can speak for the rest."

Metcalfe shook his head. "No. Let them go. You and I can–"

Carson grabbed Metcalfe by the shoulders, spun him roughly around to face him. "I'm not going anywhere," he hissed. "Get it through your thick fucking head that I will not leave you!"

Metcalfe was silent. He didn't know what to say.

Sestus nodded. "Quite appropriate. Again, I have chosen well."

"Eleusis," Metcalfe began, "what is the point of this–"

Sestus shook his head. "The point should be clear, Metcalfe; but I suppose you're too stupid and inbred to figure it out, aren't you?"

"Okay, that was definitely Sestus talking," said Metcalfe.

Carson nodded, but declined to comment.

"No," Sestus continued, coming forward to walk a circle around Metcalfe, as if sizing up a ship or ground car for purchase. "I correct myself. You're not stupid. You're just so much a product of your uneducated, backwater environment that you can't pick up on the cues around you. That's your problem. It's always been your problem."

"Eleusis–"

"Eleusis is just listening now," Sestus replied. "It's letting me do the talking. That's assuming I can get a word in edgewise with you here. Anyone ever tell you that you talk entirely too damn much? It's annoying."

"All right, Sestus, why are you here?" asked Metcalfe.

Sestus shrugged. "I was minding my own business, trying to stop an attack on the *Titan*. That reptile Ustenar fired on me. I figured I was dead. Then I was here, able to see, but with Eleusis doing my talking for me. And you don't seem happy to see me. You should be. I saved your ass when Fournier wanted me to kill you–"

"You saved Fournier's ass," Metcalfe corrected him, "and you know it. Where is Fournier, anyway?"

"Cold storage, with the rest. He might be brought back out, if we can come to an agreement here."

Metcalfe crossed his arms. "And how will we do that?"

"By experimenting. Eleusis is a machine intelligence, Metcalfe. It must be programmed. Thus far, its programming has been conflicted. The First One wanted it to save the people of this planet, but he also wanted to rule them. His interests conflicted with theirs; and, not knowing a damned thing about mortal emotion himself, he allowed Eleusis to become immersed in a miasma of feelings and sensations neither of them understood. On top of it all, he taught Eleusis violence. He taught it that the only sure way to deal with an enemy was to destroy them. And then it happened that the people of Eleusis became the enemy. What was a poor machine to do?"

"Eleusis and I agreed," said Metcalfe, "that it would employ no more violence. It would use its powers peacefully–"

"But then you didn't stick with the plan! You started whinging about emotional damage being done to your friends, and you confused Eleusis again."

"And Eleusis tried to kill them."

"Because they were distracting you! They were taking your attention away from where Eleusis wanted it. It's a child, Metcalfe! It's looking for a parent. It doesn't understand that Daddy has other friends, and it doesn't care. It just saw more enemies, and it resorted to ancient programming to deal with them, because the programming you gave it hadn't been proven to work. You told it you would show it how to handle enemies, and then you tried to walk away before the job was finished." Sestus's tone became harsh and his eyes lit with flames of anger, "Just like you always do!"

"All right," said Metcalfe, "this is just–"

Sestus put his face up to Metcalfe's. "Just what, Terran? Just pissing you off? Just making you uncomfortable? You want to walk away again? Like you did when you came here? You swore an oath to protect the people of the Confederacy–"

"And I've done it," said Metcalfe between his teeth.

Sestus patted his cheek. "Oh, yeah, you've done it. Saved ten billion lives, didn't you, hero? But you couldn't face the responsibility, either. Couldn't face the fact that, to protect yourself, sometimes you have to pick up a weapon. And if you pick up a weapon, sometimes you're gonna have to use it. You're gonna have to kill someone. You want to be the great defender, Metcalfe, you better be ready to kick some ass! But you don't want to do that. You want to go sit on a mountain and pray and reflect on your inner self... and let someone else do the dirty work!"

"This is pointless," said Metcalfe.

Sestus laughed. "No! No it's not! You see, you've confused Eleusis so badly with your nursery-school-be-kind philosophy that now it's going to need you to *show* it how to deal with an enemy. That's why I'm here! I'm the enemy. The worst enemy you've ever had."

"Don't flatter yourself," said Metcalfe.

"I don't! You don't hate anyone as much as you hate me. Corrupt admirals, terrorists, starving colonists who turn violent... you can deal with all of them. But I'm supposed to be on your side. When you do a good job, when you score a victory, I get the credit. And then I turn around and treat you like shit, don't I? You hate me because I'm one of your own, one of the kids in the compound! And you're supposed to love me and take care of me! But I still bully you, and it makes you feel little and helpless again, doesn't it, Metcalfe? Doesn't it you illiterate, inbred piece of Terran waste?" He screamed the last in Metcalfe's face.

"This isn't Sestus talking," said Metcalfe after taking a long breath. "Sestus wouldn't know to say all these things, wouldn't admit his own failings–"

"You think not? You think I don't know how much you hate me? How you see me? I fucking revel in it! I love being your enemy! You don't even hate the Qraitians like you hate me. Hell, you *prayed* for the dead Qraitians! I wonder, if I died, would you pray for me?"

"Of course I would," said Metcalfe.

Sestus clapped him on the shoulder. "Maybe we should find out.'

"Stop it!" Carson snapped suddenly. He shoved Sestus a step away from Metcalfe with one hand. "This isn't you, Sestus! You're being influenced by that machine. You don't–"

"I don't what, Carson?" he snarled. "I don't really mean it? I'm not really your best friend's enemy? You thought I was tamed now, all of a sudden? Grow up! You and I had a few laughs working together, that doesn't mean we're friends. It certainly doesn't mean I accept this earth trash as anything other than Atal's pet." He turned again to Metcalfe. "And a gutless little lapdog he is too, runs crying off the playground the first time he gets into a real fight! I'm surprised poor Eleusis didn't short circuit from the tears you probably shed all over it!"

"Stop it," said Metcalfe quietly. "I know this isn't you."

"Isn't it? You think Eleusis is feeding me the same words I've said about you in the past? You think it's inventing the animosity we feel for each other? Was it the machine's idea that I wrote a book making you look like a bumbling fool, and me like a hero? Face it, Metcalfe, you may be the stalwart boy wonder, but this galaxy is my playing field. I know how to use people to get what I want. You don't, and you never will. If you don't stop me, I'm going to grind you under my heel, stepping on your face as I climb my way to the top! I'll throw you into the launch path just like I did Carson when I made his sexual proclivities public."

"Shut up!" spat Metcalfe, the reminder of the pain Sestus had caused Carson making him angrier than anything Sestus could have said about Metcalfe himself.

"Why? So you don't have to face the fact that there are people who are a threat to you? Who will hurt you if they have to, to get what they want? Why do you think Eleusis brought me here? It wants you to face an enemy, not run away crying, and not making speeches. It wants you to show how you'll really react when faced with a genuine threat. It wants you to admit that some people have to be either controlled or killed!"

Sestus leapt forward, knocking Carson to the side, and shoved Metcalfe hard with both hands, sending him flying backwards. As Metcalfe sat up and tried to stand, Sestus stalked forward and loomed over him menacingly. Before Metcalfe could roll out of the way, Sestus had executed a savage kick to his ribs. He clutched his side with one hand and gritted his teeth at the pain, still trying to find his balance and stand.

"After I've beaten you to a pulp," growled Sestus, "maybe we can relive the time you were forced to give yourself to me sexually. Maybe that will get a reaction other than–"

Metcalfe's legs swung out suddenly and his feet caught Sestus at the knees, causing him to cry out and fall sideways. As the Quintil midshipman nursed his injured legs, Metcalfe rolled and pounced on him. Rearing up, his face contorted in an angry snarl, he punched Sestus repeatedly in the face.

Bleeding from a split lip, Sestus laughed harshly and said, "Feels good, doesn't it? Finally letting go and doing what you always wanted to do? Isn't this how you deal with an enemy, Metcalfe? Doesn't this feel right? Never mind all the ethics and philosophy–"

Metcalfe jabbed the heels of both hands into Sestus's shoulders, cracking his head against the rock floor. He then stood, shaking his head. "No," he said, coughing as his still-aching ribs assailed him with a fresh wave of pain. "No, I won't play it your way." He started to back away.

Unsatisfied, Sestus found his feet and tackled the retreating figure. While Carson and Elspeth both called for the two to stop fighting, Sestus hooked his leg around both of Metcalfe's, forcing him onto the ground on his back. He fell on top of Metcalfe, sitting on his chest, and wrapped both hands around his opponent's throat.

"No!" shrieked Elspeth. She started forward.

Carson grabbed her shoulders and held her back. "Don't. You'll get hurt."

"Stop them!" the girl cried.

Carson came forward and took hold of Sestus's shoulders, but some maniac's strength allowed Sestus to knock him back several feet with one arm. Adrenaline had kicked in, and Sestus was operating at peak physical performance. He tightened his grip on Metcalfe's throat, even as Metcalfe tried desperately to pry his hands away.

"Sestus..." Metcalfe gurgled. "Not... you... doing this..."

"No?" asked Sestus, wild-eyed. "You think Eleusis is putting me up to this? You think, deep down, I don't really want you dead? Life would be so much easier for me with you out of the way!"

Carson returned and grabbed Sestus in a headlock. His hands left Metcalfe's throat as he tried again to fight off his new attacker. Metcalfe pivoted and lurched up hard, driving his hip bone into Sestus's groin. Sestus screamed in pain as Carson dragged him backward and off Metcalfe.

Elspeth rushed to Metcalfe's side, gingerly probing his throat with her fingers. Carson forced Sestus against a wall, holding one restraining hand against his chest. "All right, that's enough," he said. "Sestus, you've got to calm–"

He was cut off by Sestus's heel driving into his instep. This was quickly followed by a solid punch to the jaw. Carson went down hard.

"Son of a bitch!" Metcalfe shouted, and, disentangling himself from Elspeth, he launched his body into Sestus's. They both hit the floor, grappling, punches flying awkwardly. After several rolls, during which knees, feet and elbows were driven hard into whatever body part could be reached, Metcalfe wound up again on top of Sestus, assaulting him with blow after blow to the face and chest.

Vaguely, Metcalfe, auto-piloted by rage, heard someone ask him to stop. A hand grabbed his shoulder. He ignored it and punched Sestus again. The plea to stop repeated, and several hands took hold of his arms and shoulders, pulling him. He registered that both Carson and Elspeth were trying to pull him away.

"Terry, Jesus Christ, stop!" he heard Kevin say. His voice was raw and laced with emotion that Metcalfe had rarely heard from him. Metcalfe allowed himself to be brought to his feet, shook his head to clear it, and only now saw Sestus. He was breathing erratically, but otherwise unmoving. Blood smeared his face, and appeared to be trickling from the corner of his mouth. Metcalfe's own blood ran cold. What had he done?

Carson fell to his knees and moved his hands crazily, as if not knowing what to check first, or where his touch might help or hurt. "Oh god," he murmured, "Oh, Jesus, no!"

Metcalfe realized that Carson was crying.

"Sestus, why did you–" he began, then degenerated into hard, wracking sobs. He reached out to cradle Sestus's head carefully in both hands and brought his own face down to touch it. He muttered words Metcalfe couldn't hear into Sestus's ear.

"Don't move him," said Elspeth. "I think he's bleeding internally."

Carson only continued to cry, his tears mixing with the blood matting Sestus's hair. Sestus coughed, blood spattering Carson's jacket as he did. A bloody hand raised slowly to touch Carson's face. Sestus's mouth moved. He was trying to say Kevin's name.

Realization dawned on Metcalfe. This was not the requisite compassion one showed any fallen comrade. Kevin was devastated by Sestus's condition, like one mourning a dying lover.

"Oh my god..." Metcalfe whispered. "I... Kevin, I..."

Carson looked up, his face a study of emotions at war. No doubt he wanted to condemn Metcalfe for his part in this. At the same time, his eyes pled to his friend for understanding and help.

Metcalfe, disbelieving, said, "You... and... him?"

"I'm sorry," said Carson. "I... there wasn't time to tell you... " He shucked off his jacket, balled it and placed in under Sestus's head as he laid it gently down. "Jesus, Terry, he's dying! You..."

"I'm sorry!" Metcalfe blurted out. "I–he attacked me... He hit you, and..."

Carson looked for a moment on Sestus's ruined face. His eyelids were fluttering, trying to stay open. "There's... more to him than you ever saw... or were willing to see." He reached to brush blood-dampened hair from Sestus's forehead. "Yeah... he's an asshole," he admitted. "So was Renfro. You never gave up on him. You said there was good in him, and you were right. He died giving Aer'La a chance to live." He looked up and leveled an accusatory gaze at Metcalfe. "Why couldn't you see the good in Sestus?"

"Do you... love him?" Metcalfe asked weakly.

Carson shrugged. A sigh that turned into a sob issued from him, and he said, "I don't know. Maybe... we were just having some fun, but... either way... I didn't want him to be hurt... how could this happen?"

Sestus coughed again, a sick, wet, spluttering sound; and Metcalfe, overwhelmed by guilt at the violence his hands had wrought, shouted at the ceiling. "Eleusis! Damn you, where are you! He's dying! You pushed him to this!"

He did not say, "You pushed me to this." He didn't for a minute try to convince himself that anyone but he was responsible for what had happened to Sestus, but perhaps he could also see that the damage was undone. Eleusis had the power. "Heal him! He may be dying!"

Elsepth came up to him, placed a hand on his shoulder. He assumed she was merely offering comfort and sympathy, but then he looked in her eyes. They were shining with laughter. She smiled and said, "Why shouldn't he die?" She looked casually at the body on the floor. "I'm not sure he is dying. I think Carson is just overwrought because you bloodied his lover's pretty face. Still, he's your enemy. I think you should just kill him now."

Metcalfe looked at her in disgust. "Eleusis," he said.

The girl nodded. "You know, this is fun, living in all these bodies. I think I'll do it permanently. I'll pick a body and live in it until it dies." She spread her arms, twirled and looked admiringly downward at herself. "Maybe this one. It's pleasing, isn't it? You certainly seemed to enjoy it the other night."

"Leave her alone, Eleusis! You can't just take other people's bodies!"

"Why not? I'm not hurting it, and it's amazing to experience sensation as a mortal! I've always enjoyed the emotions and the sensations that were passed through the mental rapport, but this–!" She reached out and placed her hands on Metcalfe's face. She kissed him. He did not kiss back. Stroking his cheek, she went on, "Do you know how it felt when you and Elspeth had sex? Of course you do, you were there! But, I mean, do you know how it felt for me? It was frustrating. I could feel the echo of the pleasure. I could quantify the biological and chemical reactions, the muscle contractions, the changes in blood pressure, the hormonal surges; but I could not *feel* them. Not like this body can feel. I had no point of reference! I want to know what it felt like!"

"Stop this now," said Metcalfe.

"Let's do it now!" Elspeth whispered. She began clawing at the folds of her tunic, pulling it up to remove it. "How do you do this? Wait, I'll just rely on her muscle memories!"

"Keep your clothes on!"

"No!" she said petulantly, but still smiling. "And you take yours off too, or I'll vaporize them and leave you naked. You should stay naked anyway. You're so good-looking without your clothes, Terry, and I can maintain the temperature so you'll never be uncomfortable." She shrugged the tunic off and embraced him, rubbing her breasts against the fabric of his jacket. "Come on, let's do it now. I want to feel you inside me. What does that feel like? Oh, and I want to know how it feels for the boy, too." She looked to Carson, still hunched over Sestus. "When we're done, I'll jump into Carson, and he can fuck the girl, and I'll–"

Carson, hearing his name, spoke without looking up. "You'll want to experience everything," he said coldly. "You'll need to help Sestus, so you can experience two boys doing it."

Elspeth shrugged. "Oh, I don't think so. You and Terry can help me with that, can't you, Terry?"

Carson flinched.

Elspeth didn't notice. She reached up to begin unfastening the clasps on Metcalfe's jacket. "And you're supposed to be naked, young man! Hurry up, if you want to keep these clothes!"

Metcalfe did not answer.

Elspeth pouted and threw her arms around him. "Come on, Terry, please?" She leaned back and tilted his face down. "If I fix stupid Sestus, can we forget about how angry you are, and just do something fun? I will, I'll fix him. I don't know why you want me to, but I will. I can always kill him later, if–"

"You think this is a game, don't you?" said Metcalfe bitterly.

She smiled. "Yes! Of course it's a game! It's a fun game, and we can play it forever! You can be here with all the people you love. I'll keep all of you safe and happy–"

"Forever?" asked Carson, standing now. He stepped over to stand at arm's length from them. "Can you really make it all last forever?"

She nodded. "I can. Kevin, you, Terry and your friends can live forever. There's nothing that can go wrong with your bodies that I can't fix! I can stop you aging, I can make your old friends young again! That Doctor Faulkner, I can make her the pretty girl she used to be, and–"

"Then why did the First One die? What happened to Eumolpus?"

Elspeth's face went blank. She chewed her lip. "He... he died."

"How?"

"He... he just died. I–"

"How did he die?" demanded Carson. His eyes were fixed on the girl, boring into her.

"Eleusis," said Metcalfe, "you've told me I can access any entry in your memories. Anything at all."

"You can," said Elspeth.

"Show me the day Eumolpus died then."

She shook her head violently. "No! I don't want to! I don't want to remember–"

"*Why?*" Carson demanded, seizing her by the shoulders. "What are you hiding?"

"You're hurting me!" she cried, struggling in his grasp.

"Answer his question," said Metcalfe.

"Stop hurting me! Make him stop, Terry, or I'll kill him!"

"You'll do no such thing, Eleusis. I won't let you. Now answer his question. What happened to the First One?"

"I can't! I can't remember!" she screamed. She began to sob. "I can't let it happen! As long as I don't remember it, it never happened!"

"You'll tell me," said Metcalfe, "or we're leaving."

She clawed at his jacket, trying to pull him to her. "I won't let you!"

"Then you'll have to kill me."

She looked horrified. "I can't! I would never! I–you mustn't say that! I would never harm you. I would never kill the One! I didn't–I didn't kill–"

"You didn't kill who?" pressed Carson.

"I didn't!" she moaned.

"You did," said Metcalfe. "Eleusis, you did something you don't want to remember! What is it, what did you do?"

"I... killed... the First One!" she managed, then devolved into heaving sobs and buried her face in Metcalfe's chest.

CHAPTER TWENTY-THREE

Idly Metcalfe stroked her hair. After a moment, he asked quietly, "When?"

She caught her breath and said, "It was after–after the uprising. Our warriors... our people were not cooperating. They... some of them rebelled. Didn't want to fight. They stood up to their brethren and... there was slaughter. The warriors killed those who wanted peace. It was... it was so wrong. I realized I had created a sick, twisted bunch of killers. There was no good in them, so I... I punished them."

"You killed them," said Metcalfe.

"Some of them. And then... and then they tried to destroy me. I... I wiped out every living thing on this planet, except the First One. I had to! I couldn't let them harm me, or him, and..."

"And he was angry?" asked Metcalfe.

She nodded. "He said... said he'd never wanted this. Said he had wanted to save his people. He said that I hadn't raised a generation of killers, that we had. And he said that he'd raised me as the first killer. I was his child and... he had to take responsibility and..."

"He was going to destroy you," said Carson.

"I... I couldn't let him. I had to stop him."

"Because he knew how to kill you," said Metcalfe in a voice almost a whisper.

"Yes," the girl said quietly.

Metcalfe nodded. It was all there, not only in her words. Reaching out with his mind, reaching into the link he shared with Eleusis, he could see it. He could see the memory... the knowledge... everything Eleusis knew, everything the First One had known, all was within his reach..

Elspeth shrugged. "Now you know."

Metcalfe nodded. "Now I know everything, Eleusis. Now I know what you didn't want me to know. What you sent Pallas away, to keep her from knowing. She would have figured it out easily, because her mind is stronger than mine. And you didn't want me to know–"

"Please," breathed Elspeth.

"You didn't want me to know," pressed Metcalfe, "that I can kill you, Eleusis. I can destroy you forever."

The girl shook her head furiously. "You mustn't! Terry, I am linked to this world! Yes, you can kill me, but... it would destroy everything! You and all your friends would die!"

"The universe would be safe," said Metcalfe.

Elspeth look into his eyes, and in a voice that sounded completely like her own innocent, girlish voice asked, "Would you kill me, Terry?"

"I can't let you go on using people. You think you're God. You're a genocidal monster!"

"Wasn't Jehovah the same?"

Metcalfe shook his head. "To the eyes of a primitive people, Jehovah was a war god who slew their enemies. I don't believe that god ever existed. True gods are loving and beyond violence. You are no god, Eleusis, and you can be killed."

Elspeth slumped into his arms, her eyes rolling back until on the whites showed. Then her eyes closed and she was limp. "Elspeth?" Metcalfe said gently. He looked to Carson. "It's left her."

Carson smiled and nodded. "Yes. I have left her. I am here now."

"Damn you, stop it!" spat Metcalfe.

"Would you kill me, Terry?" Carson demanded. "Your best and oldest friend?"

"You're not Carson," said Metcalfe angrily.

"But I am! I'm sharing his mind. Do you know what it's like, to see the world, to see you, through all these different eyes? The girl, she worships you. She's so innocent and trusting. And this one, Carson, he... Terry –"

"Stop."

"He loves you!"

"Get out of his mind!"

Carson continued to smile and began to laugh. "You don't understand! He's–he's in love with you!"

Metcalfe bit his cheek and said coldly, "I know."

"You know? He isn't aware–"

"No," snapped Metcalfe. "He's not. And he doesn't need to be. I know how Kevin feels about me. I know because Cernaq knows, so Pallas knows. I know everything Pallas knows; but I think I always knew that... that Kevin was in love with me."

The smile faded.

"And would you kill him?"

"Before I'd let him be your slave, or mine... yes. Get out of his mind, Eleusis. Get out and leave him alone. Leave all of them alone."

"Or you'll kill me?"

Metcalfe stepped forward slowly. Hesitating, with a feeling of revulsion as strong as if he were about to bite into rotten cheese, he slipped his hands around Carson's throat. "Yes," he said simply. "I'll kill you."

"You won't."

Metcalfe tightened his grip and Carson coughed. He tried not to listen. "Get out of his head. Leave everyone alone, or I'll destroy you, Eleusis."

"I'll fight you."

"You'll lose. I know how to kill you. The First One knew, and now so do I."

Carson's eyes bugged. "I'll kill you first!"

"Again?" asked Metcalfe sadly. "You'll kill the One again? And be alone... for how long?"

Carson began to cry. Tears leaked onto the hands that encircled his vulnerable throat. Metcalfe instinctively loosened his hold.

"I don't want to be alone!" moaned Eleusis in Carson's voice. "Please, Terry, don't make me hurt you!"

"Then do as you're told," Metcalfe said tightly. "Heal Sestus. Inhabit no more bodies. Take no more lives. Act to protect the Family only when they ask you to, and only in accordance with morality. You know what morality is now, don't you, Eleusis?"

Carson's eyes just stared.

Metcalfe tightened his grip again and hissed through clenched teeth, "Don't you?"

"D - do," croaked Carson, "... unto others... as I would have them do unto me."

Metcalfe nodded. "And ye harm none, do as ye will," he echoed. "It's a very simple rule, and very hard to follow. But you will follow it Eleusis. If you don't... then I'll end your existence, or die trying."

"I'll follow it," said Carson's voice, sounding like a small child's. "I promise. I don't want to die. I don't want to kill you. I... " he sobbed. "I love you, Terry."

Metcalfe closed his eyes, suddenly tired and overwhelmed.

"Terry?" Carson's voice breathed.

Metcalfe didn't respond. Relief at the end of the confrontation dominated his mind.

"Terry, what the fuck are you doing?"

He suddenly realized that it was Carson's voice—only Carson's. Eleusis had left him. His hands were still around his friend's throat. He pulled them back as though he had been burned, then cried out, "Kevin! Oh God, I'm sorry!" He pulled Carson to him and hugged him fiercely. "Oh Jesus, I–I didn't mean to hurt you!"

Carson pulled away. "For someone who didn't mean to hurt me," he said, massaging his throat with one hand, "you sure bruised the shit out of my throat!"

"You don't remember?" asked Metcalfe. "Not anything?"

"No," said Carson, still massaging and giving an experimental cough. "I guess it took me over, like it did the others. Did I attack you?"

"Not exactly. I had to make a point. Sorry about your throat."

Carson rolled his eyes. "At least tell me it was worth it?"

Metcalfe grabbed Carson's shoulder and squeezed it. "It was. Eleusis agreed to back off. It knows I have the power to stop it. And look," he nodded to Sestus, who was sitting up, blood smeared on his face and hands, but clearly no longer wounded.

"What the hell happened?" he wondered.

Carson grinned. "Rough sex. It was great. Sorry you missed it."

Metcalfe turned to Elspeth, who stood looking dazed. "You all right?" She nodded. "I think so. What happened?"

"We... reached an agreement with Eleusis," said Metcalfe. He looked ruefully toward the exit from the chamber. "Now we have to see if we can extend it to everyone else."

"Eleusis doesn't want to be alone," said Metcalfe. They sat, recovering from a mental if not a physical ordeal, in a loose circle in the grotto. "It spent millennia alone before the Family came. Over the decades you've been here, Brock, it's become..."

"Addicted?" offered Carson.

"Accustomed. Accustomed to having companions."

"Sounds to me like it doesn't know what the hell it wants," Kaya pressed.

"You're right," admitted Metcalfe. "It doesn't. In computer terms, it lacks clear programming and is proceeding based on the happenstance of random numbers. Looked at as a sentient being, it has no idea what choices will be for its good and ultimate benefit, so it moves forward by trial and error. Sometimes on impulse. Sound familiar?"

"It's a kid," said Kaya.

"It's a kid," agreed Metcalfe.

"That's meaningless," said Faulkner. "You're all kids to me. This is a bloody powerful one, whose temper tantrums could wipe out solar systems! I don't think there's a planet-sized cell in the nearest juvenile rehab facility."

"I think," said Metcalfe, "that I managed to lay some basic programming down that will protect us against that."

"That'll be the day!" said Carson. He looked to the others, "he used to copy my work in the Intro CompSci classes. Bribed me with ice cream and liquor to get him a passing grade." He shook a finger at Metcalfe. "If you programmed a planet-killer to be a little angel, we'd better get the hell out of this system yesterday."

Metcalfe chuckled. "Fair enough. I don't claim I can handle all the intricacies of the thing. I don't think any one human could. Remember, though... Eleusis can't be destroyed. We've got to figure out a way to live with it."

"But if no one can control it," Carson began.

"I chose my words carefully, Kevin," said Metcalfe. "I said I don't think any *one* of us could. Eleusis needs to learn morality the way all of us do–a little at a time from a community of people who help us sand down our rough edges; but with a strong moral core programming that keeps us from being manipulated."

"Oh, well, if it's that easy," said Carson.

"I didn't say it would be easy. I just think maybe we've started it on the right path."

"Just a minute," said Faulkner. "Mr. Metcalfe, my respect for your moral foundations knows no bounds. Goddess, you're practically Wiccan."

"Thank you."

"But you're the second One this... intellect... has chosen. Why didn't the First One imbue it with enough morality not to go killing people?"

"I... I'm not sure, Doc."

"I think I know," said Aronson. "You see, the First One, the last of the original Eleusinians, only wanted peace and to be left alone, but it was willing to impose its wishes on others. When it had the power of the Voice of Eleusis at its command, it began forcing others to its will. Once that process was started–"

"Absolute power corrupted absolutely," supplied Faulkner.

"Because the corruption was there to begin with, that being the desire to control others. Of all things, Terry recognized that he had to leave all of us our free will. He used the power to suggest, to prod–"

"He picked us up and dropped us in a cave," said Carson.

"To save your miserable life," said Metcalfe.

"Thanks. Next time how about slowing me down so I don't hit the floor at a full gee from zero, huh?"

"Noted," agreed Metcalfe.

"Eleusis learned that power could destroy and control from its original programmer. Now it's learned that it can also preserve and create," finished Aronson.

"So which does it choose?" asked Faulkner pointedly.

"We... have to help it," said Metcalfe. "I know this is probably the last thing anyone wants to do, following that last ordeal, but... if Eleusis has humans, Qraitians and other mortal sentients to commune with, I think it can find its way."

Carson's face turned dark. "So... I guess you're going to stay here and lead that effort?"

Metcalfe shrugged. "If I were to desert, it's not like the Navy could come and arrest me, with the power of Eleusis to protect me."

For the first time in anyone's memory, Pallas spoke sharply. "Metcalfe, stop it! You're being... mean!"

He laughed. "Okay. No, Kevin, I'm not staying. Assuming that the Captain can figure out how to keep us all out of Hydra Station–" He looked hopefully at Atal.

"I give it fifty-fifty odds," said the Captain.

"–I think I learned... well, when everything was falling apart, I still counted on the same handful of people to pull it together, didn't I? I think it would be a little silly for me to go off and leave you."

"Fournier will still want the planet evacuated," said Carson.

Aronson smiled. "As Terry pointed out, anyone who stays here has the power of Eleusis to protect them. If we stay."

He looked at Elspeth and Icarus, sitting by his side, the boy's head cradled in the girl's lap. He had cried himself out from the death of his father. He had still been uncharacteristically silent.

"We'll have to discuss it with all of our Family, but what do the two of you think?"

"Am I... Family?" asked Icarus hoarsely. "Will you still have me?"

"As long as there is breath in my body," acknowledged Aronson, "all people will be welcome on this world, if they will follow the ways of peace. That includes, I suppose, Eleusis itself."

"It's a big responsibility, Aronson," said Atal.

"My people descend–spiritually–from a missionary sect, Captain. Long ago, our forebears traveled old home Terra, spreading a message of peace. Sadly they often shed blood and ruined lives in so doing. That's why we withdrew from such endeavors long ago. Perhaps it's time to return to that mission... peacefully, bringing our message first to the entity we thought was God himself. In that spirit, may I invite you all to join us in Commuion? A more open, honest Communion this time."

"Captain," said Metcalfe to Atal, "you haven't had much to say. Until we bring the Admiral into the loop, you're in command of our mission. Will the Navy allow the Family to remain here and teach Eleusis?"

"I haven't said much," explained Atal, "because I learned long ago the lesson some of you learned today. Leadership is often simply the science of observing while those you are leading find their way, being available to guide them if they stray. So I don't impose my will if I can avoid it. I think the Family has found an answer. My job will be to bring that answer back and see if it sticks with Fournier and the Admiralty."

"And the Qraitians," added Metcalfe.

"Speaking of which," wondered Celia Faulkner, "just where in the name of the Goddess did all those Qraitians disappear to?"

Metcalfe opened the door to the meeting hall, through whose walls could be heard the banging and shouting of dozens of fists and their accompanying voices. Ustenar, outraged, was framed in the doorway.

"Human," she hissed. "How did you open that door?"

"With the knob, Commander," said Metcalfe.

"We have tried for hours–"

"You have been in protective custody," said Atal.

Steven H. Wilson

"Custody? We were on our ship one instant, and in this building the next! We–"

"Placed there," Atal continued, "by officers of the Confederate Navy." He winked at Metcalfe. "With a little help."

"The power of the Voice created a force field within the walls," explained Metcalfe. "Until we came to open the door."

"Handy," the Captain agreed.

"Then you have captured the weapons," observed Ustenar bitterly.

"No," said Atal. "We have arranged... a treaty. With the Family of God, and the native intelligence of this world. That treaty–"

"That treaty," finished Aronson, "is not exclusive to any race or government. The people of Eleusis... *all* the people of Eleusis... will live in peace with our fellow sentients. There are no weapons here. There is only power which will protect us, should any being not respect our treaty."

"We have agreed to no treaty!" insisted Ustenar.

"Talks will open aboard *CNV Titan* in 24 standard hours," said Atal. "You and your representatives will be welcome, Commander."

"You would trust us aboard your ship, Atal?"

"My ship will be neutral ground for the duration. Trust will not be an issue, as you will of course have a military attache to–"

"Spy on us?"

"Assist you. Your escort has already volunteered. My daughter, Midshipman Atal. I believe you know her? In the meantime, we need to arrange transport back to your ship."

"My ship was not destroyed?"

"Safe and Sound. I locked the doors and left a light on," said Celia Faulkner.

"I don't suppose we have sufficient transport capacity on hand–"

"Begging your pardon, Captain," said Metcalfe, smiling, "I believe we do." He pointed to the lake, where several dozen uniformed figures were now emerging from the woods, making their way toward the meeting hall.

"Druelinger!" Atal exclaimed. "How the hell–?"

"Out of the nowhere, into the here," said Metcalfe. "Eleusis and I were on track with our plan when the transport moved in on us. It knew I didn't want anyone killed. Because there was time and I wasn't in danger, unlike with Daedalus, it placed Colonel Druelinger and his people in stasis. They've been safe on the planet's surface since all of you reappeared in the cavern. I believe their ship can accommodate Commander Ustenar's crew."

Ustenar stepped forward to where Icarus stood, still keeping close to Elspeth. "As part of this treaty," she asked, "may I expect the return of our Qraitian citizens?"

"The treaty will require that each person be allowed his or her free will," said Aronson. "Eleusis will tolerate nothing less. Where Icarus goes is up to him."

"Well, boy?" asked Ustenar. "Will you come home and die with honor, or will you live in infamy?"

Icarus cleared his throat—a strange sound, coming from a Qraitian. "I ask that the body of Daedalus... of my father... be returned to his home world. He would have wished that. Commander Ustenar, I hope, for his sake, that you will let it be known in the Empire that he died defending his Emperor. His honor is secure."

"And you?" asked Ustenar.

Icarus reached out and took Elspeth's hand. "As for me," he said. "and my... family... I believe the phrase is, 'we will serve the Lord.'"

Ustenar started to reply, but a shout came from the direction of the lake. Standing on the porch of Aronson's house, Georg Fournier was calling the Captain's name. Behind him, trailing out the door, were Gregson and the other officers of the *Douglas*.

"The Confederates Eleusis spirted away were incarcerated separately," Metcalfe explained. "To avoid further violence."

Fournier stalked toward them, arms waving, shouting all the way. Most of the words sounded like expletives from many languages. When he came within speaking distance of *Titan's* Captain, he stopped, hands on hips and demanded, "Atal! Just what the *hell* is going on here?"

"In short," said Georg Fournier, his voice tight, "you're recommending that we abandon the mission objectives, leave the human population in place, leave the illegal aliens on a Confederate colony, leave open access to this system to hostile forces, and finally, having verified that the planet Eleusis does host the deadliest weapon discovered in all of human history, that we leave it in the hands of civilians?"

He slapped the table and leaned back in his chair. With his appearance, it had been decided that a preliminary briefing should be held immediately, here in the Family's meeting house. "Atal, explain to me, how do you define failure? Because, if this isn't it, I don't understand the concept!"

"Admiral," said Aronson calmly, "the Family of God, and our antecedent sects, have always stood outside mortal political boundaries. As our adopted home, we maintain that Eleusis is not within Confederate space, nor is it in Qraitian space."

"The existing treaty between our governments disagrees," said Fournier.

"Respectfully, Admiral, how can your governments determine the status of a sovereign world without input from its own government?"

"Sovereign—you have no government!" scoffed Fournier.

"We do. We have a king."

"Oh?" asked the Admiral acerbically, "then let me speak to him!"

Aronson smiled. "He will allow you to speak to Him at any time, in any place, Admiral. He just doesn't promise He'll answer."

"Superstition and double-talk! If you have a government, who speaks for it? A real person, not a myth!"

"I have been authorized to speak for all of Eleusis," said Aronson. "And we require that the treaty drawn beginning today preclude any existing treaty between your empires."

"One Empire, one Confederacy," corrected Fournier.

"Of course," said Aronson, "I don't know what I was thinking. Today's treaty must supercede any claims of ownership either of your governments makes on our world. The Family of God are not human, and we are not Qraitian. We are the children of God. We are all species."

"And if we do not agree to your presumptive terms?" asked Ustenar. "What are you going to do about it?"

"That depends, Commander, Admiral, on what *you* are going to do about it. No hostile action will be tolerated within our system. Indeed, as had been amply demonstrated, no hostile action will be possible."

Fournier shook his head. "Which only brings home the point–your people, who recognize no government, command supreme power. You expect us to allow that to continue? Unobserved? Without oversight by our own representatives?"

"I do not wish to be indelicate, Admiral, but you cannot allow or disallow that which you do not have the power to control. Your representatives will be welcome. They will not be allowed to interfere in our lives, but they will be welcome guests. I would venture to say that you will lose a great number of them to us, as they see the benefit of our way of life."

"And if they report back to us that you cannot control the weapons? That Eleusis is a threat to the rest of the galaxy?" asked Ustenar.

"Then, Commander, I should recommend prayer," said Aronson. "For no force of mortal contrivance would seem to be able to resist the power of Eleusis."

"Like a sword hanging over our heads," said Fournier.

"A condition humans, and Qraitians, should be accustomed to," said Atal.

Aronson smiled. "Indeed. To live has always been, after all, an awfully big adventure."

EPILOGUE

"You'll come back?" asked Elspeth hopefully. She held Metcalfe's elbows, not fully releasing him from the hug they had just shared.

He nodded. "Can't say when. I don't think I have any leave coming, or any favors to cash in for a long while."

"I think Captain Atal knows you did the right thing here," she replied. "You changed everything... for Eleusis, for humans and Qraitians... And you need to come back. You're still the only one who has real power over Eleusis."

"Not the only one." He nodded at Pallas, who stood at a discrete distance, waiting for him to board the Marine transport back to *Titan*. "I've already shared the knowledge with Pallas. From there, it can go to anyone we choose. In time, I believe everyone here will know how Eleusis can be destroyed."

"Sounds dangerous," she said skeptically.

He shrugged. "The more people that know, the more people there are to prevent it from ever being necessary. It won't be possible for one person with the knowledge to have, say, a psychotic break and wipe out everything. The rest of the Family will be there to prevent it."

She shook her head. "So we came here for peace, and now we command the greatest destructive force known."

"You don't command it. You can reason with it. In the long run, that's better."

He stepped back, put his hands on her shoulders. "Well..." he said.

"Don't be gone too long," she said quietly, never taking her gaze away from his eyes. "This has always been a happy place, but... you made it even better."

Awkwardly, he struggled for words until Pallas, suppressing a laugh, said, "Just kiss her, you idiot! Don't you know anything about girls?"

He did. That is to say, he did kiss her. He decided, for the record, that no, he knew nothing about girls.

"I'm sure you would have preferred tea, but this is all they have. You look like you could use it."

Atal held out a steaming mug to Celia Faulkner. She accepted it, sipped, and was glad to taste coffee. Not great coffee, but still, what was to be expected? They were, after all, aboard a Marine transport. It carried what could be stored for the long haul.

"Old lady witches are supposed to prefer tea, but I'm a rebel. Thank you."

He sat next to her. "Are you all right? That assignment was a bit more—"

"If you say 'a bit more excitement than someone my age can take,' I'll throw this in your face. Captain."

He grinned. "I'm too much of a coward to say something like that to your face, Doc. I was going to say, 'a bit more than we bargained for.'"

"That's better. I don't know, though. It was an espionage mission, after all. We knew Ustenar wouldn't exactly be polishing the best silver for us. I didn't quite expect to see your daughter splayed out for sacrifice like an offering to the gods in some sadomasochistic barbarian ritual, but..."

"Seriously... Thanks for keeping her safe," he said quietly.

"Thank Metcalfe and Eleusis," she replied. "I had little to do with it."

"I'm not allowed to admit this to too many people, but that shook me to my core. I thought I might really lose her this time."

She rubbed his hand sympathetically. "It's not easy, is it, bringing your only child along on such dangerous job?"

"Not easy, no. It's what she wanted, though. And Kaya gets what she wants."

"She comes by it honestly. Has anyone ever said 'no' to you?"

He laughed. "Fournier. All the time."

"Yes, but Fournier carries the curses of several gods on his head. His miserable life is its own punishment. I suppose I should ask if anyone's said 'no' and made it stick."

He nodded. "I've had many commanding officers along the way. I had to listen to them."

"And I bet you gave them every bit as much trouble as our Mr. Metcalfe gives you."

"More," he agreed.

"More? Did you enlist the services of an ancient god?"

"Okay, Metcalfe gets the prize. He's a bigger pain in the ass than I ever was. And that's an accomplishment." He stared for a moment into his own cup of coffee. "Do you think he's all right now?"

"Now? I'd say, after this he'll be overly driven, irritable, too serious by half–"

"Thank Commerce, he's back to normal!" laughed Atal.

"He'll be fine."

"Good, because I don't intend to go easy on him."

"You're angry because of what almost happened to Kaya?"

"To all of them. And I'm not angry, I'm... scared. For them. I don't blame Metcalfe. He just sets the tone for the others. They're too reckless, too convinced that they're always right. I need to reign them in before they get themselves killed."

"Lest they believe that Eleusis will now step in and save them every time?"

"That's another thing," said Atal. "What is the new... dynamic between Metcalfe and that thing? Is it going to always be in his head?"

"As I understand it," said Celia, "yes and no."

"That's helpful."

"I'm not finished. Yes, Metcalfe will always have access to Eleusis. It will always respond to him as... well, I suppose as a child would to a parent or a teacher. But it's not the genie from the lamp, Jan. It's a machine, and it's limited by its technology, coupled with the limitations of the human mind, in how far it can reach. It can lay waste this planet and perform matter-energy conversions we don't even understand yet. But when Metcalfe leaves this solar system, it can't 'see' him anymore. He's out of range."

"In a way that's good," said Atal. "In another way... he's not here anymore to reason with it. If it only listens to him—"

"A bit like leaving your child with a baby-sitter the first time, isn't it? Will the little angel surprise you with good behavior, or will it burn the house down? I believe it will begin to accept direction from the Family. It was already bonding with some of them, especially Elspeth and Icarus. They're going to command a lot of power."

"That, unfortunately, is the only way to live in peace," said Atal.

"She's dangerous," said Sestus quietly.

"Pallas?" asked Carson. The young Quintil had been staring daggers at her since their encounter in the cave. Carson supposed he couldn't blame Sestus. She had, intentionally or not, given Eleusis the keys to their minds.

He nodded. "She's the most powerful telepath alive. She can move things with her mind. She can force our bodies to do things we don't want them to do. I bet she could kill with a thought."

"All Phaetonians have some of that ability," said Carson.

"But she's... I don't know. There's something about her."

Carson grinned. "She's never slept with you?"

"Seriously. She listens to no one. Even Metcalfe, rebellious as he is, respects Atal. Pallas just does whatever she wants."

Carson thought about it. He had always thought of Metcalfe as the stubbornest being in the universe. Pallas did have a habit of making decisions and going forward with them despite opposition from others. Still, "That doesn't make her dangerous," he said.

"Maybe Metcalfe just likes danger," Sestus went on. "He's got a homicidal computer god for a pet, he tried to ram us all into the Qraitians a few months back..."

Carson reached out and brushed ruffled blond hair from Sestus's forehead. He was healed, but he was still a mess from the fight. "I think you're stressed out from all that's happened. When we get back to the ship, we can have a few drinks—"

Sestus pulled away from Carson's touch. "When I get back to the ship, I'll have to prepare a report on my part in the mission," he said coldly. "Unless maybe your friend over there would like to have his monster computer do all our reports for us."

Carson placed a hand back on Blaurich's shoulder. "Sestus—"

Sestus only looked at him and shook his head.

Carson asked, "Did I do something wrong? We were—"

"Carson," the other man interrupted, "I remember everything. From the cave."

"You do? I don't... I don't remember what happened when it controlled me."

"It didn't control me. It... I guess it influenced me but... but the things I said, I remember them. I believe them. I forgot for a while, I guess... I started to get caught up in the... the romance of it all. Metcalfe saved our lives. He's... he's amazing. He is. He's talented and brilliant and... But that's not enough, Carson. We can't go through life all wide-eyed and preaching to every enemy about loving our neighbors. We can't always stop to talk about right and wrong when there's a job to do, a mission to fulfill. It might feel good. It might make a nice public relations piece now and then, but, in the long run, it doesn't pay off."

"I don't think Metcalfe's trying to make anything pay off," said Carson, his tone sounding harsh even to himself.

"That's just it," said Sestus. "He's not practical. There was a little bit of time... I guess I wondered why he hated me so much. But... he's supposed to hate me. Someone like him can't like someone like me. He's all about moral judgment, and I'm all about what works. What gets you ahead in life. We're too different to ever be friends. I mean... I shot at Admiral Fournier! What was I thinking?"

"You saved his life."

"Good spin," said Sestus.

"It wasn't a spin, it was the truth. If you hadn't put him out of action, Eleusis might have killed him."

"I was only thinking about Metcalfe. Trying to help him. I believed..."

"Metcalfe was right," Carson reminded him.

"But for all the wrong reasons. Wait until the report on this incident is written. You'll see. It'll be a blot on Metcalfe's record."

"You could change that."

"Change it?" laughed Sestus. "I'm counting on it. There are no friendships in my world, Carson. Not in the Navy, and not in the merchant families. If I forget that, if I fall in with you and Metcalfe, I'm done." He added quietly, "I couldn't make it in your world, anyway."

"Bullshit!" hissed Carson. "You could do anything you put your mind to, Sestus! You're—"

Sestus held up his hand. "Spare me the pep talk, okay, Carson? You don't owe me anything. We're not friends. I slept with you because... because I saw Metcalfe's star rising, and I thought you were the easiest way to hitch a ride. It was a tactical error. I won't make it again."

"I don't believe you," said Carson.

Sestus started to rise. "I think I should sit somewhere else."

"But—!"

"You're right about one thing," Sestus said quickly, "I do need to blow off some steam when we get back. There's a lady marine over there I've had my eye on for a while. I hear she likes it rough. 'Scuse me."

He wandered away. Carson watching after him, mentally kicking himself for ever letting Sestus get to him.

"Don't sit there mentally kicking yourself. He gets to all of us."

Carson looked up to see Kaya standing over him, smiling sympathetically. He gestured for her to sit, though he'd prefer to have been alone. Preferably out of this ship. Preferably still in space.

"Is everyone a telepath now?" he wondered.

Kaya chuckled. "Honey, your emotions are written all over your face."

"I don't hear that often."

She pursed her lips. "No? Hmph. No, I guess you don't. You've always sort of been the iceman type, haven't you?"

"Rumor has it I sleep in freezers," said Carson.

She leaned in close to him. "Okay, seriously... How long have you and Sestus been doing it?"

"That's none of your business!"

"Sorry, won't wash. Everything to do with Sestus is my business. We're betrothed."

"You're *what?* You damn well are not! You people don't even get married!"

"We do. Sometimes. For a year or a month... or an evening. But Sestus and I are joined by the most sacred bonds of all–the ties of public opinion. Since we were first turned out of the creche–possibly since our genetic designs were first approved–the media has covered every detail of our lives. As the heirs to Quintil's two richest families–"

"How do you have families?" asked Carson irritably. "You don't get married and none of you even know your parents!"

Kaya drew herself up importantly. "I know my father."

"And your people think you're a couple of perverts!"

"Okay, fair enough. They do; and maybe we are. No other father and daughter on Quintil live together, and few work together. How we have families is by contract. Dad was designed to be the heir to Atal Holdings. He may never have met Mr. Atal Senior–"

"Mr. Atal Senior? Doesn't he have a first name?"

She shrugged. "Far as I know, it's 'Mister.' He may have another one. Who knows? Why should I care? I don't know if I've ever even seen the man. But when he dies, Daddy is CEO of the biggest merchant and manufacturing concern in the galaxy."

"Shouldn't... *Mister* Atal interview candidates for the position?"

"Good Commerce no! Daddy is the best candidate, just as he was designed to be. And when Daddy dies... well, that won't ever happen, because he's immortal. Fucking force of nature, my father. But if he decides to go missing, presumed dead for a century or so, then I inherit, also the best-designed candidate for the job."

"Genetics don't guarantee character or suitability for a profession."

"The best geneticists on my planet beg to differ with you. Anyway, about Sestus..."

"I have nothing to say."

"The sex was good?"

"Well, you can imagine–"

"Don't have to. I've had him. On camera."

"Then you know."

"I don't, actually," said Kaya pointedly. "It wasn't that good for me. May have had something to do with the salmon mousse all over my ass–we consummated our love on a buffet table–but I'm pretty sure it was because Sestus is just unimaginative and disinterested in his partner's pleasure."

"I... can't agree."

"Then he was inspired. Must have been you. Wow. You made Sestus passionate? That's like raising the dead. What is it about you? I have to know. Let's do it now."

"No."

"Right here, in the seats. I think there are cameras–"

"No."

"Okay. Shy, huh? How about one of those pressure suit storage lockers?"

"Been there, done that."

"Not with a girl, I bet."

"What do you mean 'consummated your love?' Are you saying you were in love with him–"

"Too?"

"I didn't say 'too.'"

"You didn't. What was it you didn't say?"

"I didn't say anything."

"Right, but it was a very specific something you didn't say."

"Go away, Kaya."

"I'm not finished comforting you yet."

"When will you be done, when I've bled out?"

"Nope. I insist on waiting for brain death before committing. So, you're in love with Sestus."

"I am not! I just... I thought we were becoming... friends."

"Sestus has no friends."

"Apparently."

"You might blame his design, I suppose. Personally, I think he's just an asshole. That's not in the genes. That's a gift from the gods."

"You're an atheist."

"Limited conversion. My time with Terrans has convinced me that there are supernatural forces capable of making us greater assholes than we would otherwise be. Explains a lot of your planet's religious history, don't you think?"

Carson sat back and closed his eyes.

"Nothing to say?"

"You're carrying on fine for both of us."

She reached out and massaged his neck with one hand. "Don't let him get to you, Carson."

"He already has. I was having fun–"

"Screwing your best friend's mortal enemy? Making up for the way Yank ran off and abandoned you? Getting him back for hogging all the attention these past few months with both his heroism and his celebrated neuroses?"

"Guilty."

"Yank still needs you, Carson. He's not going anywhere."

"We're not talking about him."

She tightened her grip on his shoulder. "The damned thing is, Carson, with you and me... no matter what we're talking about, we seem to be talking about him."

Finally, Carson smiled. "Really makes you want to kick his ass, doesn't it?"

"Every day, my brother."

She lifted the armrest between their seats, curled up against him and closed her eyes. They sat together, loosely embraced, reveling in companionable silence.

The silence lasted about fifteen seconds before Kaya said, "Seriously. Will you sleep with me tonight? I know I'm an ookie *girl* and everything, but I have trim, boyish hips and you can pretend."

He glared at her so hard she began to fear he would hit her, but his answer was, "Fine. You're on."

"Really?"

"Really. Tomorrow morning at least I'll know if you stop talking while you're asleep."

She grinned. "Want to know the best way to make me stop talking?"

Similarly huddled together nearby were Cernaq and Aer'La. They had not spoken since leaving the surface. Indeed, Aer'La had spoken little since being brought out of the cavern after her confrontation with Eleusis. Although she had been able to communicate effectively enough when called to, she'd been aloof, withdrawn, sticking close to Cernaq and, literally, keeping her head down. As he'd drawn an arm about her shoulders aboard the transport, he had found she was trembling. Telepathically, he knew it was not from cold.

He did not press her to speak. It was, therefore, halfway through their journey home before she said, "Something's wrong with me."

"You are suffering the after-effects of a psychic trauma."

"That thing scared the shit out of me," she said quietly.

Cernaq nodded. "It made you relive your recent encounter."

"You mean the time I almost died. Don't use words like 'encounter,' Cernaq. I almost died."

"But you did not."

"Some days... I wish I had."

"You don't." He did not know if it was a statement of firm belief, or an appeal to her not to want to die.

"I... I don't know. It's so... I never know when the memories, the feelings... when they're going to come up and bite me on the ass. Dammit, Cernaq, what if I lock up or freak out in a crisis? What if I get somebody killed? Somebody who shouldn't get killed? What if Metcalfe had needed me back there? He would have been killed! And he'd have died hating me!"

"He does not hate you."

"I hated him!"

"You did not. You were subject to a powerful sense of frustration, caused by his actions. That confused you, caused you to resent him, possibly caused you to entertain thoughts of harming him; but you did not, and do not hate him. I would know."

She flicked his shoulder. "Show off."

"Never."

"He doesn't hate me? You're sure?"

"He's a very forgiving person. Perhaps you should go and talk to him."

"He's with the bitch."

"Aer'La! You promised."

"Sorry. He's with your close and trusted friend Pallas."

"Thank you."

"The bitch," she finished.

Cernaq sighed.

"I'll talk to him," said Aer'La. "But... Cernaq, what am I supposed to do about this? I'm afraid I... No. I'm just afraid."

"I owe you an apology," said Pallas.

Metcalfe held his jaw tight so it wouldn't drop. *"You* owe me an apology?" He tried to keep his voice quiet, despite his amazement.

"Certainly. I was presumptuous. I violated your privacy and forced on you a psychic bond for which you had not given explicit permission. It was an immoral act, contextually."

"Contextually?"

"Among my people, the thought is the deed. You thought, albeit idly, and under... emotional duress, that you *did* want to bond with me. I forgot, conveniently, I suppose, that you are not trained in the disciplines which keep stray, irrational thoughts within the confines of your own mind. Had I been dealing with a Phaetonian–"

"It wasn't 'under duress.'" he interrupted, "It was in the heat of passion. And I was surprised when you appeared in my mind; but I wasn't angry, Pallas. You did nothing wrong. You did what I wanted you to do."

"Without your permission," she concluded. "I should have waited for your formal and rationally derived answer. It was immoral."

"Either way, if you did something wrong, Pallas, I forgive you. That's how this is supposed to work."

"It is?" She was genuinely surprised.

"Yes. Love and forgiveness have to go hand in hand, or love is impossible to maintain."

"Love," she said slowly, "is the recognition in another of the qualities one most treasures oneself. If you love me, it's because you see value in me as a moral and rational person."

"I wouldn't put it that way, but okay."

"If I stray from those values, that which you have recognized in me is compromised, and–"

"Pallas, don't you understand? We don't love only the good in people. We love the bad as well. I don't think I could love you if you were perfect."

"That is irrational."

"Hence the expression, 'crazy in love.' Do you really expect me never to make a mistake? Never to do anything morally wrong?"

"That would be unreasonable. But I expect you to recognize when you have done wrong, and I would expect you to recognize it equally in me. I would expect you to tell me if I'd done wrong. I... I don't want you to let me fall below the moral standards I see in you. I want to be worthy of you."

"You are." He leaned over and kissed her.

"Seriously, Metcalfe. You just fought an ancient nigh-omnipotent intelligence to a standstill because of your belief in free will. You're a hero–"

"Yeah, I'm kinda sick of that word, after these past few months. It's meaningless."

"It isn't. Oh, yes, the way the news media use it it is. A hero is anyone lucky enough to live through a traumatic event, whether they participated in their own survival or not. It's also anyone who happened to die in the same event, no matter how they died. But you are my hero. You embody my ideals. Far better than I do, I'm afraid. You fought for free will. I took a shortcut around it to get what I wanted."

"Am I supposed to be mad, when what you wanted was me?"

She frowned.

He took her hands in his. "Okay, I'll make you a deal. You try never to use your telepathy to force a decision on me, I'll tell you if you do, and I won't sleep with women I've just met, and to whom I have no right or ability to make a commitment."

"What? Where did that come from?"

"From my moral context. A man has no business sleeping with a woman unless he can offer to stay and be her partner. I took advantage of Elspeth."

"That's ridiculous! Elspeth enjoyed your lovemaking. She was honored that you would choose her for a partner. I felt the same way when you chose me."

"And you know this because you read her mind?"

"I know this because she told me."

"You... talked... about me?"

"Of course. We had something in common. We both admire you and we'd both been your lover. Why shouldn't we talk?"

He shook his head. "The rules really are different out here."

"So they are. They make more sense. Please do not promise me that you won't avail yourself of worthy sexual partners. It's healthy to do so. I've learned that, since leaving Phaeton. I'd prefer that you share your mind only with me–"

"Well, I wasn't going to start an affair with Cernaq."

"Oh, I'd make an exception for Cernaq. He's worthy of you too, sexually and psychically. If you want to share with him–"

"That was a joke."

"I don't see why. Cernaq is very attractive and very skilled sexually."

He felt his eyebrows shoot up. "You know this first hand?"

"Not yet, no. He told me."

"Not yet?"

She shrugged. "I'm very fond of Cernaq. I believe he's my best friend, as Carson is yours. Why would I refuse him? I've no doubt his curiosity will eventually lead to–"

"Aer'La would kill you."

"She would not. If she tried, I am capable of stopping her. If she tried too hard, I fear she might be injured." She paused, studying his face. "You... don't like the idea of my having sex with anyone else, do you?"

"What do I say to that?"

"The truth."

"The truth makes me seem awfully... petty... given how tolerant you're .being of my... encounter."

"There is no need for tolerance, Metcalfe. And there's no need for jealousy, either. I have no desire to interview for replacements for you. Cernaq is my friend. He's not my hero."

Metcalfe felt himself blush.

"And there's no need to be embarrassed. You are my hero. You should be as confident of my loyalty as I am of yours. I knew you would return to *Titan* and to me."

"I wish I'd known it," he said ruefully.

"That is the benefit of a more rational thought process. I can sometimes predict your actions before you decide on them."

"Guess I'm dense."

"Sometimes, yes," she agreed. Then, when he laughed quietly at her, she said, "Was that when I was supposed to say that you're not dense?"

"Probably."

"Overall, I suppose you're not. You're just sometimes a bit confused by the many conflicting philosophies others have attempted to force upon you; and so you have to do things like going off and finding legendary gods with whom to trifle, in order to derive through experimentation the things you wish to know about yourself."

"I am too tired to follow that sentence." He wrapped an arm around her shoulders and inclined his head against hers. "I'm just glad you're not angry with me."

"Not at all. I'm curious, in fact. Maybe you could share your memories with me later, of what it was like with Elspeth?"

"You want to–"

"Share the experience? Yes."

"Positively voyeuristic! I'm beginning to feel like I went to one of Kaya's parties, where they have sex on the banquet tables in front of everyone."

"Did others–" she began, then saw in his mind. "Oh. Icarus watched."

"And Eleusis was inside my head. It revels in intense emotional experiences. You and Eleusis have that in common."

She looked away suddenly.

"What?" he asked. "Is something wrong?"

"Eleusis," she said quietly. "When it was speaking through Sestus, it said that... it compared my influence over you with its own. It believed it was being rational. It believed it was doing what was best for you. It acted only in its own self-interest... Eleusis and I... we share similarities which disturb me."

He drew her chin around so she was looking at him again. "Eleusis is... incomplete. A child who grew up without adults to guide it. It's as if it never learned language. It's fundamentally flawed. You're an adult, a complete and healthy human being. And there's a universe of difference between its brand of self-interest and what your people believe. Eleusis would destroy a race, a world, a universe, to satisfy its aims."

"There are times," she said quietly, "when I think I might do such a thing to protect you."

He hugged her close. "I wouldn't want that. And you would never hurt so many people. I can't imagine you hurting anyone."

She was silent. After a few moments she said, "Perhaps we should leave our bond as it is, as Eleusis left it... broken."

"Are you afraid of what you're learning about yourself, being this close to me?"

She nodded.

"Do you... is that what you want? To be apart from each other?"

She looked up. There were tears in her eyes. "I... I never want to be apart from you!"

She kissed him and they held close to each other for a long time.

Eventually, tentatively, he reached out with his mind, as she had taught him. *Pallas? Pallas... I want you to come back. Come back into my mind... to stay.*

There was another long space of time where she was silent, where there was no answering call within his thoughts. And then, quietly, at the back of his mind, he heard, *To stay, my love.*

Aer'La balked at the doorway. "I just remembered I forgot to inspect some–"

Cernaq said, "You're lying." He looked to the others. "She's lying. I'm afraid it's hopeless."

"She's afraid," said Kaya.

"I'm not afraid of anything!"

"And again," began Cernaq.

Aer'La backhanded him in the chest. "I will hurt you! And you won't like it this time!"

Cernaq coughed, a dramatization, obviously, as he could control such reflexes.

Carson stepped protectively in front of Cernaq. "Aer'La, you promised."

Aer'La started to say something several times, then gave a groan of frustation.

"What are you afraid of?" asked Kaya.

"What if... what if there's... some sort of mind control?"

"You're sleeping with a telepath, and you're afraid of mind control," said Carson.

"I'm just saying... people have gone in and never come back out! This could be for life! I... I don't know if... "

Metcalfe placed an arm around her. "Come on, Aer'La. I've been through it."

"Yeah, but you've got... oh... spiritual powers, or something! You're sleeping with a telepath too! And I know she's controlling you!"

"Yeah," Carson nodded, "but it's not his mind she's got hold of."

Steven H. Wilson

"Aer'La," said Metcalfe reasonably, "it's okay to be afraid. It's fear that's at the root of your problem. You need to admit that. C'mon, it's not the scariest thing in the world. As long as you stay calm and in control, this is something that can actually help you."

"It's also something that can take over your life!"

He took her hand. "Anyway, you're not going in alone. I've decided I'm not going to make a break either. I need to continue doing this. So we'll face the dragon together, okay?" He put one finger under her chin and turned her face toward his. "If there's one thing I've learned in the last few days, Aer'La, it's than an Arbiter never has to go it alone."

Quietly, with her eyes closed, she allowed him to lead her through the door marked:

LUCINDA GRAE, LT, CMT, PhD
COUNSELING SERVICES

FROM: Fournier, Admiral G.
TO: Confederate Security Council, All Members
RE: Eleusis

Situation stable at present. Monitoring teams dispatched, and permanent bases to be established at strategic points. (See attached specification.) Efforts will focus on understanding the technology behind the matter-energy conversion capability of the Eleusinian defense network.

From this moment, Metcalfe and Pallas are persons of interest. Both displayed remarkable abilities to interface with the A.I. controlling the system. Close monitoring of both will be ordered. Their locations will always be known to this office. Suspicious activity, particularly return trips to this area, will be cause for mobilization of resources, and possible detainment.

The destructive capability of the Eleusinian network, while limited in reach, is immense. Will keep this body briefed on our efforts to collect intel. At the point that we are satisfied we understand this technology, the destruction of the existing site is strongly recommended.

Given the threat to Confederate security, collateral damage, including civilian casualties, will be consider acceptable in efforts to end the threat of Eleusis.

ABOUT THE AUTHOR

Steven H. Wilson has freelanced for *Starlog*, written for DC Comics *Star Trek* classic and *Warlord* series, and, most recently, served as principal writer and director for Prometheus Radio Theatre and publisher of Firebringer Press. His original science fiction series, *The Arbiter Chronicles*, currently boasting nineteen full-cast audio dramas and the novel *Taken Liberty*, has won the Mark Time Silver Award and the Parsec Award for Best Audio Drama (long form). As a podcaster, besides hosting the Prometheus Radio Theatre podcast, he has recorded Lester Del Rey's *Badge of Infamy* for podiobooks.com and voiced multiple roles in J. Daniel Sawyer's *Antithesis* and Nobilis's *Scouts*. Active in science fiction fandom since 1984, he has written, drawn, edited and published fanzines, acted and directed with a comedy troupe, and served as a gopher, a con chair or a guest at roughly a hundred conventions. Wilson, who serves as IT manager for Howard County (Maryland) Fire & Rescue, holds degrees from the University of Maryland College of Journalism and the Johns Hopkins University Whiting School of Engineering. *Unfriendly Persuasion* is his third novel.